THE LIVES SHE
LEFT BEHIND

THE LIVES SHE LEFT BEHIND

James Long

WINDSOR
PARAGON

First published 2012
by Quercus
This Large Print edition published 2013
by AudioGO Ltd
by arrangement with
Quercus

Hardcover   ISBN: 978 1 4713 2100 9
Softcover   ISBN: 978 1 4713 2101 6

For Pam

British Library Cataloguing in Publication Data available

Printed and bound in Great Britain by
MPG Books Group Limited

CHAPTER 1

Joanna's father Toby had wanted to call her Melissa but he played no part in the final decision because he died more or less in childbirth. Her mother Fleur dismissed the name out of hand and even Toby's death did not change her mind.

So it was that Joanna Mary Driscoll was born at 8.15 in the morning on the last Wednesday in May of 1994, breathing in the air of the York Hospital Maternity Unit with a puzzled and anxious look in her pale blue eyes. Toby would have picked her up and comforted her but he had been dead for over an hour by that time, driving straight into an oncoming petrol tanker as he left the hospital car park in an unreasoning panic. He was racing home to collect Fleur's bag of vital accessories—left behind by him, as she pointed out, when her waters broke.

They didn't tell Fleur about the accident until after Jo had been delivered, and something began to go wrong between mother and daughter as soon as they did. Fleur, the few remaining soft parts of her beginning to harden over, looked grimly at her baby with blame already hanging in the air between them.

Fleur had been the main wage earner in the marriage and she went back to work as soon as she could, so Jo was cared for by a succession of nannies mostly too young to show her more than an inept sentimentality. Over the next few years, the ones who were old enough to understand rapidly fell foul of Fleur when they dared to imply

1

she might do well to spend a bit more time with her daughter. It was just after one of these had left, fired abruptly the previous evening as soon as she had finished the ironing, that Fleur found she had no alternative but to take Jo with her on her day's business.

That was why Jo, as a toddler, quite baffled by the world, found herself in the village of Stamford Bridge, a few miles outside York, tagging along as her mother strode round a ramshackle Georgian mansion. Fleur was barking questions at the cowed girl from the estate agents, who was starting to understand why her more experienced colleagues had suddenly found pressing alternative duties.

Jo started to cry when she looked out of the patio doors across the farmland behind the house. Irritated, Fleur asked her what was wrong, but she couldn't explain because she didn't know. At four years and two months old, how do you decode a tide of adult grief without any protecting drainage channel of words or concepts? All Jo knew was that the bit that she was just starting to understand as herself was shredded by a turmoil of utter sorrow bowling down at her from across that bleak field.

Fleur tried to reason with her but reason had nothing to do with this. Crying turned to howling and then into such an utter loss of control that the young estate agent found herself propelled forward to bend down and clutch the tiny girl to stop her damaging herself while the mother's mouth tightened in anger as she stood and watched.

After ten minutes, all the muscles Jo was using to cry and writhe were so worn out that she heaved to a halt, rolled over towards the window and stared out in a dull torpor. That was when Fleur finally picked her up, taking care to keep the child's tear-stained cheeks away from her silk blouse.

'No more?' she said. 'You've finished then?' and the little girl pointed with an unsteady finger out across the fields as if that explained everything.

Driving back home to York brought a change in Jo that her mother was too annoyed and too busy with her own thoughts to recognise. Sitting strapped in her child seat, Jo tried to turn her head to look behind, then stared out of the window when a bend in the road allowed a brief glimpse of the receding village. She had a picture of a bridge in her head but it faded away so sharply that she gave a little sniff of surprise. It left something behind. All at once, and for the first time, Jo felt her separateness, aware suddenly that she was one single person, different to this mother in the front seat. Furrowing her brow, she began to explore herself, trying to test out where she stopped and started.

That night, Jo lay in her bed knowing she was alone, that beyond the tips of her fingers and her toes nobody else was there who knew what she was feeling in the exact way she felt it. She wanted Francesca to read her the rest of *The Gruffalo* but Francesca had been sent away. She picked up the book from her bedside table, struggling with both hands, and opened it to look at the pictures, trying to find the last one they had looked at together before Francesca had kissed her goodnight and gone to finish the ironing—before she had heard loud voices downstairs and her

3

mother shouting. She let the book fall on the bedcover and saw the bridge again, in shape after shape, all imagined, all wooden, all sad. Clutching the woollen doll another lost nanny had bought her, she held it squashed against her chest, fearing that if she let it go someone might come and bury it in the earth by that bridge. Then she began to cry silently, keeping the sobs inside for fear of footsteps on the stairs.

Lost in that misery, someone quietly spoke a name inside her head, touched her on the forehead—behind the forehead where it really hurt, kissing the tears away from the inside. In the filtered evening gloom of the curtained room someone was there with her, giving her courage, telling her she was not alone after all and everything really would be all right. Something like a story without words filled the room, sealed off the rest of the house and brought her safety. It was a story about friendship and love, a promise of the future—even better than *The Gruffalo*, thought Jo as she fell asleep.

When she woke in the morning, she was so delighted by the visit that she told her mother about it at breakfast. A week later, her mother took her to a large, quiet house near the Minster where a quiet man sat in a quiet room and asked her lots of questions with long, quiet silences in between.

'Your mother tells me you have a new friend.'

She nodded.

'She says your new friend is called "Girly". Is that right?'

It was near enough, so she nodded again.

'Is that Girly?' he asked, and it took her a

4

moment to realise that he was pointing at the woolly doll. She was so surprised at his mistake that she laughed out loud.

'That's a toy,' she pointed out in a kind voice so he would not feel hurt. You would have thought a grown-up would know that.

Afterwards she sat in the waiting room, watching *Antiques Roadshow* on television while the quiet man talked to her mother.

'It's nothing to worry about, Mrs Driscoll,' he said. 'A high proportion, perhaps even a majority of children of Joanna's age have imaginary friends. It can be a reaction to all kinds of things—a bit of stress, a bit of loneliness, sometimes neither of those. It's often the more intelligent children who need to have someone they can talk to. It may be an animal or a fairy or another child.'

'This one isn't any of those,' said Fleur. 'She talks as if it's a grown woman.'

The psychiatrist was about to suggest this might be a mother substitute but he looked at the jut of Fleur's jaw and thought better of it.

'There's another thing. She keeps eating grass.'

'Grass?'

'Well, plants and leaves. Things from the garden and the hedges. I told her she would poison herself and she just said no, she wouldn't, and it made her feel better.'

'That's probably harmless,' said the psychiatrist uneasily. 'Animals do it. Let's look at the other side of all this. What is it you *like* about your daughter?'

'Like?'

'Yes. Well, all right. What pleases you? What does she do right?'

All that came into Fleur's head was that her

5

daughter was surprisingly good at predicting the weather but that felt more like an irritation than an accomplishment, starting from the fine, warm day when Jo had developed a wobbly bottom lip when she wasn't allowed to bring her raincoat with her and they had both been soaked by a downpour that seemed to come from nowhere.

'She's very tidy,' Fleur said, but it didn't seem an adequate response.

Back home, Fleur often found herself wanting to shout 'Don't watch me like that' when she saw her daughter's eyes following her. What she meant was 'Don't need me like that', which you might say was not her fault, going straight back to her own mother and her mother's father and grandfather, and on backwards veering between genders for thirty, forty, fifty generations—all the way back to one who started the whole chain reaction without any parental influence whatsoever. Perhaps any one of them could have broken the chain by deciding to do it differently. Could have done, but didn't.

Jo became a very quiet little girl when she was at home. At school, she could talk to her secret friend in her head, but she learned to close that door when she knew her mother was around and that meant that at home she was only half a person. At night, when her mother was downstairs, she could talk again, sometimes out loud, and her friend would be there to reassure her, to go over the events of the day with her and show her how to smooth away the sharp parts. She didn't know that Fleur could creep up the stairs, leaving the television turned up to cover her. She didn't know that from the other side of the thin plywood that

6

had turned the old doorway between their rooms into a clothes cupboard, her mother could hear anything she said and write down what she heard. That was why, once or twice a year for the next five years, Fleur would take her daughter to another quiet specialist and then another, always hoping they would take it more seriously than they did. She wanted them to treat her daughter like you treat an old house for woodworm, as if a spray from some magic chemical might make her normal.

*   *   *

When Jo was nine, Fleur went to a parents' evening at her school. It was an expensive private school and she went because she had recently bought the vicarage next door. As a speculation it looked like being rapidly rendered unprofitable by unexpected problems in the roof and she thought perhaps the head might see it as a worthwhile investment to help the school's expansion. That meant serving her time by sitting down to listen to Mrs Hedges, Jo's teacher, and it soon became apparent that Mrs Hedges had something to say.

'I'm very interested in an expression Joanna used in class, Mrs Driscoll. It's not one I've heard before.'

Fleur's first thought was that her daughter had used a swear word because it would not have surprised her at all that Mrs Hedges hadn't heard it. Mrs Hedges seemed to have only a small fingerhold on the real world that Fleur inhabited, the world of business. She had no time for the whimsical and indulgent take on childhood that

7

Mrs Hedges had displayed on the few occasions they had met. She did not see it as a teacher's function to show undue fondness for the children in her care nor to bring them up in the belief that the world was a benevolent place only distinguished from fairy tales by the absence of talking rabbits.

'What did she say?'

'We were discussing proverbs, you see? It's such a good way to get them to look at language and culture and history.'

The only proverb that immediately came to Fleur's mind was 'A fool and his money are soon parted', a statement of which she thoroughly approved, so she simply raised her eyebrows and Mrs Hedges, sensing a chill without understanding why, floundered on.

'I asked them if they knew any proverbs and she put her hand up, you see? She doesn't often do that so I went straight to her and she said this odd thing.'

'Which was?'

'She said, "The mist on the hill bringeth water to the mill." Now, I wonder, is that something you say in your family?'

'No. Why on earth would anyone say something like that?'

Mrs Hedges opened a folder and Fleur noted grimly that the cover was decorated with stuck-on pictures of roses. 'Then she said, "Women's jars bring men's wars." At least I think that's what it was and, um, yes, "The hasty hand catches frogs for fish." '

'And is that supposed to mean something? It sounds like nonsense.' Fleur looked across the

8

school hall to where Jo and a group of other children were being rehearsed in some entertainment that she feared the parents would be expected to sit through at the end of the evening.

'I was hoping you could tell me,' said the teacher. 'I took the one about mist and mills to mean that good things come out of bad and I looked up the frogs one on the internet. It says it's very old and Sir Walter Scott used it in *Ivanhoe*. I wondered if you'd been reading *Ivanhoe* to her or something like that?'

'No.' Fleur hadn't been reading anything to Jo and wasn't sure if *Ivanhoe* was a poem or a book.

'And the women's jars thing? I can't find any trace of that.'

'I have no idea. Does this matter?'

'Well, yes, I think perhaps it does. Since then her writing has really taken off. She's turning out to be very imaginative. She has been writing some lovely stories.'

Mrs Hedges delved into the rose-covered folder again and any other mother there would have smiled and reached for the papers she brought out and been thrilled that their daughter was showing early literary talent but Fleur, who was not any other mother, had something more pressing on her mind. She looked across the room and saw Justin Reynolds, a member of the Council Planning Committee, just getting to his feet from another session at another table. She left Mrs Hedges stunned by the speed of her departure, though somewhat relieved.

In the car on the way home, as Jo waited without success for any mention of the songs she had sung in her first ever public performance, her mother said, 'I've arranged for Maria Reynolds to come and play.'

'With me?' asked Jo, surprised.

'Well, of course, with you. Who do you think she's coming to play with? Me?'

To Jo that somehow seemed less unlikely. The closest she had ever come to Maria Reynolds was in the brief moment before Maria had pushed her over in the playground. She said nothing.

'Where do you get all these sayings from?' her mother asked. 'All this stuff you've been spouting in class about mists and frogs and jars. Have you been reading books?' It sounded like an accusation.

'Someone told me.'

'What someone?'

But Jo had learned not to mention the friend she talked to every night when she went to bed— the friend who was there for comfort and for wisdom, who spoke to her from inside her head.

'I don't know,' she said.

'You're getting very secretive. I don't like it.'

That evening Jo sat in her room, getting ready to do her homework. Mrs Hedges had asked her to write another story.

She settled in her chair and opened her exercise book. 'What shall we write about this time?' she asked into the silence of her room and listened to the answer, smiling to herself.

Fleur came in much later, noticing the light still on. She had been on the phone for most of the evening trying to sort out the problems at the Durston barn conversion where the highways department were kicking up about access on to the

10

lane. She tutted when she saw Jo lying asleep with most of her clothes still on, unbuttoned all she could and rolled her daughter under the duvet. Then she saw the open exercise book.

'My Cottage,' she read. 'My cottage stands where it has always stood, under the edge of the hill, and it is made out of the bones of the hill. All its stones came out of the hill and its beams are made from the trees that grew on the hill. One day it will sink back into the hill but only if I am not there to save it.'

They lived in the heart of York, in a house made of good Victorian brick. Fleur tutted again. Mrs Hedges might like it, but imagination didn't put bread on the table.

Jo wriggled away from the noise her mother made, burrowing miles down to the place where she really lived, in the cottage room under the eaves where the evening air, blown by birds' wings, carried in the scent of kindly thatch.

After school the next day Maria Reynolds came to play. She loomed over Jo, blotting out the light and hissing murderous and mysterious words of ill omen at her whenever they were by themselves.

'Have you been saved?' she said. 'You're going to burn in the fire. Did you know that?'

For once Jo tried to stay as near her mother as possible to keep this fat malevolence under some sort of restraint, but Fleur shut herself away in her study, leaving her daughter to endure the pinches and the mean taunts. Even when Maria's father came to fetch her, the misery did not end because Fleur poured him a glass of sherry and shut him inside with her. Jo set up the skittles just outside the window for safety and she could see them talking inside—saw her mother unfolding plans, laughing and smiling as she never normally did. They were at it for half an hour and whenever they were both looking the other way, Maria would throw the hard wooden ball at Jo instead of at the skittles.

'I'm going to heaven,' she said. 'I've been saved. You haven't. You're a sinner. You deserve what's coming to you.'

At the weekend, Fleur announced that they were going out for a picnic, which was not something they had ever done before.

'Where are we going?' Jo asked.

'It's by a river. There's a field I want to see.'

It was usually houses and old barns her mother wanted to see and Jo was very used by now to hanging around while Fleur talked to men with clipboards and tape measures who got out of battered vans. 'It's what keeps us fed, my dear,' was what Fleur always said if she thought she caught a look of boredom. 'Your father didn't provide for us, so I have to.'

A field sounded good until she asked the next question, looking at the hamper her mother was loading. 'Will we eat all this food?'

'We will, and Mr Reynolds will, and Maria and her little brother.'

It took them nearly half an hour to drive there. 'Now, what I want you to do is take Maria and her brother off and give me some time to talk to their father,' said Fleur.

'Isn't their mother coming?' Jo asked hopefully.

'She's coming a bit later,' said Fleur, 'when she's finished doing something or other for their church. They're very religious, you know. There's no need

12

to make a face. There's nothing wrong with believing in things.'

The picnic was indeed in a field on the edge of a river, but what Fleur hadn't said was that the river flowed through a village that felt a bit like a small town because it had factories and a big caravan site on that side. The field was a bit further down the river but it wasn't the sort of field that promised fun even if Jo had been by herself. Maria's brother was called Simeon 'With an "e", he told her, 'like in the Bible,' and he joined in the game of bullying Jo with a zeal that showed how accustomed he was to being the usual target.

'You don't go to church, do you?' he asked as soon as they were by themselves.

'I've been to church,' Jo said. 'I've been to a wedding and a christening.'

'That's not real church. That's misusing the church's solemn fabric for earthly ends. If you don't go to real church, you'll go to hell. You have to be saved.'

'She won't be saved,' said Maria with contempt. 'Who would bother to save her?'

'God the Father would,' said Simeon. 'He saves anyone who wants to be saved.'

'Not her,' said his sister. 'Don't talk about what you don't know about.'

'He'd save her.'

'Who says so?'

'I say so.'

Words came to Jo's mouth. ' "They say so" is half a liar,' she said quietly.

'What does that mean? That doesn't mean anything. Are you saying I'm a liar?' Maria stepped up to her, inflating herself and butting Jo with her

13

stomach so that she had to step back.

'I don't think a real god would be like that,' Jo answered bravely. 'God tempers the wind to a shorn lamb.'

Simeon made a loopy sign with his hand. 'You say stupid things,' he said, and Maria pushed her so that she fell over backwards, then kicked her and walked off laughing. Jo felt tears coming to her eyes with the pain of the kick and reached out in her mind to her private friend, the wise and gentle one who was always there for her, but instead of that comforting strength she could only feel distant misery.

That was a shock. It was the first time there had been any distance at all between them. She could not remember the time before her friend. That calm, consoling voice had always been somewhere just there. If she could have reached inside her skull, she could have put her finger on the exact spot, towards the back and a little to the right. Now she could feel someone still close by, but not *with* her—and it was someone who was hurting even more than she was. Jo got to her feet and ran along the edge of the field, with the water flowing just beside her, past the twisted shopping trolley wedged among the stones and the pool where dark fish flicked their tails, all the way to the far hedge where she knew her friend was, where she was needed.

She knelt close to the riverbank right by her friend but there was a wall between them and she knew this best of friends didn't want to drag her into whatever was happening. She persisted, opening herself up to the misery next to her until she broke through the barrier and found out, much too fast, what death and

14

the sorrow of death felt like.

Fleur eventually found her there, curled up in a ball and weeping. The Reynoldses were close behind her, the father and the mother, with Maria and Simeon hanging back behind them, grinning.

'What's going on?' Fleur demanded, and Jo was too carried away to observe her usual silent discretion.

'He was killed,' she got out between sobs. 'They killed him. He did it to save him.'

'Who did it to save who?'

'He did. Her son. Her brave, brave son.'

'Whose son. Who is *her*?'

But before Jo could find a way not to answer that, they both became aware of a mumbling from behind them. Fleur turned sharply to find Justin Reynolds' wife, Leah, making the sign of the cross over and over again as she recited an incantation in a language Fleur did not recognise at all.

'What on earth are you doing?' she demanded.

'Asking the help of the Lord for your poor daughter in her affliction. The Lord will come to her aid.'

Fleur remembered just in time that she needed the Reynoldses and choked back her words.

Leah Reynolds, warming to her task, gesticulated ever more violently, then knelt and put her hands on Jo's head. Jo twisted to escape but the woman wrapped one arm right round her and held the girl's head back against her chest with the other hand. Her husband watched with an expression of pride on his face.

'She's done this before,' he said. 'Casting out. She has special powers.' Fleur thought hard about his position on the Planning Committee and did

15

her best to smile, as Leah Reynolds continued to intone.

'Let me go,' said Jo quietly. Leah Reynolds ignored her. 'What?' said Jo. There was a silence, then she said, 'You have no right to restrain me. Please take your hands away.'

Leah Reynolds went on speaking in a monotone. Fleur thought perhaps it was Latin and then Jo started to laugh and laugh, not hysterically but in adult amusement. 'Oh you silly woman,' said the child. 'Go on. Just get it over with.'

Next week, her mother took Jo to a new person in a new office—a woman this time who was far less quiet and told her more than she asked her. After she saw the woman, her mother started to give her tablets and Jo could hear her friend telling her not to take them, to hide them in her mouth and spit them out later, and that worked for a week or so until her mother caught her and then she was forced to drink a whole glass of water and it was impossible not to swallow. The tablets made her feel sleepy and dull and not at all herself. The worst thing was that they pushed her friend away so she could only feel her, waiting anxiously, too far off to talk—her friend Gally.

CHAPTER 2

They left the house in York when Jo was twelve years old. She got up when the alarm went off on a perfectly ordinary Friday morning. There was no milk in the fridge, just two half-empty bottles of white wine and a carton of apple juice. She looked for bread to toast but had no luck there either, so she poured the apple juice over her cornflakes. It wasn't good. She searched the ironing pile then went upstairs. Fleur was in the bath with the door ajar.

'I can't find my gym clothes,' Jo said quietly.

'Where did you leave them?'

'In the washing. That's what you told me to do.'

'Did I? Look in the machine. You should get yourself sorted out. I did my own washing when I was your age.'

Downstairs, Jo found them, twisted in the middle of the sopping wet load. There was only ten minutes to go before she had to leave and she could think of no way to dry them in time to avoid all the trouble she'd be in if she didn't have them. She squeezed them out as hard as she could but they were still completely and defiantly wet. She put them in the tumble dryer on full heat until the last possible minute and all the difference that made was that they were very hot and just as wet and the steam made her eyes wet too—unless she was crying, which she thought she might be. Somehow she had managed to annoy her mother almost every time she had opened her mouth that week, but when she cried Fleur got angry so Jo had

17

saved her tears for when she was alone in her bedroom. The tablets didn't stop the tears—they just made them seem to come from off to one side.

She put the hot, wet clothes in a plastic bag and tucked them in her backpack, imagining what the others would say in the changing room when she tried to put them on. They called her 'Dopey Driscoll' at school. Despite that, when she went to the front door she was relieved to be leaving the house. She enjoyed the moment of opening it, like a cork letting the pressure out of a bottle. The door was a wooden eyelid, blinking open to a street of old brick houses and parked cars, a street that smelt different every day, a quiet street with sometimes just a silent passer-by. Until that morning it had been a predictable process, that passage through the door, but as it started to swing open, before she could even see outside, Jo heard a noise like a mass intake of breath and a shuffling as if some large animal was preparing to pounce. A crowd of men were clustered around their steps, the closest of them actually standing on the bottom step. There were cameras pointing at her and a tall, bald man near the back shouted, 'Is your mother in, ducks?'

Jo stepped back, stunned, and slammed the door. The wet clothes didn't matter because she didn't go to school that day and Fleur told her not to go near the front windows and not to answer the phone which rang all the time.

That evening they climbed the fence into the Robinsons' back garden then squeezed through the hedge into the driveway beyond that, coming out into the supermarket car park and then walking and walking until they got to a small hotel on the

18

Fulford road. All Fleur would say was that she would tell Jo when the time came.

At breakfast next morning the time did come when the newspaper arrived with the pallid scrambled eggs. It had a big picture of her mother on the front page.

'Developer Accused in Planning Scandal' was all Jo had time to see before Fleur folded it inside out and sat on it—that and a smaller photo of her mother and Justin Reynolds cutting a tape with a pair of scissors and a big smile.

'Is it bad?' Jo asked. It was the first time she had ever seen her mother look uncertain.

'Nothing that won't blow over.'

'That was you and Mr Reynolds in the paper?'

'Some shabby little journalist has got the wrong end of the stick.' Fleur looked around and lowered her voice although there was nobody else in the room. 'I build houses for people to live in and nobody's grateful. Nobody at all.'

Jo tried to feel sorry for her but nothing much came. Surely there should be a connection between us, she thought to herself, but the old familiar voice whispered in her head. 'You're not really hers,' said Gally's voice and tears came to her eyes—tears of relief that Gally was still there. Jo's tablets had been left behind at the house, along with almost everything else. It was a whole day since she had taken one. She didn't like her tablets. They wrapped part of the inside of her head in a fuzzy blanket that stopped her talking to Gally, stopped the parade of thoughts and pictures in her head, stopped her wanting to write stories. The tablets painted her whole life grey and made her heavy. 'You're not really hers.' It felt a harsh

19

judgement but she knew it was right.

Mr Reynolds' wife came to the guest house that morning for a huddled conversation in the bedroom while Jo had to sit downstairs reading. Mrs Reynolds came into the room half an hour later.

'Hello, Jo,' she said. 'Your mother asked me to give you some more spiritual cleansing. I've got a minute or two. Just kneel by my feet, will you.'

'No,' said Jo. 'Thank you. There's no need.'

'Oh, but there is. That's the Devil speaking. We must drive him out.'

'Now listen to me,' said Jo firmly. 'You have very little understanding of these things and it is quite possible, though not absolutely certain, that you have a genuine wish to help me, although it is equally possible that you enjoy the power you can wield over less forceful people, but I have a different understanding of the way the world works. I believe there is no evil, only an absence of good from time to time. Nothing in me needs driving out and if it did, I would not choose you as the driver.'

Mrs Reynolds listened to her at first in surprise, and then in some kind of growing horror.

'That's not you speaking, Jo. Don't you see? That's the voice of the Old One. There is darkness inside you. I have to do what I have to do. You must be saved.'

She lunged forward and wrapped her arms round Jo, squeezing hard.

'Let me go,' said Jo, then louder, 'Let go of me right now.' Leah Reynolds put one hand over her mouth and began to intone 'In nomine Domini, Gloria . . .' ending in a scream as Jo bit her hand

20

and burst out of her grasp.

'I warn you,' said Jo. 'I don't like hurting people unless I have no choice, and I'm smaller than you, but if you come any closer I shall hit you so hard that it will really hurt,' and the voice in her head, the old one who was not at all the same Old One that Mrs Reynolds meant, cheered her as the other woman rushed out of the room.

*　　*　　*

There was a period after that when they lived an uncomfortable life in a chilly guest house in Scarborough. The only good thing about it—though it was a very good thing—was that her mother entirely forgot about the pills in her preoccupation, so colour came back into Jo's life to liven up the grey, and her private friend came back to her completely. It wasn't quite the same. Mostly, when Jo needed her advice or her support, she knew what Gally would say without needing to hear the actual words spoken in her head. Every now and then it was just like old times again and she would feel her friend really was right there, in her old place. Those were the times she liked best.

One day, when she was feeling queasy after a breakfast of undercooked fat sausages, she found a familiar plant growing at the far end of the guest house garden. She picked a leaf and was crumpling it in her palm, ready to chew the pieces, when an urgent voice spoke in her head—Gally's voice.

'No,' it said. 'Look again.'

So she inspected it and though it looked almost exactly like Holy Rope, she saw that perhaps it was not quite the same, so she threw the crumpled leaf away, took another one carefully from the plant and walked to the library to find a book that might explain her mistake. She could not find Holy Rope in the index, but after looking at all the pictures she had just identified it as Eupatorium when the young male librarian walked up to the table where she was bent over the book, took the leaf from her with a tutting noise and whispered, 'I think I'd better throw this away, don't you?'

Jo looked up at him in clear surprise and he whispered again, with a smile, 'Oh, come on. You and I both know what this is. You're a bit young for the weed, aren't you?'

Jo's blank expression made him stop smiling. 'It's cannabis, dear,' he said. 'All right?' When he left her alone, she studied the pictures and noted the differences.

The effect of the pills was finally completely gone and she knew she had come back to life. Her old, secret friend now dwelt nearer Jo's centre, usually silent but always there with a nudge, a thought or a different way of looking at things— more like a memory bank of wise advice now than an older sister. That left Jo a little lonelier but there were compensations. There was more acceptance at her new school, even people who were almost like friends, though she was not allowed to play with any of them outside school— for fear, her mother said, of drawing attention to themselves.

'We're like spies, you and me,' said her mother. 'We have to stay undercover for a bit. Don't say where you lived before. Don't answer any of those sort of questions.'

More than that, there was the rich harvest of

imagination that filled her head. She only had to close her eyes to see pictures of places and people, and around them she found she could spin stories that became more real for her than the alien seaside town they inhabited. At first the sea itself featured in none of them. Looking east across grey waves she had a sense of dangerous people far away, but these waves were as alien as the town itself. Just sometimes, when the wind was kind and the sun shone, she was reminded of a different sort of sea, a wide bay with headlands and a narrow strip of land separating the long beach from a lake at its back.

The other compensation was that her mother had less power over her. For a quiet life, she did what Fleur asked her to do but she knew, because she had been told, that she did not really belong to Fleur and that made it possible to endure. The only time she really put her foot down was when her mother told her that they might go to live in Greece, where the sun shone and there were more of what she called 'development opportunities'. The idea appalled Jo so much that she flatly refused to consider it and her mother was so unnerved by the icy obduracy she displayed that she let the subject drop.

For all that, Jo was yearning for something and she thought at first that it might be the old house in York, though that didn't quite seem to be it. There was another blessing. They were further away from the field at Stamford Bridge and that suited Jo, because on the occasional times when they had driven past it, she always had to force her mind closed against a wave of sadness.

Her mother spent a lot of time talking to

lawyers. After two months they moved into a rented bungalow full of the sort of furniture that wobbled and squeaked halfway to splitting when you sat down on it. One day her mother came back to the bungalow late in the evening and told her to stop reading. 'You've always got your nose in some book,' she said. 'You should watch more TV. Anyway, I've got something to tell you.'

She sat down dangerously, heavily. Jo thought her mother had put on a lot of weight since they left York. She brought cakes home every day and ate most of them herself.

'We're going to have a fresh start,' said Fleur with a bright smile. 'I need to go somewhere else— somewhere where I can do the sort of things I do best and not have to argue with small-minded people all the time. They've got it in for me round here.'

'Where are we going?'

'Exeter.'

'Where's that?'

Fleur opened the book of road maps and pointed to it.

'That's a long way away,' said Jo, though she didn't mind that, not the way she had minded about Greece. She stared at the bottom corner of England pointing down to the left like a pig's snout, and felt a stirring of excitement.

'Yes, it is a long way,' said Fleur as if that was the whole point. 'I just hope it's far enough.'

*   *   *

So they packed up their stuff and on a fine Sunday they got in the car and drove away from the

24

Yorkshire coast, along roads that got larger and busier until they were sucked into the bland and blinded motorway which hid England from Jo's avid eyes behind crash barriers and signs and services. Even when it allowed her a glimpse of a church or a wood or a hill, it whisked them away again before she could find anything real.

Four and a half dull hours brought them to signs saying 'Bristol' and a violent couple of minutes where protesting horns erupted round them as Fleur swerved from lane to lane, cursing, as she lurched from one motorway to another. Jo saw wide water to her right and learned from the map that she was looking across at another country on the far side, no longer England but Wales. She was disappointed that it looked so similar as if it should have been a different colour.

A county border sign said 'Somerset' and the countryside seemed to grow kinder. For no reason she could understand, a fierce excitement began to bubble up inside her, then not so much inside her as from the outside, like a call or a promise. She tried to locate it by turning her head back and forth as if it were a homing beacon. Out across the fields and the trees, she saw a hill rearing out of the distant skyline, a sharp cone of green all by itself, and on top was the stone finger of a tower. She checked the number of the junction they passed, searched the map again and thought it might be Glastonbury Tor.

The quiet voice in her head said 'Home' and she searched the map again hoping that might be the way to Exeter, off to their left, but Exeter was still a whole page of map straight ahead.

'Can we go that way?' she asked.

25

'Where?'

'Over there, to the left.'

'That's not the way,' Fleur said crossly.

'Please? I'm sure we'll find somewhere nice.'

'Don't be daft. We're going to Exeter. It's straight on. I just want to get there and put my feet up.'

There was a junction ahead and Jo felt an urgent desire rising in her, suppressing all her common sense. It was as simple and basic as being deep under water and needing to swim upwards. 'Just for a few miles,' she said, then louder, 'I want to go that way. I want to see what it's like. It can't do any harm. Turn left here—that's all you have to do. Please, just do that.' She didn't know she was shouting, and for a moment she thought her mother was going to do what she wanted because Fleur pulled sharply across from the fast lane to the slip road, but all she did was bump up on to the kerb at the roundabout, switch off the engine and turn round to confront her daughter with fury on her face.

'I thought you'd finished with all that nonsense,' she said. 'All right then, little miss. We'll get you straight back on the pills, just you see. Now you shut up. I don't want another word out of you.'

'Don't fight her,' said the calm voice in Jo's head. 'You're right. That's home. You'll be free to go there some day.'

'When?' she asked quietly.

'When you're old enough. Soon.'

Sorrow crept through her as the land around chilled to evening and the turning wheels took them further away from wherever it was.

CHAPTER 3

Jo woke up sure she had heard the alarm, immediately afraid she was late for school. The bell ran away to the back of her head into the dream space and she knew it for the wrong bell, a church bell tolling wildly, not the clock's calm electric buzz. Night filled the room but it was an unfamiliar shade crossed with yellow and the sounds were unfamiliar too—a quiet slapping of water and a car engine in the wrong place, with the wrong echo.

Remembering she was now in this unknown Exeter, she got out of bed on to a bristly floor that released traces of a landlord's cleaning chemicals as her toes disturbed the pile. She went to the open window, leaned out staring sideways, towards the dark water of the river with street-light splashes bouncing on the ripples. The buildings beyond rose towards the centre of the city. It felt no worse than York, a little better even, just another place to be. Up the hill, a distant bell chimed twice and she switched on the light to check again that she had all her clothes ready. They were clothes from her old school and her mother had promised that the new school would not mind. There was the map her mother had printed off for her and two pound coins. Fleur had a meeting, she said. Otherwise she would have taken Jo there, as it was her first day, but she was sure it would all be all right. Jo looked at the map. It seemed a long way. She went quietly back to bed.

In the morning, she took the map and the two

pounds and a spare set of keys from a hook by the door and went out to find herself cut off from the city by the river. She turned right, looking for a way across, wasted five precious minutes, then turned back in mounting alarm and found a footbridge to the far side. There would be a bus, her mother had said, but when she found a bus stop, the names of the destinations bore no resemblance to anything on her map. She asked a young woman who looked like a student and replied in what Jo thought might have been German, then a traffic warden who pointed vaguely ahead. At nine o'clock, when school started, her heart was pounding and she was finally in a road whose name appeared on her map, but it seemed to be a long road and the side turnings came crawling towards her, each one refusing to fit the deceptively ordered promises of her now-crumpled map.

On the edge of tears, she sat on a bench and asked Gally to help her. To her surprise, she felt a small bubble of laughter start up inside her, a feeling of how ridiculous this was. I'll get there when I get there, she thought. It has to be somewhere.

It was half past nine when she finally reached St Matthew's School. The grounds were empty so she followed the signs to the school office where they looked at her clothes in surprise, consulted the computer and led her to a classroom where every eye swivelled towards her as she walked in.

'This is Jo,' said the woman who had brought her. 'She's just arrived.'

It was a science lesson and the class was split up mostly into groups of three, mixing liquids in tubes.

28

The teacher looked around and settled on the only pair of girls. 'You can work with them,' he said. 'Lizzy, look after Jo, will you?'

The girl, who had long blonde hair, made a face and Jo's heart sank but all she said was 'My name's not Lizzy.'

The other girl, who was short, studious and quite wide, said, 'Ignore her. He's only gone and delivered you into the hands of the most dangerous girl in the whole school. I'll look after you. I'm the sensible one. I'm Ali.'

*   *   *

And that was how the three of them turned into a trio, how Jo's life became more bearable and how she let more normal emotional comforts in. Lizzy—who turned out to be Lucy—and Ali had been inseparable for years. They had met on their first day at primary school when the teacher paired them up for a spelling exercise. Ali was immediately fascinated by Lucy's insouciance, by her declared lack of interest in anything she termed boring and also by her clothes, which seemed to come from a richer and softer planet than the one Ali inhabited. Lucy was secretly impressed by the fact that Ali knew so much stuff.

It took three weeks before Fleur found a private psychiatric clinic for Jo, in a large country house half an hour from Exeter, and that was a valuable three weeks because it cemented Jo's friendship with Ali and Lucy before more tablets arrived to take the edge off her. The doctor had a name full of harsh sounds and a voice to match so that Jo could often not understand the questions he asked

29

her. He listened to Fleur more than he did to Jo, nodding as Fleur described events that Jo had trouble recognising. He accepted Fleur's account of Jo's imaginary voices and suggested a new brand of antipsychotic. 'It is mild,' he said, 'only mild. You will hardly notice but very good, I think.'

Jo noticed and Ali noticed and Lucy noticed. After school, Jo would usually go back to one or the other of their houses. Lucy's house was modern and airy and full of colour. Lucy's parents, who were both something to do with media consultancy, treated their daughter as if she was an amusing acquaintance of their own age and gave her an allowance which meant Lucy's room was always full of shopping bags and new clothes, a rainbow array of disposable self-indulgence. Ali's home, indeed her whole life, was the antithesis of that. Her family lived in a Victorian villa with narrow windows—an old and serious place where the ceilings were high, the bulbs were dim and the walls were grey. There was nothing soft about it. The rooms were full of trays and boxes of bones and broken pottery and occasionally, when her mother came back from her latest excavation, Ali would find fresh boxes had overflowed into her bedroom. Her mother, who was the prototype of Ali's short and powerful build, told her they were interesting and she believed her. While Christine Massey was away digging, Ali and her father would potter round the house in a companionable and undemanding alliance. He became much more fun. When Christine returned in a welter of rucksacks, the communication switched to Colchester colour-coated beakers, Samian bowls and the rim shapes of black burnished ware. Ali longed for the time when she would know enough to say something about them that her mother would want to listen to.

The whole house smelt of old earth and slow decay and Jo woke from her first sleepover on a mattress on Ali's floor to find herself staring into the eye sockets of a skull with a sword-cut across the top. She didn't mind that at all. She stared quietly at the skull until Ali woke up, wondering what sort of soft, flexible flesh had once turned it into a face, what sort of brain had steered it along and who had mourned for it.

That was before the new tablets came. Afterwards, few thoughts like that could penetrate the chemical barrier. 'You're a lot more normal these days,' Fleur said. 'That's a relief, I can tell you. No more talking to the fairies.'

'Why do you have to take them?' Lucy asked indignantly, sprawled across her bed. 'They're bad for you. You're much quieter. My mother says you should call ChildLine.'

'It's not her fault,' said Ali, who was sorting her homework into folders. 'You know what Fleur's like. Would you want to argue with her?'

Ali knew all about forceful mothers. When Christine Massey thought something was a good idea, other people tended to give in. Christine had never considered the possibility that her daughter's preferences might not be exactly congruent with her own. When she was seven, Christine hoisted Ali into the saddle of a small pony because she had heard that riding was the healthiest interest to cultivate in a daughter. Ali found the height, smell and muscled determination of the pony quite terrifying but that had no impact on her mother.

31

Unable to see any alternative to falling off this wobbly ridge of leather-topped horseflesh, Ali did so many times and was immediately hoisted back on by Christine, who saw this as only a minor interruption to the project. Ali rode for the next six years without enjoying a single second of it and was only released when the pony died of old age, or possibly pity for her. During that time, the idea of telling her mother she would rather not never even crossed Ali's mind. She had developed a worried look by the time she was five and it rarely left her. In her own life, she tried to be as forceful as her mother and could never quite bring it off.

The three of them only rarely went back to Jo's house. Fleur was usually busy, poring over plans and estimates on the kitchen table, or deep in conversations with builders and architects as she rebuilt her business life. Mother and daughter shared the same roof but very little of anything else.

*   *   *

The three girls grew up at different speeds and in different ways as the years passed. Lucy went on looking two years older than she really was and refusing to take any boy seriously who wasn't another two years older than that. Jo had turned from child to girl and those boys who looked first at Lucy would often find something less obvious but more lasting when their gaze slipped to Jo, though they shied away from her detachment if they tried to take it further. Ali prayed secretly for some miracle of puberty that might stretch her upwards and inwards. One winter's day at the end

32

of 2009, just after lunch, Jo found her sitting on the frosty grass behind the science block, with her back to the wall and traces of tears on her cheeks.

'I was looking for you,' Jo said as she sat down beside her. 'What's up?'

'Oh, nothing,' said Ali. 'Everything. You know.'

'No I don't. Tell me.'

Ali sighed. 'I heard Chris and Tim talking. They didn't know I was there. Chris said I'd been mooning around and he thought I fancied him and Tim said "Bad luck." He said I was a ...' She stopped.

'You don't have to tell me what he said. He's an idiot.'

'He said I was a fat dwarf with breath like a sewer.'

'You haven't got bad breath.'

Ali gave her a dark look.

'You're not fat,' said Jo, 'and you're five foot two.'

'Five foot two and a half,' said Ali and burst into sobs.

'Chris Mellon is a halfwit and Tim Smith barely even counts as a life form.' Jo put her arm round her friend's shoulders.

'That's not everything. There's Facebook. I've been getting horrible messages.'

'Who from?'

'From the Six.'

'The sleazy Six?'

The Six were the girls who thought they ran the school—the sharpest, hardest, rudest sixteen-year-olds in the place.

'Listen to me,' said Jo. 'None of that matters. When we've done our GCSEs we'll be out of here

33

and going to Exeter College and this will all be a bad dream. That's only a few months.'

'But right now, I'm here and they're here and . . .'

'And what?'

'. . . and I'm nearly sixteen and I still don't have a boyfriend and I wish I did,' Ali wailed.

'Ali, that's like crying on Monday because it's not Thursday.'

'What do you mean?'

'Your life will come along at its own speed and when you're not expecting it, and there's nothing you can do to hurry it up.'

'But it might not.'

Jo moved a little away from her and stared out at the wider world as if she were listening to something, and when she turned back Ali thought some mystery had come into her eyes. 'There used to be times when there weren't enough men or women to go round,' Jo said, 'usually men because they caught the rough end of the world. Then if you were stuck, like most people were back then, and you couldn't get away, you just had to put up with it, but even then the good ones found their match. I don't mean people like the Six, I mean the really good ones—people like you, the sort of people someone would want to spend their life with. The right person comes along. And it's so different now. You meet so many people these days, so very many people. Nobody stays in one place any more but that helps, you see? Just breathe deeply and be patient. Your time will come.'

Ali stared at her. 'You haven't been taking your pills, have you?'

'Not for three days,' said Jo. 'Mum forgot again. She's picking them up today.'

'Don't you feel the difference it makes?'

Jo shrugged. 'Yes, but then I forget.'

But for Fleur's approach to life, the friendship of the three girls might not have survived the amount of time Jo spent shut down in her chemically-dulled world. Fleur always put Jo second to her business activity and that meant there were regular periods when they ran out of pills. For three or four days, every now and then, Jo would emerge from that chrysalis and remind her friends why they stuck with her.

The other two, Lucy in her studied flightiness and Ali in her stolid determination, were on a mission to save Jo from malign adult forces.

*   *   *

One day in early May 2010, with the start of their GCSE exams only two weeks away, Ali summoned the other two to join her in a cafe on the way home from school.

'My mother's got this idea,' she said, and Lucy groaned.

'The answer's no,' she said. 'Now what's the idea? Somehow I already know it's not going to be fun.'

'No, it will be. Listen.'

'Does it involve digging?'

'That's not the point. It—'

'It's digging. Count me out.' Lucy got to her feet and reached for her bag.

'Give her a chance,' said Jo. She was dull that day.

35

'Why? I know all I need to know.'

'There are boys,' Ali said quietly, and Lucy sat down.

Lucy was currently playing the role of tragically spurned lover. She had spent the past three months entwined around sharp-tongued Matt, tall, slim and nearly twenty—Matt, with his own band which played evening gigs in some of the town's bars and cafes. Matt's drummer, Whizz, liked Jo in a hopeless and unrequited fashion but Ali knew none of them were interested in her.

The group had been broken up by Matt's sudden switch of affection to a nineteen-year-old music student.

'It's such a *tragedy*,' Lucy had said. 'Horrible Harriet's *stolen* him and it's not just *my* pain, it's yours too.'

'Don't worry about me,' Ali said immediately.

'I didn't really mean you, I meant poor Jo.'

'I'll probably survive,' said Jo.

Lucy was getting tired of the tragic role. 'What boys?' she asked.

'Twelve students from Bristol University.'

'Twelve students? They could be girls.'

Ali shook her head. 'By the law of averages half of them will be boys. That's two each.'

'No it's not. It's one each for you two and four for me.'

'One?' said Ali, 'Only one?' but the fact was she would have given anything for one.

'You can have mine,' Jo offered. She knew Lucy would be able to take her pick. Lucy had been surrounded by boys since they had first met. Jo had no obvious beauty yet, just a pleasing curve of cheek and chin framed by dark brown hair, but her smile turned heads and that smile, once so rare, was seen more often these days. The boys who were drawn to it got no more than polite interest. Jo found them all too young and wondered briefly if a Bristol student might not have attractions.

'Seriously,' said Ali, 'none of us knew what to do after the exams, did we? At least none of us could think of anything our parents would actually let us do.' She meant her parents and Jo's mother, because they all three knew Lucy's would let her do whatever she wanted within reason. 'The advantage of this is that my mother thinks it's a good idea.'

'My mother wants to send me off to some camp because she's going to a conference,' said Jo.

'Hang on,' said Lucy. 'Just before we sign up for this, what exactly is it?'

'It's a three-week dig at a place called Montacute on the site of a Norman castle.'

Jo looked at her, frowned, looked away.

Lucy studied her. 'Astonishing. You manage to sound excited about that.'

'It's three weeks of freedom,' Ali said with a note of pleading in her voice.

'Where will we be staying?'

'Everyone's camping. All the diggers. I'm glad. It's much more fun that way.'

'I have very firm views on camping,' said Lucy. 'I don't mind sleeping under the stars so long as there are five of them and they're fixed to a hotel wall.'

'No, it's really fun, I promise. They have campfires at night and they sing songs and stuff.'

'Is there a pub?' asked Lucy.

'Probably.'

'They'll serve us if we're with all the others, won't they?'

'Maybe.'

'I haven't been ID'd for *ages*. Will they have power at the campsite? I don't want my iPod going flat.'

'Power? It's a field. A field with boys in it,' said Ali hopefully.

'But I know what archaeologists look like,' said Lucy. 'I've seen them on television. They've got long straggly hair like old sheep and they're bald on top. They get incredibly excited about very small broken bits of pottery. They're always drinking beer and they knit their own sweaters.'

'Where exactly is Montacute?' Jo asked.

'Near Yeovil,' said Ali, and brought out a map.

As Jo looked at the map, some of the names on it penetrated the curtain in her head, prompting a small thrill almost like pleasure—Martock, Somerton, Wincanton. She put her finger on Montacute and knew she wanted to go there.

*　　　　*　　　　*

A month and a half later the three girls got out of the Yeovil bus in the middle of Montacute village and lined up on the verge like some demonstration poster of different body types: Lucy, the tall blonde with the aquiline profile; Jo, half a head shorter, dark and curved; Ali, who barely reached Lucy's shoulder, stocky and with hair which looked, as Lucy had once said in a far-too-honest moment, as if it had been assembled from other people's leftovers.

Jo was looking all around her and seemed to be

sniffing the air. It was the nearest to liveliness that her friends had seen all week. The other two had come out of their GCSE exams released from pressure but completely true to type. Lucy had indulged in a theatrical spectrum ranging from comic despair after the Maths exam to claiming the best answers ever written to an English paper. Ali had been quietly pleased with all of them, but anxious not to rub that in if she was talking to anyone less confident. Jo had only said they were mostly all right.

'Jo,' said Lucy, 'before we get there, Ali and I have got something to say.'

'Yes?'

'Fleur made us promise something before she agreed you could come.'

'I can guess.'

'She made us promise to watch you take your tablets every day.'

'Oh, don't worry,' said Jo with a sigh. 'I will.'

'No. That's what we want to say. We're not going to do it. It's up to you. You don't have to take them.'

'Why?'

'Because we know what you're like when you don't. That's the real Jo.'

She looked at her friends, unsure what to say, so used now to the dulled-down world that the idea of weeks away from it sounded almost frightening, then she nodded slowly.

Ali looked at her instructions and the map. 'It's this way,' she declared and set off. They made a hundred yards before Lucy stopped them.

'My straps are hurting.'

'I'm not surprised they're hurting. You can see

39

through that cotton,' Ali said. 'Didn't you bring an old sweater or something?'

'I don't own any *old* sweaters.'

'Didn't you bring anything serious?'

A Land Rover was coming up behind them.

'All my clothes are extremely serious. Those Bristol boys won't know what's hit them. Just make sure you're on my tail. Where I lead, you follow.'

The Land Rover pulled in ahead of them.

'You said they'll all have big white beards,' Ali said. 'They're not even going to notice the fact that you're hardly wearing anything at all.'

The driver of the Land Rover opened his door as they reached it.

'You look like the rest of my diggers,' he said. 'I'm Rupert. I'm running the dig. Would you like a lift?'

'Where's your big white beard?' said Lucy.

'You've got to be Christine Massey's daughter,' said the Land Rover driver, glancing at Ali as he let in the clutch. 'You look just like her.'

Ali sighed.

CHAPTER 4

The last thing Ali wanted to hear on this first day of freedom was that she looked like her mother, so she was still frowning as she pulled the components of their tents out of their bags. She was also cross with Lucy, who had sat in the front of the Land Rover deliberately swaying as it bounced through the potholes so that her shoulder collided with Rupert's, though he had seemed oblivious.

'You'll be pleased to hear the forecast is fine,' he said. 'I can promise lots of food and good company. As for the archaeology, I've made my offerings to the gods of dirt and we will see what they provide.'

He turned in through a field gate and nosed the Land Rover against the hedge on the end of a line of cars.

'Grab your stuff. Pitch camp at the far end of the tents. Tea, cake and first get-together in about an hour.'

He walked off towards a billowing pile of camouflaged green canvas where a group of young men were struggling with wooden poles.

Lucy stared after him. 'Six foot two, eyes of blue,' she said. 'Who said archaeology was boring?' Then she saw him join the men at the marquee. 'Those must be the students,' she said, 'One, two, three, four, five, six, seven. Well, seventy-five per cent of them are the right gender.'

'Fifty-eight and a third,' said Ali. 'Seven-twelfths is fifty-eight and a third per cent. You divide a hundred by seven and—'

'That's what I have you for,' said Lucy. 'You do the dividing and Jo and I will go and do the multiplying.'

Jo had been staring up at the steep wooded hill that rose two hundred yards away from their field. She smiled, glanced towards the marquee and began straightening out the tent and its tangled nylon cords. Lucy walked off towards the marquee without a backward glance and Ali stared after her a little nervously. She had gone along with the bravado of the boy talk. She had lived through

41

varied fantasies of this adventure since the first moment her mother had suggested it. All of them had a boy in them somewhere—a boy who would fit Ali perfectly, a boy who would like doing what she did, who would rather listen to the birds singing than something on earphones, who would have read Cormac McCarthy's novels and Alice Oswald's poetry—above all, a boy who wouldn't keep looking at Lucy or Jo when he should be looking at her. None of those fantasies had the flapping of canvas and the sound of strange male voices in them. The figures round the marquee were frighteningly real and only a short walk away.

Ali knew Lucy would be straight in there like a manseeking missile and she feared she would be left, awkward and unappealing. She finished fitting together one of the poles, a long snake of glass-fibre sections, and started on the other one. They put up Ali's big tent to sleep in and Jo's tiny pup tent to put their bags in and made themselves dizzy blowing up airbeds.

'Don't do it. Leave it to her,' said Jo as Ali turned to Lucy's deflated mattress.

'Oh, I don't mind,' Ali replied but before she could start, they heard Rupert shout. They walked across to where the camouflage canvas had been propped up, stretched and pegged down into a marquee so that what had been a ragged block of wind was now a tamed, friendly space—a place of tables, benches and a score of people talking animatedly like old friends meeting again. Lucy was in the middle of a group of boys.

'This is Andy,' she said, putting her arm round the shoulders of an athletic looking student with curly fair hair, 'and these are Sandy, Randy, Dandy and . . . um . . .'

'No we're not,' protested one of them, 'I'm Doug and this is Jonno, Conrad and—' He was interrupted by a shout from Rupert.

'Okay everyone, settle down,' he called. 'If you're not holding a mug of coffee, grab one quick. It's good and strong and there's chocolate cake on an epic scale.'

The girls headed for the trestle tables with the food. Lucy hissed at them, 'He's mine. You choose from the others. There's no competition.'

'What do you mean?' Ali whispered back.

'The girls. I think they dug them up but they haven't washed the dirt off yet.'

They filled mugs and plates and followed Lucy back towards the bench where all the students were sitting. Rupert called out, 'Find yourselves a seat, everybody, and we'll get started.'

The renewed buzz died down, the end of one woman's sentence left tapering in the air, '. . . shoulder brooch, second century at the very latest, as it turned out.'

All faces turned to Rupert. 'Some of us know each other from here or there. You'll get to know my students. They're moderately house-trained but don't lend them any money. You might remember Paul Tatham—he hasn't been around for a few years. Something about Australia, wasn't it? So welcome back to proper archaeology, Paul. There's the famous Dozer, of course. Every dig needs a Dozer.' There was a scatter of laughter and the girls looked round to see who he was talking about, but everyone was looking back at them as Rupert pointed.

'I don't think any of you know these three,' he

said. 'They're Alison, Jo and Lucy. If you've ever laboured under the iron rule of Christine Massey, you'll spot where Ali's DNA comes from. OK, now, down to business. The reason we're all here is because a dog disappeared down a rabbit hole. Its owner, Mr Hogarth, was shouting down into a space which seemed to echo and a few minutes later, when he was starting to panic, the dog—Heineken by name—came bouncing up from somewhere behind him covered in earth. From which we deduce that there is a large subterranean void down there. Mr Hogarth, being an unusually sensible man, called English Heritage and lo and behold, here we are in a remarkably short time to investigate Mr Hogarth's hole.'

He turned to a display board and pointed at a plan.

'St Michael's Hill, Montacute,' he said. 'The tower on top is an eighteenth-century folly but the rest is pure Norman motte and bailey, built in 1068 by William the Conqueror's half-brother Robert of Mortain—part of his campaign to subdue Somerset. There's been a bit of archaeology here over the years but there is no record that anyone found any kind of void or chamber. This is a natural pile of earth and rock which once had a timber castle perched on top. Solid is the word. You do not, in the normal way of things, fall into holes in a place like this.'

He looked around at the attentive faces and pointed to a cross on the plan. 'That's where Mr Hogarth's hole appeared, so we're going to sneak up on it carefully. There's some vegetation to shift so while Johan and Sheila get the finds tent ready and Bobby does food, the rest of us will grab mattocks, hoes and shovels and get stripping.'

         *   *   *

It was a steep climb up to a terrace on the side of the hill, in amongst the trees that covered almost all of it. The three girls were given wheelbarrows and told to dump the turf and weeds on the shoulder of the hill. Ali did it with the experienced determination of someone who had been brought up on such digs. Jo watched her and followed suit, two barrow-loads to Ali's three, using just the minimum effort required to keep up with the waste heap. Lucy found indirect routes which took her past where the boys were working with Andy stripped to the waist. Her gossamer stamina soon evaporated and she began to display a theatrical incapability which produced the entire spectrum of possible mishaps—upturned barrows, downhill runaways and uphill collisions with those trying to come down. When Rupert finally told them to pack up she was sitting on a tree stump, trying to take it all seriously enough to sulk.

They went to wash and then the other two waited while Lucy changed, complaining about the lack of a proper mirror in the tent. The marquee was already full of hungry diggers.

'Their table is full,' Lucy complained. 'We'll have to sit somewhere else. We should have got here sooner.'

As the sun dipped behind the side of the hill they ate a vegetable curry ladled, bubbling, from a vast wreck of an aluminium pot that had fed thousands since it last shone. An elderly giant of a man, white hair tied back in a ponytail and biker's tattoos on his arms, was sitting next to them and he smiled at them as they ate.

'I'm Dozer,' he said in a voice that sounded like a truck engine on tick-over. 'What was your names again?'

They told him. 'Got it,' he said. 'You enjoying yourselves?'

'It's not very exciting yet,' said Lucy, and Ali kicked her under the table.

'Exciting? You came for excitement, did you? You did know it was archaeology?'

'I want to start finding things.'

Ali cut in, her voice stiff with embarrassment. 'She knows that. I've told her. It's not treasure-hunting.'

Dozer winked. 'That's what we all say but we're all fibbing.' He piled up their dirty plates. 'Fire time,' he said. 'I'll start fixing it.'

'A campfire?' asked Lucy. 'Here? Oh good.'

'Not here,' said the old biker, sniffing the wind. 'Over there.' He nodded across the field.

'That's so the smoke doesn't affect the trenches,' said Ali didactically. 'It messes up the radiocarbon dating.'

The man looked down at her and grinned. 'Is that right? And I thought it was so the smoke doesn't blow into our tents.'

When he had got the fire going, the older diggers brought wine and beer from their cars and passed it round in plastic mugs. Dozer had dragged logs into a ring around the fire as makeshift benches. This time Lucy made sure they got in early, sitting herself firmly down next to Andy and towing the other two after her.

Jo found herself next to the one called Jonno.

46

'Did you enjoy this afternoon?' he asked. He had the build and the broken nose of a rugby player but his voice was light and lilting. Jo thought he might be Scottish.

'Enjoy?' she said. 'Endure is a bit more like it.'

'Clearing's never fun,' he answered. 'Tomorrow will be better.'

'I enjoyed it,' put in Ali. 'There's nothing like hard physical work.'

Conrad, the student next to her, nodded in approval, wiped his thick glasses and his brow with a spotted handkerchief. His pale chin was outlined by a dark, sporadic beard. 'Spot on,' he said. 'Just right.'

There was a tired buzz of contented people around the fire until Rupert stood up and called for silence.

'That's enough relaxation,' he said. 'Time for work now.' There was a chorus of catcalls. 'No, I mean it,' he went on.

'I thought this was going to be fun,' Lucy muttered.

The boys turned and grinned at her. Rupert seemed to be smiling in the darkness. 'I've asked one of my students to prepare a health and safety lecture for you tonight. Please welcome Conrad.'

Conrad sprang up into the firelight. His voice was rich and his words were confident.

'There are clear rules to be followed when working on this site,' he said, 'particularly when digging into its depths, as the following cautionary tale will demonstrate.'

He spun round and thrust out an arm to point towards the banks of the castle. 'Once upon a time, some time before now and since then, a man called

47

Jehosh dropped a coin down a rabbit hole in the castle mound and heard it clink, clink, clink as if against metal far below. Buried metal spelled treasure to Jehosh so he went to fetch a spade, intending to dig it up. But Jehosh was a lazy man.'

A log fell out of the fire in a cascade of sparks and Conrad strode to the other side of the circle. He seized a cup from a woman sitting there, drained it of wine in one gulp and tossed it back at her, then he wiped his lips and started again, turning constantly as he spoke so that his voice rose and fell, rose and fell in the thickening dark.

Ali turned, smiling, to Jo and Lucy, her eyes shining. Lucy shrugged. Jo smiled back.

'Jehosh summoned his brother Joseph to help him dig. Joseph was a better man than Jehosh but far worse than their brother Jacob, who was a holy man. They dug all evening until at last they rubbed the dark crumbs of earth away from the lid of a treasure chest made of solid silver, glinting in the last of the sun. In his black impatience, Jehosh tried to pull it out but when the earth still clutched it tight, he swore a terrible oath, damning his brother, the heavens and the earth, in a stream of words so violent that they hung, crimson and hissing, in the air after he had spoken them. As they faded, leaving a shadow of sulphurous smoke behind them, the birds fell silent, the sky turned a foetid purple, and with a scraping groan the treasure chest slipped deeper into the hole.

'Jehosh swore again, louder, and the earth crumbled again, taking the man with it so that his head disappeared below the surface of the ground. Joseph, who was a better man than Jehosh but not nearly so good as Jacob, leapt in after his brother.'

Ali nudged Jo and whispered, 'He's really good.'

Conrad glanced all around him and hunched forward conspiratorially.

'The sharp hobnails on Joseph's boots landed on the head of Jehosh and this time they both took the name of the Lord in vain. Their words hung, steaming and hissing, in the air above the hole and the earth below heaved and rumbled. Then it crumbled once more and down they both went.

'A wandering horse tamer happened by—a man from the high and frozen north. He heard their calls and ran to fetch their brother Jacob, who was, as you will recall, a better man than Joseph and a far better man than Jehosh. He recognised this as the work of the Devil so he shaved his head in the proper manner and said thirteen prayers before hastening to the castle mound. When he arrived he took great care to make sure that he walked around it in the right direction and did not go . . .' here Conrad dropped his voice . . . 'widdershins.'

'What does that mean?' Lucy whispered and before Ali could answer, Andy said, 'Anticlockwise.' Ali noticed that he and Lucy seemed to be leaning against each other for support.

'He exhorted his brothers far below to avoid all blasphemy but as he climbed down, he dislodged a shower of earth and small stones which fell on to the heads of his brothers below and he heard their voices join in a fresh invocation of Satan's name. At that, the day turned to full night and the entire mound shook. The earth tumbled in, taking Jacob, Joseph and Jehosh down into the far distant depths where voices can no longer be heard. When the sky lightened again there was not a movement to be seen and there was nobody there to see it until a roe deer stepped cautiously from the fringe of the wood to sniff at the tumbled earth. An entire night passed and in the morning, the searchers raised by the itinerant horse tamer came upon Jacob, white-faced and white-haired, crawling, shaking, from a badger's sett a full furlong from the mound. It is said to this day that if you find that same badger's sett, you may discover a human bone or two in the excavated earth around it—for that is all that was ever found of Jehosh, Joseph and the treasure of Montacute.'

Jo trembled. It was thirty-six hours since her last tablet and she wondered if this was the first touch of adrenalin anxiety that often came as the effect wore off. The flames of the fire seemed sharper and brighter. Conrad's voice still hung in her ears and she saw in her mind's eye a clear image of the hole and the treasure as if she had heard the story, or a story very like it, some time before. It felt long ago.

He stopped, bowed, and they all clapped. He held up a hand until they were silent again. 'That's the health and safety dealt with then,' he said. 'Shore up any trenches deeper than four feet. Test the ground beneath you for security and remember what happens when you swear.'

Rupert jumped to his feet and thanked him, then yawned. 'I'm for bed. Early start to catch the weather. Breakfast seven thirty. Briefing at eight. Someone else's turn to tell the story tomorrow. Night, all.'

Conrad came back to the log and Ali made space next to her. 'That was really good,' she said.

He smiled back at her. 'Thank you. Why don't

you do one tomorrow? You could do it together. It's fun.' And to their horror, Jo and Lucy heard Ali agree.

Jonno joined them and the wine bottles went round, and at some point Lucy and Andy disappeared into the dark and it was much later into the night when Lucy slid back into the tent, trying not to wake her friends and failing in the attempt.

*   *   *

They slept soundly on the hard earth, and when Jo woke in the morning from a dream she could not quite remember the tent seemed nearer to a home than anywhere else she had been. Just one day of shared experience had turned the marquee into a place full of friendly faces and kind enquiries. Dozer winked and waved at them. Conrad brought Ali a mug of coffee and she drank it as if it was what she had most wanted, though the other two knew she only ever drank tea. They stormed the slopes of the hill laughing and chattering in the middle of the group of students and when they got up to the high terrace, Rupert separated them out and gave them their very own end of a trench to work in, tucked in under a small, overgrown cliff with the hill rising towards its summit above them.

'You came back so *late*,' Jo said to Lucy. 'Come on, what happened?'

'This and that.'

'You were giggling when you crawled into the tent. How much of this and what sort of that?'

'That's better,' said Lucy. 'The real Jo is coming back again.'

51

'I don't think we should be chatting,' Ali said sternly. 'We're meant to be concentrating.' She hoped the other diggers couldn't hear them.

'Oh really, Ali? Then you won't want to hear what Conrad said about you.'

'Conrad? About me? What did he say?'

'I would tell you,' said Lucy, 'but I have to concentrate on this very, very dull bit of earth I'm kneeling on. It needs me to scrape at it very carefully in case I miss something that could change our entire understanding of the world of the wotsits, William the thingy and all that.'

'The Normans. Come on, what did Conrad say about me?'

Lucy held up a piece of root at arm's length and stared at it. 'No, no. Don't distract me. Look, this is obviously a Saxon's leg bone and it shows that they suffered from a mineral deficiency which made their bones all floppy which explains why they were beaten by the Normans because if you—'

'Stop it,' said Ali. 'Please tell me.'

'Put her out of her misery,' said Jo.

'Conrad likes you.'

Ali's voice squeaked. 'Does he? How do you know that?'

'Andy told me.'

'Really? What did he say? Exactly.'

'He said Conrad thinks you're a good sort. I do have a slight concern that his turn of phrase shows he must actually be about fifty years old and I could have sworn he was forty tops, but that's exactly what he said.'

'Stop it,' said Ali. 'He's only nineteen. And?'

'What do you mean, "And?" That's it.'

'That's it?' said Jo. 'A good sort? You get her all

52

excited and that's the best you can come up with?'

Lucy sniffed. 'There might have been something else.'

'What?' Ali demanded.

'It's not a word I care to utter,' said Lucy loftily. 'He said you were . . . no, I can't. My lips just won't form around it.'

'Please?'

'Oh, all right. He said you were . . . cute.'

'How did he say it? Just like that? "She's cute"? What did he look like when he said it? Was that all he—'

'Look at your face.' Lucy said, and she whipped out her phone and took a picture of Ali before she could compose herself. Ali shrieked. Lucy frowned. 'My God,' she said, 'I don't know why I'm being nice to you. I've just remembered what you let us in for.'

'Oh, well, I—'

'You volunteered us to tell the story tonight, didn't you? "We'll tell it," you said, not "I'll tell it." You said "we". Why exactly did you do that? No, don't answer. I know why. You were trying to impress Conrad.'

'Oh, come off it,' said Ali sheepishly. 'That's got nothing to do with it. I just thought we could—'

Lucy reached out her hands and covered Ali's mouth. 'Enough,' she said. 'I don't like public speaking and I don't have anybody to impress and I'm not going to do it.'

'Nor am I,' said Jo, and they both looked at Ali.

'All right then, I'll do it by myself,' said Ali. There was a silence. 'I don't mind standing up and speaking,' she said in a smaller voice, 'but I don't know what to say. Will you help me?'

'Maybe.'

'Please,' she begged. 'I need some ideas.'

Lucy pouted. 'I said maybe.'

Jo relented. 'I'll help you. There's nothing guys like more than a good story.'

'Really?' Lucy said. 'Is that true? Oh, all right.'

They stopped talking and got busy with their trowels because Rupert was walking towards them with a man they hadn't seen before—an older man with thinning hair and a drawn face.

'This is my friend Michael,' said Rupert. 'He's joining us for the day. I like to make sure he gets out in the fresh air sometimes. Mike, this is Lucy, this one's Jo and this one's Ali. Don't stand for any nonsense.' He smiled at the girls. 'Mike's a schoolteacher, so you've been warned.'

He walked away and the man shuffled uncomfortably. 'Ignore him,' he said.

'Are you really a teacher?' asked Lucy.

'Not at weekends.'

'What sort of school?'

'King Arthur's at Wincanton.'

'That sounds posh.'

'No, it's a comprehensive. Where are you from?'

'We all live in Exeter,' said Ali. 'My mother's an archaeologist.'

Jo was staring at him, remembering the map and the name. 'How far away is Wincanton?' she asked.

'Half an hour,' he said and pointed vaguely. 'That way.'

Jo was still staring at him, disconcerted by the disturbing feelings in her gut. Common sense told her this was another stage of the pills wearing off but it wasn't the way she was used to. Normally, she was nervous and frightened, feeling her pulse

54

racing as everything looked too bright and sounded too sharp. This was a slower feeling, a deep ache more like sorrow and a further disturbing something as if the pain written on this man's face might be somehow her fault. She dismissed it as absurd. He was a stranger, and when he looked at her there was no flicker of recognition.

'What are we doing?' the man asked.

'Just scraping this down,' Ali told him.

'Anything interesting?'

'Not yet.'

'No,' said the teacher. 'I suspected that any trench Rupert let me into was unlikely to contain anything I might damage.'

'Is that right?' said Lucy. 'That stinks. I'll show him. I'm going to find something.'

He settled himself a few feet further down the trench and scraped away with his back to them. The girls talked quietly.

'Come on then,' said Ali. 'What about this story, then?'

Fifteen minutes later they had the rough outlines of two different stories, one from Lucy and one from Ali, and they couldn't agree which one was best, then Lucy squealed, 'I've found something. What's this? It's metal, isn't it? I think it's silver.'

She had uncovered the curving top of something too smooth and regular to be natural. She rubbed away the dirt with her fingers and they stared at a thin grey rod, the thickness of a ballpoint pen, emerging from the earth and disappearing back into it three or four inches further along.

Ali knelt by it, scraping, and more and more emerged until they had a foot showing with no sign of an end. The teacher was looking back over his shoulder curiously.

Lucy levered the pointed end of the trowel underneath it. 'It's like a cable,' she said in disgust. 'I think it's modern.'

'Don't do that,' said Ali urgently. 'You have to scrape round the edges.' But she was too late. Lucy had hooked her fingers underneath it, got to her feet and yanked hard upwards. It was immediately clear that she was right about the cable and entirely wrong about the correct way to behave in a trench. The cable ran close to the exposed earth surface all the way down the long trench to where Rupert was working with some of the others twenty feet further along. It ripped up in a spray of earth, past the startled teacher and on down, all the way to Rupert who reared up on his haunches and turned with an expression of complete astonishment to look back to the culprit, caught red-handed and red-faced with the cable still in her hand.

Rupert beckoned to them and the three of them, followed by the teacher who seemed as embarrassed as they were, walked slowly to the far end of the trench.

'What on earth have you done?' said Rupert.

'Sorry,' said Lucy. 'But it's just some sort of wire, isn't it?'

Rupert looked at the damage she had done to the even surface of the trench and shook his head. 'I'll get Mike to explain a few things to you,' he said. 'You have to be more careful.'

Dozer had walked over from his trench, drawn by the fuss, and he broke in. 'Hey, Rupe,' he said. 'You know what? This is lead sheathing, old

56

electrical stuff, and it's got the jolly old broad arrow stamped all along it. War Department stuff. And guess what? It's heading straight towards our hole.'

'Five-minute break,' Rupert said. 'Let's have a think. Everyone—take a breather.'

The teacher joined the group standing round Rupert discussing the cable. The girls walked away into the trees and sat down on the grass. They were silent for a long time then Ali said, 'I wish you hadn't done that. It makes me feel like a complete idiot.'

'You? Why's it about you? I did it, not you.'

'But you wouldn't be here if it wasn't for my mother. I feel responsible.'

'Do me a favour!'

'Let's talk about something else,' Jo suggested quickly. 'What about these stories?'

There was a further long silence before the other two took the olive branch. In the end Lucy said, 'Let's tell both of them. I'll tell mine and you tell yours. They needn't be very long.'

Ali got to her feet. 'They're all going back to work. Come on.' They walked back to the other trench, where Dozer was peering at the surface of the earth. 'I'll get stage fright if I'm doing one by myself,' she said.

'You've done school plays.'

'I was dressed up as someone else. I can do it then.'

'All right, we'll dress up.'

'In what?'

'We'll find something. Old rags.'

'What old rags? Anyway, what about Jo?'

'I don't mind,' said Jo. 'I can't think of anything

57

to say.'

'Could you help me, maybe?' Ali asked. 'You could be there to remind me if I go wrong.'

'I don't know,' said Jo. 'I'd rather just . . .' but that was as far as she got because there was a loud gasp from the cliff above them and the dark shape of a body, arms spread out, crashed down into the trench right next to them in a shower of leaves.

CHAPTER 5

Miles away and hours before, a boy blinked awake from a warm dream of love to find himself in an empty bungalow, momentarily unsure of his name. The room's sour smell drove his dream away in tatters. He stared at the wall facing him, pale blue and streaked white where water had leaked down. His pyjamas were too short for him and the polyester slither of the sheet across his bare ankles filled him with a revulsion that drove him out of bed. Barry's car battery stood on the hall table, casually dumped on top of his photography project, and when he strained to lift it off it left wide black marks across the folder. He remembered it was Saturday, then that his exams were over and his holidays had started early. The thought gave him no pleasure. A note on the kitchen table said 'Luke, gone to the boot sale. Back later.' With the last tendrils of the dream still twitching, that did not feel like his name, nor did this thin and flimsy house feel like his home.

He dressed and went out to the garage, feeling a sudden magnetic pole-to-pole repulsion from this place where he had lived his sixteen years of life, knowing he wanted to get away, right away. He pumped up his bicycle tyres and every rubbery push of the pump handle injected escape magic until the bounce of the bike told him it was ready to go with him. The road led east or west, and west seemed the obvious chance with the morning sun behind him.

Leaving the house behind felt better and at the first junction he hesitated, tried one way then another then the third, which seemed the happiest choice in a way he could not have precisely described. So it was at each turning and he made his choices faster and faster, feeling a need to keep going. An hour's pedalling on empty lanes and thundering roads and then lanes again took him further from home than he had ever strayed before. A second hour wiped the signposts clean of familiar places. His legs were aching but the unknown cheered him on from somewhere far ahead and he even enjoyed the idea that he might not find his way back.

What stopped him was a conical hill, wrapped in trees, presented like a sudden invention of the earth as he laboured up out of a fold. The small tower rising from its summit snared his eye and the moment he saw it he knew he had to climb it, as if this had always been his destination. He thought he might see anything from the top: the sea or lions on a plain or a purple city or his future. On the edge of a village, he chained his bike to a fence and followed a beaten path to the base of the hill.

Where the trees started, the earth angled sharply upwards, and although a zigzag track offered an easier approach the boy scrambled straight up, using roots for handholds as the dry dirt sent his feet skidding. The trees ended before the summit plateau, circling the tower like a monk's tonsure.

Through its open doorway a hundred stone stairs twisted upwards, spiralling him to a cramped room right at the top where patches of wall-plaster were scored with the scratched spoor of visitors. He ran his fingers over some of the deep-cut words. 'Riga Latvia' said one, then below it 'F & G', and a heart surrounding the two words 'Angels—Daisy.'

Square openings barred with iron showed him quarters of the surrounding land and he looked through each in turn, hoping something might be revealed. He saw trees and fields and the distant misty hills and despaired that this might be all there was to show for his efforts, leaving him to pedal all the way back to that loveless house. He felt a scream rising in him and let it out, yelling at the sky in an abandonment that amazed him, yelling at two dots that came from those misty hills and grew into jet fighters coming straight at the tower, hurdling his hill-top wing tip to wing tip. His yell was soaked up into an immense noise that arrived at the same moment they did and persisted long after they had gone. When it diminished it had silenced him and the whole land seemed quieter, as if they had muscled all other sound out of the way.

In that new peace a twist of wind lifted the smell of early summer to his nose and carried with it a gentle murmur of human voices. They drew him back down the stairs and at the bottom he heard laughter, a call, the ring of metal, beckoning him to the far edge of the plateau. He saw red and white tape down below in the black mass of trees, a plastic barrier stretched between their trunks. The sounds came from beyond them in the darkness and they drew him on down. He picked his way, cautious and silent, intending to spy from cover, but the tape marked the start of an even steeper drop and a dead branch, shrouded by leaves, tricked his feet. They shot from under him so that he tobogganed over the edge under the abrupt violence of gravity, feet first and head back.

He fell for long enough to know fear and his lungs flattened as he met the earth below at full length, still on his back, all the air forced out of him. For a moment the world was changed by the concussion. Where there had been trees above, all he could see were purple spheres filling his vision. The shock of impact overwhelmed him and he closed his eyes to concentrate on the fight to fill his lungs. When he opened them again there were faces bent over him with expressions of alarm— three girls' faces focused on him like a fantasy.

'Where did *you* come from?' said a blonde girl, close enough to kiss, and he tried to say sorry through the head-to-toe hurt but there was still no air to make the words. The purple shapes had gone and he would have searched for them but didn't even want to move his eyes.

'Give him space,' growled a man's voice. The girls' faces vanished and a huge head with white hair strapped back in a ponytail took their place. Luke felt unbearable regret and his eyes grew damp with all sorts of pain.

'Just twitch both feet for me,' the man said, then, 'All right, matey, let's get you on your side.'

Large hands turned him gently over. 'Pull your knees up all the way. You're winded, that's all. You'll be all right in half a mo.'

Just when he knew he would suffocate he drew a little air, then more, until he was gasping it in.

'Now,' said the big man. 'Where does it hurt?'

'My back.' He felt fingers gently exploring.

'Just a scratch. You landed on my trowel. Lucky it's made of strong stuff. Can you move everything?'

The boy tried. 'Yes.' He lifted his head and saw that he was lying across a strip of bare earth and all around were buckets, shovels and plastic trays. A ring of people surrounded him.

'Show's over,' growled the man with the ponytail. 'He'll live. Back to it, you sorry lot.'

Too late, Luke saw the swing of a girl's hair between all the older people as they turned away. He sat up but she was lost to view. He looked up at the steep face of the slope he had fallen down and the man with the ponytail followed his eyes.

'Fifteen feet, maybe more,' said the man. 'Can you get up? I only ask because we need the trench. If you've finished with it, that is.'

Luke took the outstretched hand and stood up carefully.

'I'm Dozer,' the man said. 'You okay?'

'Yes. What are you doing?'

'Digging. Just started. All we've done is get the turf off.'

The boy looked at the long strip of earth and recognised it for what it was. 'You're archaeologists?'

Dozer nodded. 'So what do we call you?' he asked.

Part of the boy thought it would be good to get away as fast as he could, to leave his embarrassment far behind and take his aches with him back to the anonymous world below. 'Luke,' he answered, and the man laughed.

'Luke Skydiver,' he said. 'Just right.' Then from behind him another man's voice said, 'Hang on, I know you, don't I?'

Turning, he saw a familiar face—a teacher's face where there shouldn't be a teacher. Two hours from his school. That wasn't fair. Embarrassment would travel home with him now.

'I'm Luke Sturgess, sir.'

'Yes, of course. My History Club.'

They stared at each other in equal awkwardness. Luke had signed up for the after-school club entirely because he liked the picture on the poster. He had gone twice and it had gone badly.

'How did you get here, Luke?' The man was looking up the hill as if more people might come raining down. 'Are your parents here?'

Martin. Luke's memory gave him the name. Mike Martin. They'd hardly come across each other.

'No, I came by bike.'

'From Wincanton? All that way? Why?'

And there were so many possible answers to that question. There was Barry, who had his mum in tears. There was his birthday in two days, which would have Barry right in the middle of it for the first time ever—Barry who did sly, small things to get at him. Then there was some sort of fifteen-about-to-be-sixteen sap rising in him, which seemed to have no outlet but physical exercise. Above all there was that feeling of something

63

missing, something he might find if he just looked hard enough. If he just knew where to look. It was an overwhelming certainty that wherever he was it was not the right place, and whoever he was with they were not the right person.

'I don't really know,' was all he said.

'You'd better come with me,' said the teacher. 'Come and see Rupert. He's in charge. We might have to fill in a form or something.'

The boy didn't want to move away. He felt that the impact, the moment when there was no breath in his body and the roof of his world had been made up of three girls' faces, had bonded him to this particular earth, but obedience made him follow the teacher round a shoulder of hillside to where a man was spraying yellow lines on the grass. The boy searched for the girls as they walked but they had vanished like wood nymphs.

'Rupert,' the teacher called, and the man with the can looked round. 'Sorry to bother you but we've had an unexpected visitor.' He explained and the archaeologist looked the boy up and down.

'Do you feel all right?'

'Not really' would have been the truthful answer. Luke was somewhere outside himself, floating above his own head. Nothing was the same any more. 'A bit sore,' was all he said.

'Bad luck. Did you come to see the dig?'

'No. What are you looking for?'

'An explanation of why there's a large hole where no hole should be. Are you interested?'

He nodded.

'Really? All right. A dog fell into an underground chamber. We've peered down it and there's an echo, so we're trying to find out what it

64

is.'

And Luke's mind, still a little loose from its moorings after his fall, conjured out of nowhere a picture of scared men with spades. Burying something? Retrieving it? He couldn't tell.

'Why are you spraying the grass?'

'I'm marking out another trench. We can't go in from the top because we might ruin whatever is down there, so we're coming in from the sides.' He pointed to the spur of earth which stood between them and the other diggers like a buttress to the hill. 'I suspect our chamber lies right under *that*.'

The boy stared at it as if it should mean something to him, then shook his head.

'This is what they call the bailey, this flat area,' said Rupert, looking around him. 'It's the part of the castle where they all lived.'

The purple spheres came back to Luke as bunches of grapes. 'No it wasn't,' he said, 'this was the vineyard,' and immediately wished he could pull the words back when the archaeologist swung round and looked at him sharply.

'Oh, I see. You're an expert on Montacute, are you?'

'On what?'

'Montacute.'

'What's a montacute?' said the boy, though he felt he should know.

'This is Montacute,' Rupert said, frowning. 'Mons Acutus, the steep hill. That's what the Normans called it.'

The teacher was staring at the boy curiously. 'You mean you don't know where you are, Luke? You just happened along?'

'Yes.'

65

'So where did that vineyard stuff come from?' demanded Rupert. He sounded almost affronted.

'I don't know why I said that,' Luke replied. That wasn't strictly correct. He had said it because those brief purple shapes, just above him as he lay there, had been grapes.

'Go easy, Rupert. He's shocked,' said the teacher.

'Did *you* know about the vineyard theory, Mike?'

'There really is a vineyard theory?'

'Well, yes. There were vineyards listed in the Abbey lands and these terraces face the right way. The theory's common knowledge but only if you happen to be a keen reader of obscure archaeological monographs.' He turned to Luke and smiled enquiringly. 'Is that what you read at night, young Luke?'

'No. I must have heard it somewhere.'

'Yes, it must be the talk of . . . where do you come from? Wincanton?'

'Cucklington. It's near there.'

'How did you get here?'

'On my bike.'

'Why?'

'I just wanted to go for a ride.'

'I don't get it, Luke. You didn't come to see the dig, you didn't know this was Montacute, and you start talking about the vineyards?'

The teacher was studying the boy intently and he saw a brief trace of a hunted expression. A deep wonder stirred in him and the chilling edge of an absurd idea. He found he didn't want the boy to disappear. 'Rupert, maybe Luke could stay for the day?' he suggested, and looked at the boy. 'If you

66

want to, that is. I'll be heading home about six o'clock. I could give you a lift back.'

'If you like,' Rupert said, surprised. He looked at Luke. 'Would you like to have a go while you're here?'

'What, dig? With a trowel?'

'Yes. Mike says I should do more to educate the young.'

'You didn't let me dig anything for ages,' the teacher objected.

'You, Michael, have the deftness of a hippo and the eyesight of a mole. This young man, if I'm not mistaken, is in the first bright-eyed flush of youth and treads lightly on this earth.'

Luke suddenly found himself nodding his head, wanting to see under this modern grass into the older secrets.

'Shall I have him in my trench?'

'No,' said Rupert. 'You stick to teaching things you know about. I'll put him with Dozer.'

So Luke found himself kneeling in the same trench he had fallen into with the big man who had helped him. Dozer looked strong enough to break rocks with his bare hands despite his white hair. 'Here you go, kid,' he said, pulling a trowel from his back pocket. 'You can borrow Maureen. She's my spare.'

The boy wished he had gone with the teacher. He could see the girls in the other trench, twenty yards away, standing with their backs to him. The teacher was with them.

'Come on,' said Dozer. 'There's dirt to shift. Just take it nice and easy, like this. You can't do much damage.'

Luke crouched, stretched out his hand and

67

pulled a skim of soil towards him as he had seen the man do. He looked up again and saw the girls kneel down to work. He reached out for a second scrape and this time, as the blade touched the earth, he snatched his hand away as something travelled up through it, through his fingers and up his arm. He looked around. Dozer hadn't noticed. He reached out again and there it was, flowing through him, a flood of light and peace and knowledge and something startling that felt like love.

He knelt there utterly still, letting it wash through him like the best of gifts until it drained away so abruptly that he wanted to chase it down into the ground. There was a sudden commotion. Everyone in the other trench was standing up—the three girls at the far end and the rest of the diggers. Luke found he was touching inert earth with nothing coming from it at all. The others were hurrying towards him.

'Up, you two,' said the man called Rupert, who was leading the way. 'No questions. Just come with us, right now.' He didn't stop until they were down the hill and out of the trees where the footpath came up from the village below.

'Okay, listen up,' he said, and the diggers gathered round. Luke saw the three girls on the far side, with four boys who were a little older. The other diggers were in their fifties or even sixties and they were all focused intently on Rupert.

'Conrad had a bright idea earlier,' he said, nodding at the young man standing next to him. 'He pointed out that the dog escaped all by itself, which meant there was clearly a second hole in the ground because the owner was still looking down

68

the first one, so we decided he would go and search for it. Five minutes ago he found it. Tell them, Conrad.'

'It was in the bushes,' Conrad said. He wore thick glasses and he was sweating. 'Maybe a badger's sett, I thought, but it was big. You could crawl down it, like at forty-five degrees. I got a torch and stuck my head in but when I saw what was at the bottom, I got out again double quick.'

He looked around at their faces. 'There's a wooden crate down there at the base of a tunnel. It's a bit rotten, coming to pieces, but you can see stuff inside—round sticks. There's metal strapping around the crate holding it together, and there are four or five hand grenades wired on to the strapping.'

A murmur went up. Rupert was frowning. 'It fits with Lucy's electric cable. We think it's a wartime bunker of some sort,' he said. 'That means the grenades and the dynamite or whatever it is in the crate could be highly unstable by now. No one goes near the site until Bomb Disposal have dealt with it. I want groups of you spaced out around the bottom of the hill to stop any walkers wandering up there. Dozer, can you sort that? Anyone not needed should go down to the campsite and wait. It's safe there. I'll go and call up some help.' He turned to Michael Martin. 'Mike, I think we need to clear the site of anyone who's not camping here. I'm sorry. Can you take the lad with you?'

CHAPTER 6

'You'd think he was half dead,' Lucy had said when they were back in their trench. 'They're making such a fuss of him. What a dork.'

'Stop being horrible,' said Ali. 'Poor guy. I bet it hurt.'

After that they worked silently, thinking about the story they would have to tell that night, but Jo was starting to feel a weight of history stir and wriggle from the layers below her as if all the particles, sifted and compressed by time, had stories of their own requiring her to listen. The three of them had been first to the trench when he fell out of the sky and she had bent over him, seeing he wasn't breathing and looking at his staring eyes, terrified that he might indeed be dead. Then she saw him fighting for breath and, as Dozer pushed them out of the way, feared he might have broken his back. As they walked away she kept looking back to try to see his face, because it hadn't lodged in her memory and Gally wanted to know. Gally wanted to know? She almost laughed at herself for thinking that way but that was the way it had seemed for just a moment. She had seen so many faces when she looked at his.

It was the pills, Jo thought, as she stood beside the trench, barely aware of the others still talking about it. She felt a little sick, dizzy, her head loose from the moorings of her feet, only slightly better when she knelt down. Then she touched her trowel to the earth again, and that was when the earth

70

threw something back at her up the blade to wash through her hand and arm and head like a spinning tide of light. She rocked backwards and stared at the surface of the trench. Next time she reached out cautiously but as the trowel scraped through the loose crumbs into the undisturbed core of hard soil it came again but differently, more gently, as if her hand was a key sliding into a lock and lifting the tumblers to match it. She held herself still, entranced, feeling something flow the other way, from her body down into this ground which seemed like a door into more of her than she had ever known was there. She looked all around for the source, fixing her eyes on the other trench, and saw Conrad come marching up to it with Rupert beside him, bringing news of unexpected danger and forcing them to their feet. All the way down the hill she kept looking back as if expecting the trench to be marked by columns of flame, and down at the bottom, as the day and their plans and the prospect of summer fun drained, she felt most sad that some outstanding possibility of knowledge had been held out then jerked away. Fragments of a different story began to prod at her.

Dozer called them all around him, detailing off the diggers in groups of two or three to put a ring round the base of the hill, showing them on the map where he wanted them to go. 'You three girls,' he said, 'you're young and fit, ain't you? Go round to the main path, then up to the top of the hill. Check there's nobody up there, then take this track down to the far side. Do you see? There's another path there and I expect there's a stile. Stay there and warn off any walkers until I come and get you. Okay? Don't go anywhere near where we've been digging, will you?'

Toiling up the hill, Ali said 'Maybe it will all turn out to be a fuss about nothing.'

Lucy said, 'Yes, Conrad's pretty short-sighted. Must be.'

'Is that meant to be nasty?' Ali retorted.

'No, I just meant he's got thick glasses.'

'I think he knows what he's talking about.'

Lucy changed the subject. 'What are we going to do?' she said. 'I was just starting to enjoy it.'

'We're going to wait and see what happens,' said Ali, 'and keep our fingers crossed.'

Jo stayed silent. They came out of trees into a clearing that covered the summit of the hill and there, ahead, a tower rose from the very top. She was surprised and not at all surprised to see it.

'There's nobody around,' Lucy said.

'I'll go up there and check,' said Jo.

'I don't think you should,' Ali objected. 'The trenches must be just down there in the trees. Supposing it blew up? You'd be right in line.'

'I won't be long,' Jo said, and ran to the doorway. She saw a date over it and lettering in what she thought might be Greek. From as early as she could remember she had always liked towers, and she climbed the spiral staircase to the small chamber at the top. There was nobody there. She looked at the scarred patches of plaster still clinging to the walls, desecrated by penknives, read 'Spurs' and then just next to it 'F & G'. She stared at that one, felt the carved letters with her fingers, and a sense of contentment came to her through her fingertips. 'G,' she said to herself. 'G for Gally.' She looked down at the trees towards where she thought the trenches lay and knew the boy had

72

come this way before he fell.

She heard Ali's voice below. 'Jo, come down. We mustn't stay here.'

They sat by the path looking out across a meadow but no one came that way. They talked about their stories and Jo agreed she would stand behind Ali and prompt her if she lost her way, but mostly she sat quietly and let the other two talk because Gally was with her again, not speaking to her but with her, just as if she was sitting there on the grass. After a long time two uniformed policemen came puffing round the hill, hot with hurry and with the weight of the signs they carried. They tied incident tape across the gateway and gave the girls unnecessary instructions about going back to their camp by a safe route. Bomb Disposal would be along soon, they said, with the air of people privy to higher secrets and dangerous affairs.

Back at the campsite, there was no sign of the teacher or the boy. Before supper, Rupert called them all together.

'I'm really sorry to tell you this,' he said, 'but the dig's over. We've found some sort of wartime bunker. I've been talking to the War Museum and they think it's part of the BRO network—that's the British Resistance Organisation, put in place after Dunkirk when we thought Hitler was going to invade at any minute. It seems this one got lost in the wash.'

'What happens now?' asked Dozer.

'They're going to make it safe. If possible they'll remove the explosives, because the bunker is a pretty remarkable find. There'll be a bit of work to do afterwards if so but only for people who've

73

done the right training. That's seven of my students, basically, because we did the Lancaster bomber crash site last year.'

Dozer grunted. 'I could have sworn I was at Omaha Beach for the D-Day digs. Can't have been me then, but there was a bloke who looked just like you, Rupe.'

'I'm sorry, Dozer, I forgot you're trained too. Of course you're welcome to stay. I need all the help I can get, but I'm really sorry to say the rest of you will have to leave first thing in the morning, so let's make the best of it and have a good time tonight.'

*   *   *

For all his words, the meal was a quiet affair full of anticlimax but afterwards, when the diggers were lying around the fire and the sticks began to crackle, Rupert passed bottles of wine around the circle, clapped his hands and said, 'Right, enough moping. Where's tonight's story?'

There was silence, then Conrad said, 'The girls are doing it, aren't they?'

Rupert couldn't see them. 'Are they here?'

Three figures moved from darkness into firelight and the ring of flame-splashed faces turned to them in expectant silence. They wore masks cut from blue plastic and red tea-towel turbans wound around their hair. There was an appreciative round of applause.

Two stepped forward, one standing behind the other. 'We have two stories for you tonight,' said the one in front, 'and each story is about a castle. I am the Lady Alicia and my story is about the first earth castle from when the Normans came.'

74

The Lady Alicia was very clearly Ali and she told them a tale of an old sword, dug up as they built the ramparts. She forgot her way once or twice and the girl behind her muttered words to get her back on track, but the sword proved to have a mystical power which frightened the invading Normans, and the ghost of a long-dead British warrior made a timely appearance to free a prisoner threatened with torture. The story came to an abrupt halt and when the audience was finally sure it wasn't going to start again, they clapped.

The two of them sat down and the third girl took her place. 'I am the Lady Louisa,' she said, 'and my story is about the second castle and the wood they cut to build it.'

Her tale was of the Normans felling oaks for their new palisade and of the brave girl who came to save the woods on her white pony, and how she and the pony distracted the Normans by dancing a pretty dance together until they offered her any reward she named and she asked them to spare half the trees.

Lucy's story had been long, including demonstrations of the dance, and the audience clapped then shuffled on their logs as it ended. A buzz of conversation had just started when Jo stepped forward and held up both hands.

'I have a story too,' she said, and her friends looked at her in astonishment.

Jo hadn't known that she had a story but when she had stood at the top of the tower, when she had felt the carved initials with her fingers, a whole collection of stories and fragments of stories had come fluttering to her from across the broad

75

landscape to which the shadows were pointing. Some, just fragile shapes of stories, had passed on as if they were only reminding her they were there but one had lodged and grown into words which seemed to be Gally's words.

'I am Lady Joanna and the third castle was made of stone,' she said in a rush, then she came to a complete halt as if she had forgotten what to say next. They waited as she stared at the fire and then away up the hill into the darkness, towards the old fortress hidden above them in the night. Her audience was frozen in a separate and combined horror of keen embarrassment. The other girls stepped forward to whisper to her but she shook her head and held up a hand for silence though silence was all there was.

She began again in a slower and more certain voice. 'The third castle was to be built of stone and the new Norman lords forced the able-bodied men from all around to build it. These men had never seen shaped stone, mortared layer on layer. Their church was wooden. Their houses were mud and wood. Oppression in stone began to rise above them—everlasting oppression.'

The other girls were looking at each other in surprise but the speaker's voice gathered strength with every sentence.

'The Saxon men of the village dragged each stone up to the top of the mound. It cost them sweat if they pulled hard enough and blood if they did not because the Normans were hard, hard men and urged them on with whips.'

She paused, this time with complete confidence, and there was no more movement from her audience.

'There was a family in the village. A man, his wife and their only surviving son. The man did not believe in war—never had. He believed only in protecting his own and he had been hurt when the Normans first came to that place, cut in the arm by a sword when he shielded his wife. His son, as yet just half a man, was the pride of his life but the Normans took the boy because the father could not work.

'The boy came back that first night, bruised and flayed and trying his best to be brave, but in the morning he could hardly get up. He left the cottage in the last of the darkness trying to hide the tears running down his face and when full day came, the man and the woman went to look across the valley to the bare top of the hill, where a stack of cut tree trunks marked the skyline and the hard walls of the castle tower had begun to coil up inside their wooden scaffold.

'They went as close as they could but they could not see him so the man hugged his wife and told her his arm was healing and he would go to offer himself again so that he could help their son. She sat there alone on the grass in her misery after he had left, unable to see where he was amongst the toiling ants, but hearing the shouts of the soldiers and the screams of the workers.

'And then after the sun's shadow had moved a yard, there was turmoil in the valley and a man bursting through the bushes by the stream, and she saw it was her husband racing back to her through the grass. Then other men came after him, four soldiers shouting, and two of them seized him and held him under their knees. One raised a sword that cut the sun in silver and hacked it down, lifting

77

it again shining red. She ran at them screaming her fear and her defiance but their leader wiped his sword with a look that said it was crueller to keep her alive than to kill her too. They walked away and she knelt over her man and heard from his last breath that their son was dead.'

There was a thickness in the way of her voice as she finished, a sob strangled in her throat. She stopped, took two deep breaths and looked around at her audience. 'When castles rise, they are built with poor men's blood,' she said. Her head was suddenly flooded with a wealth of other stories—of a brother and sister in love, of brave men making a desperate stand, of a marriage, of an excavation and a burial. They swirled in her head, tripping over each other until she sat down, utterly exhausted by her words and her thoughts.

They clapped and clapped her until Rupert got to his feet.

'Thank you,' he said, 'all three of you. That was quite wonderful. We don't often think about the folk who had to do the hard work, do we?' He nudged a log back into the fire with his toe and everyone watched the fountain of sparks in silence. He turned back towards Jo. 'I know the place you're talking about,' he said.

They took off their masks. 'Of course you do,' Jo replied. 'We set the stories here.'

'No, that can't be right. Three castles? There was only one here. Are you telling me you didn't have somewhere else in mind?'

The girls were shaking their heads.

'Are you sure? There's a place just like that,' he said. 'A truly unusual place, a village with three Norman castles and only one of them built in

78

stone. Isn't that where you meant?'

'Why would one village have three castles?' Lucy asked.

'I don't know,' said Rupert. 'No one does. But that just happens to be where we're going next when we've finished here, me and these guys.' He looked across to where his students were sitting in a row. 'It's not so far. The other side of Wincanton. It's like nowhere else I know and it really is just like your stories said. Three Norman castles, all huddled next to each other round the end of a ridge, no more than a mile apart, right on each other's doorstep. It's the strangest place.'

Dozer's voice growled out of the darkness. 'What's it called?'

'Penselwood,' said Rupert, making the first two syllables sound like 'pencil' then, with a different stress, 'or maybe I should say it like they do—Pen Selwood,' and Jo thrilled to his words without knowing why.

CHAPTER 7

Luke didn't argue when the teacher suggested they put the bike in his car. His back was still aching, one of his elbows was bruised and stiffening, and he didn't want to cycle home. For the first few miles they talked about the grenades but soon they ran out of knowledge, meaning and words. Mr Martin seemed both ill at ease and a bit too interested in him and Luke looked out of the window, trying to seem engrossed in the fields and the houses they passed as if he could project

79

himself completely out of the car.

In the end the teacher couldn't keep it in any more. 'That stuff about the vineyard, Luke. How did you know?'

'I'm not sure, sir.'

The teacher studied him for a moment. 'It's time off. Forget the sir. I've never taught you, have I?'

'No.'

'You just came to my History Club? Once, was it?'

'Twice. I came on the field trip to Dunster Castle.'

'Oh, yes.'

The teacher clearly didn't remember what had happened—the row with the other kids. He shrugged. 'I feel I know you, that's all. I mean more than just knowing your face from school assembly and so on. Can you remember anything else?'

'No,' he said, which was true in a way. Luke didn't want to talk about it. The whole thing seemed best left behind, miles away and unreal.

'Have you ever had anything like that before?'

'How do you mean, like that?'

'Well, odd thoughts. Stuff from the past, memories.'

'No,' said the boy and turned away deliberately, staring again out of the side window. As if the question had sparked them off, his mind filled with brief images of men with spades at Montacute, digging on that hill, and they were not today's wispy amateurs but solid men of old. They were burying it . . . or were they digging it up? Of course there was a big hole there, he thought. It would have needed a big hole. Like recapturing a dream

80

as daytime took over, he couldn't quite capture what 'it' was. He leaned his head against the cold glass, watching the trees streaming by. They made him drowsy. Gradually, as the engine droned and the world tore past, he fell into a trance and a series of faces came to his mind's eye—tiny faces but clearly formed, one after another.

Girls' faces.

Each one hung there beyond the window glass, tipped a little to one side or the other. Each one was as clear as a photograph and utterly different from the last—fair, dark, elfin, apple-cheeked, blue, brown, green-eyed. Each one was utterly the same. The same girl lived behind the eyes.

He had neglected to breathe and now took in a long gulp of air.

'Are you all right?' someone asked. He had forgotten Michael Martin, forgotten he was in a car, and had no clear idea how long they had been driving.

'Why do you ask?' he replied and saw the teacher's eyebrows rise. As he said it, he knew it was not the way the boy Luke would have answered and it surprised him that he no longer felt quite like the boy Luke. 'Yes,' he said, 'I'm fine,' but the indrawn breath had turned around into a long sigh and left him heartsick. He turned back to the window and tried to see the faces again but there were road signs instead. They were on the A38, slowing for the turn-off. He looked up and saw the ridge rising and the thing that was in him, the thing that was pushing out the boy, rose with it.

The teacher stopped the car. 'I'm up that way,' he said, pointing at a small lane leading up the slope, 'but I can take you home if you want. Cucklington, you said?'

The sign to Cucklington pointed south. 'It's only two miles,' the boy replied. 'I can bike it.'

The teacher lifted the bicycle out of the car and drove away.

The boy laid it on the grass and sat down, looking after the car as it disappeared between narrow banks. He had been up that way before, but only once. Five, maybe six years ago? Primary school—and he had friends then. The teacher had asked him about odd stuff, and if he had wanted to answer he would have said that day might have been the start of it.

There had been three of them, always three— Zach and Ryan and Luke their leader, bursting through the woods up there on the ridge, yelling and darting, legs pumping on bikes they knew would fly if pedalled hard enough. They were ten years old and gravity held them lightly. The sun flashed green and blue in the broken roof of leaves as they swerved and leapt through a wild world beyond parental eyes, a first visit to the scene of older brothers' boasts. They wanted to be heroes too.

Passing a perfect hump where tree roots heaved up earth, they had skidded round, rear wheels locked. Zach jumped it first and landed shouting his exaggeration. 'I got air. Wow! Did you see that? Three feet.'

Ryan went next but barely hopped, fiddling intently with his gears all the way back as if thwarted by mechanics.

Their leader Luke attacked it last, taking the longest run-up to fulfil their expectations. Luke was a brave, inventive boy and they liked to see him set the standard. He rushed the ramp, jerked head and shoulders back to make the jump, then froze, still staring upwards instead of at his landing point.

They saw the bike rear backwards, hurling him abruptly to the solid earth, and went fearfully to pick him up.

'You really stacked it,' Ryan said, avoiding looking at the blood flowing from Luke's chin, but his friend was oblivious to the injury, searching up through the trees.

'Where is he?' he demanded. 'Did you see where he went?'

'Who?'

'The man on the parachute. He's come down. He must have done.' Luke was standing up and staring into the woods. 'We have to go and find him.'

He climbed the bank, questing through the trees, searching left and right. They followed, frightened by his sudden mania.

'There's nothing,' Ryan said in the end. 'There's no one here. You banged your head.'

'It was a yellow parachute. You saw the plane.'

'There wasn't any plane.'

'Come on, you must have *heard* it.'

'No.'

'You couldn't not have heard it. It was roaring and banging.'

The vivid image was still in Luke's head. Straight wings, two propellers, one of them stopped, smoke pouring out behind, a greasy burning line across the sky, its belly pale green with stark black crosses from a war that was no more

83

than history.

They all looked up at a clear and silent sky, and that was when Luke's friends began to think him odd.

Now he felt odder still, staring up the lane where the teacher had gone, pulled in two directions. Neither of them was the road that led to Cucklington. Montacute was tugging him gently back—not the place, but the brief and shocking power that had travelled up his arm. The faces of three girls swam in his mind's eye—vaguer, blurrier now, too far away. He felt a sad and fading need to see them properly but the lane ahead called him too and that was stronger. It was the right and only way to go, more like the way home than the Cucklington road with its cheerless, pointless bungalow at the other end. He pushed his bike in the wheel-tracks of the teacher's car and every step he took felt a step nearer to something.

A sign pointed left to Pen Selwood and he stared at the name, pulled by it, but the other road had a stronger pull so he ignored it, went straight on, curving around a bend until he came to a gap in the trees and a gate on the right and a cottage beyond it and knew this was what was calling him. He pushed the gate open, wheeled his bicycle through as if dreaming, stood staring at the front door and the low windows, and was amazed when that door opened and the teacher came out to stare at him in matching amazement.

'What are you doing here?' demanded the boy.

'Me? I live here. What are *you* doing here? You followed me? Why did you do that?'

'No. How could I? You drove off.'

'Luke, why are you here?'

84

'When did you buy this house?'

'What an odd question.'

'When?'

The teacher frowned in thought. 'It was nineteen ninety,' he said, and looked hard at the boy who took a few steps back from the porch and scanned the front of the house from side to side, frowning as if it was lying to him.

'What was it like then?'

'It was a complete ruin. Why?'

'I remember it like that.'

'No, you couldn't possibly. You weren't born.'

'I know you from before.'

'Before what? Before today? Of course you do.'

'From back then, from when you first saw it.'

The teacher was shaking his head. 'Oh Jesus,' he said.

The boy saw a hint of fright in the teacher's face. He repeated it urgently as if he had to get through to the older man. 'I tell you I knew you then.'

'Stop it, Luke. You fell. Are you feeling ill?' But the boy found the familiar name was no longer so familiar. It glanced off him.

'I'm taking you home,' said the teacher. 'Get in the car.'

As they drove away, three images spun, swirling and colliding in Luke's head—the girls, the cottage, the teacher's face. He could get no purchase on them. They wouldn't stick but when they were approaching Cucklington they drove past the remains of an ivy-clad barn and the sight of it altered the teacher's cottage in Luke's mind's eye. The ivy spread up the gable end beside the road. The roof sank, the glass splintered away, and a man was standing outside it. Then that man

85

changed too and merged into the teacher in the seat next to him, but younger—no grey in his face nor in his hair.

'Where do I go?' the teacher asked him at the village sign but the boy just gazed at him. The teacher looked back in blank bewilderment.

'Luke, where's your house?'

'I don't think I'm Luke. I'm not, am I?'

'Of course you are.'

'No.'

'I'm taking you home. Will there be someone there?'

'Don't.' The boy was rubbing his head as if he could massage Luke away. 'I can't remember my name.' He stared at the teacher again. 'You have to tell me.'

'I have no idea what you mean.'

'I think you do. What was I called when I met you?'

'Today?'

'No. You *do* know what I mean. I'm sure you do. Way before that. At your house. When you first came.'

All the teacher could do was shake his head in mute distress but the boy went on, pitiless, unstoppable now as other fragments surfaced. 'You were poking around. Your car was parked in the lane.' His voice sounded far away and his face was screwed up, concentrating fiercely, 'It was a dark blue car. You'd gone inside where you had no right to be. No right at all. It wasn't yours. Not then. I caught you looking in the cellar.'

'Someone's told you,' said the teacher faintly.

'I caught you there. You know I did.'

'*You* didn't. That wasn't you. That was an old

86

man. Who told you?'

'What was the old man called?'

The teacher found he didn't want to say. 'That's not the point.'

'It's the whole point,' said the boy. 'You have to tell me his name.'

'Why?'

The boy stared at him and all Michael Martin could do was flinch away as if a snake was coiled in the seat beside him, and the only explanation came to him and it was worse than having no explanation at all. Across years of sadness he was back there again, back at the cottage she had found by chance, poking around in the ruins. All those years ago, before this boy was born.

'Because it's *my* name, don't you see?' The boy was shaking. 'Tell me my name.' He was shouting now, roaring his distress. 'You must help me. I can't remember. Please tell me. Please.'

And of course Mike knew the name which filled his head—the name of the old man who had caught them in the cottage, the old man who destroyed his life, the old man who was dead before this boy was born. He could not say it.

'Stop it,' he said and reached out his arm, not sure if he was trying to keep Luke at bay or to comfort him.

The boy glared at him, jerked the car door open, shouted, 'Get away from me.'

A man and a woman were walking down the lane. The woman ran to him. 'Lukey,' she said, staring through the windscreen at the white-faced teacher, 'is something wrong?' and the man said, 'What the hell's going on?'

CHAPTER 8

In the kitchen Luke's mother pinned him in a corner and roasted him with angry concern. 'You trying to tell me nothing happened? You screaming at him in the car and him sitting there like he'd seen a ghost?'

'I went to a dig, that's all. He gave me a lift back.'

Barry, lurking in the doorway, stepped forward into their business. 'What do you mean, a dig?'

'You know—archaeology.'

'So you're suddenly an archaeologist, are you?' Luke saw fat triumph in Barry's face as he made himself the man of the house. The boy resented that deeply.

'What did he do?' his mother asked.

'Nothing. He gave me a lift home.'

'Where from?'

'The dig. I told you. I went to this place where they were digging.'

'Why did you yell at him?' demanded Barry.

'I was tired.'

'Oh, come on. Was I born yesterday?'

'Barry's right to ask,' put in his mother more gently. 'You don't yell at people, Lukey—not without a reason. You're sitting in some strange man's car, shouting at him—something's happened, hasn't it? If he was trying something on, you need to tell us. It wouldn't be right, and anyway you should have asked us before you went. These teachers might not always be very nice people. You and him, alone and all that. Barry

88

reckons he's a poofter. Said so after he saw him at parents' evening.'

Barry's not my parent was what Luke wanted to say, but all he did say was, 'That wasn't him. That was Mr Jellicoe.'

'Was it? Maybe it was, but if they've let one poofter into the school, who's to say there aren't more? Shouldn't be any,' said Barry.

'It wasn't anything like that,' said the boy, but then Barry got going all over again and it went on and on, and of course he couldn't begin to explain.

When they finally ran out of words, he took refuge in his bedroom while they watched television with the sound turned up next door, then as evening came, he opened his window and slipped out through the back garden. He walked to the place he went to whenever it got bad—to the steep hillside with a sheer view westward over the drained marshland.

The evening sun was half an hour from the horizon and he settled down, his face towards it, to think in the peace that place offered. The high ground he was on ran away north, curving back, hiding the teacher's village. Until today the name had meant nothing to him but now Pen Selwood filled his head and with it another name that he could not quite find. He searched that way in his mind, seeking the name that hung out there along the ridge.

As he waited for the sunset, his gaze wandered across the lower ground below, casting around for something to take him out of the here and now. He looked down at the farms scattered over the lowlands, Baskets Farm and Frith Farm and the one they used to call the Redhouse Farm, and was

89

thrilled to find he knew that. He saw the late sun paint the crown of the little hill above Stoke Trister and he also knew that the tufts of woodland left on its summit were all that remained of a great swathe of trees.

Now the sun was down on the horizon and the sky put on a fine evening ocean swell of clouds in line after line, purple above, orange below, growing brighter as the sun dipped. He watched, cooling to a state nearer peace in that vast proof that only the earth's thin crust was within the spoiling reach of man. He knew that he had missed something enormous at Montacute, something he would have found if he had been allowed to stay just another hour. He knew he had to go there again, west where the sunset was calling him.

*   *   *

He got up at eight the next morning, heard his mother and Barry snoring in Sunday unison, and cycled away. As he left Cucklington, it seemed absurd to him that his name might not be Luke, but as he grew steadily nearer to the rise of the ridge he passed through a no-man's-land to a point where it seemed absurd that he ever thought it was. He slowed down as he approached Bagstone Farm and he knew that was the name of the house Michael Martin lived in even though there was no sign on it. Now that he could feel its vast gravitational pull, he was astonished that it had been hidden from him.

He pushed open the gate, relieved to see no sign of the teacher's car, needing time alone. The house stood end-on to the road. He walked slowly through the yard in front of it, noticing the encroaching brambles, minding the decay, then came to the far end where the roofline sank lower and fought his way through the dense undergrowth round to the back of the house. The ground fell away into a stream valley but he knew exactly how the path had run, though little trace of it was left and the trunk of a fallen tree lay across it. Returning to the yard, he leaned to look in at all the windows, shading the glass with his hand, then stood back, staring at the front of the house.

At first there was nothing, but instinct prompted him to wait and to slow his breathing, deep and long, to a point where the world slowed down with him. The even line of the roof peak twitched and shifted before his eyes and he discovered he could pull it down a little further in his head. In his mind's eye he tugged tiles out of place, let the guttering droop at one end. As he peeled paint from the window frames the door shuffled sideways to where it had once been, the porch sagging. The house slowly loosened as ruin crept between the stones and he blessed this new trick that seemed very, very old.

A man came out of the ether like a print developing in a chemical bath and for just one clear moment he was standing there alone in front of the door facing Luke. He knew the man—Mike Martin, the teacher, as his younger self. Then she came bursting out of the same lost past, a miracle, to stand there beside the teacher where she should never have been. The girl with a hundred faces now had only one. It was wide and smiling, framed by a flood of shining brown hair.

For just a moment she was clear to him, this

glorious girl who filled his void, but she scorched his mind's eye and he could not make her stay. The house snapped and wriggled back to the implacable bleakness of the present and left him bereft. Her name mattered as much as his because he knew in his bones that all those hundred faces he had seen shared that single name.

He felt an awareness of an imminent revelation, not here but back at the place he should never have left, back at the old hill fortress of Montacute, and though this house held a million more possibilities for his imagination or his memory or both, he knew he had to go straight back there to chase it down. In a single shock he knew she was there, that she had certainly been there yesterday, close within his reach if only he had looked with the right eyes. Three girls, his age, and she was one—standing right there, and he had let her go. His mind raced back to the fragmentary memory of each girl—the blonde, the dark girl, the short girl—and found to his despair that he had no idea which one she was.

It was simple. Montacute called him and he had to go, so he got back on his bike to ride all that way again, but this time he did not trust in instinct to find the way. Stopping at a petrol station, he leafed through a road atlas and borrowed a pen from the irritated man behind the counter to write down his route. It took him longer, struggling into a strong south-west wind, on main roads this time, passing trucks buffeting him with fists of air, and then eventually he saw the hill rise once again and turned to where he knew the diggers' tents were pitched.

There was a police sign in the way, square in the

middle of the track. It said ROAD CLOSED and it filled him with foreboding. He ignored it and rode on. A great deal had changed since the day before. Most of the tents had gone from the field. An army truck and two police vans were parked alongside the few remaining cars. A policeman stood there, barring the way.

'Sorry, you can't come through,' he said.

'I know what happened. I was here on the dig yesterday. I just wanted to see the others.'

'They've gone,' said the man. 'There's only a few of your lot left. The army's up there. You'll have to wait down here.'

A door slammed in the field and a rough diesel burst into life. Luke saw a red pick-up truck start to move. The policeman stepped to one side to make way and to Luke's huge relief, he saw Dozer at the wheel. The truck stopped.

'Hello, matey,' said Dozer through the open window. 'You back again?'

'Yes, but he says I can't go up there.'

'Too right. There might be a big bang at any moment. It's just Rupert and his students and me plus the army amateurs.' He grinned at the PC, who sniffed.

'Where have the others gone?'

'Home,' said Dozer. 'Why?'

The boy sagged. 'No reason. I'd better go then.'

'Yup, 'fraid so. Where was it? Wincanton? You biked all that way again?'

'Yes.'

'Blimey.' Dozer considered. 'Well, you're in luck. I'm going to Bridgwater to pick up some gear. I could go that way. Pop your wheels in the back.'

With only a hazy knowledge of Somerset

93

geography, Luke had no idea how kind that offer was. 'Are the girls still here?' he said. 'Are they Rupert's students?'

'Some of them were, but no, they've all gone. They hadn't done the training, you see—the explosives stuff.'

'All the girls have gone?'

'That's right. It's just the lads here now.'

With a heavy heart, Luke did what the man said and settled into the ripped plastic passenger seat.

'So what brought you cycling all the way back again, young fellow?' Dozer asked as they reached the main road. 'You been bitten by the digging bug?'

'No. I mean, I liked it. Thank you for showing me how.'

'I wasn't looking for thanks. I was looking for the reason a boy shags himself out on a bicycle.'

He got no answer to that.

'Got nothing better to do?'

'No.'

'So what else do you like doing, Luke?'

The boy frowned. 'Nothing much.'

'Nothing? That's a sad word. Me, at your age I liked bikes too but only if they had engines for pedals.'

'Motorbikes?'

'Yeah. If God had meant us to pedal he wouldn't have invented the four-stroke motor. I got my first BSA when I was twelve—a knackered old two-fifty. Put it straight with some help from my dad. Thrashed it round the fields. Then it was Velocettes and more BSAs and Enfields and still more BSAs. Never Triumphs. You were a BSA man or a Triumph man—it was like the Beatles or the Stones.'

The boy listened without really understanding, enjoying the enthusiasm in Dozer's voice.

'Got the tattoos, got the leathers. Finally got a Norton Atlas.'

'What's that?'

'Back in those days it was the quickest bike you could buy, which makes it lucky I was only doing eighty-five when I came off it on the Keynsham road. Six months in hospital then six more months' recovery. That was when I got into digging. Had to fill up my time. My physio was a digger. He got me along on one. Never looked back. So come on, there must be something in your life like that?'

'Not really.'

'That won't do. I know there's something. Football?'

'No, I don't get football.'

'Another sport then?'

'I'm not interested in heroes.'

'Why not?'

'I don't need superhumans.'

'Out of the mouths of babes and sucklings. Come on then—I'm not stopping until you tell me one single thing you really like to do.'

'I like to walk round the fields where I live.'

'Come on. I need more than that. Unless you mean you're a poacher.'

'No. I just like . . . imagining. I like to look at old houses and woods and churchyards and think about how they used to be. I like to read books. Old books are best. I like to sit in the evening and watch the sun set and think how many times it has set before.'

'Wow, that's deep. Not exactly sex and drugs and

95

rock 'n' roll. You like being alone?'

'No, but I'm not a very popular person.'

'You seem a nice enough bloke to me.'

'I like talking to people who know stuff. You know stuff. People my age don't.'

'It'll come out all right if you just wait then. You see, there's someone out there for you.' Dozer looked across at him. 'Whoops! I didn't mean to upset you.'

Luke wiped his face fiercely. 'I'm all right.'

'You just haven't met them yet, that's all.'

'Maybe. So what happened back there? What was it all about, the grenades and all that?'

'Well, I guess it was all about the British Resistance Organisation. Ever heard of that?'

'No.'

'Neither had I but I have now. You know about Dunkirk?'

'A bit.'

'1940? Hitler pushed our poor old army out of France. All the little ships went across to save our lads and we thought the Germans would be across the Channel any minute. They talked about fighting them on the beaches but they knew we wouldn't stop them there so they set up the BRO. Lots of hidden bunkers with a network of wireless stations to rally the resistance. Code name for the local network round here was Chirnside and it seems our hole was part of it. Funny really, same old reason that the old guys chose their hill forts— good view, hard to surprise people. So anyway, they had a big hole as their bunker with generators and an emergency exit with a nasty booby trap to make a huge bang if the Jerries found it. They just forgot to take it all away afterwards. Turns out there were no records this one was ever there.'

'So everyone went home?'

'Like I said, everyone except me and the students.'

'And all the girls too?' Luke had to ask. If any of the girls were still there with Rupert, he needed to get out of the truck before it took him any further away.

'The girls again, eh?' Dozer gave him a sudden sharper look. 'Ah,' he said. '*Cherchez la femme*, as they say in Scotland.'

'What does that mean?'

'It means I think I've rumbled the nature of your sudden interest and the reason why your bicycle looks so tired. Now, do you mean the students or the other three?'

The boy squirmed in silence and Dozer chortled. 'I reckon you mean the other three. They're your age. No, they've gone. So, which one is it? Let me guess now. There was Jo—she's the quiet one. There's Ali—she's the dumpy, bossy one, and oh yes, there's the blonde. Now then, what was she called? Lucy, that was it. My money's on Lucy. But hang on a mo. I was with you the whole time. You never even got to talk to her, did you? Blimey, she must have made an impression.'

'I thought maybe I knew one of them, that's all. Do they come from round here?'

'No. Nowhere near. Down west somewhere. Exeter maybe? They were really hacked off when they found out they had to go.'

'So they have gone?'

'Oh yes, they've gone.'

Luke was silent. 'Funny thing, though,' said Dozer, 'they made quite an impression on me too.

97

Shall I tell you?'

'Yes.'

'Well, when they turned up I thought they didn't know their arses from their elbows apart from Ali, the dumpy one. We all know her mum, you see. Christine Massey. She's led loads of digs. You don't mess with Christine, so I guess Ali's been brought up eating with a trowel. They were mucking about like school friends do and Ali was getting cross cos she wanted to take it all a bit more seriously and Lucy, the blonde one, she was getting up to all sorts of stuff.'

'What sort of stuff?'

'Boy stuff. Those students of Rupert's from the uni. She fancied one of them—Andy, the big, gormless one. Anyway, then the girls told this story round the campfire. Oh boy, what a surprise that was. You should have heard it.'

So he told the boy his version of Jo's story, altered a little in the retelling as all stories are, and at the end Luke asked him the question that was racing round his head. 'Which one told the story?'

Dozer frowned. 'I dunno for sure,' he said. 'They were dressed up. It wasn't the little one, Ali. I could tell which one she was. She went first. I was the other side of the fire. Must have been Jo or Lucy. Anyway, her story got through to old Rupe. He told them it fitted this next place we're digging.'

'Who's we?'

'Me and him and the students. Anyway, that was just Rupert making two and two equal ninety-eight and a half. I don't think those girls had any idea there really was such a place. It was just a made-up story to them.' A thought struck him. 'You must

98

know it, matey, this place? If it's Wincanton way, it must be near where you live.'

'What's it called?'

'Pen Selwood,' said Dozer. 'Whoa there! What's wrong?'

Luke had jerked up in his seat and was trying to control a vast excitement. 'Yes, I know where it is,' he said as calmly as he could. 'It's right by my turning. You'll see the sign. You're all coming to *dig* there?'

'When we get this one done, yes. Another Norman castle site. Just a quick look at the earthworks.'

'Why did he think that was the place?' Of course it would be the place, he was thinking to himself. If she had started to tell a story from the depths of her long, long memory, where else would it be?

Dozer told him about the three castles and the conversation afterwards.

'It certainly tickled everyone's fancy. We sat round until the wine ran out trying to guess why any village needed three castles. One of the girls reckoned they were guarding the Holy Grail. Conrad—that's the bloke Ali was leaning against—said it must have been the headquarters of the Norman College of Advanced Castle Building and they were all that was left of the students' final-year projects. Rupert got all serious and said the ridge had strategic importance but that was reckoned to be far too boring. Anyway, I've volunteered.'

'Volunteered for what?'

'To go and dig with them when they get there. He said I could come along to set an example so they know how not to grow up. It'll be a week or two yet.'

'At Pen?'

'Is that what they call it round your way? Saves time, is that it? Mustn't waste that extra second.'

'So who exactly is going?'

'You haven't been concentrating, have you? Rupe and his lads are doing a quick dig there for English Heritage. There's some problem with erosion.'

'Is anybody else going?'

'Not apart from the girls.'

'The *girls*?'

'Well, maybe. They weren't sure.'

'What did they say?'

'I heard them arguing about it. One of them wanted to go there, the others had different ideas. I reckon you put those three in a room and you'll always have four opinions, maybe five.'

'Which one wanted to go to Pen?'

'Blimey, junior! I wasn't paying that much attention. What's got into you?'

'I'd just like to know,' he answered vaguely, but he was burning up with the urgent need to know exactly which one.

Dozer thought hard. 'I saw them looking at the map. They were still arguing. Wherever they were going, they had to walk there on account of not having much cash. Oh, I remember. Lucy, the blonde, said she'd never walked that far in her life and Ali, the bossy one, said it was just a matter of putting one foot in front of the other and then Lucy asked her how many times she would have to do that and it went on like that.'

'But they might be going to Pen?'

'They might be going to Timbuktu for all I

know. Come on, kid. Which one of them's got her hooks into you?'

'I don't know,' said Luke. 'I can't tell.' He was staring out of the window avidly, thinking he might see them walking along the roadside or crossing a field.

A gurgling noise which was a chuckle filtered through years of smoke and beer made its slow way out of Dozer's throat. 'Can't tell? They're not exactly identical triplets. If it was me, I'd go for Lucy. I was always one for the blondes. Second choice, Jo. Third choice, Ali. Mind you, if you picked Ali you'd get fed regular plus you wouldn't have to worry about other blokes. Anyway, Ali's mad keen on the digging—has to be with a mother like that. I think the others just came along for the ride, plus the chance of boys maybe. They definitely had an eye for Rupe's students.' Dozer chose his words deliberately. He could see something desperate in the boy next to him. He feared some sort of puppy love was stirring and it was clear to him that the students had a few years' head start on the road to manhood. His words washed past Luke. The warning was irrelevant. The feeling inside him was based on some utter and inexplicable certainty.

CHAPTER 9

Before you ever love, you can dream of love. Jo was in the delight of such a dream, held by a vibrant boy who laughed and whispered poetry in her ear. She woke with two lines running through her head.

Our halves are nothing on their own but half
  and half make one,
And halves, divided, stand alone when the
  adding's done.

Someone had shaken her and the poem had run
away, leaving a warm residue which turned to
waking disappointment as she saw dawn light
filtering through the tent, ancient bugs crawling
across the damp nylon just above her. She rolled
over, thinking Lucy or Ali had woken her, but they
were curled up asleep.

'It wasn't them, it was me,' said Gally's voice
clearly in her head. 'Come with me.'

Gally led her up the hill as if they were hand in
hand. Jo stared ahead, wondering if the police
were up there, if they had stayed all night, or
whether they had trusted to their tape barriers in
the darkness. They followed a narrow trail,
shunning the path—a way made by deer or badgers
or foxes that snaked up the steeper contours and
brought them to the terrace. There, just ahead,
were the brown stripes of the two trenches. Jo
walked to the place where she had been working,
knelt and reached tentatively down with her
fingertips extended, holding back just short of the
earth as if afraid. She thought this must be why she
had been brought here. Driven by a craving for
that feeling which had come to her the day before,
she touched her fingers to the dry surface but there
was just the crumbling earth, inanimate with the
anticlimax of finding absolutely nothing there.

'No,' said Gally to her. 'That was not why. Sit

102

down. Breathe easily. Breathe deeply.' Jo sat on a tree stump, did what she was told, slowed her breath, searching the landscape.

'Do not try so hard,' said the voice. 'Look slowly. Clear away the trees.' And she found to her surprise that she knew how to do it. She used her eyes like a brush, swinging her gaze slowly around, wiping the trees away to let in the dawn sky and the bright east off to the left. As the trees faded, something obstinate remained—plants in rows, lower. When she let them stay they grew a crop of golden green globes and she knew them for vines, and Gally nudged her to a brief vision of men stooping to tend them—men in monks' robes.

'Now leave it to me,' Gally whispered inside her. 'Watch.'

The vines had withered. Young trees grew again, little more than saplings, and the sun moved back on its course, sinking just below the eastern rim so that only dawn's fingers were in the sky. Men were busy all around her, men she could not see to start with, but then she could smell their sharp sweat, see the dark blades of shovels arcing back and forth in the dim light, see the shrinking earth pile as they laboured to bury it out of sight, hurrying to leave this dangerous place. She turned to stare back down the slope, hair prickling, a lookout, watching for the enemy: And behind her, watching at the other side, she felt the vast comfort of his presence—the other half who made her whole.

'You were here,' Gally said quietly. 'More than once. Long ago.'

Then she heard voices below, saw other men moving up through the trees, men in uniform, and opened her mouth to hiss a warning before reality intervened and she knew she was back among the modern trees, on the edge of the terrace where she should not be, where the old explosives oozed danger in the bunker below and these men were coming to deal with it. Love abandoned her again as sadly as in waking from her earlier dream, and she crept down the hillside, picking her way through the cover, anxious to avoid discovery.

Around the corner of the contour, safely away from them, she stopped to address with the swirl of sensation and memory in her head and found Gally with her. 'You know what this is,' said Gally.

'No I don't.' She said it out loud.

'Of course you do. Last night, round the fire, you told our story. How else did that happen?'

'It was the darkness and the woodsmoke.'

'Yes, but you opened your mind and remembered and you told them all around the fire. Why would you remember if not for love? Love is the fuel that fires memory. Now you must find him.'

'I can't remember him,' she wailed.

'You can. He was here,' said her voice.

'But that was long ago. You said so.'

'That was yesterday,' said the voice. 'He touched the earth as you touched the earth and you felt each other.' And Jo gasped as she understood the full meaning of that moment. 'Go to him. You know where to go.'

Jo shook her head.

'Yes you do,' Gally insisted. 'Do it by yourself. You will find me there too.' And she seemed to walk away.

Left alone, Jo climbed down the hill on the far side to the camp and circled around through the

104

fields. She sat in the empty marquee which slowly filled in ones and twos of quiet and disappointed diggers until Lucy and Ali joined her.

'Where have you been?' Lucy asked.

She didn't want to say. 'I got up early.'

'I can't bear this.' Ali was looking around. 'It's like everyone is already halfway home in their heads.'

'Real life is leaking in,' Lucy said. 'Our island is crumbling.'

Andy and Conrad came into the tent and heaped bowls full of cereal as if to emphasise that they, at least, still had work to do.

'So what about you three?' Conrad asked Ali, staring at her intently.

'We'll go back home, I suppose.'

Conrad frowned and that was when Jo sowed the seed of the plan that had come to her on the way down the hill. 'I don't see why,' she said. 'My mother's away. Ali, your parents are in Ireland, aren't they?'

'Yes. Mum's digging, Dad's painting—if she lets him.'

'Lucy, where have yours gone?'

'Who knows?' Lucy said theatrically. 'I'll tell you when the postcard comes,' although she knew perfectly well that they were in Tuscany.

'So there's no point in going home, is there?' asked Jo.

Ali looked uncomfortable. Jo knew she was worrying that her mother would be cross if she found out the dig had ended and they had stayed away. She also knew Ali didn't want to admit that in front of Conrad.

'It's a pity there isn't another dig we could go

105

to,' Jo said, and Conrad picked it up, just as she had hoped he would.

'But there is,' he said eagerly. 'There's this next one we're going to when we've finished here—the place Rupert was talking about last night. What's it called? I could ask him. I bet he wouldn't mind if you came along. That would be really super.'

'Would it?' said Ali cautiously, but her face was shining.

'Yes,' said Jo quickly, 'and you might say that the dig hasn't ended. It's just moving somewhere else. That sounds a really good idea.'

'Why not?' said Andy, putting his arm round Lucy's shoulders. 'We should be there quite soon. I can't see this one taking more than another week. Come on, guys, let's go and ask him.'

Jonno went with them and the girls saw them standing at the other end of the tent waiting for Rupert's attention. He was talking to an army officer.

'A week?' said Lucy. 'What are we going to do for a week? Hang around waiting for them?'

'We could go there.'

'Where? To the place with the three castles, whatever it's called?'

'Pen Selwood,' Jo told her. 'That's what it's called. Yes, we could go there. I'd like to see it.'

'How would we get there? Is there a train?'

'We could walk,' said Jo.

'Walk? How far is it?'

Jo looked off to the north-east. 'A day or two going slowly, I expect,' she replied. 'We've got nothing else to do, have we? Why don't we go by the fields and the paths and see the country the way it's meant to be seen?'

Ali was frowning. 'We'll have to eat. I haven't got much money.'

'Don't worry,' said Lucy, 'I have,' and they looked at her in surprise. Generosity was not usually her strongest quality. 'I can lend you some,' she added.

The students came back. Conrad was beaming. 'He says yes. He can't say how long we'll be here but probably a week or so. If you don't mind shifting dirt he says he'll feed you. How about that?'

So they said all their goodbyes and studied Ali's map. It was twenty-five miles from Montacute to Pen Selwood. 'We could do that in a day or a day and a bit,' said Ali.

'Leaving us six days hanging about in a place that barely shows on the map. Why don't we go somewhere fun first?' Lucy pointed. 'Look, Glastonbury. That's all magic and King Arthur and stuff. Let's go there.'

*   *   *

It was further north, in the wrong direction, at a tangent to the way her heart demanded, but Jo didn't argue. It got them moving and committed and once they were on their way, she was sure they would make it to Pen Selwood.

Right from the start, the journey did not go well. Lucy's rucksack straps and her unsuitable shoes and her thin socks all combined to slow them to a frequently interrupted crawl. They were still miles from Glastonbury when evening came and they began casting around for somewhere to camp. The countryside, which had seemed so open, now took on an unexpected inaccessibility. The fields contained sheep or cows or crops. They came to a wood and saw signs saying PRIVATE SHOOTING. KEEP OUT. A track led around the wood but beyond it was a farm with windows that seemed to stare at them suspiciously. Back on the road, they walked on until they came to a field that had no animals and no crops, just grass, so they climbed the gate, walked to a corner where the hedge shielded them from the road and put up the tent. They ate the pasties they had bought on the way and fell asleep, exhausted.

Engine noise and a voice, shouting, woke them in the morning. They unzipped the flap. A tractor was parked just inside the field and a young man was standing outside the tent shouting, 'Out, out! You must get out!'

Lucy crawled out and stood upright, facing him. She was wearing a long T-shirt and not much else and he seemed disconcerted. 'Go,' he said, 'Now. I must pray.'

'What do you mean?'

'I must pray. Here.' He was pale-skinned, pale haired, thin.

'You're not making sense,' she said. 'We're not doing any harm. Go and pray somewhere else. We're going to pack up in a minute.'

He held out his wrist to her, tapping his watch. 'Must pray. Right now. You. Go away.'

'You're very rude,' said Lucy. Ali and Jo were out of the tent, collapsing it and packing away the parts in their backpacks.

He held up his hands as if in invocation and said something incomprehensible.

'You're not from this country, are you?' asked

108

Lucy.

'Estonia,' he said.

'I don't know where that is, but we don't pray in our fields. We grow things in them and, if we want to, we sleep in them, so go and boil your head.'

'Come on,' said Ali. 'Leave it, Lucy. Give us a hand.'

'I don't see why I should leave it. He's got a nerve, talking to us like that.'

The young man had retreated to his tractor and was fiddling around with the equipment mounted on the back. He pulled down two long arms which stuck out at the side and climbed up to check the contents of the plastic tank mounted behind.

They walked out of the field, Lucy looking pointedly in the other direction while Ali and Jo waved apologies at the man, who gave them an uncertain smile and waved back.

'Halfwit,' said Lucy. 'He should go back to Esty . . . wherever it was and do his praying.'

'You saw that thing on his tractor?' Ali asked.

'Yes.'

'I think that was a sprayer.'

'So?'

'He was saying "I must spray." He didn't want to spray us.'

There was a long silence after that.

'Well, he should speak English better,' said Lucy in the end.

'That's how fights start.'

'What?' Lucy swung round to look at Jo, who had spoken as if her attention was elsewhere.

'Two people up against each other, and one doesn't know the language well. Normally we have all these tricks to make our point. Word tricks. We

109

can wheedle and we can half-joke and when it gets too serious we know just how much to back off, but not if we don't know the ins and the outs of the language. That's how fights start. That's how wars start. Not because people hate each other but because the wrong words drag them to a crisis.'

'Where did that come from?' asked Lucy in surprise.

'Oh,' said Jo. 'Someone told me that once.'

*   *   *

Glastonbury was not quite what they expected. They soon tired of the shops selling crystals and plastic swords and resin models of Merlin. They shared two sandwiches between them for lunch and went into the Abbey ruins.

'Look. This is where they buried Arthur and Guinevere,' Lucy declared, staring at the sign in front of her. 'I read about it in that shop. They found a huge oak coffin with two skeletons and a lead cross with lettering saying it was them. That was 1191, it says here. Then they buried them right here in a black marble tomb in 1278. Isn't that amazing?'

'They didn't exist,' said Ali. 'They were just a folk tale.'

'You don't know that.'

Ali went to buy a guidebook. Jo stood by the gate, imagining the gaunt remains as they had once been with a roof and glass in the windows and bright colours everywhere inside. She thought she preferred the ruin.

'Let's go to the Tor,' she suggested, so they walked out to the steep hill a mile to the east, climbing the path to the remains of the chapel on the summit. All the way up she was remembering that first drive down to Exeter four years earlier, when she had seen this cone in the far distance and thought it was where she most wanted to be. Now she knew it had only been a signpost, a finger pointing beyond the horizon. For all that, it felt immensely exciting because, as she reached the summit and the tower which was all that was left of the chapel, she knew this was the frontier of her territory, a border post—and she knew she had looked out from her true home to see this same tower at the edge of her vision.

They sat down together with the evening sun behind them, staring out across the wide land.

'I know two interesting things about this place,' said Ali.

'Do tell us, O fountain of wisdom,' Lucy replied.

'The first church up here fell down in an earthquake. Then Henry the Eighth hanged the abbot here.'

Lucy shivered. 'There are some things you should keep to yourself,' she complained.

'This was St Michael's church,' said Jo. 'So was the chapel that used to stand at the top of the hill at Montacute, where the tower is now. There are churches to St Michael on a lot of hilltops. They believed St Michael fought Lucifer up in the air.'

'That's the sort of thing I expect Ali to know, not you,' Lucy said. 'So where do we go next?'

Jo, without hesitation, pointed out across the fields towards high ground in the far distance. Behind them, the sinking sun dipped below a band of cloud and lit up the horizon. In that sharp, clear light, she saw another tower sticking up from the

111

ridge.

'There,' she said, and Ali, peering at her map and twisting it one way then the other, nodded. 'Yes, that's about right,' she said.

*　　　*　　　*

They camped at the edge of a wood near the village of East Pennard, tucking the tent out of sight, then they inspected the food they had bought in Glastonbury.

'One tin of frankfurters. One baguette. Butter. One bag of mixed leaf salad,' said Ali. 'A feast.' She tore the salad open. 'Correction: one bag of compost claiming to be a mixed leaf salad.' She tipped it and brown liquid dripped out. 'Just frankfurters and bread then.'

'That's boring,' said Lucy.

Jo got up and gazed at the trees nearby. 'Never mind,' she said. 'Look what we have here.'

Pale yellow crescents of fungi were growing from low down on one trunk. She broke them off, brought them back and began to clean them, rubbing them gently with her fingers. Lucy prodded one fastidiously.

'You can't be serious,' she said. 'That's not a mushroom. It's more like some sort of tree disease. I'm not eating that.'

Jo smiled. 'It's the one we call the wood fairy's saddle,' she said. 'Don't worry. I've eaten them lots of times. They're good.'

'When have you eaten them? Where? In Exeter? I've never seen you eating them. People die of eating the wrong mushrooms.'

Jo shrugged, lit the camping stove, melted

112

butter in the small aluminium pan, broke the crescents into pieces and began frying them.

'I'll try them first if you don't believe me.'

'That won't help. You might die writhing in agony in twelve hours' time.'

So the other two watched, shaking their heads, as Jo tore open a length of baguette, spooned in the mushrooms, added a frankfurter and ate them with enjoyment.

When they had all eaten, Ali got out the guidebook she had bought in Glastonbury. 'Lucy,' she said. 'Just so you know, that story about Arthur and Guinevere is crap.'

'No, it's not. It was on the sign.'

'Oh, right. The Abbot had some sort of vision so they dug a hole and, guess what? They found the skeletons and the little cross.'

'There you are.'

'No, it was all rubbish. The whole thing was a scam. The Abbey was in trouble. They bigged it up just to get lots of pilgrims to go there. That's how they made their money.'

Jo was far away, seeing the lead cross, feeling the weight of it in her hand, studying the crude letters incised into it, '*Hic jacet sepultus* . . .' Dimly, she heard Lucy ask, 'What do you mean, the Abbey was in trouble?'

'It had burnt down,' Jo said, 'just a few years before. They had to rebuild. They had to start again. It was a huge fire . . .' She remembered the call in the darkness, remembered the whole village pouring out of their houses in the dark, chattering in horrified excitement as they ran through the village to the edge of the ridge, staring out westward to the bright red glow on the far horizon,

113

which grew until, even at that great distance, they could see flames leaping. They knew what lay out there. They knew what was burning.

The other two girls were staring at her and she realised she had been talking all the time.

'Oh my God,' said Lucy. 'It's the mushrooms. It must be. Are you feeling weird?'

'I'm fine,' she said, but she could see she had shaken them, even when they woke early the following morning. After that, she was careful to say little and leave the navigation to Ali, although she could have found the way with her eyes shut. That was why they went too far north and Ali got them lost in lanes with no signs and fields with no landmarks. Jo didn't feel lost at all. From time to time she caught glimpses of the ridge to the east and as they came nearer, they all saw the tower sticking up from the trees.

'We're nearly there,' Ali said. 'If we go up the hill to that tower, we should be able to head south from there.'

They climbed the ridge, winding through the trees that stopped them seeing the tower again until they were almost on it. Three cars parked on the verge showed they were coming to something worth stopping for and then the tower seemed to burst upward beside the road as they came out of the woodland and Jo's heart lifted with it.

CHAPTER 10

Dozer had dropped Luke at the turning where the roads split to Wincanton, Pen Selwood and Cucklington. 'We'll be back this way quite soon. Come and visit when we're digging,' said the man. 'Be seeing you.'

The boy waved his thanks as the truck drove away, then stood quite still, looking back the way they had come. For a moment he thought of cycling all the way back again to search for them but he knew that was hopeless—a random line lancing out into a wide spray of possibilities of near-misses, of bad timing and hidden views. Would he sense her? From how far? A field's width on the wrong side of a concealing hedge?

Something old and experienced whispered in his head. Trust her. Wait here. Be here for her. When she gets here, you'll know.

He wished he could send his mind reaching out from his body to find them, out there to the south-west. He tried to imagine that, probing beyond Wincanton, opening up his whole head to sense something far off. Nothing came.

The road shimmered for a moment, shifted its shape, but modern noise drove it back to tarmac and the present and a green van, changing gear as it went past him. He calmed himself, breathing deeply and evenly, blotting out the traffic's roar from the main road close by. He remembered what he had just seen and played with the road, letting it dissolve from dark grey to brown and white, rough earth and broken stone, helping it narrow to a

115

track as the grass grew in from the edges and blurred the sharper modern boundaries. There were no more cars, only birdsong.

He looked up the curve of the lane towards old Pen, and in this quieter world he heard feet scuffing on the loose stone and the sounds of distress. Turning his head back towards Wincanton, he saw four men approaching, coming from the distant town. They were young men, walking awkwardly, carrying something between them, one at each corner. Without knowing quite how, he found himself walking as one of them, saw that his own hands were gripping a corner of their shared burden. Then he looked down at what they were carrying on their litter and saw the gasping girl with the white face and the blood trickling from the corner of her mouth and her eyes fixed on his. As their eyes met, the narrow channels of his schoolboy heart were filled with adult love and horror.

'I'm taking you home,' an older voice said and it came, shaking, from his own mouth, familiar and bewildering.

Back across an hour or several hundred years, he saw the two of them behind the hedge, huddled, hiding from the sudden musket fire, caught up in someone else's ambush. He saw the horse plunge, black, through the bursting branches as he raised an arm as if he could fend it off. From below its belly he looked up at the stirrups and the trooper's spurred boots as one hoof punched down into her breast. The ground drummed and as the unheeding soldier galloped away bent on his escape he looked down at her—curling, soaked in her pain, and knew she could not live.

Stumbling along the road again, he clutched the rough litter with this man's hands, listening to every hard breath, and fixed his eyes on hers as he saw her dwindle from him. He was flooded with the certainty of loss and the need to get her home before she died. The house was four hundred strides away, three hundred, two hundred, and she had to be there in time to feel its safety comforting her death.

A horn shocked him back and the dusty path grew hard and dark again. He stepped aside out of the way of the car whose driver mouthed cross words through the glass, and of course by then the litter and his dying wife had gone, back to their own time—back to the time when Dutch William marched in to deal with cruel Catholic James and a forgotten skirmish claimed her life. In that memory she whispered a different name to Luke and she had a name too, and he hadn't pinned them down in time so they had blown away with the car horn.

He came back into a world where Dutch William meant nothing to him at all and where only one thing had not changed. The house stood just ahead. Bagstone was at the centre of all this, that he knew. The teacher was squatting there and he was quite sure the teacher knew his real name. Nobody answered his knock and he sat down in the porch, determination and certainty growing with every breath as the vast shape of an old man's memory surrounded him, even if he could not yet open its doors or discern its detail. He tried to wring the past out of the house, staring at the stones as if his history was written on them, and that was when it became clear to him that the

117

cottage was not his only resource—that there was a better place to go, a place where the past really was written in stone.

He walked north through the diffuse village, past fields punctuated by the occasional cottage, knowing his way so long as he left it to his legs and not his head. He came to the churchyard at the far side of the village and wandered through the older graves until he arrived at a crooked stone splashed with lichen, its cut letters washed almost smooth by a thousand storms. A tremor from the past stopped him there. He crouched to stare at the lettering, trying to see any clear form in the remains of the grooves. He felt them with his fingers and found only ambiguous erosion but then something came out of memory into his left hand, an iron tool, and he found himself cleaning out the letters. A matching mallet bulked from nowhere into his right hand. There he was in the deeper silence of past times, halfway through the task of deepening the first cuts, chasing out sharp sprays from the new stone. He was cutting the stone for her, set up on a trestle right by the fresh grave, somewhere back in the long age of hand-power and horsepower.

He was young and she had been young, and that time a new fever got her for which she had not found a remedy.

'I'll see you soon,' she had said before she closed her eyes. The sadness got him. The letter he was shaping was a 'G' but he could not find the next one however hard he tried.

Movement caught his eye across the graveyard, beyond the trees, and brought him back. A man walking, slowly. He saw Michael Martin stop and

118

look down. The boy rose carefully to his feet, circled round between the bushes as if he were stalking an animal, keeping to the outer edge of the graveyard all the way until he stood a few yards behind the man. Here the stones were modern, crisp and upright.

The teacher was staring at a white gravestone. The boy moved forward carefully and quietly until he was just feet behind the man. He could read the simple inscription. It said 'Ferney Masters. Born November 8th 1907. Died February 7th 1991.'

'Ferney.' The name burst out of him and the teacher turned sharply at the sound of his voice. 'Ferney, Ferney, FERNEY! That's it!'

'What do you mean?'

'That's my name. It is, isn't it?'

Michael Martin's face was white. 'Don't say that. How can it be?' he said.

The boy who had been Luke was dancing in his excitement, spinning round, jumping as if a wound spring had burst free inside him. 'Because it is. You know it is. Tell me. It is, isn't it? You have to say.'

The teacher shrank away from the demonic boy, bruised by his joy and the new energy that was overflowing out of him, shaking his head.

'Say it,' said the boy, and the teacher barely breathed the word.

'Yes.'

'Thank you, thank you,' the boy called. 'I am Ferney. Of course I am.'

The teacher sat down on the grass as if his legs had given way.

'I guessed,' he said. 'I guessed but I didn't believe it. I didn't let myself. Those things you knew. The way you were in the car. You bastard.'

119

The boy flinched, looked at him in shock, took a step backwards.

'You expect me to be glad to see you?' the teacher asked. 'You think this is some sort of cause for celebration after what you did to me? Don't shake your head. You know what I'm talking about.'

'I don't,' the boy managed to answer before his voice broke up and, to his fury, tears began to run down his cheeks.

That stopped the teacher. 'Oh God,' he said. 'You're just a boy. When did you start to know?'

The boy sniffed fiercely, wiped his eyes, tried to get back in control. 'Yesterday.'

'This is too much,' said the teacher. 'I've got to go,' but the boy pointed to the bunch of wild flowers in his hand.

'Who are those for?' he asked.

The man shook his head, 'As if you don't know. They're just for ...' but then his voice failed him too and he walked across to another new stone, laying the flowers down in front of it. The boy followed him, knelt and read the inscription out loud. 'To the memory of Mary Martha Gabriella Martin and Rosie Juliet Martin, who died in love together. January 31st 1994.' It shocked him and he did not know why. He had expected one name, a different name, though he did not know what it was.

'Who were they?' he asked. 'Mary Martin? Martin? That's your name.'

The teacher looked sharply at him. 'My wife,' he said curtly.

The boy looked back at the stone, mouthing the name. 'Mary? Is that what people called her?'

120

'She was Gabriella.' The teacher chose the half-truth. He kept the other half to himself.

'So who was Rosie?' But Michael Martin turned his back on the stone and walked away. Then he stopped abruptly and looked back and his face had softened. An expression of mild wonder came over it as a spark of hope was born and turned into words.

'If you're back, then . . .' He stopped himself.

'Yes?' The boy's eyes were fixed on him. 'What?' But the teacher's face closed like a steel gate slamming. 'I'm going home,' he said.

When the teacher left the boy stood utterly still, feeling his forgotten name washing through him, cleaning out the corners of his soul. He walked slowly around the whole graveyard, staring at the stones, feeling some vague recognition of almost every one of them, like a janitor unlocking rooms for the coming day. He looked at the church with its low tower and knew that since the days even before that stone church first stood, there had always been a Ferney here. With the dying girl on her litter fresh in his mind, he saw how this walled yard contained sorrow and loss and loneliness repeated through the ages, and he walked to the western corner where he had buried her that time. There was no sign of her grave in the place where he knew she lay, but overlapping it was a grey stone slab with a Victorian date on it and a stranger's name. He minded that for a moment before he remembered how it was. Five deaths a year in the old village, thirty or more in the worst times—the sick times, the hungry times. He did the sums. Say seven hundred in a century, ten thousand since this church first stood. Of course she had vanished into the absorbing sponge of earth, dug over again and again, and so had he, time after time. Most of their memorials were long gone, wood rotting, stone washed and frosted smooth and cast away when nobody remembered any more.

He remembered.

He went back to his own gravestone, 'Ferney Masters. Born November 8th 1907. Died February 7th 1991', then searched along the eastern side until he found the one before, mossy and indistinct in weathered sandstone. He crouched and rubbed at the cuts with his finger, feeling the letters to spell them out. 'F Carter, b 2 March 1878 d 14 April 1907.' As he stood up, he saw there was more lettering below and tore handfuls of grass away to see the further words cut in later, deeper, by a different mason's hand.

There was the record of her death, his wife's death, eight months after his, and there was her name. Just five letters. The name he had been hunting for, the everlasting name that transcended every other wrong and arbitrary name with which she had ever been christened. He stared at it, traced the lettering with his fingers, said it to himself then said it again out loud, shouting it, astonished that he could have forgotten it, feeling every particle of every past version of her laughing with him from the earth now that he knew what she was called.

He looked back at the dates on that stone and found he could read a story in them. He had died at just twenty-nine. She had waited until she could bear it no longer and then she had followed him. No, there was more to it than that. Being born

122

close by was always the safest way back to an easy return. She would have stayed her hand until some local girl was expecting.

Words whispered in his head from the grave in front of him. Her words. 'We're sentenced to life, you and me. It's only bearable together.' And he thought of the girl at Montacute. He had been drawn to her, drawn all that way until they had been only yards apart, linked by the electric earth, and in any kinder world they would have discovered each other within a minute. He had missed the chance, the huge chance, and now where was she? Out there, groping her way to him or not? Had the instinct that was guiding her faded as she left Montacute? Was she even now saying 'No, let's go home' to her friends? 'I don't know why I wanted to go to Pen Selwood'? He knew there was no certainty unless she found this place and discovered the full truth of who she was. Every chance of happiness for the two of them hung in the balance. He stared down at the grass over her grave and shut out the background of the modern world and heard a voice, clear. 'We're never quite old and we're never quite young,' it said. The voice might have been his or hers. It had a lilt to it, the suggestion of a tune, and like some sort of code it unlocked an instruction in him, a deep impulse.

He left the churchyard, cycled eastward to a track through the woods on the edge of the village. He pushed his bike amongst the trees, knowing he had to find a pit—a place he could see clearly in his mind's eye. Then he saw not just one pit but hundreds upon hundreds of them, stretching out between the trees on both sides for as far as he could see, a landscape of shallow, brambled craters. He stilled his mind and cast around, testing the air for the right direction, abandoning his bike and moving into the trees along the curving honeycomb of narrow earth ridges separating them. Following his instinct, he groped and sniffed his way to the right one, far from the track, and when he was certain, he knelt to rip out roots, shovelling the earth away with bare mole hands until he found what he was looking for. His fingers touched a smooth surface and he pulled out a plastic sandwich box, taped tight shut. He sat in silence, holding it, the first real, solid evidence of the truth of what his mind was telling him.

It took a minute to gather the bravery he needed to peel away the tape. Inside he found a letter, as he knew he would—a message from his last self to the next. With it was a small package, well wrapped and heavy. He opened the envelope, sat for a while reading and thinking, then he pocketed some of the contents of the package, buried the box again and set out to follow the letter's directions, cycling slowly off to beat the bounds of his land and find the rest of himself.

He stopped again almost immediately at a field corner where a row of stones chilled him, just one stub of wall acting as a windbreak to a feeding trough. The letter had advised him what to do.

'Deal directly with your fears and her fears. There is no fear that stands up to explanation. Go open-minded through this place and stop where your skin crawls. Face it, know it and gain by it.'

He built the long-demolished cottage out of its diminished traces, saw the frantic daughter run out to seize his arm as he walked by one Victorian day, smelt the beery breath of the drunken father half his size again, a knife pressed against his wife's throat. He had spoken the same gentling words he used for horses, soothing, soothing, soothing until the angry arm had calmed and drooped. It was not like learning, not quite like remembering—more a matter of unforgetting, knowing how to see what was already there, bringing back a confidence in how to be.

Fears were only part of it. On a south-facing hillside with a fine view he went back two hundred years to rescue a troubled painter from the petulant wreck of his easel, listened patiently to his complaints about the ungrateful world of art, discussed the painting of a picture with him and came away understanding something more of self-esteem. His tour continued back and forth through the carnage of the plagues, rebellion, the brutality of purges pagan, Catholic and Protestant as he circled the village, soaking up the sight of it now with eyes which mixed it with older times, blending in its history.

On Coombe Street past Pen Mill, the landscape dragged his eyes northward. Leaving his bicycle, he walked into the wide valley and stared across the grass to the woods rising, covering the castle hilltop. Old despair touched him and he stared at the woods, seeing them waver in his sight, shrinking, growing, through a thousand indistinct variations. He had a sense of running, legs pumping, and held on to it, welcoming and retaining that despair again, and when he looked up the trees were gone, the hill ahead of him was bare and the stone keep of the castle was rising on the mound that crowned it. His son's name came back to him and he was running in sorrow and

125

desperation to tell Gally the worst of news, chased all the way, chased to his death.

When he sobbed his way back to the modern age, remembering what sharp-bladed war was like, he sensed himself in all his ages, gathered round to comfort this fresh arrival, and he knew he had learned to wake them when he chose.

*   *   *

For the rest of the afternoon he wandered the lacework paths that crossed the fields and carried on where modern roads stopped short. The field names came back to him like blessings: the Level Piece, Broom Close, Roses Mead, Starveacre and Smoke Hay, Matrimony, Christenings and Matron's Ground. He sat on the earth rampart of the second castle at Ballands, looking out at the valley westward, running his eyes over the hummocks and dips surrounding him on that open hillside, and found he knew what lay beneath each and every mound.

The young man who came to the third castle, Cockroad Wood, was no longer the half-boy who had started the journey. This castle guarded the western escarpment and the priory track. No stone keep here. No sign left of the wooden tower and the village which once sat inside the palisade, but Luke was entirely gone and Ferney had filled out, secure in the knowledge that he could conjure it back if he chose from the vast regained depths of memory.

Then he went home.

CHAPTER 11

Michael Martin left the graveyard fighting down a new hope that hurt like circulation returning to a frostbitten finger. Back at the cottage, he fumbled and dropped his front door key. It bounced under the bench inside the porch and as he reached for it his fingers met a pair of rubber boots, tucked out of sight underneath. He pulled one out. It was folded over and when he tried to straighten it, the brittle rubber came to pieces in his hand.

They were her boots, bought soon after she found the cottage, and she had last worn them more than sixteen years ago. The crumbling rubber swamped him with all the years and all the sorrow and he sat down on the bench, plunged into a well of regret, trying not to think about her and failing. He thought that if a fairy godmother granted him a second go at life, he would not have turned off the main road that very first day, back in 1990.

He knew he had only done it for her. She had become distressed in the tailback from an accident on the main road and he had turned left to get her away from it. She was often distressed in those days of miscarriages and nightmares and London life that had gone so wrong for them. They had been looking for a cottage and she had found reasons why every one was wrong until the chance diversion had brought them down this lane, as if by accident, and she had somehow seen it despite the swaddling camouflage of trees and creepers.

He could still feel the hot embarrassment of being caught trespassing by an old man who came in from the road to find them in the abandoned ruin. Brusque at first, he remembered how the man softened abruptly when he heard her name. She talked Mike into buying the house, then cherished it back to health—and he was always there, the old man, wandering in to watch over the work, coaxing on their efforts. She had seemed so much better, so much less troubled here in the deep country than at any previous time in the London part of their brief urban marriage. Then things began to change and Mike discovered the old man was filling Gally's head with nonsense about past lives and long entanglements. He began to mistrust the old man, old Ferney.

*   *   *

He thought through it all, right through the whole sad, wonderful, dismal story, sitting there in the porch, with no sense that three full hours had passed. When he heard feet on the road he looked up to see a young man coming into the yard, a sturdy youth with dark brown hair and a tanned face. It took him a moment to realise it was Luke. This Luke no longer looked sixteen. This Luke filled his body in a different way, walking in with the confidence of age and the measured tread of certainty.

'I know it all,' he said as Mike looked up. 'You don't have to pretend.'

'What do you know?'

'I know her name.'

'Gabriella?'

The young man laughed in joy, not in derision. 'You didn't call her Gabriella. You called her what

128

she always called herself.'

The teacher looked at him with eyes that said Please, don't let this start again.

'You know what you called her,' said the young man, and then spoke so deliberately that each of the four words had time to fill the air between them. 'You called her Gally.'

'That was short for Gabriella,' Mike said as if to excuse himself.

'Gally was never short for anything. It was always her name—always Ferney and always Gally, the two of us, always here, always together. You can't deny it, can you?'

'I wouldn't even try,' said Mike. 'But I was here with her, not you. She was my wife, not yours.'

The boy shook his head briefly, violently, as if to break something loose. 'That's the bit I don't understand. She married you. My Gally *married* you? She forgot so much that she did that?'

'Oh, don't worry, you went out of your way to explain her mistake,' Mike snapped. As soon as he said it, the immensity of this conversation hit him. He had openly accepted the boy's identity. It was out there in the air between them and there could be no more pretence. In the recess at the back of his disbelieving brain he had been watching out for this boy for all these intervening years, but now he had finally appeared, far from where Mike had expected him, tumbling into the Montacute trench babbling of vineyards, most of Mike still hoped it was a fantasy. He could no longer hold that hope. Old Ferney had infiltrated their lives so completely that he came to the end of his final illness in their spare room in this house which was at the centre of it all. Back then, he had proved his story in ways that even Mike, the rational historian, had found hard to reject and now there was this final proof— the young Ferney undeniably standing in front of him.

'Do you blame me?' said the boy.

'We took you in.' Mike pointed up at the bedroom window. 'We brought you here to die. You and your bloody promise. You took her away. You destroyed me.'

The boy seemed shocked. 'Why do you say that?'

'Because it's what happened, isn't it?'

'I don't remember.'

'Oh, how convenient. You remember what you choose to.'

'Not everything. It comes back slowly. Sometimes the newest part takes longest.'

For a long minute the space between them was full of silent uproar.

'It didn't work, did it?' said Mike.

'What didn't?'

'All your planning. You haven't got her back.'

'No?' said the boy, and Mike read his face in astonishment and suddenly dared to hope.

'What do you know?'

The boy shook his head, looked away.

'No, don't do that,' Mike burst out. 'Look at me. You tell me. Has she come back too?'

A woman on a horse rode past, pulled up for a moment at the sound of his raised voice to stare in at them through the gate. For a moment Mike thought she was going to say something. He opened the cottage door and ushered the boy inside. The boy sat down at the kitchen table and ransacked the room with his eyes.

'Don't expect me to have all the answers,' he said in the end. 'It takes its own time.'

'Is she coming back?' Mike demanded.

'She might be. It could go either way.'

'It's down to chance? Like it was when she and I came here?'

'You think that was chance? She didn't come back here by chance. You know how it works. She told you. She and I, we die here. When it works out right, we're born here. Over and over. That's the way it should be, the way it used to be. We're born here and the place helps us remember.'

'So why not this time?'

'Sometimes it's gone wrong, but we almost always found our way back and the other one could help with the reminding.' The boy frowned. 'It's harder now.'

'Why?'

'There were families all round the village then, always babies on the way, waiting for us when our time came. Nobody moved around much. We were safer then. Not these days. Up here they're mostly retired, aren't they? Down there on the main road, that's where the expecting mothers are and they're all tearing past at seventy miles an hour. That's what makes it hard. They take us and we could wind up anywhere.'

'You've been gone half an afternoon and you suddenly know all this?' Mike's words covered his uncomfortable sense that the boy had become formidable.

Ferney showed him his hands with the earth still on them. 'I left myself a note, a letter from me to me. I dug it up.'

'What did it say?'

131

'Just . . . helpful stuff. Things that tell me I'm not bonkers.'

'Where was it?'

'In a private place.'

'Where's this letter now? Can I see it?'

'No, it wasn't for you. It was for me. I put it back. Something else. The gravestone. My last stone. It says I died February 7th, 1991.'

'Yes?'

'So, I should have been born again some time that year, within a few months—nine at most.'

'If you say so.'

'But I wasn't. I was born in June 1994. Something happened in between. I must have been somewhere. Do you know what happened?'

Mike held on to himself and shook his head as if that didn't count as a lie. The boy didn't know the worst part of it all. That didn't let him off. 'So get to the point,' he said. 'Is she coming?'

'Call me by my name.'

'All right. Is she coming . . . Ferney?'

'Like I said, she might be. If everything goes right.'

'When?'

It was the boy's turn for evasion. 'How would I know that?' He saw hope on the older man's face. 'You think that's good news, do you? What are you expecting? What do you think it will be like when she does come?'

The truth suddenly seemed simple and Mike enjoyed saying the words. 'It will be wonderful.'

'Will it? Why?'

'To have her back? Of course it will. How could it not be?' The boy watched him with a frown that annoyed him unreasonably. 'She died, Ferney. My

132

wife died. Dead means gone. Dead means miserable and lonely and days that drag on forever so I wished I were brave enough to walk in front of a train. Dead means idiot friends finding hopeless single women they think you might like. That's while you still have friends. Dead means the worst weekends and the worst school holidays you could ever imagine and you don't know about this, do you? You don't know about it because it's just another hiccup to you. I'll die and that's it, game over, the end of Michael Martin. It's easy for you, isn't it? You pop back up like some sort of weed and all you have to do is sit on your hands for a few years to get her back.'

Ferney stared at him impassively. Mike felt judged and found wanting by those old eyes. 'I know what loneliness is,' Ferney said. 'You've only had to live it once.'

'Once is enough. This time it's my turn and I'm not used to people coming back so, yes, it's wonderful.'

Ferney looked at him, astonished. 'Your turn? She's not coming back to *you*.'

'You can't say that.'

'Oh, I can. Think about it. Will you even recognise her?'

'Of course I will.'

'Did you recognise me?'

'That was you, not her, and I suspected soon enough. Yes. Yes, of course I will.'

'How?'

Mike's forehead wrinkled. 'We'll know each other. We loved each other. Don't you dare look at me like that. We did. Anyway, why are you asking, you of all people? You've met her over and over

133

again and you've known her.'

'Sometimes I haven't been too sure, not at the start.' Ferney got to his feet and paced to and fro. 'Just be quiet a moment.' Mike waited, watching the boy's mouth working silently. He saw Ferney nod in some sort of culmination. 'It comes back,' the young man said, 'sometimes just when you need it. Maybe this will help you understand. I was up there once, up on the hilltop. I looked all the way across to the church and I saw an open carriage pull up. I'd lost her young, the way it used to happen, and she'd been gone a long time. I was waiting, every day, watching out for her. I knew that carriage mattered so I ran through the fields all the way there.'

'When was this?'

'I don't know.'

'Before cars?'

'Cars? Of course it was—way before cars. I got to the church and there they were, in the churchyard. A well-to-do family, you could tell. A father and a mother and two girls . . .'

Ferney found himself back there as he talked, more vividly than he had remembered before. Part of the roof was off, the stone tiles piled carefully against the church wall and canvas lashed over the hole. He could see both girls. They were maybe thirteen or fourteen. One of them was halfway up a ladder, climbing fast. She turned, looked at him and smiled a radiant smile.

'Well, well,' she said, and he just stared as the wind wrapped a wing of dark hair across her eyes. She giggled and took one hand off the ladder to push it back. Her face was as sweet as he could have hoped and expectation took shape in him. She looked so like his last Gally and though he was

134

ten years too old to make it easy, he was thrilled through and through. Then the other girl, kneeling by a grave, turned to look at him. She was as plain as her sister was pretty but then she said 'Hello' and just those two syllables told him all he needed to know. It was not a tentative greeting. It held calm certainty and the grave in front of her was her own. The parents came round the corner, scolding the wild beauty to bring her down from her dangerous perch, and they walked off back to their carriage, and all the way the other girl trailed behind and waved to him to show him she would be back.

'So what are you saying?' said Mike when he finished the story, but Ferney knew he had to bring the teacher slowly to the point of realisation. Mike had to find his way to the truth himself.

'She might not be coming back fresh with recent memories,' was all he said. 'The old ones are stronger.'

'I can remind her,' said Mike.

'No. I know how. If she gets scared, I know what to do. I understand this. You don't. I'm the only one can help her. You'd better remember that.'

'She'll know me,' Mike retorted. 'And if she doesn't, she soon will. You do your own reminding and I'll do mine.'

'You can try,' the boy answered.

'So it's a competition, is it?'

That's exactly what you're making it, Ferney thought to himself, and you have no idea what a handicap you're under. But all he said was, 'You have to think of her wellbeing.'

'I don't buy this. Back then, when we first saw you, years ago when we found the house, why

135

didn't you know it was Gally straight away?'

'I was a bit too old. She was a bit too young,' Ferney said. 'It had been a long time and she didn't remember anything, did she? She was blocked off.'

'She found the house and she knew her name. That's more than you did this time.'

'She was always better at that. Yes, of course she knew the house. Speaking of the house, there's something else, something I need. Will you help?'

'What?'

'I need to be back here in the village.'

Mike gestured around them. 'You are in the village.'

'I mean I need to be living here.'

'Why?'

'It's where I belong. I can't stand it over there with them. It's too hard. I feel mad there. It all slips. I'm sane here. The time's right. I have to come back here.'

'How on earth can you do that? Where would you live?'

Ferney looked around the room, turned back, and frowned as if he didn't understand. 'Surely there's space?'

'Here? You mean in *my* house?'

'Your house? Is that how you think of it?'

'Yes, because that's what it is.'

The boy stared at him so intently that Mike looked away. 'It *is* my house,' he said. 'It was mine and Gally's and now it's mine.'

'Of course that's what the law would say, I suppose,' Ferney replied in a measured tone, 'but the law only goes so far. There's justice to consider and there's history.'

'History?'

'You know what I mean. I've always lived here—almost always. We found ways to pass it on, Gally and me—ways to pass it on to ourselves, I mean. Even when it slipped out of our hands, we always got it back in the end.'

'That's as may be. I bought it and I didn't buy it from you. I bought it with a mortgage which I'll be paying off for the next ten years and I spent a load of money putting it right. You know what it was like, all falling down.'

'Isn't there space for me to be where I need to be right now?'

'Oh come on, you can't possibly move in here.'

'But I have to. Can't you see that?'

'Can't *you* see it's completely impossible?'

'I can pay rent.'

'How?'

The boy reached into his pocket and brought out a screw of newspaper. He handed it to Mike. It was surprisingly heavy.

Mike unwrapped it and found himself holding five gold coins. 'What are these?'

'Sovereigns. Queen Victoria. They must be worth a month or two's rent.'

'Where did you get them from?'

'From where I'd hidden them. Go on, take them. There's lots more and you can always sell gold.'

Mike knew there would be more. The old man had used the earth as his bank, depositing treasures to withdraw in a later generation. He put the coins down on the table as if they carried some contagion. 'I don't want them. You can't come here.'

The boy shrugged. 'We'll see,' he said.

At that moment, the certainty that Gally was

137

alive caught up with Mike. He understood that somewhere out there was a Gally with a young body, a body which breathed and moved and laughed and was not boxed in the churchyard earth beneath a sad stone. Ferney stood in front of him and that was complete proof. To his dismay he felt fresh tears on his cheeks. He looked towards the door as if he might suddenly see his lost Gally open it with that brilliant smile lighting her face, chasing the grey cold from every corner of his life. In their big bed, where he still slept to one side, lonely in the darkness, he always tried to capture that smile. In the days after her death it had been easy but now he had worn it to tatters in his head.

'Maybe I do know something,' Ferney said.

'Meaning?'

'Maybe I know something about where she is. Maybe I'll tell you if you let me stay.'

'That's disgraceful. You're not going to blackmail me like that. I'm not going to let you push me around.'

Ferney was on his feet. 'Push *you* around?' he said. 'You wouldn't even be here if it wasn't for me. Don't you talk about—'

The door shook as a fist hammered on it from the outside, then burst open. A man and a woman erupted into the house. Mike had seen them before, walking up the verge at Cucklington.

'Found you,' said the man. 'Thought as much.' He had a bright red face and slick, oiled-black hair. 'Get in the car, boy. Outside. Now.'

'Do what he says, Lukey,' said the woman behind him. 'We've been searching. There's going to be a lot of trouble. Come with me,' and she tried to pull the boy outside.

'Crying?' said the man to Mike. 'You'll be crying when we've finished with you, you ponce.'

There was nothing the teacher could do but watch from his window as they drove their son away.

*   *   *

He went to bed early, imagining the comforting shift of a body on the mattress next to him, imagining the woman he mourned, refreshed, remade. He got up early the next morning, showered, shaved and drove to the school singing. In the staffroom he read a notice about arrangements for the end of term, pulled a stiff white envelope from his pigeonhole and read its instruction to come immediately to the principal's office.

The note took the edge off his new feeling of goodwill. He guessed what it was about. The principal hadn't liked his suggestion for the end-of-term activities week. She said nobody would be interested in yet another Somerset castles tour. She wanted something more contemporary. Her secretary, Mrs Firebrace, gave him a slack-jawed, unhappy look when he went into the outer office.

'She's in there with Mr Montgomery,' she said.

Mr Montgomery was the Chair of Governors.

'Shall I come back?' Mike asked.

'Oh no. No, they're waiting for you. You're to go straight in.'

Mr Montgomery was wearing a suit. He stood up when the secretary announced Mike but he didn't put out his hand. Jennifer Foxton half stood

139

from behind her desk, then seemed to buckle back into her chair. They both gaped at him as he looked from one to the other.

'I'm afraid there's been a complaint,' she said in the end.

CHAPTER 12

The latch was hanging off, two of its screws torn out of the softened wood, and the five-bar gate sagged open just far enough for her to squeeze through, careful not to let the damp decay stain her jacket. She was running late with two more appointments to go and had hoped to avoid emergencies like this one.

The cottage stood on a slant from the lane, not quite at right angles, its slate roof dipping away. Paint curled off the window frames in grey-green flakes. Soapy leaves sprawled over newer shoots in the flower beds.

She looked around what might once have been a farmyard, arming herself for the moment when the papers in her file would merge with a living, breathing client. It seemed to her to be a lonely place. Brambles arced in from the screen of trees around the yard, barring the way to old brick sheds.

She lifted the door knocker, held it in the air for one more undecided second, then banged it down twice. A pigeon clattered out of the trees. She was raising her hand to knock again when she heard faint steps within and someone fiddling at the door. The man who opened it was frowning, grey and tired, and she could not imagine him laughing.

'Mr Martin? Michael Martin?'

'Yes.'

'I'm Rachel Palmer.'

He looked at her blankly.

'From Whitson Saunders.'

'Who are Whitson Saunders?'

'Solicitors,' she said. 'I'm here to represent you. Your union called me.' That got no response at all. 'Didn't you know I was coming?'

'No, I didn't,' he said.

'They didn't ring you?' She glanced beyond him into the hallway. In the gloom, she could see a message light winking red on a machine.

'I don't think so.'

'Tony Ferranti. Is that right? Your branch representative? He asked me to come.'

'Did he? I told him I'd be all right.'

'I'm here to help you, Mr Martin. Your union thinks this is serious. We need to do something straight away.'

'Why?'

'What did the school tell you?'

'The principal said I should stay at home while they sorted it out. She called it gardening leave.'

'When was that?'

'Yesterday.'

'But you've been suspended, haven't you?'

She saw his eyes lift to her and widen. 'Suspended?'

'Well, I'm sorry to bring bad news but I'm quite sure you have. They tell me they sent a letter yesterday afternoon by Special Delivery.'

As one, they looked at the floor next to his feet, where a scatter of envelopes spread across the flagstones. A red and white card lay on top and he bent to pick it up. 'Oh. I didn't hear the knocker. It says they tried to deliver something that needs signing for.'

'Yes. Look, can I come in?'

He shrugged and stepped out of the way. 'I'm sorry. Of course.'

Rachel Palmer had done matrimonial work and she had seen kitchens like this before, single men's kitchens which had once been shared. She could even put a rough date on the start of the disintegration. Ten years ago? No, more than that. Fifteen maybe. Time for the paint to discolour darkly above the stove, for the small saucepans to show the marks of scoured burning while the larger ones gathered dust.

'Would you like tea or coffee?' he said.

'Have you got any herb tea?'

He opened a cupboard and she saw a mess of very old cardboard packets. Some had split and the teabags spilling from them had turned mid-brown.

'Don't worry. Anything will do.'

She watched his back in silence as he searched for a second acceptable mug, then they sat opposite each other at a wooden kitchen table and her papers stuck to its surface as she spread them out.

'You've been suspended indefinitely, effective yesterday.'

He looked up then, suddenly alert, and she found that a relief. Surprise made him more human, less like the relic of some profound disaster. 'Is that normal?' he asked, 'No, stupid. Of course it's not. What does it mean?'

'It means you mustn't go near the school or

142

contact anyone else involved.' She took refuge in her notes. 'You are the subject of a complaint made by the parents of Luke Sturgess of Sandwell Cottage, Cucklington. They allege there has been ...' she hesitated ... 'an improper relationship between you and their son.'

'What does improper mean?'

She stared at him, saw he was younger than she had thought behind the fence of frown lines. 'Don't you know?'

'It doesn't mean anything . . . sexual, does it?'

'Yes, I think in this case that's a major part of their concern.'

He shook his head. 'They think that? And the school believes them?'

'The school hasn't got much choice,' she said gently. 'I suppose you could say that suspension is the necessary response after an allegation of that sort.' It felt too soon to dive into further detail. He looked prepared to pull down the shutters at any moment.

'It isn't true,' he said. 'It's a complete misunderstanding. I hope you know that? I'm not like that. It's horrifying that anyone could . . .' He seemed unable to go on and she waited for him to get control of his voice but in the end he only sighed so she talked to give him time.

'I'm sure it will be all right,' she said, though she wasn't yet sure of anything. 'We'll sort it out. Don't worry.'

'Look, I'll just quit. I had half a mind to go anyway. If they don't believe me I'll resign.'

'I'm sorry, but it's not quite that simple. They're suggesting that this may go back a little while.'

'Does that make a difference?'

143

'I'm afraid it does. The boy is only just sixteen now. If he was under sixteen when any offence is alleged to have taken place, then it's not just a matter for the school and the education authority. It becomes a matter for the police.'

'I didn't even know him until this week.'

'They say you did. They say you took him on a school trip last year—an overnight trip.'

'Oh, for God's sake.'

'You hadn't thought of that?'

'I hadn't thought of any of this.'

'All right, let's get on and see what we can do. I need to ask you some questions.'

'Go ahead.'

'You were married, I understand? Are you still in touch with your wife at all?'

He looked at her sharply. 'Of course not.'

'Why do you say of course not? Are you on bad terms?'

'We were never on bad terms. Not for a single moment. I say that because she's dead.'

That changed things for Rachel. There was sorrow, not anger, at the core of this house, although there was a disconcerting edge to the way he said it.

'Forgive me. I should have known that. I really should. This has had to be done in a rush. How long ago did she—'

'Sixteen years and five months.'

She thought he could probably have told her in days, perhaps even hours.

'You don't have any children?' There were no children here, that was clear, but the question had to be asked.

'Not now. We did.'

144

'You lost a child?'

'I lost my family. My wife and my daughter. Both at once.' There was something harsher creeping into his voice.

'I am so sorry,' she said, aware of the complete inadequacy of the words. 'I can only guess at what that feels like,' then, because she had stumbled into this and could not retreat without sounding heartless, she asked the hard and pressing question, 'How did it happen?'

He was staring down at the table. 'They died together. Gally and . . . Rosie.'

'How old was Rosie?'

He seemed unable to answer, just staring back at her, shaking his head slightly so she pressed on. 'Was it an accident?'

He shook his head more emphatically but said nothing more.

'Mr Martin, you need to trust me if I'm going to help. I have to understand a lot about you, and I have to understand that quite quickly. If this isn't the right time, I'll happily come back but it will need to be soon. I really am on your side. Please believe that.'

'Are you? Why? You don't know me.' He didn't sound annoyed, more quietly curious about how this thing they had embarked on was meant to operate.

'Of course your union's paying me to be on your side.' She saw his eyes slide away from her as if that was what he expected. 'That's how it starts,' she said, 'but that's not necessarily where it stops.'

'You make your own mind up?'

'I'm not supposed to, but of course I do.'

He looked at her then, seeming to notice her

145

properly for the first time. 'All right. What do you need?'

'It would help if you told me as much about the background to this as you can bear to. All I've got at the moment is your professional details. History lecturer at the University of London, then teaching at a Somerset comprehensive?'

'Yes.'

'Not even head of a department? Wasn't that a big step down in the world?' She was looking for the discontinuities, the chinks the other side might use if she didn't get there first, but she was also thinking he was perhaps a failure.

'It was a personal decision.'

She chose to keep her silence and that drew him into filling it.

'It changed when they died,' he said. 'There's no fun travelling all that way up and down just to be by yourself when you get back.'

'You could have stayed in London?'

'No, no. This place was Gally's whole life. I couldn't leave here.'

'Gally was your wife?'

He nodded. 'Once she found this house she never wanted to be anywhere else. We had our baby down here. It was her whole world.' He frowned. 'Does any of this matter?'

She nodded. 'It might. Look, Mr Martin—'

'Please. I hear Mr Martin all day long at school. I don't want to be Mr Martin. Call me Mike.'

'All right. Mike. I don't think you can guess what this is going to be like. You're accused of improper behaviour towards a teenage boy. They are going to be turning over stones. There could be all kinds of suggestions.'

146

'Such as?' He sounded indignant now. She preferred that to weary hopelessness. She could do something with indignation.

'Well, for example, they might suggest you switched to teaching in this school because you wanted to be with younger children. That's why I'm asking about your career.'

'That's mad.'

'I'm afraid when these things get going, you can't rely on sanity.'

He was clearly shocked. 'But I was married. I had a child. I just told you.'

'Sadly there are people out there—married people, people with children of their own—who are still capable of terrible things.'

'Not me. I promise you.'

'The police are going to need more than promises,' she said gently. 'I'm sure you've never been on the receiving end of an investigation before but—'

And that was when he astonished her. 'I have,' he said. 'That's the point. I have.' He stopped and stared down at his hands and she saw his fingers twisting around each other. She tried to keep her face calm and waited patiently until he looked up at her with an expression of defiance, a new animation.

'You'd better tell me,' she said.

'The police questioned me about Gally and Rosie.'

'About what exactly?'

'About their deaths.'

'In what way?'

'They thought it might not have been an accident.'

147

She tried to cover up her shock. 'You were a suspect?'

'I was *the* suspect.'

'Why? Whatever made them think that?'

'They couldn't tick their boxes. Gally and Rosie died by poisoning, you see. She would pick things in the hedgerows. Not just for food. For medicine too. Their people couldn't sort it out, they couldn't work out the toxins. They didn't know exactly what made it lethal.'

'So they tried to point it at you?'

'I was all they had.'

'How long did that go on?'

'Weeks and weeks.'

'How very terrible. What happened in the end?'

'They just let it go. They never said they believed me, only that they didn't have enough evidence to act.' He looked at her and it was a moment of certainty for her. 'I still feel scared every time I see a policeman,' he said.

She found herself believing in him. This was a good man, a man who had been fought nearly to a standstill but certainly no murderer.

'Tell me about Luke Sturgess.'

'Luke Sturgess?' It sounded for a moment as if he did not quite recognise the name. 'Oh, right. What do you want to know?'

'How did you come across him? In class?'

'No. I never taught him. I only really met him at the weekend.' Mike explained about the dig.

'And last year?'

'I don't really remember that much. He came to my after-school History Club once, then he came on the castle visit. They all stayed in a hostel. I was in a B & B next door. He never came again. Like I say, I didn't ever teach him.' Mike didn't tell her what he was just starting to remember—that the boy didn't come back because the other kids in the club had made fun of him and his interest and the strange questions he had asked.

'So would other teachers confirm that you didn't know him well before that?'

'It's a big school,' said Mike vaguely. 'I don't suppose they'd know one way or the other.'

'His parents allege that they witnessed Luke in a highly emotional state in your car.'

'That's true.'

'And they also say they found him here in this house yesterday.'

'Yes, he was here.'

Now Mike was facing this keen-eyed woman across the kitchen table, he knew it could not really be explained, not to someone who lived in the realm of logic. The kettle had boiled so, taking a moment to gather himself, he got up to make the tea. Rachel watched him as he filled one mug, put the kettle back down, and only then seemed to remember there were two of them.

'So can you tell me more about that?'

'He was shocked the first time. He'd fallen down a bank at the dig. I was taking him home.'

'Right,' she said doubtfully. 'So why did he come back here?'

'I don't know. He's an unusual boy. He does what he wants.'

'But his parents were worried enough by him disappearing to find out where you lived and come here to find him?'

'His mother and her current partner.'

'Whatever. Why do you suppose they did that?'

149

'They jumped to the wrong conclusions. He turned up out of the blue. I couldn't stop him.'

'But you let him in the house. Didn't you think that was unwise, having him here? You being a single man?'

'I'm not a . . . I don't think of myself like that. Anyway, it wasn't really my choice. Like I said, he just showed up.'

'Why?'

'You'll have to ask him.'

'I may not get the chance.' She had been waiting for the moment and though this wasn't quite it, there might not be a better one, 'Listen . . . I'm sorry, but I do have to put this to you as a formal question. Has there been any sexual impropriety between the two of you?'

His eyes changed as he closed down on her. He looked as if he had trusted her and been proved wrong.

'I do have to ask,' she said again. 'I'm not accusing you.'

'For God's sake. Of course there hasn't. Have they talked to him?'

'I'm sure they will, but in these things, a vulnerable boy might not be expected to tell the truth.'

'You do believe me?'

'It's not just me who needs to believe you.' She judged that he was near the limit for a first meeting, looked at her watch and saw a chance to get back on schedule. She drained her tea in one long swallow. 'I'll come back tomorrow, if I may. What's better for you, morning or afternoon?'

'It doesn't make much difference.'

'Nine o'clock?'

'If you like.'

'We'll need to talk more about your wife's death, I'm afraid.'

He nodded.

'Are you going to be all right?' she asked, a little to her own surprise. She had a strong sense that she had opened up something that had been sealed for years. All she got was another curt nod.

A little worried, she pushed it further. 'Do you have people to support you? Friends in the village?'

'Oh yes,' he said. 'Now, I must get on.'

He saw her out and watched as she drove away then he went back in, sat down at the kitchen table and steeled himself to remember, to put it all in place, feeling he could do it now that death was no longer quite so final—that he must do it to be ready for her return.

* * *

Once upon a time, Mike had led what he thought of as a normal life. He had followed his father's dusty footsteps into academia. He believed in his father's version of that world, where the people were safely removed from the story, like rocky headlands seen only on a sailor's chart. Alone, Mike had not known he was lonely until a girl had slipped into one of his lectures and come up to him at the end, admitting she was not a student and challenging him on the desiccated, impersonal way he saw history. He had stepped off a cliff into her wide smile and she had mistaken what she needed from him enough to marry him.

Mike's marriage had ended on a Monday.

He had come back home to Bagstone to surprise her. He knew just how the smile would spread across her face when she saw him and a fine, fierce anticipation hummed in him.

This return had been quite unlike him, the clockwork man committed to his four-day working week. In term-time he left the cottage every Sunday evening and came back every Thursday night, but on that Sunday he had been loath to leave her. His doubts had assailed him all the way to London. Stuck in the Chiswick traffic, he had dared to imagine asking for compassionate leave. The following morning it had proved much easier than he expected. The Dean was sympathetic and ten minutes was all it took. Two lectures were cancelled, his tutorials were postponed, and the rest of the week was suddenly his to go straight back home and help Gally care for their child.

He was back at the cottage by midday. The gate had been shut and he left the car outside in the lane to make his arrival more of a surprise. It was February and Gally had been preparing the yard for spring. The signs of her deep care were everywhere in the harmony of stone, brick and the kind channelling of nature. Rosie's toy shears were on the bench in the porch next to Gally's real ones.

He picked up a postcard from the mat, saw a sunny harbour scene, flicked it over and recognised his aunt's impossible scrawl. Hanging his jacket on the brass hooks, he noticed the answering machine was switched on and went into the kitchen expecting to see the remnants of their breakfast but the table was clear and the oak draining board was empty, pale and dry. The kettle was cold. He filled it half-full, switched it on to boil for the tea they would drink together when he found her. Upstairs, he saw their bedroom was tidy, the bed made up, Rosie's room too. The spare room door was closed. He turned the knob, feeling it wobble on the shaft because of the broken grub screw— one of the jobs for Jason the handyman on Wednesday.

The house bulged with silence. The door caught on the loose carpet behind it as he pushed it open and he saw the corner of the window through the narrow gap. That window looked out at the back of the house and he thought he might see them further down the valley. They might even now be walking back towards the house, Rosie swinging and tugging on Gally's hand. They would be so surprised to see him at the window. Gally would lift Rosie into her arms and run with her.

Edging his foot through the gap to flatten out the rucked carpet, he pushed the door right open and it came to him even before he saw what lay on the bed that they were no longer anywhere near.

*   *   *

It was late summer when they finally let him bury her. The churchyard was crowded with the people of the village and a handful of Gally's older friends. She had no close family and Mike stood by himself at the graveside separated from the rest by a gap which felt like quarantine. The mourners wondered at his blank face but inside the boarded-up man, mad despair was clawing at the walls.

He watched the disconcerting, unfamiliar coffin

153

as they lowered it into the underworld of earth and they watched him for a flicker of expression, then they all turned their heads for the second coffin, the tiny coffin, so they missed the agony that creased his face.

There was polite tea offered afterwards in the old school hall by the churchyard gate but he found he could not go in and thought perhaps the rest of them might prefer it that way. On his way home in the unfitting sunshine, he had branched uphill without any conscious decision, climbing to the top of the ridge, their place, where, alone under the high sky, there had been space to let his anger out.

'It's your fault,' he had said inside his head, staring at the stone bench on the hilltop. He said it again out loud but the words seemed no louder than the thought and were swallowed by the ocean of air. He stood over the bench, looking down as if the old man was still there to hear his accusation. 'It's your fault,' he said, and he sat down on the end of the bench, staring at the gap beside him, wishing Ferney had left enough atoms behind him to allow revenge. The three of them—the old man, the girl who had briefly been his wife and their daughter—swirled in the air, two, then three, then two.

'You got what you wanted,' he said to them. 'Well, now you're both bloody well dead and I hate you for it.'

A skylark had sung far above his head and taken the razor edge off his anger with its song. 'I fell for it too,' he had whispered to the shade of her. 'People die and they're buried and they rot and that's it. That's all there is.'

Death had dulled his life again and for all those years he had tried not to think but now, as he lifted his head from his hands and looked across at the empty chair where the lawyer had sat, thoughts filled him, rough and jostling thoughts. The boy Luke, for whom he could feel sympathy—the boy who was turning into the man Ferney. How could he feel sympathy for that man who had taken everything from him? He could feel for the child but not for the man. Why should he? What now? Was Ferney the only way back to Gally renewed? Did he have the strength for the battle ahead?

He needed air and clarity, so he walked out of the house and took the so-familiar path, worn to the bare earth these past years by just his feet and no one else's. As he climbed the gentle dome of hill on grass cropped close by sheep, he saw the squat pillar of the surveyor's triangulation point rise into view. He saw the old stone bench beyond it and to his surprise, which was really no surprise at all, he saw against the bright sky the hunched shoulders of someone sitting on it and knew exactly who it would be.

'I heard what happened,' the boy said as Mike walked up. He was staring at the ground. 'It wasn't anything I said. I just couldn't stop them.'

'You should be at school, shouldn't you?'

'I've finished my exams.'

'What are you doing here?' he asked, suddenly tired by it all.

The boy looked at him with something like a polite version of contempt on his face and his expression said, Come off it, this was my place long

155

before it was yours. 'They say you've been sacked.'

Mike flinched. 'Is everybody talking about it?'

'Yes.'

'Well, I haven't been—not sacked, just suspended.'

'I'm sorry.'

'You should be,' said Mike. 'It's all because of you. I'm not meant to be talking to you. In fact you'd better go.'

The boy looked around at the empty landscape and shrugged. 'I'll go if you want.'

'No.'

'No?'

'I need to ask you some things.'

'That won't help.'

'Why do you say that?'

'Because questions have power and answers only drain their power away.'

'I don't know what that means. You know something about Gally, about where she is now. You have to tell me.' Mike found himself looking around the edges of the hill as if she might appear at any moment, dancing towards him with a smile that would melt away the time between.

'I don't,' said Ferney, and Mike couldn't decide if he meant he didn't know or that he didn't have to tell.

'I've got a question for you,' the boy said. 'Does this tune sound familiar?' He hummed something which, Mike thought, could have been any of half a hundred folk songs.

'No, it doesn't, I—'

'Well, what about these words? Have you heard them before? *We're never quite old and we're never quite young and we . . . we something . . .*' His face

156

was screwed up in concentration.

'Listen, Luke—Ferney—I don't even know what I'm meant to call you. Why the hell should I be interested in a song?'

'Call me by my real name. I only wanted to know if you ever heard her sing it.'

'Her? Gally? My wife? You wanted to know if my wife ever sang me that? Oh, I think that would definitely be my business if she had, not yours.'

The boy shot him a startled look as if he had not expected such vehemence. He got to his feet and ran off down the hill and Mike shouted after him, 'No, if you really want to know. No, she never did.'

CHAPTER 13

It was true and it wasn't true. She had never sung Mike the song, but he had heard her sing it, just once, when she didn't know he could hear.

There was a place hidden away at the back of Bagstone where a wide path with flower borders curled down through trees into the stream valley, a green tunnel into the sunlight of the meadow beyond. When old Ferney died and Rosie was born, Mike saw a chance to start again. He craved peace for the three of them and he made Gally a private place to sit there in the shelter of the back wall. He let in the morning sun by pruning the lower branches of an old hollow tree and he moved earth by the barrow load to flatten out a small circular terrace. He had surprised himself by making two oak benches that did not wobble, and he found a cast-iron table at a local auction so that

157

Gally could sit there with Rosie in the quiet time she liked at the start of every day.

He had kept the benches and the table hidden behind the sheds until it was all ready. One Saturday morning he put everything in place and came upstairs to where she lay in bed with Rosie in her arms. He gave her the end of a piece of string with a green satin bow tied to it. She looked at it and smiled.

'Thank you,' she said. 'I needed some string.'

It wasn't sarcasm. He knew that if his present had just been string, she would have still found delight in it. 'Try following it,' he suggested. 'You might need to put some clothes on.'

'Do I get a cup of coffee first?'

'Put your trust in the string.'

She bathed him in her huge eyes, laughed in delight and handed him their sleeping child, then in her usual way she was out of bed and into her jeans and woollen work shirt so quickly that it looked like some trick film edit. Charged with Rosie's safety, he was slower down the stairs but she waited for him at the front door, laughing more and more as she saw that the trail led outside.

'Thank you,' she said. 'That's more string than I ever dreamed of. It must have cost a fortune.'

She walked slowly now, gathering it in careful loops as she went, around the far end of the house into the reclaimed wilderness beyond, to the terrace she had watched him build and to the table and benches which were his present to her, the table laid with a new chequered cloth.

'Will you join me for breakfast at Gally's place?' he asked.

158

'Today and every day,' she said and turned to hug him and their child.

With the air of a conjuror, he went behind the old tree and from the deep hollow in its heart he produced a vase of lilies, a basket of warm croissants and a pot of coffee.

*   *   *

But that was how it was in the beginning. That was how it was before Rosie turned two. They had two years of joy, then Rosie changed and the misery began. That was the in-between time, the short gap before their lives together ended. He had started to spy on Gally, to watch over her and Rosie in a desperate wish to keep them safe. The effort of holding it all together was tugging Gally away from him into an arcane world in which her old, old selves came to the forefront more and his simpler, present Gally was hidden in them. She had been back there on the terrace, comforting the toddler who refused to be comforted. There was one small window in the kitchen wall, no more than a foot square, which looked out to the terrace. It was open an inch or two and he heard her voice, calm, reasonable, strained, trying to talk Rosie into some sort of peace. 'There, I know. I know what it's like. We'll be all right. We'll get through this. Just be a little patient, my love. We've had worse.'

Then to his surprise, because she wasn't a singer, he heard her voice lift into what might have been a lullaby, but with words he had never heard before.

'No, we're never quite young and we're never
    quite old
And we shouldn't give tongue to what's best left
    untold.
For we're never quite old and we're never quite
    young
And the earth will grow cold when our last song
    is sung.'

But Rosie howled louder and Mike heard the despair in her voice as Gally tried to hug the fighting child and his blood ran cold.

*   *   *

Six thousand days had inched by since Gally died. Most of those days had started with a snatched breakfast which was no more than refuelling. Many had ended in shallow sleep with the bedside light still on and a book spilling from his fingers. Sometimes he would wake at dawn on top of the bedclothes, still dressed. In all that time he had only once faced up to that place behind the house which represented all he had lost. That time, at least five years ago, he had fought his way through the undergrowth to no avail. The terrace had disappeared under a snarl of brambles. Even their precious hollow tree had fallen and its wreckage lay across where the path used to run. How could a tree fall so close, he thought, and him not know? Because it was only a small thing, a tree, compared to everything else that had fallen.

He walked back into the yard now and looked towards the far corner of the house, seeing how badly he had let it go in the intervening years. On

160

that very first day when she had found Bagstone, mobbed by the stems and tendrils which were prising it apart, Gally had immediately stepped in to start healing its wounds. He knew she would hate to see it as it was now. It wasn't yet time to face what lay behind the house but the yard in front was another matter. His old leather gloves felt stiff until he had worked the fingers back to flexibility, then he went out to the shed to look for a scythe only to find a chest-high tangle of brambles barring the way to the shed door. Trampling them flat with his feet, he had to put his shoulder to it before the door would open, shunting a pile of debris behind it.

Unexpected joy filled Mike as he got to work as if the energy he put into each swing of the scythe was turning back the reaper's clock, preparing the way for the reversal of a death. He went on until dark and by eight the next morning, an hour before his appointment with the lawyer, he was at it again. The hour passed quickly and he was still slashing away when the woman arrived.

'Gardening leave is only a name,' she said. 'You don't have to take it seriously.'

He thought perhaps she had come searching for an icebreaker. 'It needs doing.'

'It certainly does. What a funny village this is. I was early so I drove around. It's all over the place, isn't it? There are fields then a few more houses then fields again. There's no middle, is there?'

'It's built on a non-nucleated medieval pattern,' he answered absently.

'What?'

'Sorry. It's a survival of the way farming villages used to be. Quite rare. The gaps have usually been filled in by now.'

161

'Oh. Was that the sort of thing you taught at the university?'

'Yes.'

'But not now?'

'Not any more, not at the school. School history these days is all World War One as seen by cartoonists.'

'Do you miss the university?'

'I miss having serious conversations.' She recognised thin ice in the tone of his voice, a brittle bridge over a deep hole.

She looked around the yard. 'Did you have to do a lot to the house?'

'Everything.'

'Were you living here while you did it?'

'We camped out in an old caravan. Right there.' He pointed to the side of the yard.

'What was the house like?'

'It had been empty for donkey's years. There was a stream flowing through it.'

'Did you enjoy doing it together?'

He detected a test, a question designed to open a small window on his relationship with Gally. 'Yes,' he said firmly. 'We were very happy. Gally absolutely loved it from the first moment she saw it.' He didn't say that she started seeing things, that she made him move the front door.

Back in the kitchen, the lawyer opened her folder. 'The police are likely to want to interview you soon,' she said. 'They'll be talking to the parents again and to the boy, of course. I gather they haven't seen him yet.'

'And the school? I suppose they're all talking about me there.'

'I'm sure they are,' she said. 'That's human

nature, but there's absolutely no point in worrying about that, is there? The school governors won't be discussing it, not officially anyway. They have to stay out of this sort of thing while the police do their stuff.'

'This sort of thing? I don't like being this sort of thing.'

She didn't respond.

'So what do we do?' he asked.

'We have a bit of time to get to know each other. I need to ask you more questions, I'm afraid. It will all help, I promise.'

So they sat there through a long hour of morning while he searched his memory for details from the past, groping for the reasons for things, conscious all the time that he was producing a very imperfect explanation of who and why he was. They moved on to how he met Gally, how she had wandered into his history lecture one day.

'Why was she there?'

'She loved history.'

'So you asked her out?'

'She wasn't a student.'

'I wasn't suggesting there was anything wrong.'

She went on asking about Gally but Mike thought she was taking care not to probe too far— asking about her moods, then bending the subject back to safer ground when Mike touched on her nightmares and her sudden daytime fears and hesitated in his description. It never took her long to get back to it.

'Did she ever have any treatment?'

'Not after we met. She got a lot better when we moved here.'

'And . . . from then on?'

163

'She was fine.'

He knew perfectly well what it was that she wanted to ask. It was the same question that had lurked in the background of every conversation, every phone call, and every letter from Rupert and his handful of other caring friends in the years immediately afterwards. He decided to get it out in the open on his own terms.

'Listen. The inquest decided the balance of her mind was fine, that she wasn't depressed, that she was happy and logical at the time of her death and there was no reason for her to take her own life or to ... to take Rosie with her. That's what they decided after listening to all the evidence and that's what the record says.'

The woman in the chair opposite him rocked backwards as if he had thrown a punch at her. 'Okay, I admit that was what I was getting at.'

'I'm sorry. Perhaps that came out a bit strong.'

'No stronger than the time a judge told me off for wearing distracting earrings.'

He looked at her then, sufficiently surprised to see her properly for the first time. 'Can they do that?'

'Judges can do whatever they want.'

'What did you do?'

'I took them off and suppressed my desire to tell him I didn't like his wig.'

He looked at her sober grey clothes and realised that might not be all that she was. It began to dawn on him that she was a person, not just some embodiment of the legal system foisted on him by strangers—that she might really be an ally.

She looked back at him. 'You don't think it was an accident, do you?' she asked gently.

164

'It must have been,' he said. 'I know it must have been. She didn't leave me a letter. She would have left me some sort of explanation, wouldn't she?'

'I'm sure she would,' said the lawyer quickly, but in fact neither of them were sure.

After that she stayed on safe ground—his professional history, his teaching record, and so on. Then, just as she was gathering her papers and was getting ready to go, she asked the hand-on-the-doorknob question and he knew it was the one she had really come to ask the whole time. There was a preamble.

'The police might decide this complaint is a waste of time,' she said. 'That's the best outcome we can hope for. It seems the boy's parents don't have a very good reputation apparently.'

'Not parents,' he said. 'The man isn't Luke's father. I'm sorry—I'm just being a pedantic schoolteacher, aren't I? Go on.'

'No, you're quite right. She's not the problem but he has a record of minor violence. He causes trouble with the neighbours—malicious complaints about everything under the sun. This could be just another one.'

'But?'

'Did I say but?'

'Your voice did.'

'Did it? Yes, well, of course there's a but. There's a but the size of an elephant. What was going on with you and the boy? In the car and then back here? I need the real reason, Mike. I need something that will stand up in court.'

He shook his head. 'I don't really know.'

'That won't do. Imagine it. They will demand an answer. The judge will make sure they get one.

165

You can't say you don't know.'

That word 'court' burrowed into his head. How would he reply to a prosecutor? There were no answers that could stand that test.

'All I did was give him a lift.' He explained about the dig and Luke's sudden appearance. 'I didn't even know him before that. Then he came here. I didn't ask him to.'

'But why?'

He wondered what on earth he could say and a half-truth presented itself. 'He's interested in the history of the place.'

'The house?'

'And the village. He's into local history.'

'So you talked about the past?'

He could agree to that without any hint of a lie.

'That's an unusual boy,' she said. 'I can barely get my daughter to talk about the present.'

'How old is she?'

'Twelve. Thirteen next month.'

'Do you have any more?'

'No. Is that it, then? Is it really just that you talked about history?'

Something slipped in Mike's head. The mention of her daughter had distracted him for a second and he dropped his guard. 'And Gally.'

'Gally? Your wife? You talk about your *wife*. Why?'

'Because . . .' He had almost said 'because he knew her', but he stopped himself. He said, 'Because he understands,' and that was no better. The lawyer leapt on it.

'How could he possibly understand something like that? Don't you realise how strange that would seem if you said it in court? It's . . .' She searched

166

for a word. 'It's weird.'

'You find me weird?'

She looked at him without answering for a long count of seconds. She had kind eyes.

'No,' she said. 'I'm sorry. Perhaps I should have used a different word. That wasn't very professional. But okay, yes, I find it weird. Here's a better word, a real lawyer-word. It's *inappropriate* and I expect that's a word we'll be hearing a lot more of.'

'What does it mean?'

'In this case, it means that you've been talking about the wrong things to the wrong person and that it's not fair to saddle a teenager who is a casual acquaintance with adult angst he can't possibly be expected to understand.'

Mike realised how many misconceptions were locked up in that one sentence but the truth was a path leading straight over a cliff. He tried evasion.

'He's older than his years.'

'He's an old soul, is he?'

'That doesn't sound like a lawyer speaking.'

'I'm only a lawyer in the daytime. Mornings and evenings I'm a free spirit. I meet people who seem to fit that description and I can't think of a better one.' She made a note on her pad and he wondered what she had written. It felt like some sort of verdict on him. 'So at this point, the best we can hope to say is that you found you had a common interest in history, that he came here uninvited and nothing improper ever happened between you?'

'Yes. You keep talking about court. Is it going to come to that?'

'We should know quite soon. The police will do

their stuff with everybody concerned. They'll want to interview you under caution. After that the Crown Prosecution Service will decide whether there's a case.' She looked at him hard. 'Everything you've told me about Luke, do you think that will match what he'll be saying to them?'

'I suppose so.'

'And that big question that you haven't quite answered yet, the shouting match in the car?'

'I'd say it was tiredness and a bit of shock.'

'Then him turning up here?'

'It's not my fault if he doesn't like his house or his family.'

'Are you lonely here?'

'Oh.' He was about to deny it but then he thought she deserved something nearer the truth. 'Yes.'

'All the time?'

'Not all the time. Not when I'm busy.'

'Do you have friends in the village?'

'I know people.'

'But are they friends?'

'Gally had loads of friends.'

'Are they your friends too?'

'I wave at them as I go by.'

'Do you go to their houses?'

'We used to.'

'Do you have friends at work?'

'Colleagues, yes. We talk work stuff.'

'Not people you might go to the pub with.'

'I've never been into pubs much.'

'So it's a solitary life?'

He walked out with her to her car and as she opened the door, she paused for a moment and looked at him thoughtfully. She saw a man whose spring had unwound and thought all he needed was some joy to wind him up again and he would shed ten years.

'I'll be even more unprofessional,' she said. 'I think you're a good man and I'm sorry for your loss. I know you're keeping something back. I really hope you learn to trust me enough soon enough to tell me everything, because I would hate to see you in court still holding on to secrets I don't understand. That way disaster lies.'

As she drove away, he saw just how untidy the yard still looked despite his efforts. In the long, pointless afternoon that followed he picked up and discarded four or five books, switched on the television and flicked through the channels, considered catching up with the ironing and could see nothing in the immediate future that demanded ironed clothes. In the end, he took his keys and wallet with no real purpose in mind and drove away. Later, finding himself in Yeovil, he went into a cinema where he watched an American movie all the way through without following any of it.

*   *   *

By the time he got home, it was dark. Exhausted by the day and by the questions it had brought, he went upstairs to turn on the bath and came back down to the bookshelves for something to read in bed. He was in search of comfort and distraction, history with no emotion, something dry about some place safely other than this at some time in the far, far past. He was still looking when the bubble of his solitude was burst by a loud knock. He stared at the door as he approached it, hoping

169

despite the unlikely hour that it would be a charity collector or the Jehovah's Witnesses or anybody who wouldn't need him to do any more explaining.

He opened the front door to find the boy standing in the porch. On his back was a stuffed rucksack.

'Luke?'

'Please don't call me that. You know what to call me.'

'Ferney. All right. What on earth are you doing here?'

'Can I come in?'

'No, you can't possibly.'

'Why not?'

'You must know why not. I'm in enough trouble already.'

'I've got nowhere else,' said the boy. 'I've left home. You have to let me in.'

'No, I really don't have to. You must go back.'

'I can't. It's too late. It took ages. The rucksack makes my bike wobble and I haven't got lights. I'm not going back. If you won't let me in, I'll find somewhere to sleep outside.'

Mike looked past him into the darkness and saw a silver lace of finest rain glistening in the spilled light.

'You've got no right to do this. I'll drive you home.'

'I can't go back there. Barry punched me. He asked if I'd been here again.'

'Where did he hit you?'

'In the chest.'

'Does it hurt?'

'It did. It's getting better.'

'Oh, come in then. You really can't stay but I

170

need to think.'

The boy sat down on the sofa and Mike went to put the kettle on. When he came back, he saw the sovereigns were still on the table where he had left them.

'Take those with you,' he said. They felt like a trap, a bargain with teeth.

'There's a man in Shaftesbury. He's a jeweller. He knows me. You can take them there.'

'You've sold him sovereigns?'

'Loads of times.'

'When?'

'Not lately.'

'You mean not since last time, don't you? He wouldn't know *you*, would he? Maybe he'd know an old man called Ferney, but he wouldn't know you at all. In fact he might be dead for all you know.'

'There'll be others. You can always find coin dealers. I told you, it's rent.'

'It's only rent if I let you stay and I'm not going to, so put them back wherever you dug them up.'

The boy stood up abruptly. 'You have no right to throw me out.'

Mike found himself confronted, almost nose-to-nose. He felt acutely uncomfortable. 'It's my house. I have a perfect right.'

'Listen to me,' said the boy quietly and deliberately. 'We always got this house back. Always. You bought it but that's not the point. You bought it with her. This house has always been ours, hers and mine.'

'It's not yours now, all right? It's mine and what I say goes. I'm not going to argue.'

'Gally owned half of it, didn't she? You'd let her

171

stay if she came back.'

Of course I would, Mike very nearly answered, it's our house—but he choked off the words. The boy still stood defiantly close to him, hands on hips, staking his claim.

The kettle shrieked and Mike spun round and strode to the kitchen, relieved at the excuse. He took his time, trying to get his breathing back under control. He made the boy a mug of sweet tea but by the time he went back to the sitting room, the confrontation was past. The boy had tilted over, lifted his feet on to the sofa and was fast asleep. Mike stared at him, tried to find it somewhere in himself to shake him awake and turn him out into the rain but he was too kind to do it. He stood undecided, then he drank the mug of tea himself, spread a rug over the boy and went upstairs where he found the bathroom full of steam, the hot tap still on and water pouring out of the overflow.

*   *   *

He was so deeply asleep at midnight that the hammering on the door went no further than diverting his dreams a little. It was Ferney who let them in and they kept him downstairs while they came to the bedroom, so the first Mike knew of it was a hand shaking his shoulder and three large forms around him in the dim moonlight.

He reared up, terrified by their presence, adrenalin flooding in preparation for a hopeless fight.

'Mr Martin, wake up, please. We're police officers. Mr Martin, wake up.'

172

'What? What's wrong?' he said around a slow, thick tongue. 'Has something happened?' Then he was fully awake, sitting up, and one of the men switched the ceiling light on. He screwed up his eyes. Three men—two in plain clothes, one in uniform. The older of the plain-clothes men spoke to him while his eyes searched the room. The intrusion appalled him. Their confidence in their power swamped him.

'We need to talk to you. Get dressed, please. We have a warrant to search this house.'

'What about? What's happened?' Then he remembered the boy downstairs and put two and two together. 'It's about . . .' He stopped himself saying Ferney. 'It's about Luke, is it?'

'Save that until you've got up.'

They watched him as he sat up in bed.

'Do you mind?' he said. 'Just while I dress?'

'Starkers, are you?' said the younger of the plain-clothes men. 'That how you sleep, starkers?'

'Just give me a moment.'

'We'll be on the landing. Right outside.'

Mike found pants in the chest of drawers, pulled on the clothes he had heaped on the chair and struggled to find two clean socks of roughly the same colour, feeling that somehow mattered. He heard raised voices downstairs, Ferney's voice loud but calm.

'I'm sixteen years old. I can do what I want.'

The response was muffled but then Ferney's voice was clear again. 'They're not telling you the truth. I've left home of my own free will. I'm only here because I didn't have anywhere else to go. Mr Martin didn't even know I was coming. He just let me sleep here.'

'Keep it quieter down there,' called the older policeman from the landing. Ferney wants me to hear all that, Mike realised, but they don't.

'I'm ready,' he said as he pulled a sweater over his head. Dressed, he felt more able to stand up to them. 'I want to know what's going on. Who are you?'

'Detective Sergeant Wilson, from Yeovil,' said the older man, coming in. 'We'd like to ask you some questions at the police station, if you don't mind.'

'Do I have a choice?'

'Oh yes, sir. You have a choice. You're not under arrest.' The man's voice said he soon might be if he took that line.

'Do you normally come asking questions at this time of night?'

'Only when we have to.'

Once upon a time, in what now seemed the far past, Mike had been used to assuming the police were on his side—that they weren't there to doubt him but to protect him. The long investigation sixteen years earlier had changed that.

'I don't think it is all right,' he said. 'I think you could make an appointment for a slightly more reasonable time. I don't want to come with you, not in the middle of the night.'

'Well, in that case, Mr Michael Martin,' said the sergeant, 'I'm arresting you on suspicion of downloading indecent images. You do not have to say anything but it may harm your defence if you do not mention when questioned something which . . .'

Mike was so startled that his mind went off to wander somewhere far away. He looked past the

174

sergeant and all he could see was the other man staring at him with mild curiosity on his face.

'I haven't downloaded any indecent images,' he said. 'I can hardly download anything at all on that computer. It's too old, or I'm doing something wrong—I don't know. I keep trying but it doesn't help.' He saw the younger man was taking rapid notes. 'Oh, I don't mean indecent stuff—of course I don't.'

'What then?'

'Castles mostly. Pictures of castles.'

'Bouncy castles?' the man suggested. 'Kids jumping up and down?'

'Norman castles,' said Mike. 'Motte and baileys.' He saw the younger man struggling to write that down. It was almost funny.

He was taken downstairs and straight outside to a police car. He didn't see the boy. On the way to Yeovil he had to suffer the suppressed hostility of the younger detective which showed itself in brief, sharp glances, loud sniffs and an unnecessarily tight grip on his arm as they got him in and out of the car. They told him he was entitled to a lawyer and that seemed absurd. It didn't occur to him that he knew any lawyers. They went through their procedures at the desk and then he lay meekly down on the hard bench in the cell as if he was some compliant guest in the world's worst bed and breakfast.

*   *   *

He hardly moved until dawn chilled the cell walls. It was a measure of his state of mind that he had entirely forgotten about Rachel Palmer's existence

175

until he heard her raised voice outside in the corridor and the door opened to reveal her haranguing a stony-faced man with sergeant's stripes on his uniform.

'Come on,' she said. 'We're going.'

'Are we?'

'You're released on police bail.'

'How did you know I was here?'

'I'll tell you over breakfast.'

She drove him to a small cafe that kept early hours, where she ordered coffee and bacon sandwiches for both of them. She said, 'Give me a moment,' and tapped out a long text on her mobile. Only when the coffee arrived did she put it away and look at him.

'Okay. That was what I would call a disgraceful fishing trip by a policeman who's easily old enough to know better. On the very doubtful justification of some sort of hysterical phone call from Luke's family, they've seized your computer and they're checking it for paedophile images. They tell me they've taken a box of photos too. They're not going to find anything, are they? Please tell me they're not.'

'What box of photos?'

'I have no idea, but that's not quite the indignant denial I'd been hoping for.'

'No. Of course they're not.'

'So what *is* on the computer? Any images at all?'

'I told them. Somerset castles for a project I'm doing. Other school stuff. Just things for lessons.'

'Nothing else?'

'Nothing at all. How did you know I was there?'

'You're an idiot, Mike. You don't mind me calling you Mike?'

176

'It's better than calling me an idiot.'

'Why didn't you ring me?'

'You didn't seem like that sort of lawyer. I don't know you well enough to call you in the middle of the night.'

'Luke doesn't know me at all. He called me without a second thought.'

'*Luke* called you?'

'That's what I said.'

'How did he know your number?'

'My card was on your dresser. When they took you off, he refused to go with them. They couldn't arrest *him*. He had the sense to ring my mobile.'

'I'm sorry. He must have woken you up.'

'Of course he did. I do go to sleep at night.'

'Oh dear.'

'So come on, Mike. You'd better tell me why was he there. Why on earth did you let him stay at your house after all this? Okay, he's over sixteen now, but you must be completely daft.'

'He turned up in the dark, in the rain. He said his mother's boyfriend hit him and he had nowhere else to go. He was asleep before I could get rid of him.'

'That's what he said to me. He said something else too.'

'What was it?'

She took the bill. He realised he had no money on him.

'He said—let me get this right—he said that if you wanted to tell me the whole story, it was okay by him. He said if you decided there really wasn't any other way then you could do it, but he said it was up to you and it probably wouldn't help. Now, what do you think he meant by that?'

Her mobile phone beeped twice with the arrival of a text message. She read it and frowned. 'I've got to get back to Wincanton. Can we talk as we go? I'll drop you off.'

She was preoccupied as she got in the car, silent as they drove out of town.

'Is everything all right?' he asked her in the end.

'Just domestic stuff,' she said. 'I texted a friend to see if she could do the school run instead of me. It was my turn. Trouble is, her car's in being serviced.' She glanced at the clock on the dash. 'I don't want Lulie to be late.'

'Lulie's your daughter?' He felt unreasonably glad that she had trusted him with the name.

'Yes. Oh, I'm sorry.'

'Come off it. There are daughters everywhere. I teach people's daughters every day—or at least I did. I'm quite used to the idea of daughters.'

'So, are you going to tell me?'

'Tell you what?'

'What this thing is you've been keeping to yourself, which I guess is the same thing Luke says you can tell me.'

There was a silence lasting a mile or two.

'Well?' she said in the end. 'Now I know it exists, you really must tell me what it is.'

'I don't know how I can,' he said. 'It will make no sense to you and it will take more time than we've got.'

'Just try. It's obviously central to all this, so I'm not going to be much good to you otherwise.'

'Couldn't your husband take Lulie to school?'

'That's a very bad attempt to change the subject, and of course he could if I rang him, but as he now lives in Vancouver, I suspect he might not get here

178

in time.'

'I'm sorry.'

'I don't know what for. Now stop testing my patience and tell me.'

'Even if that was a good idea, you wouldn't believe me.'

'Try me. You haven't got much choice. I know there's something to tell and I'm a good lawyer. I don't let go.'

She turned off into the lane to Pen Selwood and stopped the car.

'If you don't mind walking home from here, we've got five minutes. I'm going to sit here and if you make Lulie late for school, then on your own conscience be it.'

There was a tantalising sense of liberation in telling her what could not be told.

'This is strictly between you and me, right?'

'I'm your lawyer. That does mean I keep your secrets.' She looked at the clock again. 'Lulie's waiting.'

'Okay. I'll do my best.' He glanced out of the car window and took a deep breath. 'When we first came here, Gally and I, we met an old man at the cottage. We got to know him well. He was called Ferney. He died on the day Rosie was born.'

'Yes?'

'It wasn't always easy with Ferney. Not for me. He got on very well with Gally. He persuaded her to believe something quite odd.'

He knew suddenly that he didn't want to go on, that he shouldn't have even started, but she looked at him and tapped her watch. 'Which was?'

'Which was that they had known each other for an extremely long time.'

179

'What do you mean? They'd met somewhere else?'

'No, here in Pen Selwood.'

'How come?'

'That's the thing. He told her they had known each other many times over.'

'I don't know what that means.'

'Through many lifetimes.'

'Oh, what? And she believed that?'

'In the end.'

'That's crazy stuff.' She shook her head, 'That affected her? It must have been very hard for you. How could she fall for that?'

He looked at her as calmly as he could. 'I came to believe it too.'

'My God. Really? Well, I suppose you can get caught up in all that sort of thing if you—'

'No. He proved it to both of us.'

'Proved it?' Her voice changed as if she had stepped back from him. 'Anyway, what's this got to do with Luke?'

'Well, that's the whole point. You're not really going along with any of this, are you?'

'That's just my standard listening face. Try at least to tell me what the whole point is before I have to go.'

'Luke says his name isn't really Luke.' She looked at him and he could see the implication dawning on her. 'He says he's Ferney.'

'Oh, come on. You're not saying you believe him?'

'He had no way of knowing about the old man, Rachel. He's told me a great deal of stuff about last time round that he could not possibly know. Yes, I believe him.'

180

She stayed silent, staring at him, and in the end he had to fill the silence. 'I know it's true. I don't have any choice.'

'Out,' she said. 'Jump out now, please, or Lulie will never forgive me.'

He had intended to tell her the rest but the tone of her voice stopped him. He opened the door and hesitated. 'You think I'm mad.'

'All I can think about right now is how I'm meant to keep my mind on the road while I drive to Wincanton. I'll get back to you on the madness. Go home. Get some sleep.'

CHAPTER 14

Ferney woke soon after dawn, curled on the sofa where he had gone back to sleep after the police took Mike away. He lay quite still, in sole possession of Bagstone as was his right. The wind was rustling the trees and he knew from the precise sound of the creak in the upstairs window that it was coming from a little south of west. He listened, delighted, until it dropped to no more than a breeze, ticking off all the tiny sounds that the old house, relaxing, twisted out of silence.

He was waiting for her, he and their house together.

He looked around this room that Gally had made. There was a silver-framed photograph and he picked it up and gazed at her—the Gally who had arrived with this unexpected attachment, the Gally who had married this teacher, this temporary man, the two of them smiling together at their

181

incomprehensible wedding.

Could it still be a problem?

He went into a dream, imagining that the police might keep the teacher, might lock him up so there would be nobody to fight for possession of the house, of Gally even, but then he came back to the pressing question: what if she didn't come? He knew he needed to sniff her out, track her down, bring her home in case she wandered uncertainly by.

He made for the door but was stopped abruptly by unfamiliar guilt. Michael Martin had been kind to him, Michael Martin had been arrested because of him—surely he was no real rival? The telephone was on the kitchen table. He could call the police, tell them it was all untrue. Would that help? They might not believe him. There was a card right by the phone and he saw the word on it, 'solicitor', and he dialled the number. It felt the least he could do.

With the sun still low in the east, he climbed the slope to Pen Point and the old stone bench. At the stubby trig point next to it he turned right round twice, sniffing the high, clear air, and vaulted up on to the top of the concrete pillar, balancing on the narrow bronze plate where the surveyors set their instruments. He looked all around him again, searching the landscape for three girls walking, fearing they might be just beyond his vision, missing their target, walking past, dwindling.

He tried to send out a fierce signal, a homing beam, but could not find the power. Inching his eyes round the horizon, open and expectant, he swung back to the north as if his head were on the end of some compass needle of instinct. The north

182

commanded all his attention. A tiny frisson, like a stream of bubbles in a pond, rose from his stomach into his chest and he concentrated his gaze that way towards King Alfred's Tower and slipping left to the plain beyond, past Witham Friary, Nunney and Mells, across all the fields to the high ground in the far, far distance. There was nothing clear, nothing but the prickling inside him, dying away as he drowned it in too much attention. North worried him. They should be coming from the south-west. North meant they might be passing by.

He balanced on the concrete pedestal and had a sense of a recent time when he'd tried to climb up here and failed, of knees that had stiffened too much. He frowned, unable to pull that one out into daylight. The brief sense of age gave him a fresh awareness of the vigour of this young body of his. Jumping down to the grass, he bounced up on spring heels then thrust his arms to heaven and leaned back as far as he could to exult in his flexibility. He saw a small aircraft droning over his head in a clear blue sky, a single-engined light plane with a high wing—a Cessna he thought, but as he looked at it the plane dropped sharply towards him, flying much lower, much faster. Its wings shivered, spread out into an ellipse, and the tone of the engine deepened into the howling growl of a Rolls-Royce Merlin. The Spitfire rocketed over his head just below the overcast which filled this older sky. He had a brief glimpse of 118 Squadron markings and bent to do his duty, reaching down to crank the handle of the field telephone, a handle that disappeared back into the past again the moment his hand touched the Bakelite knob.

He looked up again into a disconcertingly blue sky in which the little Cessna had droned another quarter mile eastward. A voice in his head told him calmly, This happens. Expect this more and more. Get used to it. Use it.

Royal Observer Corps. The words came into his head with a brief scrape of a serge uniform against his wrists. RAF but not RAF. Unfit for active service. A bit too old and still a little lame in one leg from—from what? A memory of pain came back to him, a flash of a tractor tipping down a hill.

He turned to the north again, drawn back there, wide open to that war, and was shocked by a hard vision. It came and went in a microsecond—flame in fog, ripped metal and death, an air machine meeting the violent ground. He sat down, winded, with his back against the concrete pedestal. The present world and the swelling buzz of traffic from below wallpapered over the past and in this present world, the dull awareness came to him that he could not go back to the vile bungalow, that he had nowhere to live now that didn't spell trouble, nowhere but Bagstone. He remembered the phone call he had just made and the words he had said to the lawyer out of pity for the teacher—the words he should not have said. He had opened the way for Mike to tell the lawyer and he knew you shouldn't tell. You never tell people. He punched his right fist into the palm of his other hand. The schoolteacher was old enough to get himself out of his own mess. He answered himself back that the schoolteacher had helped him, had acted like his friend—that he owed him something.

I'm still too young, he thought miserably and that brought the same comforting phrase straight back to him, 'We're never quite old and we're never quite young.' Turning it in his head, he found it deeply familiar, a perfect fit with this hilltop where they had found each other so many times.

He looked to the south again, then the west and all around, searching. This time he found nothing but he knew for certain that there was someone there to find. Gally was getting nearer, he was sure of that, and they couldn't both be groping in the dark. One of them had to know the way.

At the bottom of the hill he gave in to a sudden whim and rode his bike to Zeals, to the fields where the wartime aerodrome had once filled up the wide land. The control tower had softened into a house, the busy runways had gone, but the old perimeter track still wound through growing crops. Ferney sat on that track astride his bicycle, opening his mind, searching for the flames in the mist. All that came was a pale echo of hangars and classrooms, of aircraft models and silhouettes. Training.

He went back to the village because he felt that tug again, plucking him northward, definitely northward. Before, it had all the uncertainty of a fish nibbling at the bait. This time it was a trout striking, a hard pull. It was as clear as someone ringing a bell, as thrilling as a trumpet call. Knowing with growing delight that the time had come, he cycled the old ridge road through the fortress ramparts which had been there long before the Normans. He left that road where it tilted down to Gasper, bumping on to the path through the trees, hammering down the old track towards the tower—Alfred's Tower.

The immediate future excited him, the prospect of who he might find there, but the past just wouldn't leave him alone and with every step the last war came closer to him whether he liked it or not—the second great war. He felt a rooted hunger in the pit of his stomach, the chafe of battledress on his thighs and under his arms. This old him was alert, his ear always cocked for the wrong engines in the sky, the gravelly Daimler-Benz roar of a machine-gunning Messerschmitt or the bomb-laden throb of a Junkers 88.

He came out of the woods, saw the high tower ahead of him in the clearing, and knew exactly where and exactly when he had seen those flames in the mist. 1944, soon after the D-Day invasion. There were no more fleets of German bombers to speak of, just the odd lone raider, but the Observer Corps still had much to do. The invasion was a month old, an uncertain toehold on the very edge of France, fiercely resisted, and the aerial armada was streaming south to keep the bridgehead fed. The skies were full of chaos and lost aircraft and on this July day, with low cloud covering the ridge, they had a message from a poacher that something terrible had happened at the tower.

The whole unit knew the breadth of Ferney's local knowledge so he was sent straight there with a driver in the Morris Utility. Mist covered the top half of the tower and the part he could see looked undamaged, but as the truck pulled up they both gasped at the sight of great lumps embedded in the grass. The cupola from the very top had thundered down from the clouded summit, tons of masonry half-buried in the earth. No sign of a plane.

Ferney smelt burning fuel where fierce firelight

186

flickered below the western slope. Plunging down through the trees, the driver after him, guided by the choking smoke blowing straight up into his face, he came to the edge of the fields and the funeral pyre spread across the grass around the torn hulk of an aeroplane. Olive drab paint and a white star said it was American. He ran towards the cabin, hidden under a cock-eyed stub of wing, but whatever his heart told his body to do, his head would not let him go into that furnace and cold logic told him there could not possibly be any point.

Derek the driver came up to him and pulled his arm. 'Back a bit,' he said. 'You don't know what's in there waiting to cook up. Could be bombs on board.'

Ferney nodded at the broken tail lying clear of the flames. 'It's a Norseman,' he said. 'Ferrying stuff. People, parts. No bombs. If there was ammo, it would have gone up by now.'

'Poor sods,' said Derek. 'Nothing we can do.'

'Go back to the truck,' Ferney told him. 'Get on the radio. Tell them what's happening. Tell them to come to the farm then up the track.' He pointed through the mist. 'It's just off the Hardway.' He checked himself for using the old, old name. 'Off the South Brewham road. The Captain will know.'

Left to himself, he kept vigil for the men in the plane as the wood and fabric slowly burnt away to leave the metal frame and nothing else that was recognisable. He thought about the waste of life, he thought about the hard and hopeless wars he had known, and most of all he thought suddenly and unexpectedly about his sons, his once and only sons. Like an image bouncing to infinity in two

187

mirrors, the modern boy remembered the wartime man remembering poignant lines from long ago. *Old men who stay behind, do not inflame the young with words of war. The ruin that you risk should be your own, not theirs.* The words brought the taste of tears.

He came back to the present, shocked by the remembered deaths and by the scale of his second-hand grief. Sitting down, he leant back against a tree and stared at the tower, trying to pull more of that out into clear sight. Sons? When? They had sons? He sat stock-still and stopped thinking completely, hoping it would all come back, and in that state the tower itself disappeared and the trees grew back, thick, all over the avenue cleared to make the vista, and he lost himself in the dense woodland for two, three, four hours without any awareness of the time passing.

He came back to himself with a jerk as if someone had shaken him by the shoulder. The tower stood before him, a hundred yards away across the open ground. He could see the entrance, could see a family milling noisily around it, apparently arguing. An overpowering sense came to him that he had just missed something, that he had come back to the present a moment too late. It pulled him towards the tower, filled him with the image of climbing up it so that he could feel his legs taking him up the long spiral stairs. He got up stiffly and, leaning on his bicycle, began to push it across the short grass, the front brake rubbing with a twig trapped between brake block and rim. He bent down to pull the twig free, then straightened as a shiver like a waterfall ran right through his soul.

This time it was no random wartime ghost. Something delightful was boiling up inside him, filling him to bursting. He knew it was Gally. He knew she was right here, close by, so he laid the bike down and once again he turned right round to find where this feeling was coming from. He felt it everywhere and nowhere that he could precisely locate. Then he looked up.

The top of the tower hung over him, bending back from the passing clouds. A head appeared, craning over the battlements right up there, then two others close together, too distant and too dark against the bright sky to discern separately. As he saw them the electric joy compressed in him burst out and met its pair, connecting and clutching and pulling them together, and he heard a girl scream.

CHAPTER 15

The tower was a soaring construction of dark brown brickwork, massive and so high it made the girls feel dizzy as their eyes climbed it. The stone figure of a king, crowned and armoured, stared out from a niche over the arched doorway.

They went up tightly turning stairs which spiralled up inside a corner turret. Dim light washed in from arrow slits every twenty steps to show them their footing. Halfway up, they heard footsteps coming down, echoing, long before they saw the slow-moving couple responsible. They had to squeeze against the wall to let the elderly pair by, both so intent on their nervous descent that they seemed not to notice the girls. Then, finally,

189

there was light ahead and at the top, they ducked under a low parapet to climb out on to the roof of the tower and the roof of the world.

To the west, they looked down on woodland far below, plunging down the side of the ridge to a chequered plain of tree-lined fields. A long smudge of white smoke gave a distant hamlet a comet's tail. The sun and the wind sent vast cloud shadows trudging north-east. The girls stared over the battlements at the wide earth.

'How high up are we?' Lucy asked.

'A hundred and sixty-one feet,' said Ali.

'How do you *know* stuff like that?'

'I read what it said on the way in.'

'Well, aren't you clever.'

'It feels higher,' said Jo. 'Much higher. I don't know how high a hundred and sixty-one feet is, but I feel as high as a hawk.' For the first time in her whole life, she felt in exactly the right place, surrounded by vast possibilities and the prospect of joy. This was where Gally had told her to come, but where was Gally?

She walked to the next side of the triangle and the other two followed. There were hills in the distance and something more manicured, like parkland, beyond the immediate trees. Ali had the map out.

'I think that's Stourhead over there,' she said. 'It's National Trust. We could have a look round it if you like?'

'Boring,' said Lucy.

Leaning over the stone parapet, they looked down at a wide avenue of grass stretching away below them. The old couple were making their way slowly across to their car. The tower was a triangle and they walked on to the third wall. From here they looked almost south, right along the top of a wide domed ridge thick with trees, the tallest of them barely half the height of the tower. There were patchwork fields on both sides but ahead, the promontory seemed to stretch to the far horizon, dividing the land.

Ali still had the map open. 'That's it,' she said. 'Just over there at the end of the ridge. The trees are in the way but that's where it is.'

'That's where what is?' asked Lucy.

Ali pointed at the map. 'Rupert's village. Pen Selwood, the place with the three castles.'

'I can't see one castle, let alone three. How far is it?'

'Close—a couple of miles, maybe a bit more. The trees are in the way.'

Lucy looked over Ali's shoulder at the map. 'Show me the place?'

'There. Do you see? Cockroad Wood—it says "motte and bailey" just by it and there's Ballands Castle, same again.'

'That's two. I can't see another one. Are you sure that's it?'

'Absolutely sure,' said Ali, with an edge of excitement in her voice. She searched the map. 'Look, there's the earthworks symbol, where it says Pen Pits. Anyway, the village is marked. It's Pen Selwood. Don't you remember? That's what he said—Pen Selwood.'

Jo was not listening. She was standing a little away from them, searching her mind for Gally, who had gone ahead of her and, surely, should be here. She cast around in growing panic. There was no sign of her friend anywhere, in the back of her

191

head or in the world outside. Wasn't this where he was meant to find her? She looked out, then saw a movement below and glanced down. A boy was pushing a bicycle towards the tower from the edge of the trees. She stared at him, feeling something disturbing and almost like a fever rising in her, then reached out to grip the parapet as if it might be the only way to stop herself falling towards him.

The door to the stairwell spat a squabbling family out on to the roof like a Roman candle launching star shells. Four teenagers emitting sharp, derisive yells, an angry red-faced father and last of all a large mother, puffing and out of breath. Two of the teenage boys started a strident 'It was him, it wasn't me' argument.

Ali turned the map around and looked out towards the invisible village. She walked towards Jo as if to show her. Lucy followed. They peered down to see what had caught Jo's attention. The boy with the bicycle was right below them. They couldn't see his face. He stopped and stared down, inspecting his front wheel.

'There's a path,' said Ali. 'That's going in the right direction.'

Lucy leaned over, looking down, just as one of the teenagers aimed a wild swipe at the other, who grabbed his arm. The first boy pulled away and ran, chased by the second. The running boy tripped, swore and fell headlong just as he reached the girls. Two of them had turned to face the noise. Jo was still staring down at the boy with the bicycle and the boy suddenly looked up.

However it began, the end result was horrifying. One, or perhaps two, of the girls screamed. Bodies collided, legs tangled, and in a moment Lucy felt a violent impact and found herself tilting, falling, already more than half over the parapet, head down, staring at the hard, hard ground twenty storeys below. She felt herself sliding helplessly beyond the point of no return, the stone scraping at her waist then her hips as her feet came off the ground in a second which seemed to last a whole minute. With absurd clarity, she saw the pale face of the boy with the bicycle far down below, looking up then dropping his bike and starting to run.

'He's going to catch me,' she thought, and knew he couldn't and that, quite madly, she was about to be dead. Then came an immense tug on one of her legs and on the belt of her jeans. Jo and Ali both got their hands to her and hauled her back with adrenalin strength, scraping her arm raw on the stonework.

*   *   *

Afterwards they went over and over what had happened. By that time they were sitting on a fallen tree trunk down at ground level. They were all three in shock.

'You grabbed me,' Ali told Lucy, 'then we both fell against Jo.'

'No, I don't think so,' Lucy said, still shaking. 'I think he ran into Jo and then both of them hit me.'

'I thought you fell first, Ali,' said Jo. 'You screamed.'

'That wasn't me. I thought that was you.'

'They might have taken a bit more notice,' Lucy complained as the other family, still arguing, came out of the tower's entrance and walked away without even a glance at them. 'I mean, their stupid son nearly killed me.'

'I don't think they saw how it happened,' said Ali judiciously.

'Stop being so bloody fair,' snapped Lucy.

It all went round in circles but they talked it out endlessly as they needed to do, until the remembered image of horror had been slightly dulled by the repetition. There was no single version of the true course of events, but Jo could not say plainly what she had felt. She kept it to herself because she knew she had no choice, but above all it was an enormous disappointment that there was no sign of him when they had reached the ground. The boy and his bicycle had disappeared utterly.

Exhaustion had followed in the footsteps of shock. They wanted to eat and then to sleep somewhere well away from the loom of the tower. They were all three eager to be somewhere else.

There was indeed a path through the trees but it curved off left and then hairpinned round right, twisting until they were no longer sure they were heading in the right direction. Lucy kept up with the other two as if she had a new grasp of what mattered in life. The business of finding their way allowed them to put what had just happened behind them.

They came to a fork where a smaller path went off to the right and the main track curved away. Ali's map didn't help. It had been opened too many times and a diamond of paper had gone missing from the double fold just where she thought they were.

'Which way?' Lucy asked.

'I'm not sure.'

'You're always sure—at least when there's a map involved.'

'Well, I'm not this time,' said Ali. 'There's a hole in it.'

'We could toss a coin.'

'Or we could follow the arrow,' Jo said abstractedly. She was searching the path ahead and the bushes each side, hoping to see the boy or something.

'What arrow?'

She pointed at the ground ahead. Three sticks in the middle of the path pointed down the left fork. 'That one.'

It was too perfect to be accidental. 'It's probably kids playing,' Lucy suggested, prodding the sticks with the toe of her shoe.

'Well, anyway, if I had to guess,' said Ali, looking up towards the sun as if that might help, 'I would say that's probably the right direction. Let's try it.'

It was right. It joined a wider track and brought them to a tarmac road, climbing up from a valley to their left and curving away to go straight ahead into trees.

'That's it,' said Ali, looking at the map. 'That's exactly where we wanted to be. See? There's the bend.'

They walked on into the woodland and these were higher, darker trees, closing out the sky, surrounding them with shaded hiding places and foreboding. They walked more slowly and closer together and when they saw an earth rampart ahead, coming out of the woods each side, they stopped. The road ran through it as if through a gateway, as if demanding permission to pass.

195

Lucy peered at it. 'What's *that*?'

Ali brought out her map again. 'I think it's a hill fort.'

'Is it one of the three castles?'

'No, they're Norman. This is much older.'

'Do we have to go through it?' asked Lucy.

'No, of course not,' said Ali, looking back at the map. 'We don't have to do that at all. We could go back down the road and all the way round to Stourton, then through Zeals and back to Pen Selwood that way. It shouldn't be more than—oh I don't know—fifteen miles? Or we could walk straight through here and it's a mile and a half at the outside. That's a tough call. I just don't know how to choose.'

'It's creepy,' Lucy said. 'It reminds me of *The Lord of the Rings*. There'll be a Ringwraith or something like that waiting inside.'

'Don't be so stupid. You just need to . . .' Ali broke off, suddenly noticing Jo, who was staring ahead, her face white and her lips moving almost silently. Ali strained to hear what she was saying.

'Now what's the matter with *you*?' Ali asked. 'I don't know what's happening today. The world's gone mad. Come on, let's go,' but Jo didn't move, ignored her, stared ahead as if Lucy had spoken the truth and some bad spirit was waiting in ambush. She was shivering, calling silently for Gally, needing support.

Lucy frowned at her, looked away and waded into the long grass on the verge. She came back holding a piece of paper. 'Someone's messing around,' she said. 'They've left us a message.'

Ali turned to her. 'What does it say?'

'It says, "There's nothing here to hurt you. Have

196

no fear. Walk on."'

Jo turned slowly and held out her hand for it. The pencilled message was written in capital letters on a sheet of ruled paper torn from a notepad. A rough hole had been punched in the top.

'Where was this?' she asked.

'Spiked on a stick, just there, right beside the road.'

'How could it be for us?' said Ali. 'It must be kids again. They're having some game of their own.'

'It hasn't been there long,' Lucy objected. 'It's like brand new. I think it must be for us.'

'I'll put it back.'

However it had got there, it seemed to change things. Jo walked on and Lucy followed as they passed through the gap, seeing the old ramparts flanking them on either side, making a sweeping ring out amongst the trees. Then the banks curved in on the road again, closing the circle at the far end of the old fort. They came out of the woodland to fields on the left of the road.

Ali saw it first. 'There's another message.' She ran ahead and pulled it off the stick, but instead of running back she stood there, reading it, with a puzzled expression. Lucy and Jo walked up to her.

'It's not kids,' she said. 'Kids wouldn't write this. Listen to what it says. It says "We're never quite old and we're never quite young, you and me." That's not kids, is it? Then underneath it says "Remember that?" with a question mark. It's definitely not kids.' She held it out to them.

'It can't be meant for us. Perhaps it's a treasure hunt,' suggested Lucy, 'though it's a funny sort of clue.'

'It could be a quote from something,' Ali suggested, 'or a line from a song?'

The other two shook their heads and they walked on but as the landscape opened up, so Jo was suddenly less sure about that—much less sure. In the course of the next hundred footfalls, those words began to seem as old as the bones of the ridge itself and as familiar as the palm of her hand, and they came with a tune attached to them. She tried to hum it, but she kept losing it, then she thought back to the boy with the bicycle and twisted to look behind, feeling him close by, hoping he might be coming along after them. They passed a house on the right and a farm down a drive to the left and she found there was nothing new there either, just deep familiarity. Someone else was close by too. Jo knew Gally was there in some new and startling way. She was the first to see the final sheet of paper pinned to its stick, and she went to it with her heart beating like a bird. There were three words on the paper.

'Welcome back, Gally' was all it said.

CHAPTER 16

Ferney had stood staring up until the scream from above broke the pull like snapped elastic and sent him reeling backwards, clutching at his bike for support. What he saw up there cut through him: a girl, long hair dangling towards him, sliding impossibly far over the parapet on her way down to death. Knowing she must fall, he dropped the bike

198

and ran towards the tower in sick horror and in the slow motion of the worst of dreams, believing he had caused this, knowing it was hopeless. His feet caught a root, but his speed carried him leaping beyond the stumble. The thought flashed through him, in the middle of his desperate sprint, that this was absurd—to find her and lose her again immediately. At the base of the wall he rocked back, eyes searching up in fear, expecting to see gravity's express rushing her down to him, to where her fall would kill them both. Better that way, he thought.

Everything had stopped. She was still there, halfway over the stonework, but hands were gripping her, hauling her back to safety, back out of his sight.

He walked backwards, a pace at a time, keeping his eyes on the top of the tower, as if he might have to rush to her rescue again. The girls had disappeared so he took his bicycle into the edge of the woodland, crouching down in the green cover, eyes fixed on the doorway, too shaken to know clearly what he should do next.

He saw it over and over in his mind's eye: long hair hanging down, surrounding and obscuring the face that craned towards the killing earth. It had been blonde hair. Lucy, the blonde Lucy—it must have been. Whatever had leapt between him and the girls had pulled Lucy to him.

Three girls came quietly out of the tower's doorway and down the steps. From a hundred yards away he could see her, Lucy, the tallest of them. The other two were supporting her. Ferney crept forward as far as he could without showing himself. Gally was there, almost within reach and comfortably within the pull of the village—Gally who might be Lucy. He was desperate to know for certain so that he could reveal himself to her and make sure he would not lose her again.

He stretched forward, studying each one to differentiate the overwhelming sense of Gally that was flooding from the three of them. It seemed absurd that he could not immediately tell. They walked to the edge of the clearing and sat down. He moved through the trees, closer, but had to stop short where there was a wide gap. He must not be caught skulking, spying on them. He saw the other two comforting Lucy with arms round her shoulders until time had passed and they all seemed calmer, then they studied a map, got to their feet and, to his intense pleasure, headed into the woods straight towards the village.

He abandoned his bike and took to older paths, running to get ahead, looping well away from them in the shelter of the trees. They walked slowly and he raced further on as they neared the junction where, as the first sign to Gally, he laid down an arrow of branches as they had each done before in their lives. They almost caught him. He picked up their chatter round the corner in time to flatten himself behind a tree only feet away, so that he heard all their talk, drinking in their voices, trying to match them to invisible faces, trying to discern which one fuelled this near-bursting passion inside him.

When they had gone on he cut across to the west, dropped down the slope and ran through the open trees along the lower terrace to gain ground. He stopped at the old ramparts—Kenny Wilkins' camp as they'd called it these past three hundred years, Cenwalch's as it had been way back. He knew for sure that she would be afraid there. It was where their whole long story had begun in blood and terror. In every new life she always had to pass through the fear it triggered until she remembered what had happened and recognised the root of that fear.

Knowing that, he reached into his bag, pulled out his pad and wrote her a message of love and reassurance. Skewering the note on a stick, he ran on ahead, fired by the idea that this was the kindest way to bring her home and the best way to end his awful uncertainty by seeing her reaction.

He watched from the bushes as the three girls read the second note, 'We're never quite old and we're never quite young.' The line had been playing inside his head ever since it first woke up there, prodding him to remember more, teasing him with the start of a tune. It had a power to it that felt both old and recent and he thought it must surely have the same effect on her, but as he watched them read it he could not be sure. They all looked puzzled. Now they were walking towards where he hid, getting closer and closer, and for the first time since that brief meeting at Montacute he had the opportunity to study their faces. The short one was the one with the map. Everything about the way she walked and talked showed she was bossy. She looked young, not yet woken into womanhood. The taller, dark-haired girl was blank, restrained, a little removed from the other two, and he couldn't get a sense of her at all. There was no sign of any joy rising in her. That left the tall blonde Lucy who had so nearly fallen from the

201

tower when their gazes met, just as if he had pulled her down with the force of their recognition. She reminded him of his neighbour's Afghan puppy, fine and floppy and endlessly playful. She was alive to everything around her. He looked at her, on the edge of her coming beauty, and thought he could see how Gally's purpose would blossom in her.

He backed carefully away into the thicker cover behind him, turned and raced on again, nearing the outskirts of the village, knowing that time and distance were running out together. The answer came to him and it was so simple and he pinned it all on three plain words, 'Welcome back Gally', pegged into the ground. He held his breath as they came closer but he suddenly found he already knew the answer. It was the quiet dark girl who went to it and he could see Gally's animating spirit in the way she moved. He filled with love as he watched her read it. He thought she would turn to show it to the others but instead she sank to the ground as she read the words. It was the quiet dark girl who began to cry and his heart went out to her.

CHAPTER 17

Lucy and Ali walked up to where Jo was kneeling, still staring at the note in her hands.

'Are you crying?' Lucy asked. She reached out to take the sheet of paper but Jo wouldn't let go.

Ali was craning over to see it. 'It doesn't mean anything, at least nothing worth crying about,' she said. 'I mean, who's Gally? I don't know anyone called Gally, do you?'

'Yes,' said Jo, 'Yes, I do.'

'Who?'

'It's me,' she said. 'Of course it is.' She had never told them about her friend.

'Oh, don't be daft.'

'It's always been me,' she said, 'and all the time I thought it was somebody else.' She wiped the tears from her eyes with the back of her hand and stood up, looking from one girl to the other with slight surprise, then she stared back into the woods and down the road ahead as if expecting to see somebody else.

'You're frightening me,' Ali said quietly.

'There's no need. I'm fine. Come on.'

She strode off towards the village. The other two walked fast behind her, trying to catch up, exchanging looks and mouthing silent questions at each other.

They came to a scatter of houses where five lanes curved round the corners of fields to meet in a loose group of junctions. Jo was still walking fast, straight to a gate on the far side where she stopped. They caught up to find her staring in through a graveyard at an old stone church with a squat tower.

'What's wrong?' Ali asked, breathing hard.

'Nothing at all. I told you.' Jo turned to look at them with that same unsettling expression on her face as if they didn't belong there with her.

'You were crying.'

'Was I? When?'

'Just back there. A minute ago.'

'Oh, I'm all right now. I'm more than all right. That . . . that was just a surprise.'

'A surprise? What do you mean? It's all nonsense, Jo—it was meant for someone else. The other ones too—all that stuff about being old and young.'

'The song?' said Jo from somewhere that was still some way away. 'You know it, don't you?' She sang

'For they're never quite young and they're never
  quite old
And their song is a secret that's best left untold.
For they're never quite old and they're never quite
  young
And lifetimes have passed since their song was first
  sung.'

'No, I don't know it,' said Ali, 'and I don't understand any of it,' but as she spoke, Ali found she was looking at a version of Jo she had never seen before. It was as if the reserved, slightly hidden girl she knew had been turned inside out. This Jo smiled at her with a kind assurance, her face lit by something like serenity.

'Well, never mind. Do you want to come with me?' She went into the churchyard without waiting for an answer and they followed. They heard her say 'Hello' as she entered the church porch as if she had met an old friend, but when they caught up she was standing alone, looking at the inner doorway. Above it was a stone lintel, a lamb carved in the centre flanked by lions. Jutting out either side to support the lintel were two stone heads, carved in profile, gazing across at each other. Both wore crowns.

Jo was staring from one to the other and it seemed to Ali and Lucy that she had addressed her greeting to the two heads.

'Who do you suppose they are?' Lucy asked, because it seemed a safe question.

'A king and queen,' Jo answered.

'Is that a queen? I thought they were both men.'

' 'Til Christmas falls on Candlemas . . .' Jo replied, then stopped.

' 'Till what?' demanded Lucy. 'What's that?'

'It's a rhyme.'

'You're very full of songs and rhymes and things. If it's a rhyme, what does it rhyme with?'

'Oh . . .' Jo frowned in thought. ' 'Til Christmas falls on Candlemas, the king . . . something . . .' She looked at the heads again, raised her hand and touched the face on the right. It had a sharper profile, with a hooked nose. ' 'Til Christmas falls on Candlemas, the king shall never kiss his lass.'

She stood gazing at them and both her friends thought she was shining with a happiness they had never seen in her before.

'I like that,' said Lucy. 'The two of them staring across at each other and they can't reach each other. When does Christmas fall on Candlemas? I hope it's soon.'

205

'It's not,' Ali said. 'It doesn't happen, not ever. Candlemas is forty days after Christmas. I suppose it means the king never gets to kiss her. Have you been here before, Jo?' but Jo seemed to have lost interest in the church. She had gone back into the graveyard, staring over to the far corner where rows of more recent gravestones stood in neat lines. She shivered.

The other two hung back. 'This is awful,' said Ali. 'We're going to be in such a lot of trouble.'

'Us?'

'Yes. Fleur's going to ask about her tablets, isn't she?'

'Where are they?'

'In the side pocket of my rucksack.'

'Stand still.'

Lucy took them out, started to press one out of its bubble.

'What are you doing?'

'I'm going to throw some of them away then Fleur will think she took them.'

'Put them back. We can't. Anyway, it might not be that. Maybe she just needs some food or something. I'm pretty hungry.'

'So am I,' Lucy said, putting the tablets in her pocket. She called to Jo. 'Let's go and find a shop. We need food. I'm not answering for my blood sugar level if I don't eat. Oh, she's gone.' Jo was striding across towards those further graves but as she got to them, they saw her check abruptly and stare at the rows of stones with an intensity that stopped them in their tracks as if they should not intrude. She put her hand up to her mouth, doubled up, and her friends watched in horror as she vomited on the grass.

'Oh, gross,' said Lucy.

Ali grabbed at a practical explanation. 'That's what's wrong. She must have eaten something.'

'We haven't eaten anything. That's why we're hungry—unless it's those mushrooms.'

'Oh look, she's off again.'

Jo was heading for a gate in the far wall and they followed, walking fast for another five minutes, again barely able to keep up with her, past fields as if the village had ended, then through more cottages to a junction where she turned left without a moment's hesitation. There were houses all along this part of the road.

'This is more like it,' said Lucy hopefully.

Jo took no notice, staring all around her with keen interest, then she faltered, came to a halt and looked hard at a house as if she expected it to be something else. An old woman holding a watering can was standing in the next-door garden. 'Can I help you, dears?' she asked.

Jo said nothing. 'We're looking for the shop,' Ali called.

'You're a bit too late,' the woman answered. 'It *was* here. It closed, getting on for twenty years back.'

'Is there a pub?'

'Not any more. There were lots of them once. There was the King's Head just down there and the Queen's Head right by it. Then there was the old Rest and Be Thankful before that.'

'I'd have liked that,' said Lucy. 'I would have been really thankful for a rest.'

'You wouldn't have liked it at all,' said the woman. 'It was a rough old place, that one. Always fighting in the Rest, I was told.'

Jo had said nothing throughout this exchange, staring hard at her. 'Mary?' she said faintly.

'Is that your name, dear? My mother was called Mary.'

'So where would the nearest shop be?' Ali asked.

'Right down that way,' said the woman, pointing onwards. 'You go on all the way to Zeals. It's a mile or two down the hill. You'll find something there.' She considered them for a moment. 'You look a bit done in,' she said. 'Would you like a cup of tea and a biscuit to set you on your way?'

They sat on the bench in her garden. Lucy, sneezed, fiddled in her pocket for a tissue, turned away to stir sugar into each of their mugs, then handed the tea to the other two. 'As soon as we've drunk this, let's get out of here.'

Jo said, 'There are things I need to do here. There's someone I have to see.'

'Who?'

'You two can go on without me. I'll be fine.'

'We can't possibly do that.'

'Yes, you can. There's a place I have to go. It's very near.'

To Ali's surprise, Lucy said, 'Well, all right—but come down the road and get some food with us first. We all need to eat. Please? I'd hate it if you just went off and left us. At least let's have one last picnic,' and Jo considered, then agreed.

They walked out of the village but now Jo was hanging back behind them, looking over hedges, into gardens and all around. The other two found themselves far enough ahead to talk quietly. 'Why did you agree?' Ali asked. 'We can't leave her. It could be shock from the tower.'

'If anyone should be in shock, it's me,' Lucy retorted. 'Nothing happened to *her*.'

'She might have taken something.'

'What sort of something?'

'I don't know. Ecstasy?'

'Jo? Not Jo. Anyway, Es don't do that to you.'

'I wouldn't know,' said Ali self-righteously.

'She's taken something now,' said Lucy with a grim smile.

'What do you mean?'

'I put one of her pills in her tea.'

'Lucy, you didn't! After what we said.'

'It's an emergency. We have to get her out of here.'

'How long will it take?' They turned at the final cluster of cottages and watched her walking slowly towards them. 'I don't know,' said Lucy.

'Let's see what some food and a good night's sleep does.'

'You sound just like your mother.'

Not long, seemed to be the answer. She caught up with them, smiled at them vaguely, and they walked on down the hill in a silence that neither Ali nor Lucy wanted to break. Silence seemed safer. After twenty minutes they came to a larger village.

'I like this place,' Lucy said. 'It's normal. It's got traffic and signposts and street lights and houses with straight walls—and look, it's got a real shop.' Jo shivered and stopped to stare behind her. She said nothing for a while, then she turned back to them, frowning.

They bought pasties and chocolate bars, then they took to the countryside, climbing fences and edging around fields away from the drumming of the main road until they came to a flat triangle of grass hidden away in the corner of a field where they put up their tent.

Tearing the wrapper off her chocolate and watching Jo closely, Lucy said, 'I didn't like that place, Pen Selwood. It was odd.'

Jo turned to look at her with wide eyes. 'Odd? It's not odd.'

'*You* were odd,' said Lucy. 'I've never seen you like that.'

Jo shook her head. 'I'm sorry. Was I?'

'I was a bit worried,' put in Ali judiciously. 'I thought you might be coming down with something.'

Jo turned her head and looked up towards the ridge that rose to the west. 'No,' she said, and her voice was slower, flatter. 'I'm fine. I just felt like—I don't know, like I was in a bit of a dream. I really loved it there. It was . . . calm.'

'Calm as in dead. Dead as in spooky.'

'No. Calm like walking on Dartmoor. Living in town is phone calls and being places at the right time and mobiles and text messages—'

'You never hear your mobile ringing,' Lucy retorted, 'and there's no point in texting you because you don't answer.'

'Yes, but half the time I'm with you you're talking to somebody else. It's like not being there at all.'

'And you're saying you loved that village?' Ali asked. 'And all we did was go to a church and walk past some houses and talk to one not very exciting woman.'

Jo was silent for a time then seemed to gather herself for a reply. 'You could talk up there. You could sing for yourself and not have to listen to

210

other people's voices on earphones. Down here it's different. Listen to that noise.'

'The road?'

'Yes, the cars on the road, going somewhere as fast as they can. They stop us hearing the larks and the warblers. They stop us smelling the hedges and the grass. All for the sake of taking us shopping to buy new clothes we only need because someone else tells us we need them.'

'What are you on about?' Lucy demanded. 'You wouldn't know a warbler if it pecked you. Is this the same Jo who was drooling over shirts in Topshop last week?'

'No, it isn't,' Jo answered quietly.

'Anyway, I don't want to go back there. I don't care about the three castles any more. Let's go somewhere with lights and cafes.'

'What about Andy?' Ali pointed out. 'They're going to be digging there next week.'

'Oh yes. Not to mention Conrad,' Lucy retorted. 'Well, I'll care next week but not right now.'

She got no reply. Jo seemed to have forgotten about going back up to the ridge.

Lucy yawned deliberately. 'Why don't we just go to bed?' Ali suggested. 'Aren't you tired? I am.'

So they settled in, putting Jo between them as if for safety. 'We're on a slant,' Lucy complained. 'I'm sliding downhill,' but within a minute or two she was asleep and instantaneously, it seemed to her, she was abruptly awake again. It was morning, her head was pushing against the cold nylon wall of the tent and Ali was shaking her.

'All right,' she said. 'Stop it. What's the matter?'

'Jo's gone,' said Ali. 'She's taken her backpack and she's gone. She's left us a note.'

211

CHAPTER 18

She woke herself up, and through a fading pharmaceutical fog still knew that she was Gally. The dim dawn light filtering through the nylon told her she had the world to herself. Sitting up slowly, she looked at the girls on either side of her. Ali had her mouth open and her throat gurgled softly each time she breathed in. Lucy was curled up, pushing into the side of the tent.

In her dream she had found a door in her house that she had never seen before, revealing stairs leading down to unsuspected rooms looking out on sunny fields, and he was somewhere down here in this, her proper home. She woke before she found him and the dream should have drained away to acid disappointment but it hadn't. Instead, it left a name washed up on the beach of waking reason and that name was Ferney. His name lay under everything and told her that all the comfort of the dream was within her reach somewhere near.

She looked at her sleeping friends and knew this was a moment of choice. She could hold on to Jo, take the pills to shut out Gally and go with the two of them wherever they took her, and walk and listen and waste time and not feel very much at all about anything. She could travel back home with them and unlock the door of the house in the middle of Exeter and be there when her mother came back, and carry on the difficult dance the two of them had learned. As Jo, she could do that and go on just about managing her dulled life.

Or she could be Gally and leave them behind

212

and go where she had to go.

As if there were any doubt, the song played in her head again, 'You're never quite old and you're never quite young', and this time she knew that part was just the chorus because a whole verse was suddenly sitting there, right in the middle of her mind as if she just hadn't noticed it before:

> *There's a boy on the ridge at the end of the day*
> *Who is watching the way from the west.*
> *From behind the dark hills, light is fading away*
> *And the sun is dying to rest,*
> *And the sun is dying to rest.*

She realised he would have been up there waiting for her yesterday when she had not come and she knew she must go straight back there. Dressing herself with minute movements, she pushed her ballooning sleeping bag into her backpack, wrote them a note, then inched her way past them, freezing when their breathing changed. She slipped out of the tent, excited, impatient, into a young morning.

A bearded man in overalls, standing on a street corner with a toolbox at his feet, was the only other person awake in Zeals. He mumbled a vague, embarrassed greeting, then looked up the road and at his watch. She ignored the way they had come. Now she was Gally, she could navigate with the certainty of a migrating bird, branching left on a lower road then on to an overgrown track, and every step she took, every foot of height she gained, was a step into greater clarity as the new parts of her brain weeded out the last traces of the drug. She was going to her real home and the

213

morning air fuelled her with exhilaration.

The track flattened out over the shoulder of the ridge, into a lane which twisted downhill again between high leafy banks. She felt that if she stopped walking the magnet ahead of her would still tug her gently to her destination, whatever her legs might do. Then all at once there was not one destination but two. A climbing footpath beckoned to her right, the road ahead beckoned her on, down to a junction where the fall of the land ahead was screened off by woodland. She stopped in the road and they seemed equal in their demands so, thinking quite wrongly that it made no difference which way she went first, she carried on down the road. It seemed the right choice because when she turned left at the junction she knew she was within seconds of her heart-sought place. A bank backed by trees blocked her view to the right, but as she walked around the lane's concealing curve, she saw a gateway and the gable-end of a house hidden in those trees and understood in a moment of ballooning delight that she had come home.

The sight of the gate stopped her in her tracks. It hung, crooked and decayed. She stood in the middle of the lane, disturbed and uncertain, acutely aware of her unwieldy backpack, feeling that she might need to turn and run. Taking it off one strap at a time, she lifted it over the roadside bank, pushing it out of sight in the bushes, then went nervously forward on soft feet to the gateway, craving and fearing the cottage. The sight of its sad dishevelment stopped her again as she went to push the gate open. In that frozen second she saw that although it was still so very early there was a stranger standing outside the front door—an older

214

man, someone who should simply not have been there in that house.

The disturbance in her coalesced around this man and ignited into horror. She wished she had chosen the footpath up the hill. He was facing away across the yard but stiffened as if he had heard her and began to turn his head. She had just enough time to gather herself and duck away. She sensed him behind her, coming to the gate, and felt his eyes on her back as she walked faster and faster towards the corner of the road. She kept going without looking back, knowing she could not face him for reasons she did not begin to understand.

Her feet took her quickly through the village lanes to what seemed like sanctuary at the church. She sat inside the porch, hidden from view, breathing hard. The crowned heads framing the doorway knew her well enough to forgive her anything but that did not help. This bench, the cottage, the lanes through the village—all felt like a comfortable old shoe, but this shoe had a sharp stone in it. She looked up at their age-smoothed faces and thought they were telling her to confront it so she walked reluctantly to the place where she had found herself overwhelmed the day before. She saw the worn memorials of past centuries give way to newer, sharp-cut stones in perfect ranks and looked at the names on them to delay the moment of arrival. John Gaffin, Monica Jarrett, Richard Cox. They shouldn't be dead, she thought—not John, not Mrs Jarrett. She could see them in her head—elderly, yes, but not dead. Richard Cox was a stranger.

She approached the stone obliquely and stopped short as if it might bite her. She read the

215

inscription then she looked at the date, so soon before her own birth, and understood that she had been Gabriella, that the bones of a body she had once inhabited lay down there under the grass, but she stared, baffled, at the other name—the chiselled name of Rosie. She stooped and through her fingertips, raking the roughened edges of the cuts, she felt the tangled sadness of this stone. It wasn't the whole story, just another door creaking open inch by inch, but it brought tears to her eyes and when she looked up and saw a man watching her from twenty yards away—the grey man from the cottage who was also the teacher from the dig—she did not have to search far to know who he was.

* * *

A dream had woken Mike early—a dream that he was holding Gally, her back curved against his chest. He had taught himself to reject that dream as soon as it began so as not to wake to an impossibly cold reality. He got up in case he dreamt it again and went outside, still in his bare feet, stopping on the step to inspect the state of the yard. A puff of cool wind touched his face and he felt the hairs on the back of his neck stand on end. He thought he was being watched from the road and dismissed it as an absurd fancy until he heard a faint noise, the scrape of a shoe on the road surface, and turned to catch just a flash of colour through the trees as someone walked off. Bare feet on gravel slowed him down and it took him twelve painful steps to reach the gate, and by the time he had tugged it open all he could see was the

216

disappearing back of a girl, rushing away round the curve of the lane.

Back inside, he scrabbled for socks and shoes and then went after her, making the wrong call at the junction, then turning back when he saw only clear road ahead and going as quickly as he could up the other way, catching a brief glimpse of her when the banks allowed, far ahead of him. He felt a double dose of dread—that this might all be coincidence, she might be a passer-by with nothing to do with him, someone who would panic if she saw him following. Even worse, this might be no coincidence at all and then what would he do? Approaching the church, he saw her only fifty yards ahead. She had slowed down and he hung back, watched her walk towards the porch and turn for a moment to look across the graves. That was when he recognised her as one of the girls from the Montacute dig and knew there was only one reason why she had come to the house that morning—that this was no coincidence, that she was Gally. His wife was back from the dead.

The feeling of dread did not go away because that absurd fact brought with it so many other consequences.

To his great surprise, Mike felt unaccustomed anger at the boy who had kept back the extent of what he knew. He now understood why Ferney had appeared from nowhere at Montacute. His anger didn't stop there and, watching the porch, he stepped back behind the bushes to deal with the rest of it.

He realised he was also angry with her, with what she had done and what she had put him through all these years—so startlingly angry that when she came from the porch towards the grave he stayed where he was, until he saw her kneel down and stare and touch the stone and start to cry silently. That was when he went towards her and she turned and saw him and stood and held out her hands, turning her palms outward in a gesture full of sorrow and apology.

He stumbled towards her as if drawn in dread to confront a ghost and she saw how harshly time had trampled him, and between the moment he started to move and the moment he arrived in front of her, staring wide-eyed, she even knew his name.

'Mike,' she said. 'Oh, poor Mike,' and all he could do was shake his head from side to side, until his legs seemed to give up so that he sat down heavily in the grass, collapsing back to lean against the next stone. She retreated a couple of paces and sat down too, cross-legged. It felt safer to set a distance between them but she could not face the intensity of his gaze, so that she snatched looks at him then felt her eyes ricochet away until some sort of shame dragged them back to him again.

'You knew me,' he said.

'I knew your name.'

'Is that all?'

He felt to her like one small wave in an entire rolling ocean but she couldn't say that.

'I knew you,' she said, 'but I'm not sure how.'

'Look at the stone.' His voice sounded harsher. 'Do you see? Gabriella, that was you.'

'Yes.'

'Gabriella Martin. Married to Michael Martin— to me.'

'You?' It seemed absurd to her, 'And you knew *me?*'

218

'I followed you from Bagstone. Who else could you have been? I've been waiting for you.'

She was staring at him, taking the years off his face, trying to fit the bewildering intrusion of this man into their place. She shook her head. 'You're here,' she said as if that were the oddest thing imaginable.

'Of course I am. We lived here. You know that.'

She did in a way but it felt like the last few words of a long, long book.

'He was wrong,' Mike said. 'He said you wouldn't remember.'

'Who said that?'

Mike flinched at her question. He felt an urgent opportunity to snare her memory somewhere in their joint history before he lost the chance to his rival. 'Come on, Gally,' he said. 'We lived in London. Coldharbour Road? You worked at the community centre?' She only stared at him in bewildered silence. He persisted, looking for something that might feel more light-hearted. 'The railway ran past the garden. You pretended we were trainspotters.'

Stranded on the blankness of her gaze he flailed around searching for any other happy time. 'What about Greece? Our last . . . our holiday? There was a saying painted on a restaurant wall. You—'

'I don't remember Greece. I remember here.' She steeled herself and looked at the gravestone. 'Who was Rosie? Tell me that.'

His face tightened. He looked down too, then back at her. 'You ask me that? You must know.' He saw blank anxiety in her face, eyes searching the hard, hopeless letters in the stone. 'Gally, listen. That can wait, can't it? Come with me. Let's go home. I've missed you so much.'

'Home?'

'Our home. Bagstone.'

'That's not *our* home.' She looked at him with horror, got up and began to back away. 'Who do you think I am?' she said. 'Look at me. I'm not your *wife*,' and she turned and ran away, ran from him, from the man who had been her brief, mistaken husband, and he didn't try to follow. But as she ran, she was carrying his awakening memory with her.

She came to a fence, climbed it without looking back, hesitated for only a moment then knew where to go. She followed the edge of Broom Close and Clover Ground and on up the rise to the top of the hill and there, two dark bars broke the sky against the risen sun—the concrete pillar and the outline of the man standing beside it.

CHAPTER 19

Ferney had watched the three girls enter the village from behind a garden hedge, then from the shelter of the churchyard wall, scurrying, bent low, from one vantage point to the next. Now he had eyes only for the revealed Gally and was astonished that he could ever have thought the blonde girl might have been her.

He could have stepped out and declared himself to her but he knew that moment should be just between the two of them. Nothing and nobody else should get in the way.

He watched her walk into the church porch, heard her voice say 'Hello' with a surge of pleasure and knew who she was greeting. He saw her walk out of the porch towards the newer graves, expecting her to look round at all the places where all their bones had been laid in calm acceptance. Instead she seemed to buckle as if someone he could not see had punched her in the stomach and then, as he watched in consternation, she was violently sick on the grass.

It would pass, he told himself. She would surely go on to do what each of them had always done. She would walk in a wide, sampling circle through the village, getting back the measure of it, then she would sense the pull from the high ground at the centre of their territory. She would make excuses to her friends and climb up to the stone bench on the hilltop and he would be there before her. When they left the churchyard, he trailed them to the place where the shop used to be, watched from the field as they sat drinking tea, feeling her in his head, but then they all walked away, the wrong way. He saw her begin to hold herself and to walk in an entirely unfamiliar way. She felt no longer his. He stopped then and saw them dwindle down the lane and was considering racing after her, shouting, making her come back when he heard an old instinct speak reassuringly inside his head. Don't, it said. Let it come to her by herself. Just trust.

He walked back to the churchyard, stopping where she had doubled over, so close to her latest grave, but graves held no great fear for either of them. He studied the stone again, considered the mystery of Rosie and, to his surprise, began to feel some deep disquiet stirring inside him. Gally must have had a daughter—a daughter with the teacher, this man Martin whose surname was on her stone—and both of them had died, mother and daughter.

Children had never been part of their way of doing things, not since the twins such a very long time ago. He looked at the grave and it moved. The stone faded away and the earth pushed up into a long mound half a pace to the right and he was all the way back there. There was a wooden cross, two pieces of adzed oak pegged together, and she was standing next to him, looking down—Gally with her hand in his, cloaking him in love and sorrow.

'This is where I put you,' she said. 'You and him. You are back and I am back but our two sons are not. At least we have Sebbi here within our care, but Edgar is so far away and I don't know if I can bear that. What was it like, the place where you buried him? Tell me again. Tell me exactly.'

'It was by the landing of a bridge over a narrow northland river, whose name I never knew. The river had a muddy bottom with weed growing at the edges and there were small black fishes hanging in the stream when the fighting stopped, flicking their tails. They told me that when there was a cold, dry wind you could see high ground to the north, but I didn't see it. My eyes were never clear enough.'

'I would like to see him. Will we go there some day?'

They were standing outside the churchyard hedge where she had buried them in the dark of the night, beyond the boundaries of the church. It was twenty years on and the Norman grip was tight, the troubles over. He let the wooden cross fade away and the churchyard grew out to take him back inside it. The marker stone they put there later to replace the rotted wooden cross had itself been frost-flaked to blankness and vanished in a year when neither of them had been old enough to save it. The mound had sunk away but he thought he could still trace its outline, even now.

There was a puzzle here. What had the power to hurt her so much now? Was it the new grave or the old? This modern daughter or their ancient son? Rosie still meant nothing to him that he could clearly identify. All he could find in himself was a slight sense of alarm, too fragile to inspect. Ferney walked away from the graveyard knowing only one thing for sure. He could not leave the village. She had stepped straight into some sort of trouble and he had to be the beacon to bring her back safely. She might be coming back even now.

He left the church and took the field paths to the hilltop, his senses stretching out to see her, smell her, find her. The bench was empty and he lifted himself to sit on the edge of the concrete bollard of the trig point to gain that little extra height. He knew they would need a safe place when she came back. He thought of going to Bagstone, of banging on the door and demanding that Mike let them stay, but he could not take her there with that man occupying their house and so much of recent history unresolved. He set his mind roaming to try to solve the problem and found himself standing on the grass where the trig point would one day be, staring north to where she was walking up the slope towards him. She was there and she was not, fading and shredding, refusing to

223

stick with any one physical shape. The trees were wrong. The willows were modern, out of place, keeping her out—so he felled them with a sweep of his eyes and saw five great elms thud upward in their place. The hedgerow wriggled and thickened and hooves clattered in the lane down below. He was trimming the middle elm, removing a bough which fell to the ground, and then he was standing right by it on the edge of the field, sawing the fallen limb into a pile of logs, smelling the sapwood. The handle of his saw was elm, the same wood as the logs it cut. The iron of the blade was soft but it was the best they had though the teeth needed filing and resetting four times in a working day. He turned, the saw still in his hand, and there she was. A young girl in pale green with a mop of golden hair, walking down the hill on tussocks of grass, a sacking bag slung over her shoulder. She paused, shading her eyes to stare, then dropped the bag, gathered her skirts and ran towards him, a complete stranger who was no stranger at all. He stared back, straining to make out the newest face of this old, old love. She ran straight into his arms and though he had never before held this body, he had always held the girl who looked at him from behind those bright eyes.

They folded to the grass and kissed, filling the gaps of taste and touch and smell with a devouring hunger. They held each other as hard and as close as two people can, feeling each other's faces, drinking each other in and learning the freshness of their new skins for enough time for the sun to move a handspan before either of them tested their new voices on the other, then Ferney said, 'How far?'

'Two months walking,' she said and he had trouble understanding because the two was a 'twae'.

'From where?'

'Frae Dumfries.'

He had no idea where that was.

'Scotland,' she said, and he drew in his breath because Scotland was dangerous. The Pretender had brought his troops down almost to the gates of London in the winter, driven off only when German George pulled England's army back from France.

'That's for us to know. Just us. Don't tell anyone else.'

'I'm nae fool,' she said. 'It comes back. I've kept silent. Ha' ye got the hoose?'

'The house? No. Not yet.'

'Where then?'

'There is a place.'

That brought him back to the world of modern concrete. He eased his cramped legs down from his seat on the bollard, knowing now she would not be here today and needing to sort out a shelter for them. That reminded him of Cucklington and the family that no longer felt anything like his own, so in the early evening he cycled there, found the house empty and, to keep them at bay, wrote a note to say he had left home, that he would contact them soon and his mother should not worry.

He raced back to Pen, remembering an old refuge for times like this. He could see it in his mind—a stone barn in a narrow field out of sight of the farm. Which farm? The farm towards the wood, towards the pits. He cycled up the lane, worried suddenly that the barn might have fallen

225

into ruin, even more worried as he came near that it might now be a house, like others he passed, absurdly domesticated like a pig in a party frock. He climbed the field gate and looked along inside the thick hedgerow and his heart jumped to see it was still there, magnificently unchanged from when he had last used it. When was that? he wondered. Eighty years ago? More? It had stood there in one form or another for half a millennium before that. He pulled one swaying door open enough to slip in, climbed a ladder through the trapdoor to the hayloft and found it still half-full of last year's hay. Pulling bales together into a bed on the old elm boards, he spread the remains of a horse blanket over it and lay down to think, to cast his memory back like a fly on a line, upstream on time's river, right through into the deep yellow evening, remembering the girl from Scotland and all the other girls who were all the same girl. He was filled with the saturation of the memory of love and the deep desire for things to be put right again.

*   *   *

In the early morning, as bars of sunrise slipped between loose tiles above, he woke and looked for her and remembered with a soul-scouring pang that a quarter of a thousand years had passed since the Scots Gally, but before the sorrow could take hold he knew that mattered not at all because she was close by once more.

He wondered just how she would be this time. 'I have to take care,' that one had said, the Scottish one, in the first flush of talking when she had slipped halfway back to being pure Gally again and the way she spoke had already begun to change. 'I take fire quickly. Anger clutches me. It is the way this body chose to work.' Of course he knew that. There was that steady, central core that made them who they were but there were also the different glands, different brains, different fingertips or nerve endings or retinas or eardrums that could change the way their spirit met the world—hurdles they would always learn to leap. The Scottish girl was slender, snub-nosed, wide-eyed. They were not always so lucky in their bodies and that first moment of meeting had taken many forms.

He knew he was lucky this time. That dark hair and the soft brown eyes were all he wanted, but what had met her here? Why had she found horror when their world of Pen should have wrapped its warmth around her? The tombstone was the reason and he did not fully understand and somehow he had to understand to see her through.

Although it was so very early, he saw movement in the farm's kitchen as he passed so he knocked and asked for a slice of bread and a drink of water as wanderers always used to do, and the woman there looked a little stunned but fetched what he needed. Then he walked rapidly up to the hilltop, feeling a sense of urgency, certain she was coming. As he walked, he sang the song whichwas haunting him—the song he didn't really know he knew until he sang it out loud, the song with a hundred variations in it, adjusted by the different habits of speech at each of its rebirths.

She's a girl on a hill-top who waits in the dawn
To see if he'll come from the east
From behind the bright hills where the new sun
  is born
Just when she's expecting him least
Just when she's expecting him least.

The boy on the ridge at the end of the day
Is watching the way from the west
From behind the dark hills, light is fading away
And the sun is dying to rest
And the sun is dying to rest.

For they're never quite young and they're never
  quite old
And their song is a secret that's best left untold
For they're never quite old and they're never
  quite young
And lifetimes have passed since their song was
  first sung.

He came to the bench on the hilltop and saw it through many different eyes. Most recently it sat heavily, a place for one man sitting as years passed, waiting in loneliness. It should be a place for two, a place of meeting, packed with love.

The morning birds were carving sharp curls of song out of a high and empty sky. He stared north to where the stubby church anchored the village and saw someone there, far off, running between trees then dipping out of sight into the lower ground between them, and then he knew that she was coming to him and all he had to do was wait. The sun was behind him and she came into the field that curved up to where he was with her eyes screwed up and her hand out in front of her face as if to shade them.

He stood stock-still next to the concrete pillar and she halted twenty yards from him, holding up her hand again as if to stop him approaching and give herself time. He understood perfectly. She looked all around her, breathing in the air of this place of theirs. He could see her inhaling the history to fill the vacancies inside her. She closed her eyes and he knew a storm of memory was flooding her head.

She opened them again to see him waiting patiently, still little more than a dark shape against the sun. Filled with happiness, she came forward and the two of them met afresh where they had met so many, many times before. They stood a foot apart and both of them were bubbling with delighted laughter as they searched every surprising detail of each other's face. There was no surprise when they finally let their eyes meet and see what they had always seen. Those old eyes fed starved souls. New hands searched new skin and new mouths met.

After a long while, she stepped back from him. 'Let me hear you,' she said. 'I want to know your voice.'

'That's easily done,' he replied. 'This is how I sound. Do you like it?'

'Of course I do.'

Other voices reached them—a family walking the field path.

'Where can we go?' she asked.

'Not to the house.'

'I know. Where then?'

'The old wild place,' he said. 'Will that do?'

'Take me to the wild place,' she answered.

229

She stayed out of sight while Ferney retrieved her backpack from the hedge near Bagstone, then he took her hand and led her through the fields to the stone barn. He made her wait below while he climbed the ladder, taking her backpack with him. She heard him moving up above, tracking him by the groan of the planks and the fine fall of dust through the gaps between them.

'You can come up now,' he called and she climbed the wooden ladder to see the hay bed he had made under the rafters with her old sleeping bag, spread out, unzipped, as a covering.

'Last night,' he said. 'I was here last night. I didn't know for sure that you would be with me here today. I am so glad you are.'

It seemed at first that there was no hurry at all. Nobody else would come to this private space. The tick of time had stopped and left a deep silence. They sat on the edge of the bales and stared at each other with their whole long history in their eyes, and she put her hand up to trace the shape of his face with her fingertips, feeling the tiny shock of a spark just before they touched his skin. Then they were both overtaken by an intense curiosity and began to explore the hidden shape of each other inside their clothes. A cavalcade of Ferneys came to her mind's eye as they did. Dark and fair, tall and short, handsome and less clearly so, though always pleasing to her. She saw his eyes look at her with the same look that had been in all their eyes.

There was no reticence because they knew each other far, far too well for that. There was no trepidation because they were both seasoned in the art of loving each other. Instead, there was a rising

230

peak of sheer delight that they had once again been given young and perfect instruments on which to play their old and expert music. When there was nothing left to take off and they had discovered every unmapped inch of each other, it seemed that there was a hurry after all, as the years of separation ended.

Afterwards, they lay staring into each other's eyes as if they resented the time lost even in blinking. He kissed the tip of her nose.

'When did we last do that?' she asked and saw his eyes focus far beyond her as he felt back for the answer.

'Years and years ago,' he said. 'Before the war. Seventy years, maybe eighty. You went missing. I never found you. Where did you go?'

'I don't know yet. I will soon. I know who I am now and that's a start,' she said. 'I finally know. I was there all the time but I was trapped. I didn't know why I felt so lonely until today.' She smiled and nuzzled against his cheek and then without any warning at all, she burst into violent sobs.

'It's all right,' he said. 'You're here now. It's okay.'

'No, it isn't. It should be.'

'Listen, my lovely Gally, I know this much,' he said. 'It's not easy being me and you. There's a lot of waiting and hoping and loneliness in between. We only just get by at times like that. It's easy to forget that when we're together.' He could see that just below the surface she was still on the very edge of a crisis, so he took it head on. 'What happened to you in the churchyard yesterday, when you first arrived? I was watching.'

She took in a gulp of air, tried to speak and

failed.

'Don't rush,' he said gently, smoothing the tears away from her cheeks with his fingers.

'I walked in there and I felt so happy,' she said slowly. 'I knew I had come home. I took off a coat named Jo and there was me, Gally, underneath all the time. I found that somewhere in my head I had the answer to all kinds of things if I just looked, but something was pulling me and I went to the graves and the next moment I was drowning in sadness.'

'Which grave?'

'Did we have a child?'

He watched her, not knowing how to reply.

'We did,' she said. 'We had a son, didn't we? It should have been his grave. I knew where I buried him.'

'That was a very long time ago.'

She frowned. 'Was it? I didn't think so.'

'It doesn't do to dwell on all the deaths,' he said. 'You have to balance them against all the life. There's been just as much of that,' but he could see it wasn't working. Something stronger had taken root.

She took her arms from round him and rolled away, curling up. 'I think I might have done something terrible,' she said in not much above a whisper.

'What did you do?'

'Our child died,' she said. 'I let someone kill our child,' and she began to weep.

'There's an old story you need to hear,' he said. 'Wait.' He put his hands over his ears and she understood that he was clawing his way back there for her.

He put himself in the churchyard when it was

much smaller. One old stone stood upright like a rough-cut finger, but the other graves were only mounds with here and there a simple wooden cross. He sensed a crowd around them but they weren't there for a burial or a christening or a wedding. They had been summoned for the feudal needs of war.

He opened his eyes, put his hands down and turned to her. She was watching him intently, her eyes red and wet. 'I think I know what this is,' he said. 'I can tell you part of the story but it would be easier if we went back there to do it.'

She shook her head. 'No. I can't. I went to the cottage first this morning and someone followed me to the church.'

'Mike Martin.'

'Yes. He said things I don't understand. What did he mean?' She began to cry again.

He held her, hushing her with kisses and stroking her head. 'I won't let him hurt you,' he said when she was quiet again.

'No. No, he won't hurt me. That's not it. I think I hurt him. Did I? Do you know what I did?'

Ferney said nothing.

'I should have seen you first,' Gally said, her arms tight around him. 'I made the wrong choice. Why does everything have to be so complicated?'

'The world's changed,' he answered slowly. 'We've always been a universe of two, haven't we?' But everything is mapped out now. Even our hilltop. You saw what's up there, didn't you? Our everlasting, unchanging hilltop, and now there's that concrete lump on top of it.' He saw her puzzled look. 'It wasn't there last time you and I were properly together. Do you know why they put

233

it there? To measure the whole country, to pin everything down to the nearest inch. The Ordnance Survey. "Ordnance" as in artillery. "Survey" as in maps to tell them where to aim their guns, how to destroy people. Everything's mapped. People are mapped. We're used to being left alone, aren't we? The world doesn't leave people alone any more. There are systems for everything, systems that ring bells if you're not normal—and we're not normal, are we?'

'No, I don't suppose we've ever been that.'

'So now this man is in the house that should be ours and these days houses are worth a king's ransom and people don't let them fall down any more. So many times we've just wandered back into the ruins and set it right again. Not this time. He thinks it's his but it's our house and it's our village.' He sat up and reached for his shirt. 'First things first. Let's get you right. Let's make sure you understand the things that hurt, then they won't hurt any more. I know where we should go. It's quiet and safe and nobody will find us if we don't want them to.'

That was what he thought.

CHAPTER 20

They walked, hand in hand and utterly at home, through the village's northern outskirts to a place where a cone of earth rose in the trees. Climbing to the top, they sat and looked down through the fringe of trees to the wide world where the ridge dipped down to modern times.

'We must untangle this,' Ferney said. 'We must put your old sorrow back where it belongs. It was before they made this place. It all started at the church.' Gally felt him move a little bit away and knew he was only partly in her own time. 'Imagine the church, not like now. Timber.'

She could see the wooden building and was excited by the clarity of her vision. 'Yes,' she said, but the silence ran on and he seemed to be losing the trail, breathing hard, frowning.

'What was the weather like?' she asked on a hunch.

He nodded. 'It was raining,' said Ferney. 'Drizzle. Britnod didn't like rain.'

The name brought a broad face to her mind—often suffused red, a deep ravine of scar-tissue diagonally across one brow.

He started again with new strength in his voice.

'We were called to the church in the autumn,' he said. 'You, me, all of us. The thane, Britnod, said he needed twenty men. He was a short man, wasn't he? He stood up in the pulpit wet through, in an ugly mood, and told us we owed him our service.'

He seemed in his stride now, talking from a place a thousand years away. He had his arm round her and she could feel the drops of water from his soaked sleeve trickling down her shoulder blade and into the wool as they stood together towards the back of the nave. She was no longer listening to Ferney's account but to Britnod himself. They both were. Ferney might have fallen silent for all she knew.

'You can come forward of your own accord or I can force you. It's your choice.'

'What's it for?' called a voice, and there was

laughter because they all knew the answer.

'William the Bastard, that's what it's for. Keeping your homes and your loved ones safe from the godless Normans, that's what it's for. Who's first?'

She felt Ferney shake his head and knew he had no intention of stepping forward. Harold and William were equally godless to him, as foreign as each other in the longer scheme of things. She knew exactly what he thought about war or riot or rebellion—that when you let the fever, the bloodlust take over, you lost the triumph of humanity over the animal. Eight men volunteered right away. The six brutes from the forest hovels who enjoyed any sort of fight, the scarred youngster with the wild eyes who was always boasting of his sword skills though he possessed no sword, and muddled old Dern, who put his hand up to anything and usually did it badly.

'Eight,' said Britnod. 'Well, I'll count that as seven. I need thirteen more.' There was silence. 'I remind you it is the King's service. It's for Harold Godwinson who is master of us all.'

'He's not my master and he's never been my friend,' called the same voice.

'Harold needs you and Harold will pay you. If you don't have weapons, I will provide.'

That brought three more shuffling forward.

'What's more, I will feed you on the way to the muster. After that the King will feed you.'

Two more joined them.

'Where is the muster?' called a voice from the back.

'A week east.'

'That's a long way.' It seemed to douse any

236

remaining enthusiasm.

'No more? Right then. I gave you your chance, now I'll choose the rest.'

Standing near the back, Ferney and Gally were keeping their twin sons Edgar and Sebbi behind them as if to hide them—their fine twin sons, their wondrous mistake. Gally's brews had not stopped the twins' conception. They told each other Edgar's energy had overpowered anything she could have done to stop him. He showed every sign of having hogged her womb too. Sebbi was a much weaker baby and always in the physical shadow of his twin. They had arrived to make a world of four where they had been two for so long and fifteen years of delight followed, full of a fresh and different love.

'They're like spears,' she had said one day, watching them breaking in a colt.

'How?'

'We hurl them forward into the future. They follow their own course, but they carry the faint trace of our hands on them always, and on the spears they hurl in turn.'

'We have our own futures.'

'Yes,' she said. 'We have both but this is just as wonderful.'

Britnod called Edgar's name out first.

Gally gasped as her son stiffened and stepped forward, then gasped again as Britnod called for Sebbi too. That was when Ferney discovered there was one single thing that could still make him go to war.

'Wait,' he called. 'Leave them be. I'll take their place.'

Gally clutched his arm and he whispered

237

urgently in her ear, 'Let go. I know how to stay alive. They don't and they only get one chance.'

Britnod glared at him. 'You offer one of you for two of them?'

'They're boys. I'm a man.'

'I don't give a toss. They're big enough and I have to come up with the numbers. You don't make two, you make one. Come if you want. You're a hard sod and I'll be glad to have you, but one of them comes too. You choose which.'

'I can't make a choice like that,' said Ferney, horrified.

'Then get your woman to choose, before I count to ten.'

The same rude voice from earlier said, 'Didn't know you could,' which prompted a gale of laughter and left Britnod flushing even darker.

'Choose now, woman, or all three of them go, I swear.'

And Gally was trapped in a mind-stopping moment of wanting to refuse but knowing Britnod held the power of the King's law. Her arm went out of its own accord to pull weak Sebbi to her. She saw Ferney step forward and Edgar follow him and called out in anguish to them and a voice was calling back—two voices calling 'Jo, Jo!'

*   *   *

The note she had left behind in the tent said she was going back to the village. 'We'll have to look for her,' Ali said and got out the map. The same picture was in both their heads—the moment when they would have to tell Jo's mother they had lost her daughter.

238

'Where?'

'The castles,' said Lucy. 'This all started with our stories round the fire.'

So they climbed the ridge in search of their friend, feeling like rescuers, but what seemed precise and easy in terms of symbols and inches on a map was much less obvious on the ground. The first castle proved a disappointment. A field path led to a gently sloping valley.

'Where is it?' Lucy asked.

'Look at the ground. Can't you see the ramparts?'

'Ramparts? Those are speed bumps. My granny could storm those and she's got bad knees.'

'Well, they would have been much deeper back then and they would have had palisades running along the—'

'I think you've mistaken me for someone who's interested.'

They could see down into the valley ahead and along the fall of the hill to both sides and there was no sign of Jo. Back on the road, a car pulled up opposite them and the driver called to them. He was middle-aged, powerfully built in a dark jacket—a little bit dangerous.

'You two,' he said. 'Do you know a boy called Luke Sturgess?' Ali and Lucy eyed him warily and shook their heads. 'You might have seen him,' said the man. 'He's about your age. Take a look at this.' He held out a photo but they stayed where they were, too far away to inspect it.

'Don't be stupid,' said the man. 'I'm a police officer. Here.' He pulled out a card.

Lucy walked slowly closer and the policeman held the photo up to her. 'What's he done?' she asked.

'Never mind that. Do you know where he might be?'

Lucy frowned at the photo. 'No,' she said, 'but we're looking for someone too. A girl with dark hair and a blue backpack? Red jacket? We're a bit worried.'

'When did you lose her?'

'This morning.'

'Then she won't be very far away, will she?'

'Oh thanks,' said Lucy as the car drove off. 'That helps.' She turned to Ali. 'Shall I tell you something really odd?' she said. 'I did recognise that photo.'

The way to the second castle was a muddy ordeal, edged by a honeycomb of overgrown craters spreading through the woods as far as they could see. Half a mile in, they left the track and climbed up the hill to their right. On the top, a steep mound rose amidst the trees. They scrambled up it to where a curve of stonework ran round its summit.

Ali inspected it. 'This is it. This is the motte, you see. Look at the stones. It's wonderful.'

Lucy cupped her hands and shouted, 'Jo! Jo? Hello? Jo-oh!' There was no answer. 'Come on,' she said. 'She's not here either. That leaves one more.'

'Let's have a proper look at this one first—it's interesting.'

Lucy glanced around her. 'No, it's not,' she said. 'It's a pile of earth. There is nothing remotely interesting about that.'

'Can't you imagine the Normans up here?'

'No. I can hardly imagine me up here. I can

240

imagine me down there and I can just about imagine one more castle, then I can imagine a hot bath and a huge meal. Which way do we go now?'

'We've done Ballands. This is Castle Orchard. That leaves Cockroad Wood.' Ali was studying the map. 'It's back the way we came, past the farm.'

'More puddles. How lovely.'

Half an hour's trudging took them through a gate into a well-kept wood and a track which curved around the contour of the ridge's western flank, the ground falling away to their left. They met a woman with a glad-to-be-alive Labrador.

'Is the castle this way?' Lucy asked to Ali's annoyance, because the map showed it was.

'Not far,' said the woman. 'Fork right in a hundred yards. It's just along there. Down, Jessie.'

'Don't worry,' said Ali. 'I can't get any muddier. I don't suppose you've seen our friend, Jo? Dark hair. Backpack, red jacket.'

'Oh yes, I think I did,' said the woman. 'There was a girl sitting up on the castle mound just now. A girl and a boy.'

'No, she'd be by herself.'

'Well, the girl was definitely wearing a red jacket.'

'A boy,' said Lucy as they walked on. 'She's been gone for five hours and she's found a boy.'

'No, not Jo. She wouldn't be in the middle of a wood with a stranger. That's just not her, is it?'

Lucy was thinking about the photo the policeman showed her, thinking and wondering. 'Walking out on us isn't her either.'

Two hundred yards on they came to the fork. The carcass of a deer lay on the track right by it. 'That's funny, isn't it?' said Lucy. 'You would have thought

241

she'd have said "Turn right at the ribcage", wouldn't you? I mean you can't just walk past something like that and pretend it isn't there.'

'It's the countryside. I expect she sees things like that all the time.'

Lucy prodded the bones with her foot. 'That woman probably killed it. We disturbed her in the act of eating it. They're like that in the country. She only just had time to wipe her face.'

'Look,' said Ali. 'She was right. There's Jo, up in the trees.'

A girl in a red jacket sat on the top of the mound, looking away from them. A boy in green sat close beside her.

'Oh my goodness. It *is* Jo, so who's *that*?'

'He's got his arm round her,' Lucy hissed. 'I don't believe it. Let's creep up on them.'

'No, let's not,' said Ali. 'Jo?' she called. 'Jo? Hello!'

The girl above took no notice and for a moment they doubted it was her, but when they called again she turned slowly to stare down at them then turned back to the boy beside her. They dumped their backpacks at the bottom of the slope and climbed the steep bank.

'Well, this is a surprise,' said Ali somewhat crossly when they reached the top. She looked hard at the boy, who looked calmly back at her, then she looked at the girl next to him and looked again, harder. 'What's wrong with you, Jo?' she asked, shocked, and swung back to the boy. 'What have you done to her?'

'She's a bit upset. I'm looking after her.'

'What upset her? She's our friend. What did you do?'

242

'Come to that, who are you?' Lucy stood over him with her hands on her hips.

'I'm called Ferney, I'm—'

'Balls,' Lucy said. 'You're not called Ferney. You're called Luke and you're the one who fell into the trench at the dig and now the police are looking for you. Jo, I think you should come with us, right now.' She pulled out her phone and snapped a picture of him as if that might control him.

The girl blinked and seemed to come back to them. 'It's all right,' she said. 'I know about that. Yes, his name is Luke but he's always been Ferney to me.'

'You already knew each other?'

'Oh yes.'

'How come? You didn't say anything about him at Montacute. What happened—you just bumped into each other in the middle of a wood?'

'More or less.'

'*How* do you know each other?' asked Ali.

'From way back. Don't worry about that now.'

'What about the police?'

'That's not important,' said Ferney. He seemed calm and assured.

'Well, what now?' Ali demanded. 'It wasn't very nice just to go off like that. We've been looking all over the place.'

'I'm sorry. I suppose it wasn't. Why don't you both sit down?'

'I don't want to sit down,' Lucy broke in. 'I want to go. I'm tired, I'm hungry, I'm muddy, and I'm pissed off with fake castles which are just piles of earth. Well, okay, the last one had a rockery on top but I'm bored stiff and somebody should tell

243

somebody to stop writing "castle" on maps when all they mean is "giant molehill".'

'Oh, they were deadly places once,' said Ferney. 'Imagine it. A big timber tower right where we're sitting. Soldiers on watch, ready to kill. Stakes driven in all the way round for a wall. The bailey down there, where they all lived.'

'Are you making that up?'

'There's an information board,' he replied calmly, pointing towards the track. 'See it? They've even done a picture—you know, like a reconstruction. You can go and read it.'

'All right,' said Lucy. 'We'll do that. Jo, would you come down with us? Just you. You don't mind, do you?' she said to Ferney. 'We need a girls' talk.'

They clambered down to the board and Ali began to read it. 'Oh, for goodness sake! Don't bother with that,' said Lucy. 'That's not why we're here. Jo, what are you *doing*? Who is he? Where did you get him from? How could you just go off like that?'

'I had to. I didn't mean to upset you.'

'Then this policeman showed us his photo. He could be a murderer for all I know.'

'Of course he's not. He's the best man in the world, I promise.'

'Man? He's not a man. He's our age. Anyway, you've never mentioned him once. I know everything else about you. How come I don't know that?'

'There are lots of things you don't know about me.'

'Oh really. Jo Driscoll, woman of mystery. I suppose you have a secret cave where you dress up in your cape. I know your bra size. I know you

244

prefer Grape Nuts to Sugar Puffs, though I have no idea why. I know who you snogged first.'

'Well, for all that, I do know him and I promise you don't need to worry.'

'Please, Jo, you're going to come with us now, aren't you?' said Ali. 'You're not yourself. All that stuff about your name yesterday and now him. I think we should head for a station and get back home. There's a bus from Zeals to Gillingham. The woman in the shop said so. I think there are trains to Exeter from there.'

'Why do you want to go?'

'Because of you going off like that. It feels like things are falling apart. Where's your backpack?'

'No, I'm sorry, I'm going to stay here for a while. There's stuff I have to sort out.'

'But we can't leave you here. What will we tell your mum?'

The girl facing them, who seemed so serene and certain of herself, suddenly faltered at that. 'My mum? My mum.'

'Your mum,' said Lucy. 'Your mum, Fleur. Remember her? Your just-ever-so-slightly-scary mum?'

Jo ignored her, staring at Ali. 'I don't know. Let me think. She won't be back for a few more days. I'll write to her.'

Lucy took Jo's head in both hands, turning it and forcing the other girl to look at her. 'You'll *write* to her? Are we in the same century? Nobody *writes*.'

'We can't just abandon you,' said Ali. 'She'll think we're completely irresponsible. What can we possibly say? You decided to stay in a tiny little village with someone none of us has ever heard of who's wanted by the police?'

'Ali's right,' said Lucy. 'Listen, Jo, I never thought *I'd* be telling you to be more responsible but I have to say this is completely mad and I'd rather not be eaten by your mother who, as we both know, can be a bit extreme.'

'I'm staying here. It's as simple as that. I'll sort out my mum.'

'But there isn't even anywhere we can contact you.'

Jo frowned. 'Yes there is. There's a house called Bagstone Farm. It's the far side of the village. There's a man there called Mike. I'll make sure he knows where I am.'

'Mike? Who is Mike?'

'Mike Martin.'

'How do you know *him*?'

'He's a teacher.'

'The teacher from the dig? That Mike? Did they brainwash you when we weren't looking? How come you've only just realised you know this place? You never said so yesterday. One minute you're in the tent with us and the next minute you're called Gilly or Golly or something weird and you know a boy called Ferney, which doesn't sound at all like a real name either, as well as a man called Mike and a farm called whatever it's called, not to mention an entire village.'

'Please believe me. I'm fine. I'm not in any trouble and you don't have to worry about me, okay?'

'Have you got this man's number?' demanded Ali and Gally found, somewhere amongst the most recent shards of her memory, there was a number that she still knew. She wrote it down for them, thinking as she did so that there didn't seem to be enough digits and realising, too late, that this was a number from 1990.

'Keep your phone charged,' said Ali. 'Have you got it on you? No, of course you haven't. I bet you've left it in your backpack. Get it out. Switch it on. Listen, Jo. You've got our numbers. Lucy's phone is flat but you can call me.'

They had one last go at persuading her but she wouldn't budge, so in the end the two girls walked reluctantly away, looking back frequently until they were out of sight. Gally climbed back up the slope to Ferney.

'That wasn't easy,' he said.

She didn't answer and he realised that she was crying silently.

'What is it?' he asked.

It was a while before she replied. 'I'm not their friend any more, am I?' she said quietly. 'I've lost them and the person I used to be. It's like she's dead.'

'You're still her but you never were just her. You're Gally. That's much bigger than just her.'

'Jo. I was Jo.' She gripped his hand so tightly that he tried to pull it away and his eyes widened in surprise. 'That's my life walking away from me down there. Those are people I care about.'

'But we've got ourselves back. That's everything.'

She relented a little then. 'Yes, of course we have, but give me space to grieve.' She let out a shuddering sigh and put her hand to her mouth. 'They'll tell my mum.'

'When?'

'When she gets home. A week maybe.'

'We'll sort something out. A lot can happen in a week. Let's live for now. Please don't be sad. You are my lovely Gally who is finally back where she should be.'

'That's not all of it, is it? There was Mike and there still is Mike.'

'He's not important in this.'

But Gally was remembering the distraught look in Mike's eyes and her acute uneasiness at the message in the stone and feeling a tangled net of responsibility and guilt. 'You can't say that,' she said. 'He seems so hurt. Why do I feel so terrible? Isn't it because of Edgar and Sebbi?' She said the names as if they were children only just lost.

'No,' he said firmly. 'That's all far too ancient. Yes, it ate away at your soul for a very long time, five or six hard lifetimes, but you were cured of that. Someone helped you recover. We'll come to that.'

She shivered and Ferney felt it. 'You don't like it here.'

'It's just a grassy mound,' she said. 'I like the way the grass has covered it and softened it and taken away its teeth, but I know it used to have teeth and I still hate the castleness of it.'

'You always have. You've never had any time for armies. The land soaks into us and we soak into it and all that happens there gets stirred up and dissolved in time and we're just on the end of all that. Did you hate Montacute too? I bet you did. I think something led me there, not just you. Montacute matters.'

'It's a powerful place,' she said. 'When I was there, I told a story round the campfire. It came to me and took me over.'

248

'I know. Dozer told me when I went back to look for you.'

'You went back?'

'Of course. Anyway, that wasn't about Edgar. That was Sebbi.' He sighed. 'Edgar was already dead. I buried him myself, a long way away. I'll tell it all when I get it straight, but not now. Listen, we don't carry these hurts with us any more. They would overwhelm us if we did. That first time it took years and years to get beyond it. We learnt that lesson.'

'So why do I still feel so bad?'

'We've been buried all over that graveyard, you and me. There's hardly a spot in it we haven't occupied. You were looking at the old grave but there's a newer one on top of it and I think that's what makes you want to cry. It says Gabriella Martin on it. That was you, you know that.'

'And I was married to Mike,' she said, as if that part still made no sense. 'You've seen it. Who was Rosie?'

'That's the bit I don't quite know yet,' he said. 'We will have to remember exactly what happened. Fears are easier to fight when you can name them but right now I think we have to move on. There's good and bad in every place round here. Look around you now. Let's try and get back to the good. Forget the castle. Remember later on.' He pointed down to the flatter mound of the bailey below. 'Do you remember the woman with the pigs?'

'What woman?'

'See if I can help you get there. The palisades. Imagine the stakes still there but pretty rotten. Lots of them broken and lashed together with twine, bits of branch filling the gaps, anything she had lying around. Okay? She kept the pigs in there, rooting around. She lived up here in what was left of the old tower. She stretched pigskins over the beams to keep the rain out.'

'Wait,' said Gally, looking slowly around with eyes focused eight hundred years away. 'Was there a skull on top?'

'That's it. A stag's skull with only one antler, up on the roof peak.'

'Yes. Let me get it.' Gally stared down, imagined the gap-toothed wooden poles, caught a shred of them and pulled them into focus. 'She was the wise woman. She was Freya or . . .'

'Freda? Is that right?'

'Freda. I liked her. She showed me how to use cowslips.'

'You showed her more than she showed you. You just did it so she never knew she was being shown.'

'I don't remember that part.'

'Things come when it's time for them. It's time for us now. We've found our way back and we're the right age.'

She held both his hands in hers and stared into the deep familiar comfort of his eyes with huge joy unfolding inside her. 'Yes. I know how good that is, even if I can't quite see the edges of it yet.'

'It doesn't have edges.'

'But what do we do now? We can't stay sitting here forever. Where do we go?'

'We have to ask him to let us use the house.'

'Bagstone? How can we do that?'

'It's your house too.'

'Be kind, Ferney.' Gally sighed. 'If it's my house

250

too, then I'm his wife. How do you think that will feel? It was me and him, wasn't it? You were an old man.'

'That was a mistake, no more. You married him when you had forgotten about me. You were far away. We know what that's like when you're far away.'

Gally went on exploring the growing knowledge and growing disquiet within her. 'That's no excuse. You have to face it. For quite a few years he was the centre of my life. I married him. I'm afraid I am still the centre of his. I can't be hard on him.'

'We need somewhere to be, you and me. It has to be there. It's not just a house. It's our root.'

'The village is our home. We've lived in other houses.'

He looked at her with eyebrows raised.

'I know,' she said. 'Only when we had to, but it is possible.'

'Imagine trying to move into somewhere else. Two sixteen-year-olds. Have you even got a bank account? I haven't. That's not the point though. Bagstone is the only place where we fit. You know that.'

'How's this going to work?' she asked. 'I haven't got much money left.'

'I've got money. You remember?'

She screwed up her eyes. 'Remind me?'

He pointed down the hill. 'See that tree? See my mark on the trunk? Six feet this way, two feet down, a box with something in it. I never know exactly what until I dig them up. Sovereigns, often. All over the place—here, the Pen Pits, the woods by the house. Stuff from the good times.'

'A week,' she said. 'We've got a week to sort it

251

out before my mother gets back.' She got up. 'I'm going to talk to him.'

'Be careful. Don't let him drag you into his world again.'

He walked with her to the southern edge of the village then he climbed to the hilltop and she went on towards the house. When she got there, she saw two cars parked in the yard.

CHAPTER 21

Mike knew he had got it badly wrong as soon as Gally ran from the churchyard, but he was in a state of such complete confusion as he walked home, replaying the scene word by word, that he had no idea what else he could have said to change the outcome. There was already no room for doubt by the time she called him by his name in the churchyard. He had known who she was with a lurch of his heart as soon as she had come to his gate. Her strange new shape did not matter. The eyes were all it took, but her eyes had only shown pity and then fear at his response.

He sat in his kitchen, hoping she would come back so much that he thought he had conjured the knock on the door out of pure imagination. He opened it to Rachel Palmer, who looked at his expression and stepped back.

'Is this a bad time?' she asked.

'Oh,' he said. 'No. Come in.'

'I think we really need to talk.' She looked grim. There was no trace of the foothold of friendliness they had established before.

252

'You got there in time?' he asked.

'In time for what?'

'For your daughter.'

'Yes. Look, we haven't got long.' She stared at him. 'I did leave you a message? You must listen to your machine, Mike. It was important.'

'There's been a lot going on.'

'They want to interview you under caution this afternoon. They're still trying to find the boy. They might come back looking, you know. They mustn't find him here. Do you know where he is?'

'No.'

'He's not helping by hiding.'

'I don't suppose he's hiding. He's just . . . being himself.'

'Himself? Well, that's the other thing, isn't it?' Here it comes, he thought. She sat down at the kitchen table. 'You left things on a pretty strange note last time,' she said. 'We do have to talk about that.'

'Perhaps we should just pretend I never said it.'

'In many ways I wish we could, but I have to deal with it because I think you meant it, didn't you?'

He opened his mouth to answer and closed it again.

'I've thought about it a great deal, Mike. I want you to understand something. I have to be able to rely on you and your answers to my questions. The whole thing falls to pieces otherwise. If I can't rely on logic, we're both lost. Now, look—I realise it's not uncommon when people have been bereaved for them to take comfort in believing all sorts of things they would never have considered before. There's no shame in that. When you've had a great loss, you have to find ways of dealing with it. I

253

come across it surprisingly often. Sometimes people just need to kid themselves a bit and there may be no harm in that. Do you know what I mean?'

'Yes, I think so.'

'I would suggest the best way forward would be to talk to somebody about it, someone with a bit more professional experience.'

'I'm very happy with you. You're very professional. I don't need another lawyer.'

'I don't mean another lawyer. I mean a counsellor or perhaps a psychotherapist even. Someone who would help you come to terms with everything.'

'Oh, I don't need that,' he said in surprise.

'I think you do. What are you going to say in court? If I could tell there was something odd going on, then believe me, the court will spot it just like that. What will you say when they ask why you were spending time with the boy? You can't tell them all that stuff you told me, can you?'

'But what difference will it make if I go and see someone? It won't make any difference at all, will it? Oh, no—now I get it.' Mike spoke in mild surprise as he realised where this was going. 'It will, because then you'll be able to say to the court that I wasn't right in the head because of grief and—'

'No. Stop. That's not why I'm suggesting it. At least it's not the main reason. Please don't think that. I'm suggesting it for your own benefit.'

'Not the main reason?'

'The main reason is that it would help you. You've put me in a very difficult situation—you must see that. If you just go and talk to someone, I will at least have done my professional duty.'

'That's it, is it? You have to do the right thing?'

'No, but I have to think about your interests and I need some firm ground to stand on. It's really not fair to tell me something as crazy as that and then expect me just to go plodding on as if it hadn't happened and yes, I'll be honest, it would give us a defence of some sort, which at the moment would be a very good idea.'

'I've got nothing to defend myself against. I've done nothing wrong.'

'Those two aren't the same thing at all.'

'But they'll soon see I've done nothing, won't they?'

'Mike, you need to understand this. I'm a big fan of the court system. I didn't use to be before I came to sit in courts day in, day out. When I was a student I was quite sure that money talked louder than truth and that fuddy-duddy judges screwed up all the time. I thought juries were rigged and racist and middle-class and blinkered. That was before I saw the machine working. What courts are really, really good at doing is sorting out the good guys from the bad guys. They can smell someone who's not telling the truth. They just can. If you go into court not telling the whole truth, then they're going to know. They're going to sniff you out and put you in with the bad guys and I wouldn't want to let that happen to you.'

'You wouldn't?'

'Of course I wouldn't. As a client. I get some really tricky people. You're not one.'

'So you want me to see a counsellor and then you'll be happy?'

'Then *you'll* be happy, or happier anyway. At

255

least I hope you will. I'd love it if you could get your life going again instead of sitting here waiting for your wife to come back.'

'Waiting for Gally? I'm not waiting for Gally.'

'I'm very glad to hear it, but I don't think I believe you,' said Rachel, leaning over to look out of the kitchen window towards the little terrace at the back of the house. 'Have you got a gardener?' she asked.

'No. I wish I had. It's an awful mess.'

'But I just saw someone.'

'No.'

She got up and looked through the glass. 'There's a girl out there, clearing up. Who is it?'

Mike stood up, leant over the table and peered out. He saw Gally, quietly pulling out dead plants from the little terrace, and he had to catch his breath. 'Oh. That's—that's the girl who's . . . um . . . who's come to do the gardening.'

'The gardener you haven't got?' Rachel stared at him.

'She's new,' he said.

The lawyer was out of the front door before he could gather himself. He went out after her and saw her disappearing round the end of the cottage. Forcing his way through the undergrowth in her wake, he heard her voice ahead of him.

'Hello?' she said. 'You're working hard. I'm Rachel. Who are you?'

As he caught up with the two of them, standing facing each other on the terrace, he heard the girl answer, 'Oh hello, I'm Gally.'

'Well, now I've heard everything,' said Rachel, looking at Mike with a fixed expression of forced brightness. 'Shall we all go back inside?'

256

Gally looked at Mike. 'I'm sorry,' she said. 'I saw you were busy so I came round here. I couldn't bear it. When did the tree fall?'

He saw beyond her the long wreckage of the trunk swathed in bramble bandages and only realised then that it was her tree, the tree whose hollow had provided that first breakfast. He looked at her and could see her as she would be at his age. She seemed to be any age he wanted.

Gally came into the kitchen slowly then stood, rooted to the spot, staring all around her, and her eyes filled with tears. Rachel guided her to a chair.

'I'm Mike's lawyer,' she said. 'I'm here to try to help because he's in a bit of trouble. You say your name is Gally? Gally what?'

That threw her for a moment. 'Driscoll,' she said in the end.

'Gally Driscoll?'

'Jo Driscoll. Jo for Joanna—that's what I was christened.'

'But now you call yourself Gally?'

'That's my name.'

'Do you live here in the village?'

'I came yesterday. I live in Devon.'

'You came yesterday, for the first time?'

'In a way.'

'Mike's wife was called Gally, but you knew that, didn't you?'

The girl nodded and tears started rolling down her cheeks. Mike stood awkwardly watching.

'I'm sorry, pet,' said the lawyer. 'I'm not trying to be horrible. Mike's already told me some things that I've found hard to take on board.'

'Ferney said I should,' Mike added quickly.

Rachel looked from one to the other and sighed.

257

'Can I ask you both a big favour?' she said. 'Will you just suffer me for five minutes so I can sort my head out?'

Mike nodded and looked at Gally, who did the same.

'I think of myself as a rational person,' said Rachel. 'If someone told me the moon was made of green cheese, I would only believe them if I could go up there and taste a bit. That's the way I am. So I want to do a test. You should be flattered because I should simply walk out of here and never see you again, but I look at both of you and I know that would just leave me wondering about it for the rest of my life, so do you mind if we do it this way?'

'I've only just come back into this,' said Gally slowly. 'This time yesterday, I was somebody else. This morning, I still knew so little. Now it's all changed. I've woken up to myself. Right now, I can hardly remember being Jo but it's still quite a shock being me. What I'm saying is I might fail your test.'

'Is it all right to try?'

'It might be.'

'You don't look certain.'

Gally studied her. 'This is a private thing. It always has been.'

'Yes?'

'We mustn't become some sort of spectacle.'

The woman nodded. 'I see that. Well, I'm Mike's lawyer. I am absolutely bound by professional rules. This will stay between us unless you say otherwise.'

Gally looked at Mike, who said, 'I trust her.'

'All right,' said Rachel and opened her bag. She took out a pad of paper and tore off two sheets.

258

There was a mug with a broken handle on the dresser, full of pens, pencils, screwdrivers and other refugees. She sorted out two ballpoints that worked.

'Gally, you sit there. Mike, you sit over here. I'm going to ask you some questions and I want you both to write down the answers without saying anything. All right? Okay. Oh God, I hope this is a good idea. First one. Mike, I remember you said you and Gally first saw this cottage together. When was that—nineteen or twenty years ago? You must have driven here. What sort of car did you come in?'

Mike thought, nodded, and wrote something down. Gally just stared at Rachel.

'Can't you remember?' said Rachel kindly.

'I've never been good on cars,' the girl said.

'Oh, I see.'

'I can remember the colour and what we called it. I *think* I know what it was.'

'Write that all down. Mike, you write down the colour and whatever name you called it, if you know.'

'Oh yes, I know,' said Mike and started writing again.

'All right,' said Rachel. 'Now, I also seem to remember Mike said you met Luke here. No—I suppose I don't mean Luke, I mean Ferney. Can you describe what happened and maybe what he was wearing?'

'Oh yes,' said Gally. 'That's easy.'

'Is it?' said the lawyer. 'Is it indeed?'

'What else?' Gally asked when they had both finished writing.

'Let me see what you've written. Then I'll know

259

if there's any point in going on.'

She took the two sheets of paper, read Gally's first and raised her eyebrows, then she read Mike's and as she did so, her whole posture changed. She stared at his page, then at Gally's, then sat down at the table.

'Now I wish I hadn't started this,' she said. 'Well, here we go. Mike. You said the car was a Ford Orion. Gally said it was a dark blue colour with black seats and you called it Humphrey and it might have been a Ford. Mike, you added that it was blue and that you called it Humphrey.'

'An Orion,' said Gally. 'Yes, that's right. I said it was a three-star car. Like Orion's belt? It always smelt of cigarettes.'

Rachel stared at her.

'What about the second one?' Gally asked.

'Oh. The second one. We have a car called Humphrey, and we still need a second one, do we? All right. Gally, you said you were looking round the house and you'd just seen there was water filling up the cellar when Ferney came in. He was wearing a tweed suit and a green tie. Mike, you say you were in the kitchen, looking down the steps at the flooded cellar when you heard him walk in. You asked if it was his house, and he said, "No, not now." You think he was wearing an old-fashioned jacket and a tie.'

'Is that close enough?' asked Mike.

'Oh, I should think we could say that,' said Rachel. 'Yes, at some risk to my sanity, I think we could say that. I suppose there is just an outside chance that you two are much more devious than you seem.'

'How would that work?'

'Well, casting around for some sort of logic, I suppose I'm starting from some of the very few things you've told me. You could have worked up something around that just to fool me.'

'You can ask us about anything else you like.'

'No.'

'You believe us?'

'You're not devious. More important perhaps, I might prefer to keep a little bit of space in my head for my rational mind to reject this later on when it all seems further away, if that moment ever comes.'

'And you'll keep it to yourself?' asked Gally nervously.

'Dear girl,' said Rachel, 'I most certainly will. In fact it's rather the other way round. If you ever dare tell anyone I took part in this conversation, I will hunt you down. It's more than my professional life is worth. Are you going back to Devon?'

'Oh, no.'

'So where are you staying?'

'I've been camping,' said Gally. 'With friends.'

'And now?'

'I'll . . .' Gally looked at Mike and then around at the kitchen. 'I don't know. We'll sort it out.'

'If either of you should see Ferney, he needs to ring the police.' Rachel wrote down details on a sheet from her pad and held it out towards them. Gally took it and Mike looked at her sharply.

'I must go,' said the lawyer. 'I'll pick you up for the interview, Mike. It won't do to keep them waiting. They're still taking this very seriously.'

She turned to Gally. 'I'm going towards Mere. Do you need a lift anywhere?' she said, as if it might be better for her not to stay.

261

'No. I need to talk to Mike. It's all right.'

Mike followed her to her car. 'Do you still want me to go to a shrink?' he asked as he opened the door for her.

Rachel studied him. 'Is that a joke?'

'No. Why?'

'I'll be back in two hours. Be ready.'

Back in the kitchen, he found Gally wiping the worktop.

'You don't need to do that,' he said. 'There are more important things.'

'It's sticky.'

'You've seen him then?'

'Yes.'

'And?'

'And what?'

'Did angels sing? Did bands play?'

'Don't.'

There was a silence. 'Is there any Jif?' she asked.

Mike opened a cupboard, looked vaguely inside and fished around at the back. He held out a plastic bottle. It was ancient, encrusted with a stalactite dribble of whatever was left inside.

'How long's that been there?' Gally asked, then realised she knew exactly how long and that this domestic conversation in the house they had inhabited as man and wife was a bad mistake.

She put the cloth down and washed her hands under the tap.

'Mike, I hurt you back there by the church.'

'Not as much as you hurt me before.' He felt like a bully as he saw her flinch. 'Do you know what you did?'

She held out both hands as if to push his words away. 'There's a lot I can't reach yet.'

262

'It's pretty fresh in my memory,' Mike said flatly. 'Let's sit down next door.'

'I know it is.'

In the sitting room, she went to the mantelpiece and took the framed photo in her hands and stared hard. 'Me and you,' she said.

'Our wedding.'

She nodded and picked up the photo next to it with her other hand, looked from one to the other and sat down as if her legs had given way. 'Oh no,' she said. 'Please, no.'

'You and Rosie.'

She laid it face down on the table, her eyes averted, and he felt uncomfortable and unsure of how to deal with her distress.

'We don't have children,' she murmured.

'You and him?'

'Me and . . . him. It just leads to trouble.'

'Rosie was ours,' he said as gently as he could.

She took a deep breath. 'I've seen the grave. I can see what happened. I don't know quite how.'

'Poison. The coroner called it an accident.'

'Oh no.'

'Come on, Gally. You did it. You should know.'

'What did I say to you?'

'If you had said anything I would have stopped you. I wouldn't have left you alone for a moment.' She reached her hand out to him and to his surprise he ignored it. 'You left me nothing,' he said. 'You know what the police thought? They thought I'd killed you both. Can you imagine that? You left me hung out to dry.'

'I didn't leave you a letter? I didn't explain?' She sounded incredulous.

'No you did not. You left me alone to try to work
263

it out.'

'Oh, that's not right.'

'You're telling me.' He found he could not stop himself. 'You took away my future,' he said and saw her recoil from his bitterness, but it only spurred him on. 'When I die there will be nothing left at all, no one to come after me, and all because of you.'

'The spear,' she said almost to herself.

'What?'

She closed her eyes. 'I need to think.'

Mike sat back and watched her and found that helpful. With her eyes closed and her head still, this girl was someone else. Then she opened her eyes and he knew her and wanted her back again.

'I can't really believe you're here,' he said simply. 'You and me, sitting in this room again.'

She looked at him and the pity in her eyes was not at all what he wanted to see. 'Mike,' she said slowly, 'the "me" who met you loved you as completely as I knew how at the time. Nothing changes that, but you know that was only a part of the whole me.'

'But you didn't tell me that.'

'I didn't *know* that then. I didn't remember anything.'

'You knew your real name was Gally.'

'Yes, but not why and where and for how long.'

He stared down at the table.

'I have put you through horrible things,' she said in the end. 'I know that's true and I don't expect you to forgive me for it.'

'No.' He looked up with a stranger's eyes. 'I don't think I can do that.'

'I'm not surprised you blame me.'

264

'I blamed myself for letting you believe him, but above all I blamed him. Ferney. That's who I blamed. I blamed a malicious old man who saw a vulnerable young woman and twisted her brain round to believe a ridiculous truth. I blamed him for leading you up some fantastical garden path all the way to suicide, and do you know what? The days I felt like that were my best days by far. That anger was what got me through. Other days I just sat on top of the hill, staring around, hoping he was right and I might see you coming back. I even took a crappy teaching job down here just so I wouldn't be away if you ever did come back, and now you are back I can see that was utterly, utterly pointless, because how on earth can I hope to compete?'

'Oh Mike.'

It would have been easier if he had still sounded angry but his voice had none of the energy of anger left in it. She couldn't answer him. She sat there with silent tears trickling down her cheeks, looking as young as her body, and he could have tried to let her off but he didn't. He just stared back at her for a minute or two until she was able to stop crying. She wiped her cheeks with spread fingers.

'And now?' she asked quietly. 'Do you still blame him?'

'It's harder.'

'What changed?'

'A day or two ago he was a troubled kid who needed help. I've seen him become himself in just a matter of hours. I know there's no malice there. It's something else.'

'What?'

He spoke slowly, as if to make sure each word

265

was exactly right.

'I would say there is a heedless intent in him, in both of you, that knows it has to fulfil its purpose whatever the cost to anyone else. It isn't his fault and it isn't your fault. It's a black joke on a cosmic scale—utterly implacable. It doesn't exist for love or hate. It just is. There's no point in wondering at it. The rest of us should turn and run.'

'But you didn't turn and run. You stayed here.'

'My decision. My mistake. Maybe. Here you actually and undeniably are and that is wonderful, and no, I'm not going to give up easily and just cave in because you did love me once and you owe me that and a whole lot more. There's time for you and him but you've got each other forever. I've only got this one time and I think you could give me that.'

'Can I tell you something?' she asked gently.

'You can try.'

'You could see this the other way round.'

'How?'

'When we first came here, you and me, when he first explained to me who I was, he was shocked that I was married to you. He was deeply hurt. It was as if I'd been unfaithful. I had never been with anyone else before.'

'Never?'

'Never. You were the only other one there has ever been. I'm still floundering a bit. Can you imagine? Last week I was Jo and I lived a quiet life looking out over a dead river in a city with a hill up to an old cathedral that didn't reach me in any way, and friends who helped fill the time with nothing much at all. Now there's this other me and there's him . . . and there's you.'

266

'We weren't just an accident, you and me,' said Mike. 'I don't want to hear that. I really wish you and I had never come to this place but as it is, I've had to live through something that you never have to. When I saw you were dead, it was like tripping over the edge of a cliff and seeing the rocks are coming up to meet you, and you only made a tiny mistake but there's no way back. It was like a bulb blew in my head and I felt myself go dim. Do you know what it's like after that? I bet you don't. I bet it's different for you. There's a crazy exhilaration and it burns you out to utter exhaustion and finally you go to sleep, and where does that get you? That gets you to the moment you wake up again and the sun is shining and everything seems fine for just a second, and that's the cruellest moment of all. You think it was a bad dream, then the horror takes you and you know the bad dream is with you for the rest of your awful life.'

Gally shook her head. 'You think it's so very different for me? It's like that every time.'

'How can that be? I've been by myself for sixteen years because of you and your way of doing things. I've missed you every single day. You say you had friends who helped you fill your time with nothing at all? That lawyer, she asked me the other day if I had people to do things with. That's not what it's about. It's about having somebody you can happily do nothing with. That's what matters. You two have got that forever, for lifetimes to come.'

'It doesn't always work like that.' Confronted by his sorrow, his bitterness and her own guilt, she found herself thinking perhaps he was right—that she did owe him some sort of loyalty, some sort of

267

repayment.

'Can we be friends, do you think?'

'You and me?'

'Yes.' That suddenly felt cowardly to her. 'And Ferney,' she added.

'Allies in a common cause?' To her surprise, Mike laughed. 'He wants my wife and he wants my house. What could possibly come between us?'

'Well, that's another thing,' she said.

CHAPTER 22

In daylight, the five-storey concrete block that was District Police Headquarters was more frightening by far than it had been in the dark. As they walked towards the entrance, it brought back all Mike's memories of repeated visits sixteen years earlier when he had been questioned and questioned and questioned about how and why his wife and daughter died. Those had all been in daylight and the place had not changed. The same phones rang just as faintly beyond thick doors in corridors used to enduring drunken assault, blood and vomit, which still carried the same tang of disinfectant, floor polish and testosterone. What came back sharply enough to sting his eyes again was the bewildering mixture of sorrow and resentment, that she could have gone and that she could have left him to suffer this as well.

She owed him happiness, he thought as they waited at the desk.

Mike and Rachel were led to an interview room by a WPC who unwrapped tapes and loaded them into recorders. She sat down opposite them. The door was flung open and Detective Sergeant Wilson came into the room flushed with expectation like an invader coming to pillage a city. He switched on the tapes and recited the words of the formal caution.

'Last time we met, Mr Martin, you denied any suggestion of improper behaviour with Luke Sturgess when he was fifteen years old.'

'That's because there wasn't any.'

'Do you recall a pupil called Caroline Oaks?'

'No,' said Mike, surprised.

'Come on now. You taught her, didn't you?'

'I don't think so.'

'A pretty girl. I'm sure you would remember her.'

'I don't think of students in terms like "pretty".'

'Oh, I'm sorry. You prefer boys, don't you?'

'Don't respond to that,' said Rachel. 'Sergeant, that is disgraceful. Please conduct this interview according to the guidelines.'

Wilson smirked at the WPC who kept her expression wooden.

'Listen,' said Mike. 'I taught three hundred children last year and another three hundred children the year before that. I'm sorry if I can't remember all their names. Some of them only bothered to turn up once or twice in the whole year.'

'Caroline Oaks has made a statement to the effect that in October last year she saw you and Luke Sturgess in your classroom during the lunch break. She saw you through the window in the door as she walked past. She says that you had your arms round Luke Sturgess and appeared to be

269

interfering with his person.'

'What does interfering—'

'Don't say anything,' said Rachel.

'Can you tell me where you were at lunchtime on Thursday, October the eighth last year?'

'I haven't a clue.'

Rachel Palmer leaned forward. 'My client cannot be expected to answer that question without notice or without recourse to his diary.'

Wilson gave her a frosty look and turned back to Mike. 'Do you deny that you had your hands inside Luke Sturgess's trousers on that day?'

Mike glanced at Rachel for support but she was looking down at her mobile phone.

'Hold it there, Sergeant. I wish to interrupt this interview for a private discussion with my client,' she said.

They stopped the recorder and Wilson left the room with ill grace. Alone with her, Mike shook his head in disbelief. 'I don't know what they're talking about.'

'I think I do,' said Rachel. 'Give me a moment. I just got a text message from someone who might know the answer.'

She made a call. 'It's me,' she said. 'Are you free to talk?' She listened. 'No, it will only take a minute. Am I right in thinking you mentioned a girl called Caroline Oaks?' Mike saw her eyebrows rise. 'Oh really?' She listened again. 'Are you quite sure that's true?' she said, then finally, 'Got it. Thanks a lot. Talk later,' and put the phone away.

'What was that about?' Mike asked.

'Wait and see.'

She opened the door and told the policewoman outside that they were ready to restart.

Wilson and the WPC came back in. 'I hope you've persuaded your client to be more helpful,' he said.

Rachel smiled pleasantly.

When the tape was running, she said, 'Before we continue, Sergeant Wilson, I should tell you I have received information from the school where my client teaches and where the girl who has accused him is a student. I hesitate to tell you how you should do your job but I presume you are aware that the girl in question has a history of disturbed behaviour?'

Wilson looked at her without answering. 'Specifically,' she went on, 'that Caroline Oaks has been excluded from school on two occasions for inappropriate public sexual behaviour, that she is presently undergoing psychiatric treatment and that she has recently told other students that she is pregnant by her own father?'

Wilson blew out a noisy breath, tapped his pencil on the table and looked at the WPC as if he expected her to step in and say something. The WPC looked pointedly the other way.

'Well?' Rachel demanded. 'I wouldn't like to think that you had some sort of vendetta against my client, that perhaps your judgement has been clouded by personal antipathy. Could it really be that you haven't made a single enquiry about the character and reputation of this girl before deciding to accuse Mr Martin?'

'We'll check this,' said the WPC. 'I'll call the school.'

Wilson gave her a dirty look, said 'Interview terminated', stabbed the stop button and left the room, slamming the door behind him.

'I'd like you to record my objection to that as unacceptable,' said Rachel to the WPC. 'No time of cessation given, no proper logging of the tape details, no check with my client to ensure he is happy with the procedure so far.'

'I'll write all that down, Mrs Palmer,' said the WPC, and the tone of her voice said it might even be a pleasure.

'I would like to point out that my client is here voluntarily and that the matter under investigation relates to the alleged downloading of indecent images which he utterly denies, not the ramblings of an unreliable witness concerning something entirely different,' said Rachel. 'I require you to sort this out within no more than half an hour, then we shall leave.'

'Noted. If you don't mind waiting here, Mr Martin, I'll make some calls.'

Left to themselves, Mike turned to Rachel. 'That was amazing,' he said. 'How did you find that out? Of course, I remember hearing her name now. Who do you know at the school? Someone on the pastoral team? It must have been to know all that. Was it Jenny Johnson? Dave Matthews? I'm amazed they told you.'

'It wasn't amazing at all and it wasn't any of the staff. It was a real expert—my daughter.'

'Your daughter, Lulie? She's at my school? I didn't realise.'

'She is and she keeps her ears open. Tales of Caroline Oaks and her wicked ways are apparently legion.'

'Well, say thank you from me, will you? What's next, do you think? Is this sort of thing going to keep happening?'

'As long as there are pregnant teenagers with fertile imaginations and as long as there are bad apples like our DS Wilson, then yes, I'm afraid it is. You're a convenient whipping boy for a lot of whips at the moment.'

The WPC came back into the interview room.

'I've talked to the school,' she said. 'They more or less confirmed what you said.'

'Is that all?' Rachel demanded. 'No apology?'

'That's not for me to say.'

'Well, it's not your fault. I take it we can go now?'

'Do you mind waiting a moment? Detective Inspector Meehan would like a word.'

'Ah,' said Rachel. 'That will be the apology then.'

DI Meehan came in with a laptop under his arm. He put it on the table. He was older than Wilson, thin and sandy-haired with a quiet intelligence about him.

He introduced himself. 'I have to remind you that you are still under caution, Mr Martin,' he said. He started the tape again, listed the people present and the time. Rachel looked at him sharply then frowned at Mike.

'As you know, Mr Martin, you were originally arrested on suspicion of downloading indecent images of minors. The investigating officers removed a computer and a large box of photographs from your house. We have now examined both of those. We have copied some of the images on the hard drive of that computer to this laptop to facilitate this interview.' Meehan pressed a button on the laptop.

'For the purposes of the tape,' he said, 'I am

273

now showing Mr Martin images MM thirteen to nineteen copied from the hard drive of the Dell desktop computer removed from his house.'

He turned the screen to face Mike and Rachel and a slide show of images cycled before their eyes. Mike laughed in recognition.

'You find these funny, do you?' Meehan asked.

'They're torture instruments,' said Mike.

'And that's funny?'

'Only when the police think a history teacher shouldn't have them on his computer. They're medieval. I was teaching my class about life in the fourteenth century—the Hundred Years War.'

'So if we were to ask your head of department, Mr Martin, he would confirm that this was part of the course, would he?'

'Well, my present head of department has only been in the post for six months. His predecessor would have but I'm afraid she had a stroke. She's in a home now.'

Rachel held up a hand to silence Mike and stepped in. 'I don't think it would take very much to justify a history teacher having historical images on his computer, do you?'

Meehan shrugged. 'Maybe. For the tape, I will now show Mr Martin twelve more images scanned from photographs in the box removed from his house. These are numbered MM one to MM twelve in our record.'

Both Rachel and Mike stiffened a little at his tone. It was clear that what went before had been a sideshow. This was the main event. Mike looked at the first picture. His vision misted over as his eyes filled with involuntary tears. He wiped them, glared at the policeman and then looked back at

274

the screen because he could not do anything else. Gally in the bath at Bagstone, Gally holding tiny Rosie up out of the water, both of them laughing.

'Can you identify the subjects for us, Mr Martin?' asked Meehan.

'That's my wife and daughter,' said Mike.

'Mr Meehan, you should know that both Mr Martin's wife and his daughter died,' broke in Rachel. 'I don't feel this is suitable for your—'

'I know they did, Mrs Palmer,' replied Meehan. 'Mr Martin may have forgotten, but I was one of the investigating officers at the time,' and Mike did suddenly remember a quiet young man with a dogged politeness about him. He looked at Meehan and nodded almost as if meeting an old friend.

'In that case, why are you showing my client pictures which are personal to him and very upsetting and can have nothing whatsoever to do with the accusations made against him?'

'The accusations about Luke Sturgess are no longer my main concern, Mrs Palmer, and the pictures I have shown you so far are not nearly as upsetting as the rest of these images, which, strangely enough, I don't remember Mr Martin showing us at the time of the original investigation.' Meehan pressed another key, gestured for Mike to look, and the bottom dropped out of his life as the other pictures marched out of the screen, one after another.

'I thought she had thrown them away.'

'She being your late wife?'

'Don't answer that,' interrupted Rachel. She was staring at the screen with horror on her face. 'Inspector Meehan, I would like to suspend the

275

interview to speak to my client.'

'I thought you might,' said Meehan. He logged the tape off, stood up, and he and the WPC left the room. Before they closed the door, Detective Sergeant Wilson peered in at Mike with a dark look of triumph.

There was a long silence. Mike had his head in his hands. Rachel continued to stare at the screen.

'Is there something you want to tell me?' she asked in the end. 'Because right now I'm wondering if I've been the biggest mug ever. What the hell did you do to that little girl?'

'No, no,' said Mike. 'Not me, not us. Nothing. We did nothing at all. We were just trying to protect her.'

'Protect her? Look at the pictures, Mike.' He lifted his head, glanced at the screen for a moment then turned immediately away. 'I can't.'

'Then I'll tell you what I see,' she said. 'First picture: Rosie, black and blue down one side of her face with a swollen eye. Second picture: Rosie with a deep cut across her forehead and fresh bruising. Third picture: Rosie's thighs with cuts and puncture marks. Fourth picture: well, I don't even know what that one shows but she doesn't look like any two-year-old should. She looks like a child from a concentration camp. Fifth picture . . . Do I need to go on?'

'No, please don't.'

'In that case, start talking, Mike. Tell me what the hell you did because my sympathy is running out very, very fast.'

'I didn't know they were there.'

'I don't give a toss whether you knew they were there or not. Who did it?'

'She did.'

'Gally did that? She did that to her own daughter?'

Mike looked at her in astonishment. 'No, of course not. I don't mean Gally. Rosie did it. She did it to herself.'

'Mike, those are pictures of a tiny toddler who has been systematically assaulted. Bruises, cuts. They are horrific. No child that age could do that.'

She stared at him and in the long silence he looked steadily back at her, then he reached out a hand and turned the laptop round so that it kept cycling its accusations at the wall.

'Well?'

There was a bluebottle in the room, buzzing at the window. A car engine burst into life out in the yard. Tyres squealed and he heard the two-tone siren start as it disappeared up the road. He knew why. He also knew how absurd it seemed in this place of simple facts and accusations and narrow rectitude, and he found he could not call up the energy to defend himself.

'Rachel. She did. There's something else you don't understand. Rosie wasn't . . .' but the lawyer was still staring at the laptop.

'Oh, I'm supposed to believe this is something about Ferney and all the rest of this story, am I?' He nodded. She muttered something angry. It sounded to him like 'Bull-shit'. Then she drew several long, slow breaths while he watched her in dull despair and gave up hope of explaining.

'I've had faith in you,' she said eventually, the pain in her voice showing through a fading attempt at professionalism. 'I think I just lost it.'

The silence stretched and he knew time was

running out. Words would not come.

'I need to think about this,' she said. 'I'd better go and talk to them.' She went outside. Mike heard muffled words in the corridor and a young policeman came and stood by the door.

The lawyer came back with Meehan. She didn't seem able to meet Mike's eyes.

'Mr Martin,' Meehan said, sitting down, 'I have to tell you that I am now reopening the investigation into the death of your wife and daughter. I'm not yet in a position to charge you but I wish to interview you again at noon tomorrow. Mrs Palmer has agreed that you will voluntarily surrender your passport to her and that you will not leave your village without notifying her and me.'

Mike followed Rachel out of the police station, trying to keep up with her. She was walking fast, not looking back. As they drove out of the car park, she crunched a gear. 'Bugger,' she said. 'All right, now listen to me. The bad news is that Meehan always thought you were guilty and he's watched too many cold-case dramas on TV. I don't think he's ever had one of his very own. He would just love to reopen this case.'

'What will he want to know tomorrow?'

'He's been looking at the toxicology report. That was what got you off the hook last time, apparently.'

'Yes.'

'It showed you were in London when they took whatever it was?'

Mike was silent.

'Come on,' said Rachel. 'Don't clam up. There's no time for that.'

278

'Yes, that's what they said. They decided Gally took the stuff no earlier than eight in the morning. I was in London then. People saw me.'

'Toxicology has come a long way since then. He's having the findings checked out all over again.'

'He's out to get me, isn't he?'

'He thinks he's on to something.'

'And you're not sure he's wrong, are you?'

'That shouldn't surprise you, not after those pictures. Now you tell me, Mike. Why did you take those photos?'

'We were desperate. Gally heard about a healer, somewhere up in the Lakes. We took the pictures because she wanted to see them.'

'Did you go to a doctor?'

'No,' he said after a long time.

'Meehan will want to know why not.' He heard a formal distance in her voice.

'I'd rather be dealing with Meehan than with Wilson,' he said, 'but even then—'

'Meehan's a lot smarter than Wilson and a good man, I'd say.'

'I'm glad of that.'

'You shouldn't be. A good man on a mission is a lot harder to stop than a bad man with a grudge.'

That was the last thing she said until she pulled up at his gate and he opened the door. He went to find his passport and when he came back, she got out too and they stood there facing each other.

'I've decided,' she said. 'What I would really like is to turn time back and not have you tell me anything crazy. I'm going back to my office and I'm going to tell them that I can't represent you any more for personal reasons. I'll have them put

279

someone else on it. Then the only advice I can give you is that you don't tell them what you told me. Don't say anything that they can't say to Meehan and his sort. That's really all I can do for you now.'

'I'm sorry,' she added in a distorted voice, then she got back into the car and drove away.

CHAPTER 23

Two subdued girls got off the train at Exeter St Davids and walked slowly towards the river. The journey back had been hard, waiting for a bus which turned out to run only on Wednesdays, then trudging all the way to Gillingham. They arrived at the station as dusk fell to find a points failure at Axminster had destroyed their last hope of getting home that night. They had pitched their tent in darkness on a sloping and stony piece of waste ground and were barely talking to each other when they finally arrived.

'We shouldn't have left her there,' said Ali yet again as they climbed the steps to the road.

'What could we have done? Knocked her out and tied her up?'

As they expected, there was no answer when they rang Jo's doorbell, so they used the access code which they had seen her punch in so often and let themselves into the flat.

'Fleur won't mind, will she?' Lucy asked nervously.

'Of course she will. She always minds everything. She'll mind a lot more if we don't tell her.'

280

'But she's not what you'd call a caring mother, is she?'

'Frightening comes closer, but she'll want to know.'

'I suppose so. When she crashed her car she hired another one, but you can't hire daughters.'

'Where do we start?'

'She's got that big red diary. I hope she hasn't taken it.'

They found it on her desk. The word 'Pecon' was pencilled in two days earlier with arrows across every page until the next Wednesday.

'Where's Pecon?' asked Lucy.

'She was going there for a conference.'

They googled it on Jo's laptop.

'That's not good,' Lucy said. 'It's in Brazil.'

Ali clicked through to the next page. 'No, look at this. PECON, the Property Entrepreneurs Conference, Edgbaston. That's her sort of stuff. Yes, see? She's down as a speaker—Fleur Driscoll on "The buy-to-let market: profiting from the downturn". That was yesterday. Today she's doing workshops.'

She dialled the number.

A woman's voice said, 'Gemini Conference Centre. Can I help you?'

'I'm trying to get in touch with Mrs Driscoll. She's speaking at your property conference. Fleur Driscoll?'

'And you are?'

'We're friends of her daughter's. We've got a message for her.'

'She'll be in a session right now. Is it urgent?'

'Um, no—'

Lucy had leaned across with her ear near

281

enough the receiver to hear. 'Yes it is,' she said. 'It's definitely urgent.'

'Yes, I suppose it is,' said Ali. 'We must talk to her. I didn't want to worry her too much, that's all.'

'Can you give me some idea of what it's about? We don't like to disturb the programme.'

'Well, we've been camping with Jo, her daughter, and, um . . . things got a little odd and, I don't know, she, er . . .'

Lucy grabbed the phone from her. 'She met a strange guy and she wouldn't come back with us, so she's in this village in the middle of nowhere with him and it's not like her at all.'

'Okay. Wait. I'll go and get her at once. Don't hang up.'

'Lucy,' said Ali crossly, 'I was trying to be careful so we didn't scare her.'

'All you said was mumble, mumble, um, er, um. You have to use words, Ali, in the right order.'

A breathless voice at the other end said, 'Ali? Lucy? Where are you? What's happened?'

'Well, go on then,' hissed Ali as Lucy tried to give her back the phone. 'Tell her.'

'We're in your flat, Fleur,' said Lucy. 'We just got back. We let ourselves in. I hope you don't mind.'

'Where's Jo?'

'She's just—well, she's—she wouldn't come back with us.'

'From where?'

'From a village we went to.'

'What village?'

'Um . . .' Now Ali grabbed the phone from Lucy.

'It's a place called Pen Selwood, in Somerset, near Wincanton.'

'What's she doing there? I told her to stay with you two. Is that where you're digging?'

'No, not exactly. She met this boy—'

'Jo? Jo met a boy? And she wouldn't come back with you?'

'She said she'd get in touch with you. She didn't think you'd be home for a few more days,'

'When did all this happen?'

'Yesterday.'

'She met him *yesterday* and she wouldn't come back? Jo?'

'Yes. We'd camped there. She was pretty odd when we got to the village, then she got up early and went off and we found her with this boy sitting in the woods and she said she'd known him for years.'

'What's he called?'

'Ferney.'

'I've never heard of him.'

'Well, the police called him Luke something.'

'What police?'

'These policemen we met in the village. They were looking for him but they wouldn't say why. Jo said it was okay.'

'Has she been taking her tablets?'

'I don't know about yesterday but she had one the day before,' said Ali, crossing her fingers though it was technically true.

'For heaven's sake. You promised you would make sure she did. Well, I'm not having her rattling round the countryside. I'm leaving here right now and I'm going straight to this place, wherever it is. Let me write it down. How do you spell it?'

Ali told her.

'Did these policemen give you their names?'

'No.'

'Is there anything else you can tell me to help me find her?'

Lucy hissed, 'The teacher—you've forgotten the teacher.'

'Oh yes, she said you could get messages to her. Hang on. I wrote it down. A teacher called Mike Martin. He lives in a house called Bagstone Farm. It's nearby. This is the number she gave us.' She read it out. 'I tried it on my mobile but it didn't work.'

'That's an old code. It needs a one after the zero. Give me your mobile numbers. Have you got mine? I'm going straight there but I may need to get hold of you. I'm very disappointed in you two.'

*   *   *

When she left Bagstone, Gally climbed the hill to the old stone bench where Ferney was waiting.

'Did you ask him?' he said.

'His lawyer was there. I had to wait for her to go.'

'And?'

'Yes, I asked him. I said could we come and stay and he said, "Will that be one bed or two?"'

'That's all right then.'

'No, of course it isn't. There were tears in his eyes.' She hunched up. 'It's terrible. I can't ask him again.'

He stood up. 'I'll go and talk to him.'

'Don't. She's taking him back to see the police. They still want you to call them. This is their number.'

'You met her?'

'She found me in the garden, then she tested us to see if we were telling the truth.'

'He should never have talked to her.'

'Ferney, you told him to.'

'Don't get caught up with him. Not again.'

'He's a kind man. Don't be unkind. I put him where he is.'

'Till death did you part. That was the promise you made and death did part you.'

She looked at him and they both knew that was not a simple matter. 'Let's go back to the barn,' she said, but when they climbed the gate, they saw the doors were wide open and there was a tractor inside, with a pair of overalled legs sticking out from under it and the noise of a spanner turning a screeching nut. Ferney looked at the sky. 'We've got five hours of daylight, maybe six. We have a right to be in our proper place. I'll talk to him again.'

She was on the edge of tears as they walked back to the hilltop. He put his arms round her and felt that slight, disturbing resistance before she moulded herself to him. 'I hate to see you like this. It shouldn't be so hard.'

'I feel so guilty and I don't know what's happening to me. I need to know exactly what I did and why. I should be able to remember, shouldn't I?'

'It will come. Don't let it get in the way. Do you know how long it's been since we were last here together, properly together? I mean at the right age, just the two of us?'

She shook her head.

'I lost you years before the war,' he said.

'Nineteen thirty-three. You went missing, gone, just like that. I didn't get you back until you arrived with him in tow—that man.'

'Mike,' she said. 'You can at least call him Mike. What happened to me?'

'You were done away with, then the next time went all wrong somehow. We never quite got to the bottom of where you were.'

She looked at him as if she didn't quite have the courage to ask and he didn't want to tell her what he knew. 'I didn't get you back properly until now,' he said. 'Nearly eighty years apart, you and me who fit together like one.'

'It's lonely being away.'

'I promise you there is nothing so lonely as being here by yourself. That's why it's us that matters.'

'But it's not just us this time, is it? It's got so complicated.'

'Let's pretend it isn't. Come on, we'll go and see some more of our old places.' As evening approached, they walked back to the hilltop, feeling a chill creep into the air.

'I expect he's back,' said Ferney. 'I'm going down there. I can make him see he's got to let us be there.'

'Let's both go.'

'No. I won't be able to say it the way I need to.'

'You will be kind?'

'As kind as I can be.'

As Ferney approached Bagstone, he saw an unfamiliar car parked by the gate and could hear a woman's voice, raised in anger. He climbed the bank that ran along the road and slipped into the bushes.

Upset by Rachel's departure, Mike was carving into the brambles around the yard with a freshly sharpened scythe. A silver BMW stopped by the gate and a woman got out. She looked at him and called, 'Is this Bagstone Farm?'

'Yes,' he said.

'Are you Michael Martin?'

'Yes again,' he said. 'Are you from Whitson Saunders?' He hadn't expected Rachel to send a replacement so quickly and he found himself resenting this woman's presence. She looked polished, self-assured, with expensive hair.

'No,' she said, 'I'm not from anybody. I'm looking for my daughter and I wonder if you might know where she is.' Her voice was harsh.

'Your daughter?'

'My daughter, Jo. For some reason she's given her friends your name.'

'Jo?'

'Yes. Jo Driscoll. Doesn't that mean anything to you?'

Of course, he thought. She must mean Gally.

'Oh, I see,' he said. 'Don't stand in the road. Come on in.'

The woman pushed the gate ajar and walked slowly into the middle of the yard, keeping her distance.

'Yes,' he said, 'Jo. Yes indeed, she was here . . .' Another explanation he couldn't give. Another woman staring at him with doubting eyes. 'I'm afraid I don't know where she went.'

'Is she with someone? The girls said she was

287

with a boy.'

With a boy. 'She could be,' he said.

'He's called Ferney but he's also called Luke? Is that right? Do you know him? How does she know you? Why did she come here?'

'Look, you don't need to be worried.'

'Worried? I'm bloody furious, that's what I am.'

'Would you like to come inside?' He saw her eyes stray down to his hand and the scythe he was clutching. He put it down but that didn't seem to help.

'No, I'd rather stay out here. It's a simple enough question. How come she's given them your name?'

'What about a cup of tea? I could bring it out?'

Another car drove up and stopped.

'I don't want your bloody tea,' she said. 'I don't want to go inside your house. I just want to know what the hell is going on and if you don't tell me, I'm going to call the police.'

At which point, as if orchestrated by a malign fate, a new voice spoke from the gate. 'There's no need to call us, madam. We're right here.'

Mike saw Detective Sergeant Wilson, accompanied by the same policewoman they had met earlier.

'We're from Yeovil,' said the man. 'And if you don't mind me asking, who might you be, madam?'

'My name is Fleur Driscoll. I'm looking for my daughter, Jo. Her friends told me this man knows where she is.'

'Her friends would be two girls with backpacks, looking for a girl with dark hair and a red jacket?'

'Oh God. Have you found her?'

'No. I saw them yesterday. And she was coming

here, was she?'

'I don't know. I'm just trying to find out where she is. She's with some boy named either Ferney or Luke.'

'Luke Sturgess?'

'I haven't a clue.'

'We'll need to talk to you, if you don't mind, but there's something we need to do first.' He turned to Mike. 'Michael Martin, I'm arresting you on suspicion of the murder of Gabriella Martin and Rosie Martin.' He stopped as Fleur Driscoll screamed, glanced round at her with a wooden face and went on, 'You do not have to say anything but it may harm your defence if you do not mention, when questioned, something which you later rely on in court. Anything you do say may be given in evidence.'

'Does Meehan know you're doing this?' asked Mike but found himself ignored, turned roughly round by the sergeant, and felt the click of cuffs pinning his wrists together.

*　　　*　　　*

Mike was taken to the same interview room and Wilson sat down opposite him. The WPC put her head round the door. 'We let your solicitor know we were bringing you back in,' she said.

'Why the handcuffs?' he said. 'We were coming back tomorrow.'

'You'll find out soon enough,' Wilson answered as the door opened.

A fat fair-haired man with a flushed face followed Meehan in and stuck out his hand to Mike. 'Leo Avery,' he said, 'Whitson Saunders.

Seems I've drawn the short straw.' He looked at Mike as if waiting for a laugh. 'Never mind. Just skimmed through the old paperwork. Soon be up to speed, I'm sure.'

They went through the same preliminaries as before then Meehan put a sheet of paper down on the table.

'Mr Martin, where were you on the evening before the death of your wife and child?'

'The evening before? I was at the cottage and then I drove to London.'

'What time did you leave?'

'You're asking my client for a precise time of departure on an evening sixteen years ago?' said the lawyer. 'That's not a reasonable question.'

'Yes it is,' said Mike. 'I've been over it a hundred times. I left at seven in the evening. I heard the news headlines on Radio 4 just after I drove out of the gate, then *The Archers*. It's carved on my memory, believe me.'

Meehan pushed his sheet of paper across the table to them. The lawyer picked it up and began to read.

'From our lab people,' Meehan said, 'the toxicologists. They've gone over the case again. Like I told you, things have moved on. They've got a better idea of how it might have worked. Now they reckon it could have taken up to eighteen hours to produce a lethal effect.' He looked hard at Mike. 'That puts you right back in the spotlight, Mr Martin. By your own admission, you were still at the house eighteen hours before death occurred.'

The lawyer was still reading the paper.

'Ingredients partially degraded? That doesn't

sound very certain.'

'Certain enough, they tell me, Mr Avery.'

'Inspector Meehan, are you telling me they now know precisely how this mixture worked?'

'Ninety five per cent, that's what they say. Ninety five per cent is enough for me at this stage.'

'That's a bit slender.'

'Not when taken in conjunction with this.' Meehan produced a sealed plastic document holder. In it were two scorched twists of paper. 'I found this with the other evidence. Again, we didn't have the technology to enhance it properly at the time.'

'What is it?' asked Mike.

'There were burnt pieces of paper in the fireplace. It's your wife's handwriting, Mr Martin.'

'What does it say?'

'It's an incomplete sentence. What we can now read is "unbearable for her to . . ." then a gap, then "tortured by a so much older man". I believe it said "unbearable for her to be tortured by a so much older man". Anything you would care to say, Mr Martin?'

'Is it your intention to charge my client?' Avery said.

'It is my intention to keep him here for further questioning for the time being. We are expecting more detail on the toxicology. I also wish to re-examine the records on your client's movements at that time.'

They were left alone.

'That's not very good, is it?' said the lawyer. 'There's not much I can do right at this moment. You're in for the night, I'm afraid. Anybody else I should be telling?'

291

Mike shook his head.

'My colleague, Mrs Palmer, er . . .' He seemed unsure what to say. 'She said it was something personal?'

'Yes.'

'Would it help to start at the beginning, old chap?' He looked at his watch.

'No.'

When he was sitting in his car, about to drive out of the car park, Leo Avery rang Rachel Palmer as she had made him promise he would. 'I've just left him,' he said. 'Funny bloke. Wouldn't lift his finger to help. I'm afraid they've got him bang to rights.'

'Why do you say that?'

'Dick Meehan said so. The toxicology is damning. It was the only thing they were short of last time. If anyone knocked off the wife and the kid it had to be him. Now they can put him there at the right time, it's open and shut.'

'Meehan's not necessarily right.'

'Dick? He's pretty sound. I play golf with him.'

'We need someone to look at that report.'

'We? I thought you'd passed it over to me, old girl. To be honest, if there's something personal in this, I would say you should definitely stay out of it. I'll do my best, but at the moment I think we'd be better off discussing a guilty plea and thank our lucky stars if we can get some form of mitigation.'

CHAPTER 24

She watched Ferney walk towards her in the quietening evening, wondering what news he brought from down below, still wrestling, as she had been all the time he had been at the cottage, with the impossibility of making everything work for all three of them.

'It's fixed,' Ferney said when he came to where she sat on the bench. 'We can stay.'

Her heart leapt. 'He said so?'

'We can use the house. He's had to go away.'

'Where? How long for?'

'I don't know how long. Definitely for tonight. I saw him off.'

She so much wanted to believe it was as easy as that, so much wanted Mike's understanding, that she didn't question him further. The simplest fact in her life was that she wanted to be with Ferney in their old, old home, and they arrived at the door in burning excitement. He took the key from under the flowerpot, opened the door and led her inside, through the hall to Mike's untidy study at the back. He switched on the light and pointed.

'Do you remember this?' he asked. 'If you want proof it's really ours, you couldn't ask for better.'

It was a large painting in a gilt frame. 'It's Bagstone,' she said.

'Not just Bagstone. Do you see the people at the gate?'

She stepped forward to look at the two small figures. 'Oh. You and me.'

'You and me, in the place where we belong. You

remember it?' Ferney thought back to the disconsolate artist he had found in the field, taking his irritation out on his easel. 'He called himself John Poorman, remember that? Back in eighteen hundred and something, that was. Look at us, there forever as we have every right to be. Come upstairs with me now.'

She climbed to the floor above, where the eaves curved in to claim her with their old familiarity. He let her go ahead, looking in on Mike's room which had been theirs and closing the door quickly, then on to the spare room where she stood staring at the bed with tears coming.

She turned and said, 'Here. We will bring life back here,' so that he came into the room and they lay down together and let the evening slowly wrap itself around their bed.

*   *   *

When Gally opened her eyes again she was startled to find that ceiling above her with sunrise slipping through the window and an arm across her breasts and breath warming and cooling on her neck in the even pulses of sleep. She knew that she had woken there under many older roofs and she heard Ferney's breathing change as he joined her in the new day. She gently turned her head to look at her lover's body and his eyes opened so that there was nothing else there but the thin river of light between their eyes.

'I was dreaming,' he said.

'A good dream?'

'Yes, but far better to be awake with you.'

She lifted the blanket and looked down the

length of both their bodies to remind herself. 'I must go and find the herbs.' She recited the old country names—Lord's Balm, Maiden's Blessing and the rest.

He laughed. 'Your morning-after method. The natural way.'

She was silent, thinking of other, harsher herbs, and that led her back to Rosie and the boys, children who had died. 'Do you remember them well, our lovely sons?'

He saw tears starting to bead in the corners of her eyes. 'It was a thousand years ago,' he said. 'You've mourned them fully, in thought and in deed.' He knew the old sorrow was still tangled into this much more recent past and felt the dangerous depth of her sadness.

She turned and wrapped her arms around him and they held each other through the memory of the memory of the echoes of that old tragedy.

'What do you mean I mourned them in deed?' she asked.

'You always told me there's no hope for humans while we still slaughter each other.'

'Did I? Yes, I still believe that.'

'You said the world stumbles backwards every time we spill life. Few things would make me go to war.'

'Young men beware, to make you fight they first must make you hate ...' She stopped. What is that?'

'That's the man who made you better. I said we'd get to that part. I think this is the time. He was called Guy and we didn't know him when he first came.'

Gally sprang off the bed, put her clothes on in a

295

moment, urged him on. 'Come downstairs,' she said. 'I have a glimpse of it.'

She had the front door open when he caught up with her. 'We were standing here. We were looking out at the puddles by the gate . . .'

*　　　*　　　*

It had been a wet night and now those puddles were turning to mist in the morning sun. 'Listen,' said Ferney. 'There's a horse on the lane.'

He meant an unknown horse or he would have said 'There's Thomas's cob coming' or 'That's the Wyncaleton cart'. In those days, they had a good ear for strange footsteps and strange hoofbeats. He took up the thick staff that stood ready for unexpected visitors, gestured her to stay back while he held the door just far enough open to look. The horse and its rider walked into the yard. The man swung down, hitched the reins to a post and looked towards the house.

'Is anyone at home?' he called.

'I'm here,' Ferney answered. 'What's your business with me?'

The stranger faced the door but came no nearer. He smiled. He had a weather-beaten, open face and he wore a leather jerkin over wool. The sword at his belt had a soldier's plain grip and a strong and simple scabbard.

'I'm your new Lord,' he said, 'in a manner of speaking.'

'That's not Molyns,' said Gally behind him. 'Open the door, Ferney.'

They walked out into the sunlight, though he kept hold of the staff.

'My name is Guy de Bryan,' said the man.

'Of the King's household?'

'You've heard of me?'

'I've heard nothing but good,' said Ferney. 'This is my wife, Gally, and it surprises us that you say you are our Lord.'

'Sir John Molyns has incurred the King's displeasure,' said the other man drily. 'His manor of Stoke Trister and the attached lands at Chaffeymoor and this end of the ridge have been put in my keeping for the time being. I hope that comes as good news to you because we have some business together.'

'Very good news,' said Ferney. 'Come inside and share what we have.'

In their parlour, the man politely refused everything they offered from their small supplies until he wrinkled his nose and enquired after the source of the smell from the kettle on the fire.

'That's mint, my Lord,' said Gally. 'An infusion.'

'Then that's what I should like. You may have heard that Molyns has gone into hiding?'

'It takes time for news to reach us here,' said Ferney, 'and longer to make sure it's true, but we heard something like that, yes. I would be pleased to hear the reasons. He was not much loved around here.'

'Or anywhere else. King Edward sent him home from the French campaign to raise money to pay the army. A royal and urgent mission. Instead, Molyns dived straight into the Treasury like a robber's dog, feathered his own nest and left the king trapped across the Channel, a hostage to his own mercenaries and to the Archbishop of Trier who seized the great crown of England as security for his debts. Imagine that. The king was forced to escape by ignoble means. Molyns is now on the run and hotly sought.'

'And nobody knows where he is?'

De Bryan gave Ferney a sharp look. 'Not too far from here, if I am not mistaken, but well protected by a powerful patron. I'm making enquiries and I will discover him if my suspicions are correct.'

'In the Montacute household perhaps?'

'Your words, and probably wise words, but not yet mine and not yet proven.' He gave a tiny shrug and Ferney knew there was need to tread lightly. Montacute, Earl of Salisbury had a strange weakness for his violent henchman Molyns. He knew there was a long history between Molyns and de Bryan. Rumour had it that de Bryan's estranged son, wanted for a dozen misdeeds and turned against his father these many years by Molyns' coaxing, also had sanctuary in the Earl's household.

'You say we have business?'

'I would like to understand the estate before I go knocking on my tenants' doors. The accounts show some of them are slow payers.'

'I'm not one of those. I rent a barn, that is all. The house is ours.'

'Indeed I know that and I believe I owe *you* a duty because I see your barn roof needs patching. I have come to you simply because whenever I ask who is the authority on the history and workings of the area, yours is the only name I ever hear. I want you to tell me which of my tenants deserve my patience and which are only pretending to poverty.'

'I can answer the first part. I am not one for

298

blaming so you will have to search for answers to the second part in the gaps in what I say.'

Gally left them to go about her business in the village and the two men talked on about the history of the ridge, the special problems of the eastern slopes and the chance of any worthwhile return from renewed quarrying in the greenstone pits.

'I've enjoyed our time and I will come back if I may,' said de Bryan in the end, 'but I have to go to Stavordale. Will you direct me?'

Ferney told him the way through Cockroad Wood past the Norman castle.

'Wake up, Emily,' de Bryan said to his horse. 'I look forward to talking again.'

He had been gone a short while when Gally came flying in through the door, shouting for Ferney.

'There are men chasing after him,' she said. 'Three men with swords, running through the fields. They mean no good, I can tell you that for sure.'

'Where are they?'

'Heading for Cockroad.'

Ferney took his staff and went as hard as he knew how, running, then walking, then running again as soon as his breath allowed, only slowing when he came into the wood and saw the corpse of the great horse Emily, flat down on her side with the tail of an arrow sticking upwards. Thirty paces on, a man was curled around a leaking sword wound, quite dead. Into the trees, collapsed into a bush was another man, equally dead. Both had cloths tied round their mouths to disguise their faces. Ferney went on, gripping his staff, and heard the slow clashes and grunts of battle continuing. He saw de Bryan, white in the face, bleeding badly from his right shoulder but still holding his sword with a loose grip, prodding and swinging to keep at bay a man with his back to Ferney. The man was jeering at him, playing with him. De Bryan looked past him, saw Ferney coming, seemed about to say something. His adversary laughed, said, 'You don't fool me. There's no one to rescue you, Guy, and you have just committed mortal sin,' and was still laughing when Ferney brought his staff down hard on the man's skull.

*　　　　*　　　　*

They were still standing outside the cottage door. 'I remember you bringing him home,' said Gally. 'I met you by the church. Someone helped us carry him.'

Someone did, thought Ferney—some nameless villager amongst all the bit-part players.

'You nursed him,' he said as they went back inside.

'What year was that?'

He thought for a moment. 'The fight? The third of the Edwards. The French wars. Six hundred and sixty years ago give or take a bit. He was quite young then.'

'What happened then?'

'I need breakfast, then I'll tell you the bit that matters.'

'What day is it?' Gally asked as they looked for food in Mike's meagre cupboards. She was happy again.

'The day after yesterday. The day before

300

tomorrow. The first day of our new life, with just you and me and nobody in the way. Heat hanging from a high, blue morning and the old birds singing.'

'Old?'

'Who's to say they're not? They sound the same as ever and they look the same as ever.'

When the phone rang, she answered it without thinking. It seemed so natural. It was her phone and her house. By the time she realised that was wrong, she had already recognised the voice at the other end.

'*Jo?*' it said, 'Is that you?'

She nearly said no but before she could, the voice had dragged her back through the ploughed-up soil of the past day to the point where she had to say yes.

'Where are you?'

'Outside the church. Stay there. I'm coming. How do I get to you?'

'No. Don't come here.' She didn't want her here, in their house. 'I'll come and find you.'

'But I—'

'No. I'm going there now.'

In the last hundred yards of her walk, seeing her mother's car by the church gate, Gally stopped in her tracks with pity in her heart trying to be Jo again. What could she say? She had thought she could work out some way to deal with this given a week. There wasn't a week, there were thirty seconds. She had been here, walking on this same tarmac with Ali and Lucy when she was still partly Jo. She pulled a bit of that old self into the here and now, searching for more as if a butterfly could remember how to be a caterpillar.

Her mother was out of the car, looking all around her, giving her agitation away in the staccato speed of her movements.

'Hello,' Jo called. 'I'm here.'

'Jo, oh Jo!' Her mother ran towards her, seized her as if she wanted to shake her, then stepped back to look hard at her, holding on to her shoulders. 'What on earth have you been up to?'

'I'm fine. I'm sorry they rang you. There was no need.'

'Oh, I think there definitely was.'

'What about your conference?'

'I had to abandon it. I could murder you.'

'I was going to call you.'

'It's a bit late to say that. Now, come on, Jo. What's been going on?'

'Shall we go and sit down?'

'In the car?'

'In the church porch. There's a seat.'

So they sat under the old king and queen and both pairs stared at each other blankly. Gally looked at this stranger next to her and the part that was Jo was just as baffled, unable to remember whether the space between them had always felt so unbridgeable.

'I don't get it, Jo.' There was barely contained anger in her mother's voice. 'Lucy and Ali said you met a boy you knew. I couldn't think of anyone that could possibly be.'

'You haven't met him. It's quite hard to explain.'

'I don't care how hard it is. I have just had a horrid day, driving all the way down, then sitting around at the police station for hours, then I had to stay the night in some ghastly little bed and breakfast hovel.'

'The police station? Why?'

'Because I came to that man's house and the next minute the police arrived and arrested him.'

'What man?'

'Martin or whatever he's called.'

'They arrested him?' Gally could only think of what Ferney must have known, what he had concealed from her. She felt sick at the knowledge. 'What for?'

'You don't know? For murder, that's all—for murdering his wife and his child. What on earth has he got to do with you and why were you at his house? He could have killed you too. Now, what is all this about?' and Gally, head spinning, could see no way to tell her or not to tell her.

'You won't believe it,' she said.

'Try me.'

She looked up at the two stone heads and they gave her no help. 'All right. You've never been here before, have you?'

'I've driven past, but I've never turned off the road.'

'Well, that's the thing. I have.'

'Not with me.'

'No.'

'I don't see how then, but anyway, you think you know this village?'

'I know this place better than I know anywhere else on earth.'

'Go on,' said her mother but her voice was a little fainter than it had been.

'I've lived here.'

'Of course you haven't. Wait a minute. Is this some past lives thing?'

'Yes, in a way.'

303

'Oh, I see. Now I know what you're talking about. Fleur gave her daughter a tight smile. 'The thing is, Jo, that's all crap. Do you remember Stella? My screwy bookkeeper? She did that past life regression therapy and she was convinced she was a soldier who ran away from some famous battle. It was just her way of looking at what she was, which was bloody useless by the way. All it meant was that she was the sort of—'

'Mum. I mean this absolutely literally. I have lived in this village many times over and for many, many years.'

'I know you haven't been taking your tablets. This is just your old crazy stuff coming back,' but as Fleur looked at her daughter she was abruptly disconcerted. There were things about Jo that were different—the way she held her head higher, the way she kept a steady gaze on you as she spoke, the jut of her jaw. Fleur was thrown by that without fully understanding why. The stone king and the stone queen could have told her if they had the power to speak. Enough human sorrow had been aired on this bench below them over the centuries for them to understand when a mother mistook a daughter for a part of herself, a part that stood for something she did not like. Two people suffer whenever that mistake is made. Blank stone eyes had seen it. Blank stone ears had heard it. But stone does not speak and the moment passed, unexplained. Fleur had to wait under that steady gaze until Jo was ready to say more.

'When I first came here,' she said in the end, 'there was no church.'

'Oh no, Jo, that's impossible. This must be medieval—well no, it's Norman, isn't it? That's a

304

Norman doorway. Do you see? The round arch?'

'Yes, that's a Norman doorway. Before that there was a wooden church here and the Saxons built that.'

'Well then, how could—'

'It had a thatched roof but that rotted quickly so they put on another one made out of little wooden shingles.' She looked at her mother, who was staring at the heads over the door as if hoping they would interrupt.

'That got burnt down in the end,' the girl went on, 'but I was here even before the wooden church. That was more than thirteen hundred years ago. I've been here ever since.'

Her mother turned to stare at her, frowning. 'Stop it. That's enough.'

'I'm sorry. I have to tell you.'

'How can I believe this?' She stood up, opened the heavy oak door and pushed past it into the church. Gally followed. Fleur searched around, found a table with a pile of guides. She picked one up and opened it. 'Have you been reading this?' she demanded. 'Is this where all that came from? Is it?'

Gally shook her head and watched as her mother ran her finger down the pages.

'It doesn't help,' she said in the end. 'It doesn't help at all. Uncertain dates, Saxon influence, Norman zigzags. Nothing about a wooden church.' She collapsed on to a seat. 'I'm an atheist.'

'I'm not asking you to believe in God.'

'I believe that when we die, that's it. There is nothing else afterwards.'

'I'm not saying this is some universal thing . . . Mum. As far as I'm concerned, it's just us.'

305

'Us?'

'Ferney and me.'

'Ferney? This boy? Is he called Luke or—?'

'Ferney. He's Ferney. He always has been. His mother called him Luke but that's not his real name.'

'What? You mean it's just you two. In this whole huge world, it's just you? That's a bit arrogant, isn't it?'

'I didn't say that. I have no idea if it's just us. Maybe it's everybody but we remember it—that's what separates us.'

'Separates. Yes, that's a good word. That's just the way it feels. This feels very separate from me. Hold on. You said his mother called him Luke, but his real name is Ferney?'

'That's right.'

'But your real name's Jo and *I* called you Jo. *You* didn't choose it. What are you saying—that I somehow guessed your real name? Because that doesn't . . . Oh, no. Oh my goodness.'

'Mum?'

'No, wait. You're not saying that at all, are you?'

'No.'

'You're saying your real name is something else.'

'I've been Jo for sixteen years, Mum. For us that's my real name. I'll go on being Jo for you.'

Fleur looked at her, recognising that she truly was a stranger and was perhaps even to be feared. 'What is it? No, I don't want to know. Don't tell me.'

'All right.'

'Are you saying you can remember all the times you claim you lived here?'

'The ones that mattered. Most of them, I expect,

306

if I work at it.'

'How did it start then? Tell me that.'

'Walk with me,' said Gally. 'Let's go up the lane.' She wanted to get out of the village, away from chance meetings.

'Tell me about something—anything,' her mother demanded as they left the churchyard. 'Tell me about Henry the Eighth, for example.'

'It's not really been about kings and stuff, not in my experience. It's just been about people.'

'That's the way I learnt my history,' said her mother. 'The proper way. Kings and battles.'

'We let the wrong people tell our story for us, don't we? The newspapers, the TV news, history books are all the same. We let the big egos tell us about the wars and the business deals—all the testosterone stuff. We let the drama enthusiasts tell us about the disasters and the tragedies and the accidents and we end up thinking that's what the past is, that's what the present is, that's what our country is, but it's not.'

Her mother was looking at her doubtfully, 'What is it then?'

'Mostly, it's a lot of ordinary friendly, generous people over a very long time, doing the best they can in a quiet sort of way. Most of them don't go round chopping other people's heads off. We shouldn't let the people take charge who want to be in charge. They're the last ones we should trust.'

It was clear her mother didn't understand any of that. 'Is he very left-wing, this Ferney person? I've never heard you talk like this, Jo.'

'A lot has happened.'

'Where are we going? My shoes aren't meant for this.'

'It's not far. I'll explain when we get there.'

They walked on in difficult silence until they saw the ramparts of Kenny Wilkins' camp ahead, straddling the road.

'You see this place?' said Gally. 'This is as far back as I go. Do you want me to tell you about it? It might help you understand.' She raised her voice as a truck laboured past, filling the air with a roar of harsh combustion.

'It was so different then,' she said. 'Can you imagine a world where you don't have noises like that? Until there were church bells, the loudest man-made sound was the smith beating iron. When a storm came, the thunder was unimaginable, God tearing the sky to shreds, almost enough to make you mad, but we were all good at little noises. We could hear a lark sing a mile away. We knew the voices of every cow. Come with me.' She led her baffled mother up on to the camp's earth bank and they pushed through bushes until they faced east out across the valley.

'Now, imagine the noise an army makes as it approaches. Imagine how that is. You're on watch up here and you know they're coming. Scouts have come back to tell you but the rain's beating down and you can't see and you can't hear and you're hoping they've got it wrong. Then the rain lets up and the curtain lifts. For a moment there's nothing but cows below and a fox barking, until something changes in the valley out of sight so that there is a far murmur, no more than that.' Her voice had fear in it now. 'Add up ten thousand breaths and ten thousand footfalls and the rattle of ten thousand blades in ten thousand sheaths and with every footstep and breath and rattle it gets just that

308

tiny bit louder. Then it is no longer a murmur and you can no longer pretend it isn't there. It is a mumble, then a mutter, then a clatter, then a roar, and by that time it is already far too late to do anything to stop it.'

She turned and faced her mother.

'This is where it started,' she said.

CHAPTER 25

She had gone as soon as she put the phone down to her mother. The phone call left Ferney stranded, alone and anxious in a house which belonged to a man who might return at any moment and worried to his core about where his lover had gone. He walked to the hilltop knowing he could see the church from there, hoping to keep a distant eye on Gally. His heart sank as he saw there was already someone sitting on the bench—a complete stranger where no one else should be, a stranger who turned and said, 'Hello. I think you must be Ferney?'

'Yes.'

'I'm Rachel Palmer.'

'You're his lawyer.'

'Maybe. Maybe not. I think that depends on the conversation we're about to have.'

He looked across the dip to the church far beyond and saw a silver car parked outside but he could see nobody there.

'Michael Martin has been arrested,' she said.

'I know. I was watching.'

'Were you? Where's Gally?'

He pointed to the church and as he did so, they saw her walk out of the churchyard with a woman and the pair go off up the lane.

'Who's that with her?' Rachel asked.

'Her mother.'

Rachel studied the boy standing in front of her. 'There is something I need to know,' she said. 'Mike's in real trouble but I don't know if I want to help him.'

'That's up to you.'

'Don't give me that. You and Gally and your peculiar schemes have got him into this. You owe him some straight answers.'

'I don't see that that will do any good. You can't tell any of it to the police. They'd lock you up too.'

'Ferney, I'm getting a strong feeling that you don't really want to help. You haven't told her, have you?' said Rachel suddenly, on a hunch. 'You know perfectly well he's been arrested and you haven't told her.'

He didn't deny it. He just looked straight at her and said, 'I have to do what I have to do.'

'Where were you two last night?'

He didn't answer immediately. 'Oh, I get it,' she said. 'You selfish boy. Don't you care what happens to him at all?'

Ferney shrugged. 'I don't owe him anything.' He was chafing at the bit, staring in the direction they had disappeared.

'Listen to me, you little horror,' she said, and that startled him. 'If I chose to, I could make life pretty difficult for you. If I start rattling your cage, you'll know all about it. You'll have psychiatrists strapping you to a bed before you can say knife. Do you understand me?'

310

'There's no need to be like that.'

'Oh yes there is. A man who may or may not be a good man is sitting in a police cell right now because of you.'

'What do you want from me?'

'A clear explanation of why the police showed me photos of Gally and a little girl called Rosie who looked like she'd been through a mincer.'

'I don't know about Rosie. I don't understand about her. I can't help you.'

'I think you're not trying very hard and I think you do know. I've worked it out. Haven't you?'

'Exactly what have you worked out?' He didn't want to hear what was coming because in the back of his mind, he knew it was true.

'Mike told me Rosie did all those things to herself. At two and a bit years old. I thought he had to be lying, then I went back and did my sums. I'm right, aren't I?'

'I don't know.'

'Oh yes you do. It's the only way the dates work, isn't it? I know your birthday. It's part of the police case, for heaven's sake. I can read an inscription. I've seen your old gravestone. There was a gap, wasn't there? Well?'

'If you say so.'

'I do say so. You got me believing this stuff. Don't start pretending now. There's a stone saying Ferney Masters died in February 1991. He was eighty-three. Rosie was born the very same day. What a coincidence, eh? There's another stone saying Rosie died on January the 31st, 1994. You do the maths. You were born in June 1994. That's what the police file says.'

'That's all I know.'

She jumped to her feet and, to her own great surprise, grabbed him by the shirt with both hands. 'Rosie was you. It's obvious.'

He shrank back and she let go, then he sat down on the bench, curled into himself, and she sat down next to him. He covered his face with his hands. 'I can't go back there,' he said.

'You have to.'

'Why do I have to?'

'Because I will fight for Michael Martin if you tell me that's what happened and if you explain why a small child does that to herself, but if you don't then I'll walk away and I am almost sure he will go to prison for many, many years. It's up to you and your conscience if you have one.'

'Surely they'll let him out?'

'They've got new evidence.' She told him about the toxicology report and the damning fragment of paper. 'They're serious. They're going to be questioning him again at any moment, so come on. Start remembering and start talking.'

'It's very hard to go back there.'

'Why?'

'I know how to get back to other times, times when I was older, because I can—oh, I don't know ...' He was casting around for a way to describe it and she sat patiently waiting. 'I can see it through their eyes if I try. If I know what I'm looking for, all I need is just one little something to tag on to, then I can go back, but this ... I have to be two years old and a girl and I don't know how to.' He sounded so desperate that she was moved to let him off the hook but she couldn't afford to do that.

'Yes you do. Think of hurting yourself.' She thought of the photos and shuddered. 'Think of

312

grabbing a pair of scissors. They would seem huge to you. Think of holding them in one hand and jabbing them into your arm.'

'No.'

'Go on. Do it.' And she saw his eyes widen then fill with tears and all of a sudden he was on the ground, rolling round, shrieking his affront and his anger, and she made herself sit still and watch for minute after minute until he gradually subsided, lying on his side in a foetal curve, shuddering to a halt.

'Not a girl,' he said, and his voice was high and quavering. 'Won't be a girl.'

'Ferney,' she said, 'it's okay.'

'Not okay. Don't.' The boy on the ground writhed violently, pushing out the palm of one hand at her. 'Let me go. Let go.'

She knelt next to him. 'You're here on the hill. You're a boy. That's all over. It's all right.' But he went on shaking and calling out and she kept on talking, saying calming nothings as if he were a child having a nightmare. In the end he quietened and lay still, his eyes closed, and she wondered if he was asleep. She sat there, watching out for him, looking towards the church. Part of her still wanted to walk away from all of them and lead the simpler life she had known before, but another part had begun to care for him in a different way and to understand the harsh reality of his fate. She looked out at the scattered landscape of the village and wished she could see into its past as he could.

After ten minutes or so, he straightened abruptly, gasped and sat up.

'Are you happy now? I don't want to do that again, ever,' he said.

313

'I won't ask you to. Has that happened before?'

'Which bit of it?'

'I meant being a girl instead of a boy?'

Even that seemed a dangerous question at first. He looked at her like a creature cornered, then nodded. 'Once. Once that I know of. The other way round. Not me, Gally. It made her mad. I think that's what it does.'

'Only once before in all that time?'

'There was a time when we were brother and sister. That didn't work too well either.'

'What happened?' she asked to keep him talking, feeling that she needed to get him all the way back to normality, to talk about other lives before she dared push him harder on this most recent one.

'That time? They hounded us out.' He went silent, looked far away, oblivious to her. 'Our halves are nothing on their own,' he said in a distant voice, 'but half and half make one and halves, divided, stand alone when the adding's done.'

'A poem?'

'What?'

'It sounded like a poem.'

'Yes. A poem from that time. Poems and songs, they stick in the memory. They're good signposts.'

'What do we do now?'

'I have to wait for them,' he said. 'Do you mind waiting with me?'

'Do you want me to?' She was a little surprised.

He nodded. 'I was frightened,' he said in a very small voice. 'That was so horrible.'

She saw a chance to make friends with him. 'Will you tell me a bit more about this place?' she asked.

314

'I've read a bit now—in fact I've become a bit of a swot. I bought the local history book.'

'So you know about the battles?'

'The seventh century, Peonnum?'

'That was the first one. We never called it that. This was Pen then and it still is.'

'Mike must have been interested in that?'

'Frustrated more like. He said the books don't say much because nobody knows the facts except that I'd told him where it happened, how it happened, what they looked like, what the weather was like, and there was nothing he could do with that—nothing at all. An eye-witness account and he couldn't write the best thing ever on a seventh-century battle because he'd be laughed at. It's just like it would be with the police now. You understand. You can't tell people, can you?'

'Couldn't you show him where they buried the bodies? Then at least he could do some digging.'

'No.'

'Why not?'

'Because I don't know where that was. We were dead before they were buried.'

'But next time round people here must still have been talking about it. Wasn't there anything about a burial ground?'

Ferney shook his head. 'I can't remember that next time. Anyway, it wasn't just the one battle. There was the one against the Danes.'

She thought. 'Edmund Ironside?'

'We just called him Edmund.'

'When was it?'

'I don't know. Whenever.' He pointed to the north of the church. 'Beyond there, Heath Hay and the next field, towards Pen Ridge farm. The Danes were waiting up at Kenny Wilkins, in the old fort, but Edmund was too crafty. He pretended he didn't know they were anywhere near, started to set up camp in the open fields like he was having a picnic. They were too drunk to think twice so they rushed out to attack and the rest of Edmund's men came out of ambush and slaughtered them. Like cutting hay, that was what I heard. The Danes were reeling around seeing double and roaring their heads off.'

'You heard, you say?'

'My father hid me in a hole but I heard all about it when I was old enough. Edmund chased them away past Bourton, but they left seven hundred Danish dead behind and I do know where *they're* buried.' He looked towards the church again and frowned. 'Where have they got to?'

'Give it time.'

'We could get your car and go looking.'

'And miss them if they come back? Be sensible. So go on. I suppose it's odd that there should be two battles in a tiny place like this.'

'Two?' Ferney looked at her in surprise. 'There weren't just two.'

'There was another one? There's nothing in the book.'

'Isn't there? No, I don't suppose there is.' He looked all around him. 'It left its mark though. One castle over there, a second one that way, another just down there, plus there was a wooden watchtower right here and an outpost at Kenny Wilkins. Five Norman strongpoints round one little village, all because of what happened here.'

'Are you saying that's something that's not in the history books?'

316

'Yes. It's not a good idea to start talking about that kind of stuff.'

'Because I'm an outsider?'

'If you like.'

She judged her moment. 'So is it true, Ferney? Did . . . did Rosie do all that to herself?'

'You mean did I do it to myself? Yes, it's true. I can't exactly remember but I'm sure I did. Does it make a difference?'

'It makes a huge difference to me. Why did you do it?'

'I was in the wrong body. We live for each other, Gally and me. That's the only thing that makes it bearable. We made a promise, she and I. We had to stick to it.'

'And that's the promise that put you both in that grave? Mother and daughter?'

'How could we be mother and daughter? Not once the memories came back. It wasn't possible.'

'So Gally did it? She killed herself and she killed you?'

He frowned. 'Until now, we only ever told one other person in all the years. Then there was Mike and that doubled it. Then there was you and now there's the mother, and that doubles it again. It's not good. It's hard enough doing this with just us two.'

'How did you get away with it for all that time? People must have asked questions, surely. Didn't they find you strange?'

'There were strange people everywhere. That was how things were. Touched by God or the Devil depending on your point of view. You should have seen it in early spring when the stores ran low. People went off their heads then. The hungry

317

months. You would be down to the leftovers, the mouldy grain. If you didn't eat it, you starved. If you did, it sent you mad.'

'I've heard about that. It was called ergot, wasn't it?'

'We called it mould, but it wasn't just that. It was the births that went wrong, the rest of the crappy diet, the illnesses nobody could treat, and then there were the misbegottens, the children of cousins or worse. We weren't expected to be normal. If they thought we were odd, they left us alone.'

'Is that what it was like?'

'Only sometimes. People loved Gally. They always do. I usually get a bit of that, like a reflection, but it wasn't like that this last time. People left me alone. I was by myself, years and years and years, right up until she and Mike came back. I wasn't going to let that happen again, not if I could help it. It's the two of us—that's all that counts.'

'Is that really how you think?'

'Time was we'd stick our necks out to help other people. It never works. We knew stuff but we couldn't solve everyone else's problems.'

'I bet she tried to.'

'Often enough, but do you know what happens when you do that? People start turning to you for everything. They'll hand over responsibility just like that and then you're lost. I made that mistake when I was green. I never made it again. If they think you've got the answers, they'll put you on a throne then they'll watch for a reason to pull you off it and give you a good kicking.' He broke off. 'Look,' he said. 'They're coming back.' Two far-off

318

figures were walking towards the churchyard gate.

'Mike needn't be the enemy here,' she said. 'There has to be a kind way out.'

He didn't look convinced.

Those words 'a kind way out' turned in her head and led back to the main matter. 'So she brewed up some sort of mixture and she gave it to you too?'

'It was the old country way. Time to bring out the black teapot. That's what they used to say if someone was dying in too much pain. There were different potions but hers was the best. It was gentle. She had all the old knowledge and she'll have it again.'

They saw Gally and her mother go into the graveyard.

'So, just to be brutally clear,' Rachel said, screwing up her eyes to try to make them out, 'your promise to each other was that you would do away with yourselves and start over again if anything got in the way. Yes?'

'It wasn't brutal. It was the only way that worked for us.'

'It was brutal when other people got involved. Do you ever stop and think what you've done to Mike? You've destroyed him.'

He looked at her defiantly and for a moment she thought he would try to shrug it off, but he let his eyes drop. 'I know,' he said quietly. 'That's why I don't like letting other people in. That's why we don't have children. It only works if we keep it to the two of us, but that's getting harder all the time.'

'You can help me put it right. Mike Martin is carrying the can for you two. Would Gally remember exactly how she made that potion?'

'I think so. She will if I help her.'

'I need to talk to her. Would she remember what the rest of that piece of paper said?'

'It's obvious, isn't it?'

'Not to me.'

'She was talking about Rosie getting back an old man's memories and how that must have been torture for her. She can hardly say that to the police, can she? I don't know what . . .' Whatever else he was going to say was forgotten because they saw people coming out of the graveyard. This time there were three, and two of them seemed to be having difficulty getting the other one into the silver car.

Ferney stared across the fields between them. 'Something's gone wrong.'

'With Gally? Your eyesight's better than mine.'

'Yes, Gally. She's in a bad way.'

'You can see that from here?'

'They've put her in the car. No, Gally. Don't do that. Don't!'

'What's wrong? Maybe they're just going round the village.'

'No they're not. She's only just got back. She mustn't leave.'

They heard the faint sound of the car door slamming shut, the noise finally reaching them three or four beats after the sight of it, then watched as the car drove away, dipping out of their view below the hill.

'No!' The word burst out of Ferney, overflowing with anguish.

'Calm down. They might not be going far.'

'It's too soon to go anywhere. She knows who she is because she's here. If she goes away, she'll lose it.'

'She won't remember?'

'Worse than that. She'll bury it and mistrust it and it will turn round and bite her.'

'They might be heading back to the house for all you know. Let's go down there.'

Ferney strode ahead in desperate silence, listening to every distant car. Rachel watched, disturbed, as he found the key and unlocked the door.

'Just remember, it's not your house,' she said, 'and I'm not happy about you walking in like that, but I need to look for something while we're here. I need to see if he kept their old diaries, but I want you to know that I'm doing that in my client's interests and that means it's all right for me to be in the house. I'm not so sure about you.'

He took no notice of her and sat looking out of the kitchen window towards the gate while she searched. The cupboards were full of boxes, a messy avalanche of books and papers. When she found the diaries for 1993 and 1994, she leafed back through them. There were five or six entries saying 'Phone Angela' with no number, then she came to the first entry and there it was—'Angela, healer', but when she dialled, all she got was a message saying it was no longer in use. She ruffled through the pages again and a small piece of paper fluttered out. It was thin, brittle, stained and yellowed—an oblong label. She angled it to the light and saw writing—"November 1823". There was something else but the ink was faded. She went over to the light. It said "For F and G, with affection JO." She took it to show Ferney.

'Do you know what this is? F and G, is that for Ferney and Gally? It must be, mustn't it? November, eighteen twenty-three? Who was JO?'

He was staring at the label.

'You know something, don't you?' she said. 'I can tell. Have you seen it before?'

'Are you sure it says JO?'

She looked again. 'I can't tell exactly. It's very faded.'

'JO,' he said. 'Well, maybe you're right.'

'Does that matter?'

'Oh yes.'

'Will you tell me?'

'Not now. It doesn't matter now. There are far more important things.' He sounded frantic. 'They're not coming back, are they?'

CHAPTER 26

As Jo, she would have kept it all to herself, but in this place Gally was supreme and Gally knew only the plain truth would do. They stood on the ramparts of the old camp, staring east between the trees. Gally talked as if to herself, half surprised by what she knew. 'It didn't look like this,' she said. 'They kept it clear. The forest grew all round but up here, you had to be able to see. We knew they would be coming from over there and we took our turn watching.'

'They? Who are they?'

'The Saxons, Cenwalch's men. They never forgot his name round here. They call him Kenny Wilkins these days.'

'Exactly when are we talking about?'

Gally had to think. 'We didn't do dates. It was five summers after this or ten winters before that or in the eighth year of the reign of some king, but Ferney's told me since then. It was the year 658.'

'658. You mean over thirteen hundred years ago?'

'Yes.'

'And you *remember* that?'

'I remember remembering it. Ferney says—I mean, I think every time we go back to an old memory we change it a bit.'

'So you're not sure.'

'Yes, I'm sure.'

'It's all Ferney this and Ferney that with you. This boy you've just met seems to have a lot to say about this.'

'This man I've always known.'

Her mother let it pass. 'So why are we here?'

'There's nothing before this. Right here, this was the first time. That's why I've brought you.'

'And what happened here that made you so special?'

Gally looked sideways at her mother, who was staring straight in front of her, tight-lipped.

'Go on,' said Fleur. 'Just tell me whatever story you've got to tell then we can get out of here.'

'A lot of men came here. It seemed like all the men of Somerset,' said Gally. 'They knew it was the best place to stop the Saxons. They camped down by the village because there was no water here. Villagers like me did sentry duty because we knew the land. You had a fire you kept burning and a pile of green leaves to put on it to make smoke. Horns to blow too. But while I was on watch, it poured down and my fire went out. Then all at once we could hear them down in the valley through the mist and the rain, all those feet and

323

their swords rattling. I grabbed the horn and I ran as hard as I could.'

She turned and looked south, found herself gasping in her attempts to blow a warning, twisting back as she ran to see Saxon men pouring from the trees. Something brave in her made her stop in her terror, made her stand still as all those men charged towards her, made her take breath after juddering breath as they came nearer and blow and blow the warning until the sweating, stinking men surrounded her. They pulled the horn from her hands and crushed it under their boots. In the present, she became aware that she had stopped talking and knew she must not drift into this silent reverie.

'They caught me,' she said. 'They carried me back here to the camp and left me tied up in the rain. Later their men started coming back, hundreds of them with blood on their tunics and their swords. They brought in girls, my friends, tied wrist to wrist in a line. Nobody else. All the time I was thinking it was my fault for not sounding the alarm fast enough, my fault my family were dead. Then the big red-haired man started giving the girls as prizes to his soldiers. He was Cenwalch. He kept me back for himself.'

'Jo . . .'

Was it concern? She couldn't tell. 'No, this is the part that matters. There was a boy about my age left behind to guard me until the men came back. I thought he smiled at me when nobody could see.' She turned and looked back into the old rampart ring. 'It was still raining and the men were building a shelter for their king. I was tied to a tree just over there. Then the boy was in front of me, cutting my

324

ropes, with his finger to his lips for silence. He looked at me as if to ask where we should go and I didn't argue. We ran over the bank and along the hunting path and down to the village, where all the dead were lying like sacks of meat, then round the hill to my family's house. There were no bodies there.'

'This boy. Could you talk to him?'

'No, but he pointed to himself and said his name and I told him mine.'

'And those names were? No, let me guess. He was Ferney and you were?'

'Gally.'

'Gally? Is that what it is then, your other name? Your so-called real name. Is it Gally?'

Her daughter nodded.

Fleur shook her head as if to clear it. 'I can't call you that. It turns you into someone else.'

'You don't have to.'

'Go on.'

'We were tired and scared and wet and we lay there holding each other in the hut. Before dawn they came looking and we ran for it down through the pig fields towards the trees with them whooping and chasing, and they threw a spear which cut my leg and this boy, this thin Saxon boy, picked me up and ran with me until there was no more time or breath. We came to what the village called the place of life, a little clearing round a stone, and he turned his back to shield me between him and the stone and that was where they . . .' she fell silent, stunned by the force of that memory.

'Where was this?'

'It's the Bag Stone.'

'Bag?'

325

'From the old word for life, *beagh*. They brought sick people to sleep next to it.'

'That house. That's Bagstone Farm?'

'Yes, that's where the stone is.'

'So then you say you died and, the next time, you were both born here again?'

Gally looked at her mother, surprised at her tone of reasonable acceptance. 'Oh. Yes, we must have been.'

'You don't remember that?'

Gally realised to her surprise that it felt nowhere within easy reach, as if this second life had not been part of the canon of her central memories. She saw her mother turn away to stare bleakly across to the far hills.

'I didn't know this would happen,' said Gally. 'It was round the campfire. They were talking about the old castles here. Then the dig ended. Did they tell you?'

'Yes. You went walking and you came straight here?'

'We came to Alfred's Tower,' said Gally, remembering her sight of Ferney and his bicycle.

'Oh, I think I've been *there*.'

'Have you?'

'Before you were born. Is it the same place? It sticks up through the trees, all by itself. You climb up a spiral staircase. Is it near here?'

'Very near.' She nodded towards the north.

'I'd like to go there,' said Fleur, so they did and on the way, moving further from the village's packed core of association and memory, Gally felt herself and her certainties stretching thin and her mother moving back into the vacuum. Fleur too was going through some sort of change. As

326

they came out of the trees and saw the tower in the clearing she said, 'Yes, that's the place,' with a catch in her voice, and then, 'Can we go up to the top?'

Gally felt a froth of anxiety at the centre of her being. Ferney and Pen were still out there but they felt at full arm's stretch, like a rescuer just clinging on.

They climbed to the roof and the girl saw tears streaming down the woman's face as she stood there looking out. She was astonished. In all their life together, even when they were running from the press in Yorkshire, even on the one and only time they had visited her father's grave, she had never once seen Fleur cry.

'What's wrong, Mum?'

'We came here.'

'Who did?'

'Me and Toby—me and your dad.'

'Why are you crying?'

'I'm not crying,' Fleur said fiercely. She looked away and they stood in silence. 'He didn't want me to climb up here,' she said after a while. 'He didn't want me to but I did anyway.' She sounded much younger, but only for a moment. 'He wasn't going to stop me,' she said, and she was Fleur again.

'Why didn't he want you to climb up?'

'Because of you. I was five months pregnant. He thought the stairs might be icy.'

'Icy?'

'It was a freezing day, just after the New Year. It wasn't open, but it was for his work. He used to advise on a lot of ancient buildings. That was the part of his job he liked best. They put us up in a nice pub, somewhere near here.'

327

It was the first time she could ever remember her mother talking about him. Fleur's face changed shape as she talked, as if what had been bones were only muscles after all and had finally relaxed. She went on talking as if to herself. 'He ran all the way up to the top to make sure it was safe for me before he'd let me come up too. I had a bit of a wobble when I got there and that upset him.'

'What was he like?'

'How can I answer that?'

'Well, were you happy? Was he a kind man?'

Fleur turned away, facing into a swirl of wind which lifted a twisting cloud of leaves towards them. When she turned back, her face had set into its familiar shape again 'He left me.'

'Left you? He died.'

'That wasn't the deal.' She blinked. 'Come on, tell me what happened here.'

But distance had its effect and as the girl tried to tell the story of the boy below with his bicycle, she faltered. It sounded to her as if she was relating a tale told to her by someone else. The boy with the bicycle was now everything that mattered to her and she could not see him, could barely even feel him any more through Jo's eyes and the cladding of Jo's mind. The land stretched out below her was scenery in a film, not the setting of her life as it had been. She stared south down the ridge, reaching out towards him, but it was faint comfort and it did not help her with her words so in the end she stumbled to a halt, leaving the story half-told and her mother unmoved and incurious.

They walked most of the way back to the village in silence but for Gally it was a happier silence,

328

strengthening with every step. Fleur stopped by the car and put her hands on her hips. 'Right,' she said, 'enough nonsense. Now you'll kindly explain the main thing you keep dodging.'

'What's that?'

'Let's forget about all this past lives stuff for a minute. The simple question is, who is this man Martin and why have you been visiting the house of a murderer? I'd like an answer, please.'

Gally turned to the church gate, knowing that she had gone too far down the path of explanation to turn back now. 'This is difficult,' she said, 'but the best way I can explain it is to show you something.'

She led her mother to the grave and Fleur watched, baffled, as her daughter knelt on the grass in front of it. 'Who is it?' she demanded, then bent to read the inscription. 'Gabriella and Rosie Martin? They were the names the policeman said. What's this got to do with you?'

'Gabriella was Mary Martha Gabriella when she was christened, but as she got older she preferred Gabriella. She didn't know why, except that she liked to shorten it.'

'To what?'

'To Gally.'

Gillian looked back down at the gravestone. 'So what's this supposed to mean?'

'Do you see the date on the grave?' She bent and traced it with her finger, 'There, January 31st 1994.'

'That's before you were born.'

'Four months before I was born, yes.'

Fleur knelt down next to her and stared at the gravestone. 'Are you trying to tell me this Gabriella was you?'

'Yes.'

'So who was Rosie?'

'My daughter.'

'So Gabriella Martin was married to Michael Martin, the man I met at that cottage, the one whose phone number you gave the girls, and he's the one who *murdered* his wife and his daughter? Murdered you?'

'It's not true.' She didn't know exactly what happened but she knew it wasn't that.

'So you tell me. How did they both die?' Her mother stopped herself, got to her feet, rubbed dry grass cuttings from her skirt and reached out to touch the gravestone as if she needed to know it was really there.

Gally could not respond because a kaleidoscope of deaths was whirling through her from all corners of the graveyard earth. A middle-aged woman came out of the church carrying an armful of wilting flowers and walked past them towards the gate. Fleur swung round.

'Excuse me,' she said. 'Do you live here?'

'Oh yes,' the woman answered. 'Just down there.' The armful of flowers turned her gesture into a vague and hampered movement which took in half the available three hundred and sixty degrees.

'I wonder,' Fleur said, 'could you possibly tell us what happened to these two?' She pointed down at the gravestone and the other woman read the inscription, looking surprised.

'Oh, the Martins. We only moved here the year before but I remember it well. Everyone was talking about it.'

'How did they die?'

'Well, that was the question, wasn't it? Still is. We all thought at the time that he'd done it, the husband, but he got off.' She dropped her voice. 'He still lives in the village. I don't think anybody talks to him but my neighbour knew them and she reckons it wasn't him at all.' She nodded towards the stone. 'She reckons it was her, the mother, that did it. Said she went a bit bonkers. Post-natal depression, she thought. Poisoned the poor little thing. You're not a relation, are you?'

'No.'

'Are you just passing through then?'

'Yes.'

'It's just I ought to ask. Neighbourhood Watch, you know. We have to keep an eye on the church and everything. Oh dear, what's wrong with your daughter?'

Gally had sunk to the ground and was clenching and unclenching her fists. Her face was white, her eyes wide and staring.

'Jo?' said her mother. 'Now what's wrong?'

'Ferney, I need Ferney.'

'Come with me. Let's get you in the car.' But the girl seemed unable to walk so Gillian and the other woman had to take an arm each and half carry her to the BMW.

'Is she ill?' the other woman asked.

'I'll see to her. Don't worry.'

'The cottage,' said Gally in tones of desperation as her mother started the car. 'Take me to the cottage. He'll be there. He must be there. Or the hill.'

'Yes,' said her mother and drove south, but at the junction below the village, where the cottage

331

lay to the left, she turned right.

'No,' said Gally, urgently. 'It's back that way. Turn round.'

'It may be,' said her mother, 'but I'm not going there. Home's this way. We're going home.'

'I have to go back to him.'

'You're not going anywhere near him, whoever he is.'

'No. Stop the car.'

They came to the slip road on to the A303 and Fleur accelerated.

'Don't. Stop it. I'm not coming. I can't. I don't belong with you.'

'Yes you do,' Fleur shouted back at her. 'You bloody well do. I've had enough of all this rubbish. I should never have trusted those two. You're going to stop it right now and you're going straight back on the pills.'

Gally tugged the handle and tried to push the door open against the wind. Fleur lunged past her, the car snaking and a horn blowing behind her. The door slammed shut and she hit the central locking button.

'Why are you doing this to me?' the girl cried.

'I'm responsible for you. I'm doing it *for* you, not to you.'

She tried to reach the ignition key to turn the engine off but her mother slapped her hand hard. She flinched away, looked back, and there was the heart-punching sight of the receding ridge through the back window. The village and him and love and safety and her future were all leaving her, disappearing backwards at eighty miles per hour, and she knew she could not stand it.

'You don't believe me, do you?' she said

332

wretchedly.

'No, I don't. I need to get you home.'

'But *that's* my home,' Gally wailed.

'Home is where your family is. I'm your family, in case you'd forgotten.'

'Can't we just stop for a minute?'

'I'm not stopping.'

Her mother accelerated again, pulling out to pass a truck. The speedo was touching ninety.

'But I owe them.'

'Who's them?'

'Ferney and . . . and Mike, for what I did.'

'What did you do?'

Five miles back Gally could have answered that clearly, but they were still doing over eighty and her clarity was fading away at more than a mile a minute.

'You saw, back there.'

'I didn't see anything that made sense. You tell me, what did I see?'

She couldn't answer. Fleur glanced at her and she was frowning, her mouth working as if words were reaching her lips then turning back.

'I don't know any more,' she whispered in the end, and all she did know was that something was dying inside her and she might never see him again and she didn't even know who it was she might not see again. Her head was full of ghosts and there was nobody to save her.

Fleur shot a quick glance at her daughter as she braked for the Ilchester roundabout, wondering if she would make another bid to open the door, but her eyes were closed. They opened again a few miles further on and she jumped as her daughter screamed.

333

'I killed him,' she said. 'I know I did. Edgar. I sent you off and you died. Sebbi, why did they take you? Ferney, don't go. Keep away. You can't have him. No, don't do that. It's not your fault. It will be all right.' Her mother looked at her in horror, seeing the girl's head jerking from side to side and her eyes focusing far away, then she dropped her voice as if talking to a child or maybe a pet. 'Sebbi's dead, poor Sebbi's dead and Ferney too. Why should Gally stay? What's to keep me?'

'Jo,' said her mother. 'Stop it. I don't like this.'

'Put it down, Rosie. Don't be frightened, darling. Don't be frightened. I'll explain when you're older.' The girl began to sing in a harsh voice,

> *'Alone on the hill in the mist's winter smoke*
> *That's when loneliness cuts like a knife*
> *For death still has power to play its old joke*
> *When it takes away only one life*
> *When it takes away only one life . . .'*

'They can't hurt us, brother,' she called, and her voice was different again. 'There's only you and me. Leave him. Don't hurt him.'

For the rest of that interminable journey, she alternated between eyes closed silence and sudden outbursts of what seemed to Fleur's ears to be increasingly random nonsense, until at last Fleur nosed the car into the garage at the Exeter flats and turned the engine off. Jo suffered herself to be led up the stairs by the arm, and when Fleur opened the door she went straight to her bedroom. When her mother looked in five minutes later she was asleep with her clothes still on.

At eleven the next morning when Ali and Lucy rang the bell, Fleur beckoned them into the kitchen, holding a warning finger to her lips. 'She's in her bedroom,' she told them. 'Can you go and see her?'

'Yes, of course,' said Ali. 'What's she told you?'

'Nothing at all,' said Fleur. 'She hasn't said a word since she got back.'

'What, you mean she's refusing to talk to you?'

'I wish it was as simple as that, but it's more like she can't talk any more. She looks at me as if she wants to but she just can't. I don't know what's going on, but you're going to tell me, aren't you? Right now.'

CHAPTER 27

Fleur interrogated the two girls, making them describe the whole trip from the moment they left Exeter to the moment they came back.

'Did anything else happen?'

'Nothing that matters,' Ali said. Lucy shook her head.

'She didn't bang her head or fall over or anything?'

'No.'

'Did you take any drugs? I won't be angry. I just need to know.'

'We drank wine round the fire at the dig. We had a beer in a pub when we were walking,' said

335

Lucy. 'We looked old enough because of the dirt. She ate some mushrooms.'

'Magic mushrooms?'

Lucy flinched. 'No, the ordinary kind.'

'I would say Jo's psychotic,' Fleur said. 'She's never been as bad as this before. It must be drugs of some sort. Come on. You have to tell me.'

'I've never taken any drug,' said Ali indignantly, 'and I'm sure Jo hasn't.'

Fleur swung round on Lucy, who turned pink. 'What about you?' she asked, and Lucy said, 'I haven't either,' in a small and unconvincing voice. She was pink not because she was lying but because she had recently tried to give her friends the impression that she was dangerously sophisticated in that direction.

Fleur immediately forgot her promise and became angry. Drugs were the only explanation, she said. She was going to get to the bottom of this. Did they have Jo's backpack? she asked, because she wanted to search it.

They had no idea where Jo's backpack was. It was still sitting, quite forgotten, in the hayloft over the old barn.

'Have you talked to a doctor?' Ali asked to try to deflect her.

'I'm going to,' said Fleur, 'oh yes, but that will have to wait until this afternoon. Then there's the other thing—this boy Ferney and the man, Michael Martin. You've hardly said anything about them.'

'There's not much to say. We only met the boy for ten minutes.'

Fleur thought of telling them about the arrest but decided to keep that to herself for the moment. 'Now,' she said, 'I need you two because I can't stay here all day. I've got a site meeting to go to and the architect's coming all the way from Bath.'

'We can stay with her,' said Ali.

'No,' said Fleur. 'Definitely not. You will have to come with me, all three of you, then you two can look after her while I'm at the house. It's down near the sea so I can drop you at the beach. She can be as crazy as she likes on the beach. She's in bed. I get her up but she goes straight back there as soon as I'm looking the other way. Can you try? We need to go in half an hour.'

On the stairs Lucy hissed, 'What a bitch. She thinks it was our fault.'

'She's just worried, that's all.'

'The only person she's worried about is herself.'

They stood outside Jo's bedroom door nervously until Lucy plucked up her courage and knocked lightly. 'Jo,' she called, 'it's only us.'

There was no answer so they pushed the door open. Neither of them wanted to go in but neither of them wanted to go back downstairs to face Fleur. Jo was lying on her bed, flat on her back with her hands together in an attitude of prayer as if modelled in marble. She sat up when they came in and looked at them with hardly a hint of recognition. There were shadows under her eyes.

'Jo? How are you feeling?' Ali asked.

'I killed him,' said Jo in a tired voice.

'You didn't kill anybody. Come on, let's get you up.'

'You don't know.'

'I do know. I've known you for a long time.'

'No you haven't.'

'I have to say you're freaking me out a bit,' said Lucy. 'Can we talk about something else?' But Jo shook her head.

Ali thrust clothes at her, orchestrated with a false and cheerful chatter, helping her put them on. Jo was clumsy in her movements. They led her downstairs, out to the car park, and with great difficulty, because it was a two-door coupé, they persuaded her into the back of the BMW, next to Ali. The girls made brittle conversation and she showed no interest while Fleur drove in a grim silence out of Exeter and south-west on the A38. At last they came to a narrow road, undulating south through gentle hills. Fleur kept looking at the time and was driving fast, braking hard when they met anyone coming the other way.

'They should widen this road,' she complained.

'My father says it takes sixty years to drive down here,' said Ali, 'because you have to go back to 1950. He says it's the land that time forgot.'

'Does he? He's full of that sort of thing, is he?'

A long hill took them down to Slapton. The first few houses were a modern rim around the village, then older cottages crept inwards to a width intended for horses. A church stood on the right, down the slope of a wide graveyard. Ahead, a dark stone tower thrust up from the trees. At the sight of it, something inside Jo seemed to switch on. She turned and leant over, staring at the tower through the side window. The road passed into a narrow canyon of high stone walls, then twisted through right-angle bends. Jo turned and gazed at the tower through the rear window as it came back into view.

'I've been here,' she said in a voice croaky with disuse.

'Of course you have,' said Ali encouragingly.

338

'We had a picnic on the beach before exams. Slapton Sands, remember?'

'No, I mean here. I've been here.' She stared back until another gentle slope took the village out of sight, then slumped into her former torpor.

They came down to the junction with the coast road, into the great sweep of Start Bay. Fleur slewed to a halt in the car park where the American war memorial stood.

'I'll be an hour,' she said. 'I'll pick you up here. Be ready.'

Jo opened the door by herself and the girls smiled as if a child had just learnt a new trick. Her mother drove away, back to the village.

'Come on then,' Lucy said. 'Race you to the sea.'

They plunged down through the shingle towards the waves, Lucy out in front, then Ali shouted, 'Wait! She's not coming.'

It took them longer to scramble back up the steep shingle bank. They stared along the beach and couldn't see her anywhere, then Ali turned to look inland. Jo was already far away, walking fast back towards the village and the tower.

'What's she doing?' Lucy asked in exasperation.

'I haven't a clue, but we'd better go after her.'

They had to wait for a line of summer tourists' cars to go by, then run to catch her up, but even then she wouldn't slow down or respond to them. At the outskirts of the village she stopped dead and stared up. The black wreck of the massive tower loomed ahead above the walls, haloed by a dozen rooks wheeling and rasping.

'It was new,' she said in a tone of wonder.

'What was?' asked Lucy.

She pointed at the tower.

339

'Well, of course it was, once. Everything was new once. I weighed six pounds three ounces once.'

Jo was looking all about her. There was no obvious way to get to the tower. She walked up a short drive to locked gates and rattled the handle, then she came back down to where the two girls stood.

'Come on,' she said. 'It's further up.'

'What is?'

'The way in,' was all she answered and they followed her along the road.

'What's she doing?' Lucy whispered.

'I don't know,' Ali whispered back, 'but she sounds different, more like she's making sense.'

Jo turned into a narrow entry. A whitewashed pub stood in a yard at the end. Its name, The Tower Inn, was lettered in a gap between the upper windows. The tower itself hulked over it on the far side of a high wall. Round turrets ran up its four corners. One still rose to its full height above the main walls but the other three had crumbled, broken off level with the ragged top of the parapet. An elderly couple were sitting at a wooden table outside the pub.

'It was here,' said Jo.

'What was?'

'The Chantry. This was the guest house. We stayed here.'

'Who did?'

'Ferney and me.'

'Ferney? The boy from the village? When?'

'For the opening.'

'Did they used to open it?'

The elderly couple had stopped drinking and were taking an obvious interest in the girls.

'When it was new. When he built it.'

'Oh, ha ha,' said Lucy. 'It must be at least three hundred years old.'

'More like six hundred,' said the woman at the table. 'We've just been reading about it. This man Sir something or other built it in thirteen something.'

'Thank you,' said Lucy. 'It's always nice to get precise information. See, Jo? Thirteen something.'

'It was an honour that he invited us. He let Ferney read it out. Ferney could read, you see.'

'I should hope so,' said Lucy. 'If you came here with Ferney, why doesn't your mum know? She's never heard of him,' but Jo just frowned and turned away.

Ali put her mouth up to Lucy's ear. 'Be gentle,' she whispered. 'Don't put her off.'

Jo turned back to them. 'He read it well,' she said. 'I was proud.'

'What did he read?' Ali asked in her encouraging voice.

'Would you like to hear it?'

'Yes, please.'

Jo looked at the ground, concentrating, then turned to stare back at the tower again and delivered her words to the stones.

'Old men who stay behind, do not inflame the young with words of war,' she began, and her voice had a rich depth and an intonation that was entirely unfamiliar to them. 'The ruin that you risk should be your own, not theirs. Young men take care. To make you fight they first must make you fear, then out of that shape hate.'

'Mould hate, dear,' said the old woman at the table. 'It's "mould", not "shape".'

341

They turned to look at her in surprise.

'You know it too?' asked Ali.

'Well, I don't *know* it but it's what we've just been reading. I've got it here.'

'What is it?'

The woman looked at the sheet of paper. 'It's called the Declaration of Sir Guy de Bryan.'

'Where did you get it from?'

'The village shop. Sorry, do go on, dear, I didn't mean to interrupt. It's lovely to hear the words out loud. Do you know the rest of it?' but Jo took no notice of her. She seemed to have lost her thread.

'When did you learn it?' the woman asked.

Now Jo finally seemed to register her. 'Long ago,' she said.

'Long ago? Well, that's a shame,' said the old man. 'The shop woman's been telling porkies and it was such a good story.'

His wife continued for him. 'She said they'd only found it recently. Dug it up or something. She said it was so good they thought they'd print it. It was a lovely tale.'

'They've only had it in the shop two weeks,' her husband added. 'We're one of her first customers. This is a first edition, this is.'

'It talks all about it on the bottom here. Shall I read it out?' The woman bent her head. 'Sir Guy de Bryan's Declaration was inscribed on a stone tablet on the wall of his Chantry tower at Slapton, built in 1372 so that masses could be sung for his soul. The Chantry fell into ruin in the sixteenth century after Henry the Eighth's dissolution of chantries and monasteries. Only the tower and the walls of the Tower Inn, on the site of the original guesthouse, still remain. Broken fragments of the

Declaration survived in a worn condition. When further missing pieces were discovered in recent years, it was possible to assemble the whole text. It stands out as a heartfelt rejection of war by one of the most honourable warrior knights of the fourteenth century.'

Jo looked round at them and her eyes were shining with pleasure. 'That's right,' she said. 'Now shall we go back to the sea?'

'Oh, yes please,' said Ali. This time Jo walked more slowly and to start with she seemed to have a clear awareness of her two friends, though still with a reserve as if they had only recently met.

'What did you mean back there?' Lucy asked her. 'You said you stayed there.'

'Did I? I thought I had.'

'It must have been in the pub.'

'It probably was.'

'Your mum would know.'

'Perhaps she would.'

'Are you feeling better?'

'I'm—I'm glad to be here. I'm pleased to see you,' but that was it until they got to the sea, where she seemed at first to be looking for something she couldn't find, then became fascinated by the Start Point lighthouse at the western end of the bay, until all at once distress swept over her and she sat down on the shingle, wrapping her arms around her knees, and began to weep.

The girls sat down each side of her. 'What's happened to you, Jo?' Ali asked gently, stroking her arm, but she got no response at all.

'Look,' said Lucy. 'Shall I show you the pictures I took on the dig?' She held her mobile phone up in front of Jo. 'See? That's you two putting up the

343

tent, and there's Andy and the boys. That's the tattooed bloke—what was he called? Dozey? There's Ali and Conrad.'

'I didn't know you'd taken that,' said Ali, embarrassed.

'Now we're walking. That's Glastonbury and that one too, and that's the view from King Arthur's Tower—'

'Alfred's,' said Ali.

'Whatever, and that's—oh no, you don't want to see that. Let me . . .'

But Jo had reached out to grab the phone from Lucy's hand and was looking at it with an expression of delight on her face. 'Ferney,' she said and looked eagerly around her as if the phone was a mirror, reflecting him somewhere behind her. She frowned when she couldn't see him, looked at the phone again and turned it over as if that might help.

'Where is he?' she asked. 'That's his picture,' as if the other two might not understand. 'I need him. Do you see? He knows how to make it all better. He was here. We sat on this beach and the men with the boats had houses here. They've gone. They've all gone.'

'He's not here, Jo.'

'I'm not Jo.'

'You are.'

'I'm Gally. That's my name.'

Lucy looked at Ali, eyebrows raised. 'All right . . . Gally,' she said, 'why don't you tell us about Ferney?'

'I love him,' the girl said, and her face had come back to life, her eyes glistening as she looked from one to the other of them. 'Where is he? Do you

344

know? I have to find him. It's not worth it without him. It never has been. He knows everything about me. He knows how to make it right and I know how to make it right for him. He brought me here when I needed healing and Guy needed healing too, and we talked here until we had the words that said exactly what we felt. Do you see?' The girls were stunned by her utter certainty. 'Will you help me find him?' she said.

'When you say Guy, is that the same Guy the woman just told us about?' Ali asked.

'Yes.'

'In . . . um . . . 1370? You remember that?'

'I can remember bits of all our lives, all the way back. Ferney and Gally, Ferney and me.'

'And this man, Guy?'

'Oh, poor Guy,' said Gally. 'We had him in the cottage, you see. I was looking after him. The cuts were bone-deep and they weren't clean. Then Ferney heard noises outside but when he ran out the men had gone, ridden off, but they had left him lying there.'

'Who?'

'The dead man—well, a boy still really. Guy hadn't known him, you see? In the fight, he had a cloth round his face and it was kill or be killed. He had no choice. It was awful for him. He shouldn't have got up but when he heard the fuss he came limping out, leaning on the wall, and he saw what we had lying at our feet. He knew him then. He knew his own son and in case he didn't after all those years apart, they had painted Guy's own crest in blood on the boy's shirt. So do you see? It was Molyns' revenge. Guy was grieving and I was grieving because we both killed our sons, and that's why Guy did it. That's why he built his Chantry here.'

'Are you sure you killed somebody?'

'Oh yes. I killed her.'

'You said you killed your son.'

'That's right.'

'I don't even know what a chantry is,' said Lucy to get back to more solid ground.

'It was for his soul, so the priests would say prayers for his immortal soul to free it from his sins. He thought he would suffer eternity in purgatory otherwise. Ferney told him he was wrong.' The girl's voice became matter-of-fact, almost amused. 'He told him there was no purgatory and we should know, but Guy said that might be true for us but not for him. So we shared our sorrow and we wrote the words for both of us because I had killed my son too, you see?'

'Poor Gally,' said Lucy in a soft voice.

'Did it help?' Ali asked.

'Not the building, not all the priests, not all the masses they sang. But the words helped.'

'Your mother's here,' said Ali, looking up the shingle bank to the figure of a woman beckoning to them from the top.

'She's not my mother. I must find Ferney. Will you help me, please? You're my friends. He's the only way for me. Please?'

They heard Fleur shouting.

'We'd better go.'

They steered her back to the car, one each side, and Fleur looked at them questioningly.

'It's fine,' said Ali. 'We've been just fine.'

'I'm actually quite hungry,' said Lucy. 'Do you mind stopping at the shop?'

346

Fleur pulled over with a bad grace in Slapton's narrow street and Lucy came back to the car with a carrier bag, offering sandwiches. Jo took hers but inspected the triangular plastic box with puzzled fascination, tapped it against the window, then handed it politely back.

It all stopped being fine as soon as they drove out of Slapton because Jo's distress mounted to the point where she was twisting violently to see behind her, clawing at the door handle, sobbing and calling out in strings of disconnected and mostly incomprehensible words.

Fleur pulled over, got out slamming the door, and made a call on her mobile. 'We're going straight to the surgery,' she announced when she got back in. 'I'm not taking her home like this. I thought you said she was okay.'

'She was.'

As they approached Exeter, Jo quietened down and curled herself up, twisting to one side as much as the seat belt would let her. The surgery was a private practice in a leafy street just outside the city centre and a nurse came to the car to help them get Jo inside. Halfway in, Jo seemed to come to herself for a moment. She stopped, clutched Lucy's sleeve and said, 'Find him. Tell him. Tell him I'm sorry,' then the girls had to sit and wait while Fleur and Jo were taken into the consulting room.

'This is all wrong,' said Lucy when they were alone. 'I sometimes think her mother doesn't give a toss for her.'

'It's very difficult,' said Ali, judiciously. 'I mean, she is saying some pretty weird things.'

'But supposing it's true? I think it is. I really

347

think it is. Imagine if they've been lovers forever, those two.'

'How can it be? It's not one of your stories, Lucy. This is real. It doesn't happen.'

Lucy said nothing in reply. She reached for a magazine and stared at it without reading it until Fleur came back into the room.

'We're taking her to a private clinic,' she said. 'She'll be better treated there. Can you two get yourselves home?'

Something brave stirred in Lucy. 'Does she want to go?' she asked.

'That's neither here nor there,' Fleur retorted. 'It's what's best for her.'

'She's over sixteen,' Lucy said. 'Can't she make up her own mind about that?'

'She's having delusions,' Fleur said evenly. 'She thinks she's killed somebody and sometimes it's a boy and sometimes it's a girl. She doesn't even know her own name. She keeps asking for this boy you left her with. If she won't go voluntarily, she will have to be sectioned—that's their advice. Now go home before I lose my temper.' She spun round and left them staring after her.

'What does sectioned mean?' Ali asked faintly.

'I think it's that thing where they cut your brain in half, isn't it?'

'That's called a lobotomy.'

'I'm not letting them do that to Jo,' said Lucy.

348

CHAPTER 28

Detective Inspector Meehan was having a difficult day. The Duty Prosecutor thought the case against Michael Martin was evidentially weak but that was because, Meehan had belatedly discovered, his Detective Sergeant had missed out one page of the toxicology report in the evidence file. Just as he had put that right, the Duty Prosecutor had managed to get himself stung by a bee, suffered a severe anaphylactic reaction and had been carted off to hospital. The Crown Prosecution Service was sorting out a replacement but had warned him it might take another hour and his time was running out. Meehan could only hold the teacher for twenty-four hours without a very good reason for needing more time and yet he knew in his bones something had always been very wrong with this case.

When the CPS finally rang back, he found Anna Murray on the other end of the phone—the person least likely to be impressed by his argument.

'There's a hole in this file a mile wide,' she said before he had a chance to say more than hello. 'There's all their new thinking on the timing of the lethal effects but you're still relying on the original analysis of the poison by the old methods. His lawyers will say you can't change the rules on one and not the other.'

Meehan knew the lawyer in question was Leo Avery, who had never been known to say anything nearly so clever. 'So what are you suggesting?'

'That you need new samples.'

349

'I need to dig them up?'

'If you haven't still got original tissue samples in good condition, then yes. You need an exhumation order.'

Meehan looked at his watch. 'In that case, I'll need an extension. It's coming up to the twenty-four hours.'

'Frankly, I think you're out on a limb here. He's not going to run away.'

'If I get the order, can I hold on to him until the forensics come through?'

'I very much doubt it but call me if you get it in time.' She hung up.

He stared at the phone, resisting the temptation to throw it at the wall, then he called downstairs and set things in motion. He looked at his watch again and began working it out. Something in him did not want to let Michael Martin go, even if he could be rearrested later. He wondered if the news that Martin's wife and child were going to be dug up might be enough to shock a confession out of the man. Leo Avery seemed at least halfway to believing in his own client's guilt. There wasn't quite enough time but Avery might just allow him the few extra minutes he needed for the questioning and Martin himself certainly had no idea about proper procedures.

The front desk buzzed him to say the lawyer had arrived.

'Show him to the interview room,' Meehan said. 'Don't bring Martin up yet. I'll have a quick word first.'

He walked in with a forced smile and a quip ready on his lips about the mess Leo had made at the third green last weekend, but there was a tiger

350

waiting for him in the room. Rachel Palmer, crouched and ready to spring, looked at her watch and said, 'You have exactly eight minutes to charge my client or release him, Meehan. Which is it going to be?'

Mike didn't say a word until they were in the car. 'Thank you,' he said as they drove away. 'I thought you had given up on me.'

She looked at the harsh lines on his face. 'So did I.'

'What changed your mind?'

'That can wait,' she said. 'We need to talk to Gally.'

'Where is she?'

'Her mother took her away. We have a very short time to sort this out because the only thing holding Meehan back is a technicality.'

'What's that?'

Rachel hesitated, understanding how upsetting this would be. 'He has to get permission to exhume them.'

'Oh no. He mustn't do that. I don't want them disturbed, not now.'

'You don't have the power to stop him. He just has to persuade a magistrate.' She glanced at him. 'There's a chance Gally could cast some light on this. It looks like our only way forward but I haven't a clue how to persuade Meehan to listen to anything she might come up with.'

*   *   *

When Rachel had left for Yeovil, Ferney had gone back to the barn. He approached it carefully but the tractor and the mechanic had gone. He was

351

going through Gally's rucksack, looking for anything that might have her address in it, when a soft series of notes began to sound. A mobile phone was ringing in the side pouch.

He pulled it out. The screen said 'Lucy'. A voice said, 'Jo? Is that you?'

'No,' he said. 'She's not here.'

'Who are *you*?'

'I'm a friend of hers. She left her phone here.'

'Where's here?'

'Pen Selwood. It's a village in—'

'Oh my goodness, is that Ferney?'

Ferney wondered if he should admit it, but there was something in her tone that sounded more like relief than suspicion. 'Yes.'

'Oh, that's amazing. She was out of her mind and then we took her to the seaside and that seemed to help, then I showed her your photo and that helped even more, and then she started telling us all about some man called Guy who seemed to matter. Then her mother came and took us all away in the car and she went peculiar again and now she's taken her off to some clinic and I think they're going to do something terrible to her brain and—'

'What clinic? Where?'

'It's near Newton Abbot and it's called the Maple Tree Clinic and there's a doctor there who's going to force her to have some sort of horrible treatment so you've got to do something about it.' She paused. 'You will, won't you? She wanted me to find you. That's so lucky. I thought she might still have the phone with her—that's why I called it. Listen, I'm sorry I was nasty to you but she's talked about you now and I believe you and I think it's

352

just the most beautiful story and you've got to help her. You will, won't you?'

'Go back a bit,' Ferney said. 'You were at this place by the seaside and you said she got better. Where was it?'

'Um, just up from Torcross? In Start Bay?'

That meant nothing to him, nothing that would explain why she had started talking about Sir Guy. 'I don't know it.'

'It's near Dartmouth?'

'No.'

'The beach is called Slapton Sands.'

And then it made sense to him and he felt his spirits lift because all at once, he could see the shape of it. 'And Slapton village, is that about a mile or so inland from there?' he asked.

'That's right.'

'Is there still a big chapel in Slapton—a chantry?'

'There's a big old tower and she knew it. She said you were there for the opening.'

'All right, Lucy. Listen to me. What have they said they're going to do to Gally?'

'To *Gally*?' Lucy tried the name on for size. 'To Gally. Okay. Her mum said they would have to section her. That was the word. We can't let them do that but I don't know how to stop them.'

*   *   *

Ferney was waiting when Rachel brought Mike back from Yeovil. He was keyed up and scarcely able to wait for them to get inside the house.

'They let you go?' he asked as Mike walked into the kitchen. The teacher was withdrawn, grey-

353

faced, hardly even aware that this boy was intruding in his house. He seemed to find it hard to answer.

'I got him out but we've only got twenty-four hours' grace,' said the lawyer. 'We're back in there at five o' clock tomorrow come hell or high water, and that's our last chance. I'm pretty sure they're going to charge him. We need Gally. We need to understand the poison she used.'

'And I need you,' Ferney said. 'Gally's in trouble.' He explained the phone call from Lucy. 'So here's the deal. You help me and I'll help you. You stop them doing whatever they're planning to do, this sectioning thing, and I'll talk to her. I'll take her back to it to see if she can help.'

'Calm down,' said Rachel. 'Sectioning doesn't mean cutting into her brain, it just means using a section of the Mental Health Act to keep her in there against her will.'

'And doing what to her?'

'Drug treatment, electroconvulsive therapy— that sort of thing.'

'And that's better, is it? She doesn't need it. She needs me to explain to her what's happening, that's all.'

'All right, all right,' said Rachel. Her phone rang. 'Oh lord,' she said, looking at the screen. 'It's my office.' She put it to her ear. 'Hello? Yes, Pauline, I know. I'm sorry but you'll have to cancel her. Yes, I'll be out tomorrow morning—at least I expect so. I may have to go to Devon.' She listened again. 'Well, just tell Leo not to bother his little head about that. It's my client, not his. I'll sort out who pays the bill later. No, tell him I'm quite capable of handling it and anyway, he hasn't been charged

354

yet.' She listened again. 'Then tell him he can stuff himself,' she said and put the phone in her pocket. She looked at them. 'Okay. It's time for some very plain speaking. I am going to suspend what's left of my disbelief. I just need to know I've got this right. Ferney, you died here. Gally gave birth the same day. She gave birth to a girl who was your child, Mike? You two called your daughter Rosie but when she was still tiny, you realised she was Ferney? Am I right so far?'

Mike could only nod. Rachel went on. 'Rosie began to show signs of great distress. When she turned two, she started self-harming. Ferney, you've more or less told me that she—you—let's just say Rosie for simplicity—was being driven mad by the whole thing? The mess of being the wrong sex and the wrong relationship?' She saw there were tears in Ferney's eyes.

'Well,' she said, 'I seem to be the only one capable of speech around here so I'll just carry on, shall I? In the end, Gally decided to stick to some old agreement that you two had and she killed herself and Rosie so that the two of you could come back for another go—a sort of "better luck next time" kind of deal. A bit harsh on Mike to say the least.'

'She's not harsh,' whispered Ferney.

'If you say so.'

'I do say so. You think it would have been easier the other way, do you?' He flung out his arm, finger pointed at Mike. 'You think it would have been easier for him to live with *me* as his daughter? Me going mad with it? What would you have done?'

'Not that.'

355

'You don't know that.' He stopped and shook his head. 'I'm sorry. Yes. That's what happened but she couldn't find another way.'

Rachel stared at him. 'I don't know what to say to that,' she said. 'Anyway, we have to persuade Gally to remember enough about how she did it to get Mike off the hook. After all, we do know that whatever she mixed up must have taken effect a lot quicker than the police are now suggesting. That is the very slender hope on which everything now rests and because it seems to be the only game in town, I'm going to take a huge professional risk and pick you up at eight o'clock tomorrow morning so that we can go down to Devon and see what she has to say.' She looked hard at Ferney. 'So yes, we need you with us. You are going to help, aren't you?'

'On condition that you help me get her back here, safe, into this house, to be with me. That's the way it has to be.'

'That's blackmail and it's an absurd thing to ask.'

'It's not up to you, it's up to Mike.'

Rachel looked at Mike, who closed his eyes. 'Mike's helped you all he can,' she said flatly. 'He's in a lot of trouble because of you. You should give something back.' Then in a moment of inspiration, she added, 'That's what Gally would say, isn't it?'

Ferney's head dipped in the suggestion of a nod and she stared at him but he said nothing else.

'I don't think we can do anything more right now. I've got to go. Lulie needs her supper. Ferney, are you going home?'

'I've left home. I've told them. I wrote a note.'

'Won't they be straight round here?'

356

'Oh sure. They care so much they've gone to Doncaster for the racing. Don't worry, I've got somewhere to go.'

'Really?' But she was distracted, thinking of time and Lulie and school finishing, so she took him at face value as he pedalled away.

She had only been gone five minutes when Ferney came back, rapped on the door and came in before Mike had a chance to get to it.

'We've got some things to sort out,' he said, standing in the kitchen.

'Oh?'

'You think you have rights to Gally.'

'She's my wife.'

'She was your wife. She's not now.'

'Maybe what matters is what she thinks about this, not you,' said Mike.

'She's feeling guilty about you,' Ferney admitted. 'That makes it worse. She needs my support every second of every day to see her through this. She needs life to be simple—her and me.'

'I can look after her. I did before. You could let us have this time. What have I got? Thirty more years if I'm lucky? You'll have her again after that, for ever and ever according to you.'

'Sit down,' said the boy. 'Sit down and listen to me.' Great age filled him out and Mike did as he was told. 'You think we've got all the time in the world, do you? What a world it's turning into. You've got only one life sentence in it. I may have it for as long as it lasts and that's supposed to be some sort of blessing, is it? Every day, that looks like a worse and worse deal. You can be vaguely sorry that the ice will melt and the sea will rise and

357

the summer will boil us and the winter will freeze us and we will have to fight over the food that's withering in the fields and water that's draining away. You can be sad for a future world and you know you will never see it and you won't have to deal with it, but I will and she will. Have you thought about that? We won't have the convenient escape of death. And you would deny us the chance to have one more good life together, would you? Even without all that it's harder and harder, not knowing how long it will take us to find each other, not knowing if we'll be the right age and if the police and the whole snooping world will let us be together.'

'The right age? You think I'm too old for her? You know very well age has got nothing to do with it. She's not really sixteen. I don't think I'm too old for her.'

'Too old?' said Ferney incredulously. 'I'm not saying you're too old for her. I'm saying you're far, far too young.'

That was when Mike finally got it, and in that moment something inside him shifted from hopeless hope to plain hopelessness. He sighed and nodded and let go of his flawed claim. 'All right then,' he said in the weariest of voices. 'I see.'

The boy stared at him and Mike stared back. 'Look after her,' he said. 'That's what matters. Are you hungry?'

'Yes.'

'So am I.' He went to look in the cupboard. 'There's eggs and beans. That's about it.'

'I'd prefer beans and eggs, if that's all right with you.'

Mike gave a surprised laugh and something

eased in the atmosphere between them.

When they had finished eating, he went to take Ferney's plate and stopped. 'What's this?' he asked, picking up the ancient label lying on the table where Rachel had left it.

'I think it's off the old picture.'

'Which one?'

'The one I left to Gally in my will.'

Mike shook his head and put it back down.

* * *

It wasn't like having a guest in the house, more like a visit from the landlord. Mike was woken in the morning by a series of bangs and went downstairs to find Ferney standing on a chair in the kitchen inspecting the ceiling with a hammer in his hand.

'There's a wedge in that beam, do you see?' he said. 'It works loose and you get a shake in the floorboards upstairs. Just needs knocking back in once in a while.'

'How long is a while?'

'Twenty years maybe.'

'But the builders did all that when we came.'

'They freshened up her make-up,' said Ferney, 'but she's still got the same old bones,' and that didn't disturb Mike. He felt as if something that had loosened the previous evening had shifted further out of the way in the night. The boy was busy round the kitchen, cooking him scrambled eggs without asking, and he didn't even mind that.

CHAPTER 29

Rachel collected them at eight on the dot. 'I emailed the clinic an hour ago,' she said. 'I told them I was a lawyer, coming to represent their patient Jo Driscoll, and I wanted to visit her this morning. We'll see what happens.'

They drove out of the village and picked up speed on the main road. No one spoke but five miles on, Mike sensed Ferney was becoming increasingly uncomfortable. He turned round to look at him, 'What is it?' he asked.

'Leaving here is harder than I expected.'

'You've done it before.'

'Not since all this got going again. It's different now.'

'Do you want me to stop?' said Rachel.

'Just for a minute.'

She pulled into the next lay-by and they got out. Ferney stood looking back the way they had come.

'What does it feel like?' Mike asked.

'Like a rubber band that might snap if I pull it too hard. I think it's like this when we first come back. We need to stay in the village for a while to feel safe, but there's no choice, is there? Think what it's like for Gally. We've got to go.'

Another car drew in behind them. It had L-plates on.

'I need to keep a tight grip on who I am,' Ferney said. 'That's all.'

A boy of eighteen or nineteen got out of the passenger's side. 'I don't know, Dad,' he said.

His father, an older version of him, was walking

360

round to swap places. 'Go on,' he said. 'You can do it.'

'There's a lot of cars today. Can't we go back to the little roads?'

'Look, Adam,' said his father, 'you have to tackle the big ones sometimes. If it gets too hard, you just pull in and I'll take over. I won't let you get into any trouble.'

They watched as the car kangarooed out into a gap in the traffic and ground away in a low gear.

'So what shall we do?' asked Mike. 'Give up or go on?' and Ferney didn't answer. He just gazed up the road where the other car had disappeared.

'Ferney?'

The boy turned back to him. 'There's a story right at the heart of all this. I think maybe it's the key. Shall I try telling it to you? It might get me there in one piece. Just give me a moment.' He stared back at the ridge, slowing his breathing down, blotting out the noises, taking away the road and the signs and the modern buildings, but he couldn't get to the precise moment in all that long, dull time. Then he knew what had set him on that path, concentrated on the father and son he had just seen and what the man had said—'I won't let you get into trouble'—and there it was.

'It might last the whole way there,' he said as he got back in the car.

'All the better,' said Mike.

He began to talk as they drove away and very soon, the car surrounding him was no longer really there.

'The church,' he said. 'It started at the church . . .'

He told them the story of Britnod the thane, and

361

his call to arms, and how he stepped in to volunteer but found his son was taken all the same. He told them of Gally's moment of choice.

'That's what's hurting her now,' he said. 'It's Edgar and what happened, and she's mixed it up with Rosie, so now she's grieving and guilty and muddled all at the same time. She thinks she killed her children twice over. It's undone all the good he did.'

'Who did?'

'A man who helped us.' He fell silent then, after a moment, he said, 'The battles of 1066. You know about them. Stamford Bridge, Hastings.'

'Yes.'

'Good. I'll skip that. Everything I know about Hastings was second-hand anyway.'

'Yes, all right.'

'So it was a few months later, after Christmas. Now, do you know about—'

Then Mike's brain caught up with his ears. 'You just said everything you knew about Hastings was second-hand.'

'Yes.'

'So does that mean that everything you knew about Stamford Bridge *wasn't* second-hand?'

'That's right.'

'That's right it *wasn't*?'

'Yes.'

'You don't mean you were there?'

'Yes, I was.'

'You fought at the battle of Stamford Bridge in September 1066?'

'Yes, I had to, but it was a very long time ago.'

'Indeed, Ferney. That's what makes it interesting. Tell us about it. Leave nothing out.'

362

The boy tried to conjure up his son again but felt only a wall of sadness. He cast around for some other point of purchase on the story and had a sense of unaccustomed weaponry, the sword belt and the helmet. It was the helmet that did it—the helmet with the nose guard that rubbed the skin of his nose raw until he heated it, bent it to fit, and then re-tempered it for strength. In his mind, he put on that helmet again and the past rushed back to meet him.

'We had to get to the muster as fast as we could. Somewhere on the Thames. Near London, I suppose.'

'How did you know where to go?'

'Our thane knew. He took us east and when we got close they'd set beacon fires to lead us in. We got there in five days' hard going.'

'But that must have been thirty-odd miles a day.'

'I suppose so. We had horses.'

'Oh, I see.'

'Well, it wasn't that easy.' Ferney sounded nettled. 'You don't gallop like they do in cowboy films. The horses would last half a day if you did that. It's walk, trot, canter, trot, walk when you're trying to do the distances.'

'I'm sorry, I didn't mean to imply it was easy.'

'Anyway, that was only the start of it. The weather was rough, gales blowing, and all the way I tried to tell Edgar enough about weapons to give him a chance. He'd never even used a sword before so it was a tall order. There were only a few hundred who beat us to the muster. We hardly had a moment to feed when three riders came tearing in, lathered up and shouting. New orders. Everybody with horses to ride north to join the

363

King. While the storms were keeping the Bastard's ships in France, Harold's rotten brother and the King of Norway had landed an army on the Yorkshire coast.

'Now *that* was a ride. I was lucky, I had my good old saddle. We fitted each other well, that horse and me, and Edgar had youth on his side. We went hard at it, from first light to after dark, and this time we galloped whenever the ground was good. We caught up with Harold halfway and we got to Tadcaster in four days flat. The history books say we did fifty miles a day on that ride. I've looked it up. They're not wrong.

'Edgar was excited but I was dreading it. I felt we were rushing to our deaths too fast to stop. There weren't nearly enough of us and we knew what those Norsemen were like. There was bad news waiting at Tadcaster, but it had good news wrapped up in it. The locals told us the Norsemen had wiped out the northern army near York but they weren't expecting us, not for days yet. They were calmly sitting there, five or six thousand of them, waiting for the losers to bring them food and horses and hostages. I doubt there were even two thousand of us, probably less, but Harold decided it was a God-given chance to catch them napping.

'Honour is a luxury when it's three to one against you. The scouts told us half of them were larking around in the river, playing games and sunbathing, no armour to be seen. Big mistake. We came charging at them over the top of the hill and there was nothing they could do but run. Very few of them got back across the bridge to their mates.'

The boy shook his head in sad wonder. 'Even then, there was this huge Norseman who nearly

364

stopped us. He was standing there in the middle of the bridge, screaming his head off. He had the biggest axe you ever saw and he was hacking everyone who came at him. I can't tell you how many of ours went down. He kicked them over the edge into the river. We were still game for it. Our men had their blood up. Not me. I never played it like that.' He fell silent again.

Mike was focused intently on Ferney's account. 'What happened?'

'It was our man Britnod. He could think sideways. He found a rotten old punt further down the bank. He ordered Edgar and this other youngster to get in it because they were the lightest. He said he would float the punt down on a rope's end, right under the bridge, so they could spear upwards between the planks. I saw what was going on and I got to the bank in time to pull Edgar out and take his place. They pushed us off and paid out the rope but the other kid was too wound-up. He gave out this ludicrous yell before we even reached the bridge, trying to shout down his own terror. The Norseman saw us coming, flung a spear, and skewered him right through the guts. Then he picked up another spear and I knew I was a sitting duck. I saw him look the other way. I heard yelling and feet pounding on the bridge and I realised they were attacking him to make a diversion. Then I was under the bridge and I could see up through the planks, where blood was running down on to me and into my eyes, and I rammed that spear up into his calf. He came down hard and they got him. He died and that was that.' Ferney paused, then he said, 'I've never been one for killing and I paid the harshest price.'

Rachel shot Mike a glance as though she could guess what was coming.

'I scrambled ashore beyond the bridge,' he said. 'We were streaming across it by that time and they were running. We were armoured and they stood no chance. It felt good for just a moment until Britnod stopped me and told me why I was still alive. That diversion was just one man, you see? One man who saw what was happening and took his sword and went for the Norseman with everything he had, which wasn't much because he wasn't even a man, he was really only a boy. He was . . .'

He had come to a halt, unable to say any more.

'He was Edgar,' said Rachel, and the boy in the back seat just nodded through grief that was almost a thousand years old.

He collected himself. 'It's never worth it,' he said. 'We shouldn't have gone. Simple as that.'

'It was an invasion,' Mike pointed out.

'Is there some special rule for the people who got there first? Think about how I arrived in Pen. I was with the invaders then. It didn't do Gally's people much good, being here first.'

'What about Hitler? What about 1940? Did you fight then?'

'I did what I could. I wasn't fit enough to fight. I did other things. That's not the point. If you're part of a tribe, you fight for your tribe. All I'm saying is don't get too high-minded about it. I went to fight so that my son didn't have to risk his life. It went against everything I believe in and it didn't work. Do you see why we didn't have children after that? It's been simpler that way.'

'What happened next?'

366

'I buried Edgar, that's what happened next. Britnod helped me. I sat with my boy all night and talked to him, then we dug him a grave right beside the bridge and we stuck the Norseman's sword in the ground as a marker, but I'm sure someone had it as a souvenir as soon as my back was turned. After that I went off to speak face to face with my sorrow and puzzle over how I was going to tell Gally. Britnod had volunteered us to stay behind and guard the bridge. The rest of our lot slaughtered the Norsemen as they ran. By the time they surrendered, there were only one in ten of them still breathing. Our lot were celebrating. We'd had to put up with the Vikings for ever and a day.'

'But how were you?' Rachel asked.

'Me? I was at the end of my tether. For the rest of them, that was when the exhilaration hit them and they could have gone on for days like that.'

'Except if I remember my history,' Mike said, 'they didn't have too many days.'

'You know that, do you? Am I wasting my breath?'

'Don't mind him,' said Rachel. 'I don't know any of this and I'm all agog.'

'It wasn't even a week later we were getting set to go back south. I had to get back to tell Gally.' He made a face. 'I was trying to tie the Norseman's helmet on my saddlebag—not for a souvenir, more because I wanted her to know the size of the man Edgar had taken on to save me. I looked up to see a horseman coming fast from the south and my heart sank because horses in a froth are seldom good news. We all watched him head for the king and then the call went out for the commanders and

367

I knew I would soon have to leave Edgar by himself.'

'William the Conqueror had landed.'

'That wasn't what we called him. He hadn't conquered us yet. We called him Gwillam the Bastard, or Guillaume if you knew the French. He'd found a gap in the weather and slipped across the Channel while we were busy. He was camped out on the coast and we had to do it all over again—to burn down the road south before any more of his army made it to dry land.'

'How long did that take?' Mike asked.

'Four days for the first leg.'

'To London?'

'Ah, you really don't know all this story then. No. We stopped short of London at an abbey. A place called Waltham.'

They had come to a sudden halt and the story got passed back down the line. Divine help was on offer. A monk on horseback had met them in the road and asked to see the king. It was a chance to water the horses and to shelter from the strong wind. The whole procession turned off on to a track which led to a clutter of huts. Ferney edged his horse through the milling mass of men and saw a stone gatehouse ahead.

Two monks, each carrying a brace of pigeons, came out of the woods.

'What's this place?' he asked.

'Waltham Abbey, chosen resting place of the Holy Rood,' said one of the monks, crossing himself. The other monk giggled, stroked Ferney's horse and then his leg.

'The Holy Rood? The Holy Rood from Montacute?'

368

Coming from Pen, all Britnod's men knew the legend of the Holy Rood, from their grandfathers' days. In the time of Canute's peace, the story ran, a blacksmith had dug up a stone near the top of the pointed hill at Montacute, not so far from Pen. It was a natural miracle, they said, shaped by unearthly hands into a near life-size figure of Christ on the cross.

'On the hill? Where we were digging?' asked Mike.

'Right there, on that same terrace. They put it in an ox cart but the oxen wouldn't budge. The story said that a priest, recognising the signs of a miracle in the making, began to recite the names of nearby holy sites but the oxen would not stir. He listed places further and further away until he came to the name of Waltham Abbey. At that, the oxen set off, not stopping once until they reached the Abbey ten days later. It was a popular tale, even in Harold's army, where I was one of the few who didn't believe in miracles.'

Mike knew better than to interrupt because he sensed the boy was somewhere else, living it all out in his head, and the words were an almost accidental outcrop of that experience, but he couldn't help making a noise at that point.

The boy stopped, looking around as if he had forgotten the others were there. 'What?' he said. 'I've never seen one and I've had my eyes open long enough.'

'Some might say you're the biggest miracle of all.'

'You won't hear *me* saying that. There's a rational explanation for us. We just don't know what it is yet.'

The boy stayed silent. Rachel prompted him. 'If it wasn't a miracle, what was it?'

'It was a scam,' he said. 'Just a low trick, no more. I know how it got to Montacute in the first place. I saw the carts on the road when they brought it. Finishing the milking we were, and a boy came running in to tell us, so we went to look. A strong guard and a covered load, heading west.'

'I don't follow,' said Mike. 'When was this?'

'Oh, a whole century earlier, I suppose. About a hundred years before Harold was even born.' Ferney seemed to get back into his stride. 'When the Danes and the Norsemen were burning and plundering the east. Anyone with any sense in that part of the world was sending their valuables somewhere safe so these carts were bound for Montacute, and guess where they were coming from?'

'I haven't a clue.'

'From Waltham Abbey. Forget about miracles. It was as simple as that. Waltham and Montacute both belonged to the same man. Tovi owned both of them and he sent all his precious stuff from Waltham to be hidden away. You see? They buried the Rood at Montacute to keep it from the Vikings.'

'So why was that a scam?'

'That part wasn't. It was what happened afterwards. All these abbeys needed a good story to draw the pilgrims in and get their money. Waltham was a backwater, falling apart, so when peace came back and it was time to take it home again, some smart person saw a chance for a bit of marketing. Lo and behold, the blacksmith with the spade digs up the miraculous cross and it's not very

370

surprising that the oxen take it to Waltham, because that was where it had come from and that was where it was always going back to. After that, the pilgrims came pouring in.'

'You're a cynic,' said Rachel.

'Only when there's reason to be cynical. Anyway, it doesn't stop there. It was no coincidence that Harold took us that way and ran into a monk. Tovi's estates including Waltham Abbey and its miraculous Rood had passed to . . . can you guess who?'

Rachel and Mike glanced at each other and shook their heads.

'To our King Harold, no less,' said Ferney. 'He owned the place but by that time the old Rood had gone a bit out of fashion with the pilgrims and it needed a shot in the arm.'

'So you're saying Harold took his army to the Abbey as a publicity stunt for the Holy Rood?'

'Not just that. What do you most need if you're heading for a battle?'

'A good army?'

'An army that has God on its side and knows its leader is God's chosen one. When Harold came out of the Holy Rood chapel, the monks blessed us and sprinkled us and leaked their latest little miracle into all the waiting ears.'

'Which was?'

'The Holy Rood was a solid block of stone held up on the wall by iron bands but the monks all saw the Christ figure lean forward, hold out its stone hand and bless the king. That hit the spot. The men howled their cheers. The whole army galloped off, out of sheer high spirits, and we watched them go like nobody could beat them, least of all a

371

godless bastard.'

'You watched them go?'

'We'd been given another little job. Britnod volunteered us—him, me and useless old Dern. We had to load the Rood on a cart, find horses to draw it because oxen would be too slow, and follow the army as fast as we could. Harold thought its presence might help swing the day.'

'But it didn't.'

'It didn't get a chance. It took us three days to do what the troops could do in one. We were struggling along south of London when we saw a procession coming towards us half a mile away, horsemen surrounding a closed wagon, and they weren't proud, brave, joyful men. They were shambling, sad and fearful and they looked behind them with every second stride, and that wagon— oh, that was a pitiful sight. It was decked out with torn banners draped on broken spears, daubed with muddy charcoal to darken it. By the time it got to us, we didn't need to ask what it meant.'

'Was it Harold?'

'Yes, it was.'

'They were taking his body back from the battle?'

'Not just his body.'

'What else?'

'The breath that was still in it.'

'He was killed, Ferney. Everybody knows that. An arrow in the eye.'

'Not the Harold I saw.'

CHAPTER 30

They were near Honiton when Rachel's phone rang. She pulled over to take the call. Mike watched Ferney for signs of stress.

'It's good to stop,' the boy said. 'I'm not that happy with speed.'

'She hasn't been over eighty the whole way,' Mike said mildly.

'A gallop used to be the quickest I ever went, and that wasn't often.' He leaned forward between the front seats and tapped on the windscreen. 'It's all because of sand, you know.'

'Sand?'

'Yes. Suppose when you melted sand, you didn't get glass. Supposing you got something you couldn't see through.'

'Well?'

'Then you wouldn't have windscreens, and without windscreens you couldn't go quickly because the wind would get in your eyes, so no fast cars. Better still, you couldn't have bombers and fighters and things. It's all the fault of sand.'

Rachel got back in the car, looking cross. 'That was the clinic. They say that Miss Driscoll's mother insists that Miss Driscoll does not want me to represent her, and as Miss Driscoll is in a fragile condition they cannot allow visitors from outside the family.'

'Is that it then?' Mike asked. 'Do we turn round?'

'No we do *not*,' Rachel said. 'We go there and we argue our way in, because once she says she

373

wants me to act for her, they can't stop her. Are you up for that?'

Mike kept quiet. 'Oh yes,' said Ferney.

'Are you all right?' she asked, looking at him.

'The story's helping. Where were we?'

'On a road south of London,' said Mike, 'meeting Harold coming the other way, and I think you're about to threaten my understanding of English history by telling me he was alive.'

'Oh.' It took him a while to pick up the thread again. Mike watched him out of the corner of his eye as he muttered and held something in his hands that was invisible in this time.

'The man in the wagon was still breathing,' he said in the end. 'Only just, though. He was wearing Harold's surcoat. He had hair like Harold's, what you could see of it that wasn't caked in blood. His face? You couldn't tell. He had a dreadful wound half across it.'

'The arrow in the eye?'

'Nowhere near his eye.'

'Ah,' said Mike, as if that suddenly made sense. 'William of Malmesbury says one thing, Henry of Huntingdon says another. You can't trust the Bayeux Tapestry. It was just a stick next to someone's head until they added the flights when they were restoring it. But are you saying you couldn't identify the man in the wagon?'

'No, it was Harold. He still had the power, even though he was at death's door. It's like an aura, a bit like gold. It sticks to kings. All I'm saying is there wasn't much of his cheek or his nose left undamaged, and the nose was the first thing you always noticed about him. I was sure and it never makes sense to change your mind afterwards when

374

you're sure at the time.'

'Where were they taking him?'

'To his grave. They weren't expecting him to live. Two of the Waltham priests were there. They'd gone with him to sing about the Holy Rood and they were bringing him back to bury in their abbey.'

That was when Britnod said 'Why take him to Waltham? He's not dead yet. Why wish it so?'

'The Norman King gave us permission.'

'Well, sod that. All the more reason to take him somewhere else.'

'We swore an oath.'

'You did. We didn't. He's our king, not Bastard Gwillam. The game's not over yet. We'll take him somewhere they won't come looking.'

Britnod seemed to have grown taller now that he could aim his ill temper at a righteous target.

'Where?'

'Better you don't know. We'll take that cross of yours too. It hasn't done him much good yet but there's still time.'

'It bowed to him,' said the taller priest indignantly.

'Oh really? I thought you told us it waved at him. Maybe it was waving goodbye.'

'It belongs at Waltham.'

'You won't miss it.'

'Why do you say that?'

'Because I happen to know you've got another one just like it.'

'How dare you! There is only one Holy Rood.'

'True,' said Britnod, 'but there is a hollow copy of it which you are in the habit of taking out in the annual procession so the pilgrims can be impressed by the miraculous strength of the monks who hold it high above their heads.'

'Who told you that?'

'A drunk monk.'

There were a dozen soldiers in the escort and they liked Britnod's idea. The priests could do nothing so they rode home to Waltham while the wagons turned westward. The king was groaning in delirium but at Winchester the Bishop sent secretly for a woman with a precious knowledge of infected wounds. By the end of three weeks there, he no longer looked likely to die though he still had little clear interest in life. In that third week, news came of the Norman King's arrival in London and of the burial of Harold under the protection of the Holy Rood at Waltham. They laughed and wondered what poor corpse had been elevated to royalty in death.

After Winchester the soldiers went home. Britnod, Ferney and old Dern, still enjoying his private world, took one wagon. The man on the straw in the back was in an even more private world, lying inert beside his precious cross, his face swathed in bandages. They arrived at the ridge after a slow and careful journey and Gally knew they were coming. She came out of the cottage door with Sebbi behind her and looked at the three men, then out at the lane as if a fourth might be coming in after them on foot. Then her eyes were dragged back to the anguish on Ferney's face and she knew. Tears welled up in her eyes.

'We have an injured man in here,' Britnod told her. 'He needs your help.' Then when he saw the flash of hope in her face, he shook his head. 'No, I'm sorry. It's not your son. It's only the King.'

376

Ferney went to her and held her, and she looked into his eyes then set her sorrow aside for later. She went to work, unwrapping the king with care, inspecting the wounds. It was a slow job. Right through that winter and into the spring, she poured her grief into his care, nursing him with all the skills in her possession.

The word spread.

However careful they were to keep him a secret Britnod was less so, and as life returned to the hedges and fields, small deputations of the Wessex Saxons came to see if it was true that not all was lost. An appetite for resistance began to show its shoots around on the ridge. The news was bad. William was so sure of his victory that he had gone back to France, leaving his half-brother, Robert of Mortain, to crush the west. In Somerset they soon came to hear that Robert was a vile man, and he began to ring their county with new fortresses. Montacute was one of the first and that was designed to rub Saxon noses in the dirt. Robert knew what the legend of the cross of Montacute meant to the Saxons. Robert had faced the Saxon ranks as they howled the name of the Holy Rood. He knew the legend of the blacksmith's find on the steep hill and it pleased him greatly to defile that sacred Saxon mound with Norman walls.

Ferney fell silent. Mike prompted him. 'So where was the Rood?'

'We kept it in the church, under a blanket.'

'And Harold? Did he stay in the village?'

'Oh yes.'

'Where exactly?'

'With us.'

'*Harold* was living at Bagstone?'

377

'I told you, yes, but he was never going to command anyone again. He spent most of his days asleep. That didn't stop them. They said he'd wake when the time came. They needed a symbol.'

'Who's they?'

'The Saxons. Hugo from Exeter way and his followers and all the other hotheads and tough guys who'd come to the west to bide their time. They were the resistance and Pen was the place they chose.'

'Because Harold was there?'

'Because of that and because of the ridge, the best way through for an army and the best place to stop one—the same old damned reasons battles always came to the poor place. Anyway, they gathered there. They marched on Montacute more like a gang than an army, planning to throw the Normans out so they could take the Rood back where it belonged. They got slaughtered of course. Only half of them made it back to Pen, chased all the way, and that was where they made their final stand.'

'Where were you?'

'I stayed in Pen, looking after Gally, telling her it wasn't her fault Edgar died, trying to find her some peace. I was glad when they marched away and not nearly so glad when they came back, bringing their war with Robert's troops at their heels. It was a running fight all along the western slope, in the trees and fields. We were digging a big hole when they arrived—the deepest hole we could.'

'What for?'

'For the cross, the damned Rood, the cause of all the trouble. I didn't want them to find it. I thought at least I would deny them that satisfaction.'

'So you weren't in the fight?'

'The fight came to us whether we liked it or not. We could hear the shouts and screams. I turned back to get Gally and Sebbi away but then I saw Harold, standing there like a sleepwalker. He'd followed us. He looked past me and began to shout and I turned round to see a dozen Normans coming up the slope at us. That wreck of a man rushed at them with nothing but my spade in his hands. He went for them like a lion and he even got a blow in, just one, before they stuck their swords in and let the life out of him. They had no idea who they'd just killed. They kicked him out of the way and came on after us and we had to stretch our legs to get away.'

'But you did? You escaped?'

'They cut my arm but I got Gally and the boy out of there. We knew the hidey-holes. It was Hugo and his remaining men who stood and fought and it didn't do them any good. When it all went quiet, we came back and we took what was left of Harold and we buried him in the hole we dug for his cross then we kept very quiet about it. We had to.'

'Why?'

'Word got round. The story spread that Harold was sleeping in a cave under the ridge, waiting to be woken—that same old story, just like Arthur. They came looking for anyone who might be planning to have another go. Then they decided no Saxon should ever make a stand up there again, so the castles started going up. That's why they're there, you see. Three castles to control the ridge, the rallying point.'

379

'And afterwards? What happened to you?'

'We got the Rood out of there in the end. If they had found it, we would all have felt the sword. Two slow nights on a wagon. Hiding in the day, then eight men got it up the hill and we buried it where it belonged.'

'Back at Montacute?'

'On the terrace, right by our trenches.'

He looked bleakly ahead and his eyes began to shine with the trace of tears.

'We were slave labour to the Normans. Everyone was forced to work. My arm made me useless but they took Sebbi, our remaining son, to build their castles.' He sighed. 'He was weak and I went to take his place but they killed him anyway. They killed my son for not working and I tried to stop them and they killed me too. Both my lovely sons. That's why we don't have children. We come back but they don't.'

A trill of soft notes came into the car and Ferney realised as they got louder that Gally's phone was ringing in his pocket. 'Hello?' he said.

'Is that you?' Lucy's voice was a whisper.

'Yes. I'm in a car. We're coming down to see her.'

'I'm there now. You won't get in. It's like Dartmoor Prison. Electric gates. She's told them to keep you out—Fleur, I mean. She's on the warpath.'

'Is there any other way in?'

'No, but listen. I think I've got an idea.'

CHAPTER 31

Fleur had made Lucy and Ali wait outside while she talked to the doctors at the clinic. 'I might ask you to walk her around the gardens,' she had said. 'See if you can get any more sense into her. Sit in the car while I sort it out, will you? Don't leave the car without locking it. They have mad people here.'

When Fleur disappeared inside Lucy immediately rang Ferney, and Ali listened to the course of their conversation with mounting horror. 'You can't be serious,' she said when Lucy stopped talking.

'Never more so,' said Lucy. 'You be Thelma and I'll be Louise. Are you up for it?'

'No.'

'Are you a real friend?'

'Yes, I am, but we'll be arrested.'

'So you don't really believe what she's been saying? Not enough to take a risk?'

Ali found herself thinking of Conrad and wishing someone would appear with a car to take her back to him and imagining how it would be if they had loved each other for ever and ever.

'But you can't even drive,' she said. 'Can you?'

'Yes I can. My dad let me drive our car round an airfield last year. Twice. I'm OK if this is an automatic. Is it?'

They looked at the gear lever.

'I think so. It says P and D and R.'

'R must stand for Road,' Lucy declared.

'Or Reverse?'

381

'No, if R was for Reverse, there would have to be F for Forwards, wouldn't there? Nice of her to leave us the keys.'

'Lucy, you might kill us.'

'I might, but I probably won't. It's got airbags.'

'Where will we go?'

'I think I know just the place.'

They saw a nurse come out of the front door with a patient in a wheelchair, curled and inert, and it was a moment before they realised that this semi-conscious half-girl was Jo.

'We have to do something,' said Lucy. 'Look at the state of her.'

'All right,' said Ali, sucking in her breath. 'All right, but I don't like Thelma. I want to be Louise.'

'Done.'

They took the wheelchair from the nurse, wheeled an unresponsive Jo round to the side of the car that was away from the building, and manoeuvred her with difficulty into the back seat.

'Here goes,' said Lucy grimly, getting into the driver's seat and trying to find a way to slide it forward. It seemed to be electric and nothing made any difference.

'It could be on the steering wheel,' Ali suggested. 'Hurry up. They're going to look out of the window at any moment.'

'How about this one? Oh no.' The horn blared. They saw movement behind the curtains.

'Oh dear. Let's stop now,' said Ali.

'I haven't even started. Ah, now I have.'

The engine came to life. Lucy pushed the lever on the gear selector to R, pressed the accelerator hard and bumped backwards over the lawn into a flower bed. She saw Fleur come out of the front door and look at them in astonishment.

'Try D,' said Ali. 'Quickly! And by the way, none of this was my idea.'

Spraying earth, grass and then gravel from spinning tyres, they snaked down the drive to the gates.

'They're closed,' wailed Ali.

'No, they're opening. It must be automatic when you're going out.'

They were indeed opening, but very, very slowly, and when they looked behind, they could see Fleur running as hard as she could down the drive, getting closer and closer.

*   *   *

Rachel had just said 'I think this must be it' when a silver car shot out of the clinic entrance ahead of them, bumped up on to the grass verge and veered away up the road in a series of curves. She slammed on the brakes to miss it and as the car came to a halt a woman wrenched open the rear door, hurled herself in, pointed forward and shouted, 'That's my daughter. They're stealing her. Can you go after them? Please?'

Rachel and Mike turned round to look at her. The woman was looking at Ferney in the back seat next to her. She stared from Rachel to Mike and back again. 'Wait a minute,' she said, 'I know you,' but by that time Rachel had the car moving, accelerating after the disappearing BMW. When Fleur pulled her mobile out of her pocket and began to dial, Ferney said, 'Let me help you with that.' He took the phone from her, lowered the window and threw it out. 'Whoops!' he said.

383

'Butterfingers. Rachel, can you lock the doors? By the way, my name's Ferney.' He held out a hand, which she ignored.

'You can't do this,' she said faintly. 'You're abducting me.'

'Well no,' said Rachel, 'technically not. You asked us for a lift and you asked us to follow your daughter, so I'm doing that. Anyway, I have to see her to check that she wants me to represent her as her lawyer, you see, so I'm acting in her best interests and I'm not sure that you are. I would suggest you sit back and enjoy the ride.'

'Where are we going?'

'I don't know yet.'

'I think I do,' said Ferney. 'We'll see.'

By the time they reached Totnes, Lucy had mostly got the hang of steering and was learning about braking, but she hadn't thought of looking in the rear-view mirror. The GPS was the same as the one in Ali's parents' car so she had put in their destination and everything seemed to be going quite well. Gally was lying out of sight, curled up on the back seat.

'How far is it now?'

Ali played with the GPS. 'Twenty-six minutes.'

'I don't know what difference you think this will make,' Fleur said in the car behind. She was breathing in deep gasps and her face was flushed. 'As soon as we get to wherever we're going you can't stop me phoning, and then you are all going to be in such deep shit. You think you're looking after her, do you? No one's going to believe your crackpot story.'

'I can see why you would think that,' Rachel said calmly, 'but maybe you should suspend your disbelief just for a short time. I had to.'

'You're supposed to be sensible, you are,' Fleur retorted. 'What do you think the Law Society is going to have to say about all this when I get on to them, eh? They'll have you banned or whatever in no time flat and as for you, Mr Teacher, I reckon your teaching days are over.'

'Is that a promise?' said Mike. 'Please don't raise my hopes unless you mean it.' Rachel giggled and Fleur sank back into a brief and frustrated silence.

'Let your daughter explain to you,' Rachel suggested after a while. They had reached the narrow lanes and Fleur was gazing ahead, wincing at Lucy's near-misses with the hedgerows and oncoming traffic.

'Oh, she's done that. She's full of moonshine about Saxons and battles and this, that and the other. As for you, young man, don't you go thinking I'm going to let the two of you get together. No way. I'll get a court order if I have to. I can stop all this, just like that. Don't you see what you're doing? You're making it worse for her. The minute I get her back, they'll have her inside and put away and you're all going to have a lot of questions to answer.'

'That's a good way of dealing with her, is it?' Ferney asked quietly.

'It's worked so far.'

'Oh yes. She told me. You've had her on tablets for a long time, haven't you?'

'Best thing for her,' said Fleur defiantly. 'She used to babble nonsense all the time when she was tiny. I couldn't stand it. Her and her daft friend.'

'What did she call her friend?'

385

'Girly.'

'No, not Girly. Gally,' said Ferney. 'Her real name.'

'Don't give me that Gally crap. She's made all that up, just to fit,' and Fleur saw three heads shaking in unison.

The car in front slowed down as they drove into Slapton. 'Here's the deal,' said Rachel. 'I can't stop you calling the police and I won't try, but you had better understand this. I will represent your daughter and I will fight my very hardest to stop her being sectioned. If you want to avoid that, this is my offer. Sit down with us now, for one hour only, with a mind as open as you can manage, and if you're still determined to do it your way—well then, so be it.'

Fleur only grunted, which might or might not have been acceptance. As the chantry tower came into sight, they saw a third head lift up from the back seat and peer out.

'She's responding,' said Ferney. 'I knew she would.'

They could see her gesturing emphatically as the tower came closer and then the BMW came to a complete stop, its driver oblivious to the car behind. The reversing light came on as it backed uncertainly for a few yards, and turned left into the narrow alley to the pub, leaving silver paint on the corner of the wall.

Rachel parked out on the road. 'Why the hell are we here again?' said Fleur.

'Because she knows this is where she needs to be,' Ferney answered calmly.

They got out and walked into the pub yard, Fleur following unwillingly. The three girls were

386

standing there, staring at the tower. Lucy and Ali turned round, astonished. 'Jo?' said Fleur, but her daughter took no notice. 'Jo, I want you to tell these people to go away. I'm taking you home. And as for you, Miss Lucy, I'll have my keys back right now.'

'Gally? I'm here,' said Ferney, and the girl turned with a cry of utter delight, rushed to him and wrapped her arms round him. Ferney held her tightly, stroking her hair with one hand.

'It's all right,' he said, 'I'm not leaving you now. Rachel's here to help you, as your lawyer.'

'Don't you do that,' Fleur shouted.

'That is what you want, isn't it?' said Ferney urgently. 'Just say yes,' and Gally whispered the word.

'That's good enough for me,' said Rachel. 'Now, do we have a deal? One hour, that's all.'

Fleur looked at her watch. 'One hour then I call them. I don't know why you're bothering.' She stared, speechless, at the boy and girl in front of them, hugging each other close.

'Don't you see?' said Mike. 'We can't get in the way of this.'

Ferney released Gally, keeping her hand in his.

'Sit down, everybody,' said Rachel and they all sat down around a table. Gally was smiling through tears.

'We've been here before,' Ferney said calmly. 'Would you like to know when?'

Fleur didn't respond.

'December,' said Ferney. 'A week before Christmas.'

'We were in Exeter for Christmas.'

'Christmas in the year thirteen hundred and

387

seventy-two—that's when we were here. It was brand new. We came for the consecration of the Chantry. He invited us himself—Sir Guy.' He looked up at the tower and turned to Gally. 'It's the first time I've seen it since. It's taken a bit of a battering, hasn't it?' She gave him an uncertain smile but said nothing.

Mike looked at Fleur. 'Would you like a brandy?' he asked and she stared at him wildly, then nodded. 'Coffee for me, please, Mike,' said Rachel. 'This is going to be a good day for staying alert.'

He brought the drinks back and found them sitting in silence, Ferney and Gally leaning together with an arm round each other and Fleur staring at them as if they might bite her. She took the glass from him and looked at him equally warily.

'We came here together,' said Ferney, 'because the man who built it was a friend. Do you remember where we stayed?' Gally pointed at the pub. 'That's right,' he said encouragingly. 'That was the guest house and over there was the chapel and the monks' quarters and kitchens. Poor Guy.'

Gally looked down and mumbled something.

'Yes,' said Ferney. 'That's right. He was terrified and there was no need.' He turned to Mike. 'He held King Edward's standard at the battle of Crécy, held it through thick and thin, the bravest of men—but he had been tricked into killing his own son and then the priests got him. They told him he was bound for purgatory—a million years of torment, worse than hell. He built this place and hired teams of priests to sing for his soul every hour of the day and night. He thought it was his

388

only chance.'

Mike looked at Fleur as she took a swig of brandy. Her eyes were fixed on the boy, glaring from a tight face.

'Your daughter was in torment too,' Ferney told Fleur. 'She had been trapped in a choice which killed one of our sons, but it was no choice really because in the end both our sons died and it filled her head for years and years. Guy listened to her, helped her shape her feelings into ideas that healed both of them.' He looked at Gally. 'You gave him his purpose back. What you told him, saved him.'

She was trying to speak and they all watched her in silence until it became unbearable.

'You told him what you thought about war and death and life. Do you remember that?' He held her shoulders, gently urging her, but she still didn't answer. 'Think about being here that day. You and me, in the clothes he gave us—the finest clothes we had ever worn. Red and green.'

There was still no response.

'He asked you to read out the words you gave him at the consecration ceremony. He wanted you to be the one to read them out. He begged you to and you said no.' Ferney was looking intently at her face. 'Then think about our sorrow,' he said. 'I'm sorry, but I think you have to remember our loss,' and her face began to crumple.

'They mustn't hurt him,' Gally said, and they all froze. 'I'm not losing him. Edgar, my son. My beautiful Edgar. My Edgar and my Sebbi.'

'Yes, that's it,' said Ferney. 'Don't let go of them. Where did Edgar die?'

'In a field by a river,' she said. 'You took me

389

there. A river by a bridge.'

'Do you remember what they called it?'

'Stamford,' she said, 'Stamford Bridge,' and they all looked at Fleur as she was unable to suppress a sharp intake of breath.

'They made Sebbi build the castle,' she said in a voice that grew in strength with every word, 'and they killed him when he could not.'

'And then?'

'And then they killed you.' Her face was stricken.

'Gally, listen,' said Ferney. 'That was long ago. You turned your mourning into words. You told Guy there is a life force and we're all part of it and when we damage that we damage our chance of getting anywhere worth being. You said every army thinks it has God on its side and he winced at that.'

'Taking life,' she said. 'Rosie. I took Rosie's life.'

'That was different. It doesn't count when it's us. I'm back. You're back. You did nothing wrong.'

'I did.' She looked at Mike, pointed at him. 'I hurt him.'

'Yes,' said Mike, 'but I'm trying to understand.'

The girl's face changed, eased a little. She got to her feet, gazed up at the old tower above them and held out her hands, turning to face each of them one after the other as if to bless them with quietness. 'Old men, who stay behind,' she said.

'Hold on a minute,' said Lucy. She reached into her pocket, unfolded a piece of paper and thrust it at Fleur. 'I bought this yesterday when we stopped at the shop,' she said, 'and I haven't shown it to her, I promise.'

'Old men who stay behind,' said Gally again, and her voice took on a rich depth that was entirely unfamiliar to them, 'do not inflame the young with words of war. The ruin that you risk should be your own, not theirs. Young men take care. To make you fight they first must make you fear, then out of that shape hate.' She paused, wiped a tear away. Fleur was staring down at the printed sheet.

Gally began again. 'Take arms when all else fails, but mark you this: before the battle starts remember what it is to see friends bleed. In the battle's midst, remember peace is both behind you and ahead. When the battle's done, remember how it is that wars begin.' She turned back towards the tower and her voice rose. 'Kings and captains, you who order war, know that your people, left alone, would choose to eat not fight, would choose to love not hate, would chose to sleep not die. Be careful what you say to turn them to your will. Tell them that you fight for God not gain, and know your enemy has preached the same. You who read this, pray for me. I have heard blind fury roar and sow the seeds of future war and I have wept as heroes died.'

Fleur was looking down at the sheet of paper, then back at her. 'So when *did* you learn that?' she asked.

'When we wrote it, the two of us.' She drew in a long breath and looked hard at Ferney. 'I'm back,' she said. 'I think I'm all right.'

Fleur read the description on the piece of paper, shaking her head. 'This is just a trick,' she said. 'It's no proof of anything. You're all in this together. I'm not buying this.'

'You want proof?' asked Ferney. 'I can give you proof.'

'Oh really? This I have to hear,' said Fleur.

391

'Before this week, when were you last in Pen?'

'He means Pen Selwood,' Mike put in.

'Never,' said Fleur. 'Not once. So how does your proof look now?'

'What about close by? Driving down on the main road?'

'Sometimes. Me and ten million others.'

'The tower,' Gally said so quietly that they almost missed it.

'The tower? This tower? How does that help?' Ferney said.

She shook her head, 'Alfred's Tower.'

'What about it?' He turned back to Fleur. 'Have you been there?'

'We went there after we left the village,' said Fleur.

'Not before?'

'Once. We climbed right up to the top.'

'Wait,' said Ferney. 'You'd never been to Pen before?'

'No.'

'But you had been to the tower? Just the once?'

'Yes.'

'Then I can prove it. If I can tell you the exact date you went to the tower, will you start believing me?'

'You could tell me any date you like. How would I know if you were right? I know the year and the month but I have no idea which day it was. I can't remember things like that.'

'Your diary,' said Gally.

Ferney looked at her and back at Fleur. 'Have you got your old diaries?'

Fleur didn't answer. She had turned her head away. There was a long silence.

392

'Who was with you?' Ferney asked. 'You said "we"?'

Fleur's shoulders shook. She got to her feet and walked away, down the narrow entrance towards the road, leaving her car keys on the table.

Ferney turned to Gally. 'What happened there?' he asked.

Gally was frowning, 'She was with . . . with my father.'

'What happened to your father?' Mike asked.

'He . . . he died when I was born.'

'How?'

'I don't know. She never talked about him.'

'Never?'

'No. Never.'

'What was his name?'

Gally frowned again as if she might not know even that.

'Toby,' she said in the end. 'I think it was Toby.'

'Right,' said Mike. 'You stay here, all of you. I'm going to talk to her.'

He found her in the graveyard, standing looking at the gravestones. He stood outside for a while and she didn't move so he walked in.

She turned sharply when she heard his footsteps and he saw she was crying.

'I don't want to intrude,' he said.

'Go away then.'

'I think I know how this feels for you,' he said. 'In fact I'm probably the only other person who does.'

'I don't know anything about you that makes me want to listen,' she said.

'I'm just me and I'm harmless and I've lost Gally too, twice really. I know you lost someone.'

393

'What do you mean, twice?'

'Once when she killed herself and once when she came back.'

'And you really believe all that stuff?'

'Not by choice. Yes, I have to. I've lived it.' He waited. 'What was he like?' he asked gently in the end.

'Who?'

'Toby.'

'She told you his name? What else did she say?'

'Only that you never talk about him.'

She looked away again.

'How did he die?' he asked.

'In a crash,' she said. 'It's none of your business.'

'How old was Jo?'

'She was . . . she was just being born. We were in the hospital. He went back to get something that I . . .' she faltered.

Then somehow he understood. 'You think he died because of you,' he said, and she swung round, erupting in fury, punching him on the chest and the arms, screaming at him, 'It's got nothing to do with you. Shut up, just shut up!'

He did nothing to stop her but she stopped herself, put her hands to her face and began to cry with the force of a sixteen-year-old dam breaking. He stood and watched her, then opened his arms and she crept into their comfort, sobbing and sobbing and sobbing.

At the end, when she quietened enough, they sat down next to each other on a grave slab.

'You didn't kill him,' he said. 'Accidents happen. So, what was he like?'

'He would have believed this. He was a softie really. He would have been just what she needed.'

394

'You can still be what she needs now.'

'Can I really?' Fleur said. 'I never have been. Anyway, is that Jo, that girl? Is there anything much of Jo left, I wonder?'

'I think there's probably most of her left,' Mike replied. 'When I first met my Gally, before we ever came to the village, before she ever remembered anything about their past, she was pretty much the same person as she was later.'

Fleur shook her head. 'This isn't the Jo I know.'

'If you can trust in this and bring her back to the village, you'll see Jo again. You'll see quite a special version of her. Tell her all about Toby. She will understand, you know. She's got so much wisdom.'

'This is impossible,' Fleur said. 'Look at all these dead people.' She swept a hand round the wide graveyard. 'Do they stay dead, or have I got to change the whole way I think about the world?'

'I think they're all safely dead.'

'I don't get you. I mean, as I understand it, my daughter married you then turned out to have been in love with somebody else for ever and a day, then, if I understand this right, she did away with herself and your daughter at the same time. How can you stand that?'

'Sometimes I can't.'

'Don't you hate them?'

'I pity them. It never ends for them. All they've got to make it bearable is each other.'

'All right,' she said. 'I'm going to try going along with this but I need the proof.'

'Then let's go and look for it. Will the diary thing help?'

'It might, and you had better do what I say

395

because I've just realised I'm your mother-in-law,' she said and made a noise that was almost a laugh.

*　　　*　　　*

Back at the Exeter flat, Fleur delved in a cupboard and brought out a green desk diary. She held it in both hands, hiding the year marking on the cover, and stared at Ferney.

'What exactly am I looking for?' she said.

'All right,' said Ferney. 'Did you stay the night somewhere local?'

'Yes. A nice hotel, more of an inn really, just by Stourhead.'

'The Spread Eagle at Stourton?'

'That was it.'

'Was that the night before you climbed up the tower or the night after?'

'The night before, then we went up the tower in the morning.'

'All right. I'll tell you the exact date you stayed at the Spread Eagle. Is that a deal?'

'Wait. I'll see if I can find it.' She opened the diary, leafed through, stopped sharply and sighed. 'I've got it.' There was a catch in her voice. 'I'm sorry,' she said, 'It's just ... it's his writing, you see.' They waited for her to recover. 'Well, anyway, here it is. "Booked one night Spread Eagle, Stourton, sent deposit cheque." Right then, smart boy. It's all or nothing. Tell me what I'm looking at.'

'You must have stayed at the Spread Eagle on the night of January 30th, 1994 ...' Ferney paused as Fleur made a small noise ... 'and then you must have gone up the tower on the morning of January

396

31st.'

'How could you know that?'

'The simplest way you can imagine. Because my Gally died early in the morning of January 31st.'

'Gally and her little girl?'

'Yes. It's right, isn't it?'

'Oh God.' She closed her eyes, opened them again. 'Yes, it is. Then Jo was born in May. The 26th.'

'And I was born on June the eighth,' said Ferney.

'Why does that matter?'

'Because Gally and her little girl died together. I was Gally's little girl. I was Rosie.'

Fleur gave him a shocked look and fell silent, thinking. 'I had a bit of a turn when I was up the tower,' she said eventually. 'Was that it, do you think?'

Ferney simply looked straight back at her and she gave a shrug of silent resignation. 'What now?' she asked.

Gally was clinging to Ferney, listening but saying nothing. 'If she stays here she'll go quiet again,' Ferney replied. 'I can promise you that. We have to get her to Pen. She needs to be there and we need her there.'

'All right,' said Fleur, 'but I'm coming too.'

On the way there, Ferney held Gally in the back seat of Fleur's car with Ali in the front while Lucy, increasingly proud of what she had done, travelled with Mike and Rachel. 'She's not so bad,' said Mike after a very long silence.

'Who?' said Rachel.

'The mother, Fleur.'

'She's a cow,' said Lucy indignantly. 'She's never shown much care for Jo—for Gally, I mean.'

'I thought she came round to it quite well,' said Mike. 'It's not easy, you know. After all, she's been on her own dealing with it.'

'She's hard,' said Lucy and Rachel said nothing.

The traffic was bad and it was only when they turned off the A303 towards the village that Mike realised he had forgotten all about the probability of his imminent arrest.

CHAPTER 32

'Be ready. They might be waiting for us,' Rachel said nervously as they turned off the main road. 'We're late.'

She drove into the yard. There was no sign of Meehan or his men but as she stopped the car, her phone rang.

'That's him,' she said. 'What am I going to say?'

The policeman gave her no chance to say anything. They could hear the metal rattle of his voice though she pressed the phone hard to her ear. 'We got held up . . .' she said quickly. 'Oh, right. What about tomorrow morning? Tonight? An hour? No, I don't . . . ninety minutes. Yes, yes. We will. No, you don't need to do that.' She switched it off and hung her head then looked up at Mike. 'We have to be there in an hour and a half. If not, he's coming to get you. I'm sorry.'

'Well, I suppose that's that, then.'

They got out of the cars. Gally seemed to come fully alive as her feet touched the ground. She sniffed the air like a dog.

'Let's go inside,' Rachel said. 'Gally? Will you

come and talk to us? There's very little time. We need to know how you made your mixture.'

The girl took no notice. She walked slowly across the yard to the old stone poking up through what was left of the brambles. She knelt down on one knee in front of it, spreading her hands out on the ground, palms down, like a runner taking up her position for a race. Rubbing her hands on the ground as if making proper contact with the earth, she gazed at the stone through the foliage.

'This is where we died,' she said. 'The first time. They killed us here, by this stone.'

Fleur frowned, took a pace towards her. 'Jo,' she said, 'we didn't come back here for this.'

'That's not her name,' said Ferney. He put a finger to his lips. 'Just listen a moment,' he said. 'She'll get to it her way.'

Gally stood up, reached a hand out to him and turned to face them, her back to the stone.

'When we met, we were terrified and terror was with us all that short time, all through that night. To lessen it we began to love each other, and there was nothing but those two passions from the moment we met until the moment we died. They killed us here, pinned us hard against each other with a spear, killed us in love and in terror. We were enemies, then we were lovers, then we were dead, all in the snap of a finger. We died right here against this stone.'

They stood in a wide ring as if anxious not to crowd her.

'That's why I was born here the second time,' she said.

'The second life?' Ferney spoke with sharp surprise in his voice. 'You *remember* the second life?'

'Can we save this for later?' said Rachel.

'No. Leave her be,' said Ferney. 'This matters. We've never remembered it before.'

'But Mike needs to—'

'Trust her. Just listen.'

But it seemed the damage was done. Gally was shaking her head, pursuing something as ephemeral as an interrupted dream.

'No,' she whispered. 'I've lost it.'

'What do you see?' Ferney asked.

'The stone and the trees. Trees?' She turned her head, lifted her hand to point towards the house, but her eyes seemed to look beyond it. 'The tree by the hut—the old ones' hut. That tree.' She stood up, took Ferney's hand and her voice came again, strong and clear. 'I know something,' she said. 'Come with me.'

They followed her around the side of the house to the ruined terrace. She stopped there and looked at Mike with the sunlight glinting on the tears in her eyes.

'I thought you would know,' she said. 'I thought this was the sure and certain place for it. I'm so sorry to have put you through it all.'

'What place?' he asked, then looked behind her at the rotten wreckage of the tree that had fallen ten years earlier. It stretched out from the sideways claw of roots to vanish into brambles, sagging into soapy disintegration under its own weight. The hollow tree in which he had hidden their breakfast on that birthday, the place she used afterwards for surprises, for the concealment of small things to delight him.

'I thought you would look here,' she said.

'For what?' he asked, sensing the answer as he said it.

'For my letter. I put it in the tree.'

'Why?'

'So you would find it, not some stranger. That's why I left it there, inside our hollow.'

'What did it say?'

'The words are too far away from me,' she said. 'I just have the shape of it.'

'Gally, tell me.' Rachel's voice was urgent. 'How high up was the hollow?'

Gally reached forward into mid-air. 'Level with my chin.'

The hollow was underneath. They paced it out from the roots, bent and pulled the rotting wood apart in handfuls. The bark and the sapwood broke away and they piled the dead meat of the tree to one side, all of them working urgently—all but Fleur, who stood immobile, her eyes fixed on the scene with the expression of someone watching a snake. When they reached the heartwood they found it still as hard as it had ever been, so they took to saws and axes to hack it away until one last axe-cut showed the corner of a yellow plastic bag, poking through the pulpy wreckage underneath. Mike pulled it clear, brushed it clean and turned it over in his hands. It was intact, firmly sealed, wrapped round with thick grey tape.

'This?' he asked.

'This,' she answered.

'Would you rather do this alone?' Gally asked him when they were all in the kitchen.

'No,' he said. 'It's all right. You all have a stake in this, one way or another.'

The bands of tape had melted together with the

pressure of the wood and the stewing of heat and age. Adhesive clung to the knife as he tried to slice through it and stuck to the blade in ribbons. He wrestled with the wrapping, hurrying to get to its contents and at the same time increasingly afraid of them. When he finally pulled the envelope out of the remains of the plastic bag, he sat down at the table.

He knew the envelope. He knew the sheet of paper inside. It was the writing paper she had always used and the rest of the sheaf it had come from was still in the desk drawer where she had left it. He knew the ink and he knew the handwriting as if it were a warm hand tucked in his. A hollow sense of grievous loss came with the sight of it but then a real hand touched his shoulder—a warm, living hand. Gally's hand.

He began to read and the others watched him as his eyes tracked down each page, sometimes lifting again to read one section a second and third time. They saw tears form, bulge, run slowly to halt at the top of his cheek until pushed by others behind to make the first sliding line down the dry skin, opening up a faster track for the rest. At the end he frowned a little, turned to pick up the envelope from the table and shook it. Something green fluttered out and fell to the floor—a torn half of a five-pound note. He bent to pick it up, turning it in his fingers and inspecting the ripped edge, then he held the letter out to Gally. 'Why don't you read it to everybody?' he asked. 'I think that would be the right thing to do.'

Her hand moved towards it as reluctantly as if it were a flame. Her fingers stopped short of it and it was Mike who pushed it into her hand. She took it, looking into his eyes, then dropped hers to it.

'My dear, dear Mike,' she began, 'I know I am doing the very worst thing to you that it is possible . . .' her voice broke and she stopped. Without looking she passed it to Rachel. The solicitor looked at Mike, who nodded, and she began it again, speaking clearly and deliberately. 'My dear, dear Mike, I know I am doing the very worst thing to you that it is possible to do. I want to tell you over and over again in this letter that I am not doing it to be cruel to you, although I know just how cruel it is and that distresses me so very much. You will think I'm doing it because of the promise that Ferney and I made. You will think, I'm sure, that I made that promise at a time when you did not exist and it should not hold me. Please believe me when I tell you in utter truthfulness that our old promise is not the first cause of what I have to do. I am doing it only because it is the least bad of all the alternatives and I know it is what I have to do for Rosie's sake. But it is also what I have to do for your sake.'

She paused and looked at each of them in turn. 'Is this all right?' she asked, and no one said it wasn't.

'I didn't take you as second-best, Mike. I didn't take you until something better came along. I have been thrilled to be with you. I love your endless kindness and your patience and your care. I had no idea at all that the things that have happened to us were possible and if I had known, I would have run away from you that first time we met to avoid dragging you through this. Above all, I feel so terribly sad that I have brought us to this point.

'I have come to realise that there is no way out.

403

There is no treatment that will turn Rosie into a different child. She seemed like your child and my child, and you have loved her like a father loves a daughter, but that was just in her first months before she found out who she really was. She is not our child. You know that really, I am sure. Now she knows that too. That is why she wants to harm herself and that is why she will destroy herself as soon as she is strong enough to find a way. He will make sure of that, won't he? I can only see unhappiness ahead for all of us and it seems to me that this way you do stand a chance of happiness again at some future point, even though you will not think so now.

'Please know that there will have been no suffering. It should not come as any surprise that I have, over the years, learnt how to do this in a gentle and painless way and I promise you, I know that is the way it is.

'You won't want to read this now, but later when you can, there is something I want you to do. Take the Poorman portrait to a gallery—the Tate or somewhere like that. Let them look at it and when they tell you who painted it, believe what they say. Sell it and use the money to start again somewhere new. Please do not sell Bagstone. At some future time, a different Ferney and a different Gally will come back to find it. Please let them have it. I think you will know them, but if you have any doubt I am leaving you a token. Ask her and she will show you the other half.

'Please, please give yourself the chance to start afresh. Remember that for us, this is not death. Don't wait for us. There is no happiness to be had

404

in that. If I could save you the sorrow that lies immediately ahead I would, but unless I do this, there will be far more sorrow. Your Gally loves you and feels, at this moment, utterly cursed by her history. Please forgive me.'

She fell silent and Mike looked at Gally as if there was nobody else in the room. 'Thank you,' he said. 'I should have thought to look but I forgot everything when I opened that door.'

She went to him and they clung to each other but then he stepped back, took her hand and Ferney's hand and put them together.

'I don't want to sell your picture,' he said.

'It's pretty modern really,' Ferney said. 'It's not important.'

Rachel looked at her watch, 'I really, really hate to say this but we have to go, only because I'd like to keep you out of prison.' She stopped. 'But I don't know if I can,' she said. 'All this is extraordinary but it gives me nothing to say.'

'Take the letter,' Gally said. 'Let them read it.'

'They'll think it's mad.'

'That's no bad thing.'

'You don't mind?'

'They won't arrest me, will they? Take it and show them and come back here.'

'Yes, all right,' said Rachel. 'I don't know how long we'll be. Anything from two hours to twenty years, I suppose, depending on how good a lawyer I am.'

'Go on,' said Fleur. 'Get on with it. We'll still be here. We have a lot of talking to do.'

'I don't think Lucy's right about her,' Mike said as they drove out of the village.

'Fleur? Don't you?'

There was a long silence until Mike said, 'How are we going to play it?'

'If you mean how am I going to play it, wait and see.'

The next silence carried them all the way to Yeovil.

*   *   *

When they arrived at the front desk they were shown not to the usual interview room, but to Meehan's office. He shook Rachel's hand but merely pointed Mike to a chair.

'This isn't another interview under caution,' he said, 'not yet anyway. I expect you to be straight with me. I understand you've got something to show me?'

'We have,' said Rachel. 'My client has found a letter from his wife written immediately before her death and dated. He has brought it for you to read.'

'You kept this to yourself, Mr Martin?'

'No. She left it in a hiding place. We didn't find it until now.'

'That's a bit convenient.'

'I was there as a witness when it was found; so were others,' said Rachel. 'There's no doubt it's genuine.'

Meehan raised his eyebrows. 'You'll have to show us the place later. Does it explain anything?'

'If you read it, I'll think you'll understand,' said Rachel.

The policeman held out his hand and she gave him the envelope. He studied the outside then took out the contents with care and unfolded

406

them. He turned slightly away to get the light from the window and put on a pair of reading glasses that made him a little less like a policeman. They watched as he read, and saw him look up at Mike with an expression of curiosity on his face. He reached the end and went back to the start and read it all over again as if committing it to heart. When he put it down on the table, he went on staring at it in silence as if not sure where to begin.

'All right,' he said in the end. 'Of course we'll have to check this to establish the authenticity. We have specimens of the late Mrs Martin's handwriting on file. Then I'll have to talk to the Crown Prosecution Service.' That means Anna Murray, he thought to himself, and I can guess what she'll say. He looked at Mike. 'I have no grounds for detaining you, Mr Martin. You may go. Did you ever think of getting medical attention for her?'

'I never knew anything like this was going to happen.' said Mike truthfully. 'I had no idea she might do it.'

'I suppose it's pointless to ask what she means by all that at the end?' said Meehan. 'There's no logic to it, I dare say.'

'No logic at all,' said Mike, and that was the only lie he was called upon to utter.

'I have also now made contact with a woman who can explain the taking of the photographs,' Rachel put in. 'She's a healer from Keswick who—'

'Spare me all that,' said Meehan. 'I'll ask for it if I need to know, and the stuff with the boy is dead in the water too. I'll have to keep this until we've checked the handwriting.' He waved the letter at Mike. 'Will you want it back? I'd burn it if I were you. No point in hanging on to past sorrows.'

*   *   *

'Thank you,' said Mike to Rachel when they were approaching the village. 'I can't really thank you enough for everything you've done.'

'All part of the job,' she said, sounding far away. 'It's what I get paid for. What was all that stuff about the painting?'

They got back to the cottage to find the others cooking supper from a motley collection of ingredients. He took Rachel to his study.

'Ignore the mess,' he said. He pointed to the picture hanging on the far wall. 'It's a bit dark. I'll switch the light on.'

It was an oil painting of a cottage and the light showed her it was Bagstone. The stone itself poked out through the bushes on the right. The house was surrounded by trees. There were two figures standing by the gate. Mike carefully unhooked it from the wall and turned it round. 'She had it cleaned,' he said. The back was dark brown but for a small amber rectangle slanting slightly.

They fetched the little label she had found and she held it against the paler space. It fitted perfectly.

'Oh Gally,' he said, 'You meant to stick it back, didn't you?' He propped the painting against a chair and stared at it.

'It's a good picture,' Rachel said. 'Let me guess. Ferney left it to Gally in his will.'

'Yes, he did. He met the painter nearby. They got on very well. I'm trying to remember the story. The painter was in some kind of money trouble.

408

Ferney suggested he paint the house for them.'

'So, that's them? That's really Ferney and Gally at the gate?'

'Yes.'

She went close and stared at the two little figures.

'That's utterly extraordinary. I wish they were larger. You can't really see their faces.'

'That's what Gally said.'

'So who was this itinerant artist?'

'He called himself John Poorman, according to Gally.'

'John Poorman is JP, not JO.'

'That's right. It wasn't his real name. He was a bitter man, I think.'

She was still staring at the picture. 'But . . . doesn't it remind you of something?'

'It's definitely this house.'

'I meant the style.'

'What about it?'

'A million prints? Birthday cards? Biscuit tins? The Hay Wain?'

He pursed his lips and looked at her, reluctant to say it for fear of sounding foolish. 'Surely not.'

'Give me that label again. It might not be an 'O'. It could easily be a 'C'. J for John, C for . . . now, what do you suppose C might stand for?'

'Stop it. You're meant to be the sensible one. How could that be?'

'You should do what Gally said and ask an expert.'

'I can just ask the two of them, can't I? But perhaps some things are best not known. I'm not sure it's mine to sell. I'm their custodian really. What would my lawyer say about it?'

409

'Your lawyer would say there is no part of English law which applies to this.'

Ferney and Gally came quietly into the room. 'The painting doesn't matter,' Gally said.

'But it's the two of you,' Mike pointed out. 'You don't have photos. It must be the only image from all those years. Of course it matters.'

'Yes, it's us, but it could be anybody. Two tiny figures and he was no good at faces.'

'Anyway,' said Ferney, 'we have other ways to remember. We have a song or two and a poem. They take us back. We don't need the picture.'

Ali called that supper was ready. Rachel looked at her watch. 'Oh my goodness,' she said. 'I've got to go.'

CHAPTER 33

Mike woke abruptly from deep sleep, cradled all night in the forgotten comfort of a full house. That fled in a moment. Adrenalin had him gasping upright, staring at the window, dawn-dim with the first of the pale sun. Another hard knock on the door joined the echoes of the first in the shreds of dream.

'Who is it?' he called.

'Can I come in?' demanded Fleur.

'Wait.' He scrabbled for a dressing gown under the clothes on the chair, pulled it on and opened the door with some vague and startled idea in his head that she might want to join him in bed. Instead she glared at him, fully dressed and wild-eyed, pushed past him into the room, tipped his clothes in a heap on the floor and sat down on the chair.

'I have to talk to you,' she said. 'I haven't slept.'

'I'm sorry to—'

'I don't know who's behind all this, but I think it has to be you and that boy together, and you've stumbled on a girl who's not all that well, who isn't strong in her head, and you've twisted her thinking and you've even got that lawyer believing in your crap and I just want you to know this, my friend— I'm not fooled and I'm not having it and as soon as I've finished here I'm going to call up that thick policeman who seems to have taken all this hidden message bullshit hook, line and sinker and I'm going to tell him what's really going on here.'

'Oh, all right,' said Mike, 'and what is really going on here?'

'I don't know,' Fleur said, her voice sliding into a wail, and she burst into tears.

He sat down on the end of the bed, watching her, waiting for her to stop, but she didn't. Tears streamed down her face from eyes which swelled redder and redder, while the pale blue blouse she was wearing developed a growing arc of darkness, spreading downwards like the tide coming into a bay.

'If it's any comfort,' he started hesitantly, and she looked at him with just enough hope in her eyes for him to carry on, 'I think this happens a lot. I know Gally never got on with her mother. I mean, *my* Gally, last time round. The two of them were never like mother and daughter at all. I just don't think the parent and child thing works for them. How could it?'

'Why not?'

'There's meant to be part of them that's yours

411

right away, but not with those two.'

'She was never mine. When I first held her, she glared at me.'

'All babies do that, don't they?' said Mike doubtfully, remembering Rosie.

'I don't know.'

'Nor do I.'

'Toby was dead, you see? They had just told me, and there she was, and if it hadn't been for her he would have been alive.' She stared at him as if willing him to understand. 'I needed him to make it all work. He helped me be nicer, and he would have lived if it hadn't been for . . .' She stopped.

'What happened?'

And so she told him, stiffly and briefly, then going back over it, going deeper as she relived those last moments of Toby's life and the first moments of Jo.

'He would have lived if it hadn't been for me,' she said.

'Come on, there's no point in that blame stuff. Believe me, I'm an expert.' He meant to go on, to tell her how old Ferney had died in this very house, how Gally had gone into labour, fully expecting to give birth to a son, knowing it would be Ferney renewed. He wanted to tell her what he had known for certain—that she was ready to follow him through death as soon as the baby was safely delivered, how only the startling news that the baby was a girl had made her think again. At this moment he thought she would understand, but he had come just that last inch too close to a nervous animal and she snapped back, 'That's not the point. It's still bullshit.'

'Ferney proved it's not. You can't get away from

that.'

'That wasn't proof.'

'It was. You believed him yesterday even if you've forgotten that today. How could he possibly have known the date?'

'He found out somehow.'

'How?'

'He asked Jo.'

'How would she have known?'

There was a silence, then she said, 'It goes against everything I believe. She's not safe here. She's not normal.'

'Listen to me,' he said. 'Those two have no idea what it's like to be a normal child—no idea at all. From the moment they take their first breath there's already this vast thing inside them trying to get out, and they may not have words to say it but you see it in their eyes. It's hopeless. They should be left to themselves.'

'I wanted to love her.'

'You can. That's entirely up to you, but I think you mean you wanted her to love you.'

'Both.' She spat the word out and he could detect nothing like love in her voice. 'But what's it got to do with you? That policeman should never have let you off the hook.'

'There is something you should remember,' he said. 'She cared enough to explain it to you.'

'She had to.'

'No she didn't. She felt a responsibility to you. That's rare. I was only the second person they ever told in all this time. You're the third. Don't you see that's special? If you let her, she'll love you.'

She jumped to her feet, stared at him with an intensity that made him turn his face away. 'We'll

413

see about that,' she said, then turned abruptly and left the room. He heard her feet pounding down the stairs, the slam of the front door and the revving of her engine as she turned the car and raced away up the lane.

There was no point in trying to sleep again. He dressed sadly and slowly, his mind filled with images of her arriving at Yeovil, forcing them to summon Meehan and listing all the madness she had witnessed, persuading him her daughter was in danger, in need of medication. He could only measure how much the pressure had lifted the previous evening by the thudding weight of its return.

*   *   *

He went down to the front door and sat on the bench in the porch, staring towards the gateway and the road beyond like a sentry expecting an overwhelming enemy. With Fleur gone and the rest of the house asleep he thought he was alone, but when he tired of watching the gate and let his eyes drift round to the far end of the yard he saw two figures standing quite still by the trees watching him—Ferney and Gally, hand in hand. When she saw him look at her Gally beckoned him and led Ferney across to the grey finger of the old stone, still partly swathed in briars. He walked to her, stopped in front of her an arm's length away, and she stared at him with calm compassion. 'Where did Fleur go?' she asked.

'To the police. She changed her mind in the night. She woke me up to tell me.'

'Oh.' It came out like a gasp and Gally shot a

414

look at Ferney, who closed his eyes and nodded as if he had expected this.

'It's not your problem,' said Mike.

'Of course it is,' said the boy. 'Like it or not, we're all in this. I won't let her take Gally away.'

'Perhaps you should go before they come back.'

'You think they wouldn't find us? We could give them the slip for a day or two but what chance have we got against dogs and helicopters and all the stuff they've made for tracking people down? No, we'll be very plain.' Ferney looked towards the gate as if rehearsing his words. 'We'll tell them Gally is just fine and we're old enough to be together whatever that woman thinks.'

'And what about Mike?' Gally said.

'What can she say that they'll believe?' It sounded hollow to all three of them.

'Let's wait for them together,' said Gally gently. 'We've been remembering our own children, our two sons, but there was something else as well— something we need to bring back. It will pass the time. You don't mind?'

Ferney shrugged.

She turned back to Mike, 'Yesterday I nearly got it,' she said. 'Our second life. I saw it for a moment and then I lost it. I think I might be able to find it again.'

'Go on,' he said.

She crouched by the stone, just as she had the day before, staring at it intently. 'My mother built a hut,' she said. 'This was the life stone and she needed healing. She was heavy with me. I can't quite call it back but it wasn't just her. There was the old couple and yesterday, I saw their hut.' She stood up and turned to the house, pointing.

415

'I could see through to the tree behind. That was where they built it from skins and branches and whatever Cenwalch's men had left behind. Come on. It will be easier.'

They pushed through the undergrowth beside the house to the terrace where the remains of the tree were scattered. She stood for a long time in silence, then walked to the edge of the terrace where the old path had led down to the valley beyond and drew lines in the air with her hands to conjure up the hut. 'They built it here,' she said.

'Who were *they*?' Ferney asked.

'The old ones.' She thought again and shook her head. 'No names come back. They were left under all the bodies and the Saxons took them for dead. My mother had slipped away into the bushes when the men had done with her and the army moved on. She came down here because the stone meant life and there was death everywhere else, bodies and burnt houses. The old ones helped her. She told me they did what they could. They dragged all those dead people one by one into the pond and in the end, there was no more pond, just a slough of heaving mud which slowly settled until the sun blessed it with a lid of clay. That was their work and they did it and used themselves up doing it. My mother's time was near and she thought she would die too, but a man came from the west—a runaway. He took to my mother and put his work into saving her and so I was born.'

'And me?' asked Ferney. 'What of me?'

'Let's go back to the stone,' she said, and when they got there she turned all around, drinking it in. 'It was just me,' she said. 'Until I was big enough to fetch logs. But I think I can make you remember.

A morning when the leaves were turning and the fog was thick as milk.'

There was a long silence and Mike looked from one to the other of them, seeing them as they really were, so immeasurably ancient, so utterly rooted in this place, and finally fully understood in his heart as well as his head that this was their home and not really his at all.

In the end, Ferney shook his head. 'Nothing.'

'Think of a line of tired children, walking with each step hurting.'

He shook his head again.

'Think of you leading them, making them sing songs to keep them going.'

'Songs,' he said as if he saw the first pinpoint of a distant light.

'I was snapping twigs for kindling,' she went on, 'and I thought it was birds. A shrill from up the slope, lifting then choked by the fog's muffle and rising again, then coming clear in chanting like soldiers marching but so much higher.'

'I had to make them sing,' said Ferney suddenly. 'They wanted to stop. We'd been a dozen days walking and our legs were short. They'd had enough of believing in me.'

'You told them you were taking them home.'

'Weren't there women with us?'

'Only two by the time you reached us.'

'Four when we started. One died. One went in the night. Many children. A dozen?'

'More.'

He put his arm round her and they stood there silently remembering until Mike said, 'Don't stop talking. Tell me too.'

'You brought them back, you see?' Gally

417

prompted. 'Back from a Saxon camp. The girls from the village—the few left alive—and the orphans of those who died. When you felt the pull, you led them back here from the faraway west, back home. We settled them around the stone to learn to live and breathe again.'

'How old were you?' Mike asked.

'What were we?' Ferney looked at Gally, smiling. 'Ten? Who knows. It's not like being ten now. We never left each other after that, did we?'

'You led them all back here at ten?'

'Of course. Do you know the sorrow that is like a death sorrow?' Ferney asked. 'That sorrow you feel when a blade comes at you and you have time to know there is no escape. It came back clear to me, ten or not, and I knew my sorrow wasn't just for me. It was for someone I had been with and if I could find her, I could change that sorrow to something better. I discovered that I knew where it was. I would look towards the sunrise and know it was there, where the sun came up. I knew where to go and I knew I should bring the others with me.' He looked at Gally. 'I brought them back here but she put them back where they belonged. The village was ash and cinders, charred posts in the brambles, and Gally led each child back to its rightful house and helped the women look after them so that in time, as they grew up, they brought Pen back to life.'

Gally reached out, took Mike's hand and squeezed it. 'All the future was contained in those children. That is how it went from then until now.'

'There would be no village here otherwise,' said Ferney, but he broke off. 'There are cars coming,' he said.

418

'Already?' Mike groaned. He had no sense of how much time had passed. They turned to face the road, all three tense, poised as if for flight with nowhere to go and their backs to the stone. The engines grew louder. Fleur's car nosed into the yard. There was a large white van behind her but it went on by. Fleur got out and took two bags out of the back.

'I hope you're all hungry,' she said.

'What happened?' Mike asked.

'You happened. I drove off and before I got to the main road, I knew you were right. Now let's go in and cook. You look like you haven't had a decent breakfast in years. You two can help me. Mike, for God's sake go and have a shower. You look truly horrible.'

*   *   *

Mike came back downstairs to a smell of bacon and a buzz of conversation. He opened the door to a full table, overflowing with jugs of juice and milk, teapots, coffee and a large dish he had forgotten he owned, piled with sausages, mushrooms and crisp rashers. Ali and Lucy were buttering toast, Gally was pouring peppercorns into a grinder and Ferney was stirring a pan of baked beans.

Ferney and Gally ate their breakfast with the assurance of people who were utterly familiar with this kitchen and its corners and the space between things. Lucy and Ali watched them as if they were exhibits in some exotic zoo. Mike and Fleur shared some quiet wonder and only spoke to ask for food or offer it.

When they had all finished, Gally looked around

419

at them. 'I've got something to say and I know Ferney will agree. I know what I wrote in that letter.' She picked up the torn half of the five pound note and waved it in the air. 'Mike, I asked you to pass this house on if a different Ferney and a different Gally came back to find it, but now I see how hard that would be for you. With your blessing—I mean you, Mike, and you, Mum—we will try to find a different way for the time being.'

Fleur looked at her. 'You don't have to call me "Mum",' she said. 'I'll try to be as much of a mother as you want, but I doubt that's very much, eh? You haven't had a mother so far, so I don't suppose you'll be needing one now'. She took the torn note from Gally. 'Just so I know, just to make quite sure I don't wake up one morning and start causing trouble again, what about doing this anyway? I'd like to see it.'

Gally looked at her and nodded. 'The green cheese test,' she said. 'All right. Let's put everything beyond doubt. Let's find the other half.'

'Now?'

'Why not? We should tell Rachel. She should be there.'

'I can't. I've got Lulie,' she said when Mike called her. 'I'm going to be on the road most of the day and I'm taking her with me.'

'Bring her along.'

'How would I explain that?'

'You don't have to. We won't say anything. It can just be some sort of treasure hunt.'

'I don't know.'

'We're going in half an hour. You won't want to miss this.'

'I have to be in Yeovil at eleven thirty. I don't

think I can.'

'You've got time if you come right now.'

'I'll see. Where are you going exactly?'

* * *

They finished washing up and set off along the road that marked the western fringe of the village. Ferney and Gally walked in silence, hand in hand. Fleur walked with the two girls. Mike brought up the rear, looking behind him whenever he heard a car coming. They were yards away from the field entrance which led to Ballands Castle when he was rewarded. Rachel's car pulled in and parked on the grass verge and two Rachels got out. The first was the Rachel he knew, the second was Rachel seen in a trick mirror, stretched thin, a little blurred and paler but with so much about her the same. Her eyes locked on his as soon as she got out of the car and she came straight up to him with the direct confidence of someone twice her age, calmly assessing him then smiling as she held out a hand. 'I'm Lulie,' she said. 'I know who you are because I've seen you at school.'

'I owe you some thanks,' he answered. 'You saved me from Caroline Oaks.'

'I enjoyed that.'

Mike introduced her to the others.

'Where are we going?' she asked.

'In here,' said Ferney.

'This is the boring castle, isn't it?' said Lucy. 'The one with the little bumps that's hardly there at all,' but then they stopped in surprise as two worlds came together. A line of cars was parked inside the field. Six tents and a familiar green

421

marquee were lined up along the far hedge.

'That's Rupert's Land Rover,' said Ali.

Conrad was waving from the marquee. 'Hello,' he said. 'Hurray! You found us. I'm doing tea. We're a bit short-handed. Hello, Ali—how lovely to see you. Lucy, Jo, how are you? And who's this?'

He led them in a stream of words through the line of trees to the slope that steepened to the valley below, and there, across the grassy swell of the old ramparts, they saw a handful of diggers working in a long trench.

'Rupert,' he called. 'Look who's here.'

Rupert got up from his knees and walked over to join them. Dozer followed him, waving.

'Hello, Mike,' he said, 'Hello, girls and, let me see . . . Luke too. Well, well.'

Ferney stared at the trench. 'What are you doing?' he asked.

'Just trying to sort out the site. There's some confusion over the Norman features. There's supposed to be a church here but I can't see it myself.'

Mike looked enquiringly at Ferney, who pointedly looked the other way.

'We'll be back in a minute,' Gally said. 'We're just going to do something.'

'We'll stick around here,' said Ali quickly. 'I'm sure they could do with some help.'

'Lulie, you can stay if you want. We won't be long. Perhaps you might like to see what they're doing?' Rachel suggested.

Dozer grinned at the girl. 'Come and take a gander at my trench. Your keen eyes might spot something I haven't noticed.'

Gally led them north along the edge of the slope. She was casting around, looking hard at the trees and the line of the hedge. She stopped a hundred yards from the diggers, where three rough stones broke the surface of the grass, the soil dipping away beside them where a sheep path had worn down the ground.

'Here,' she said. 'Stand in front of me. I don't want them to see.' She knelt and got to work with a knife, scraping away around one of the stones until she could rock it forward. The underside had damp earth embedded in it, filling rough chiselled lines of lettering.

'This is their church, by the way,' said Ferney. 'You can tell them later on, Mike, after we've done. It can't do any harm.'

Below the stone was a square of opaque plastic. Gally freed its edges with the knife blade and lifted out a shallow box. She handed it to Mike.

'Here's your token, but like I said, it doesn't have to mean anything.'

Mike passed it to Fleur. 'You open it. If you've got any doubt left in your mind, this should fix it.'

She peeled off the tape and levered the lid open, looked inside and nodded slowly. 'I'm sure it will match,' she said, 'but let's do it anyway.'

He fitted the two halves of the banknote together.

'That may be the most interesting thing anybody digs up round here this week,' Ferney said, watching the diggers.

'Oh really?' said Mike. 'It's a castle. There must be something worth finding, surely?'

423

'Plenty, but nothing over there except earthworks, unless of course they move their spoil heap.'

'Why's that?'

'Because Harold is right underneath it.'

Walking back to the dig, they could see Lulie laughing with Ali, Lucy and Dozer. 'They're looking after her,' Gally said.

'You may find it's the other way round,' Rachel replied. 'She has a way with people.'

'You sound like a proud mum.'

'Do I? Sorry. Well, no, you're right—I am a proud mum.'

On the way back to Rachel's car, Gally walked with Lulie. 'Did you enjoy that?' she asked.

'I think Mum should go on a dig,' said the girl. 'She spends too much time at home. She'd like Dozer—he was the one with the ponytail. I mean just as a friend. He's way too old for her. It's just the sort of thing she needs. Simple stuff—a trowel and some dirt and good chat.'

'Do you spend a lot of time thinking about what your mum needs?'

'Yes,' said the girl. 'Someone has to.'

'I've got to get on,' Rachel said to Mike as she unlocked her car. 'I suppose that's it then?'

'You've been amazing,' Mike replied. 'I can't begin to thank you.'

'I'll certainly never forget it. I suspect that's the high point of my professional life.'

'What now then?'

'Next on my list? A briefing ahead of an employment tribunal for a redundant office manager. Oh what fun.'

He shook her hand and it seemed wrong, then

she got in the car and Mike saw Lulie talk to her urgently. Rachel frowned, asked her something, raised her eyebrows at her reply and got out again.

'Mike, just on the off chance, are you free next Saturday? It seems I've got a spare ticket for *Carmen* in Salisbury. You wouldn't like to come, would you? I bought one for Lulie but she's just told me opera's not really her bag.'

'Oh, thanks, but it's not really mine either.'

'It's a touring production and they're quite good. They—oh, never mind.'

Mike stared at her blankly and she looked away, fiddling with the ignition key. 'I wanted to ask you something,' he said.

She looked up quickly. 'Yes, what?'

'Do you do property stuff—what's it called, conveyancing? I want to do something about the house.'

'I don't. The firm does. Ring the office.'

He stepped back as she drove off in a spurt of gravel then he saw her brake hard. Lulie jumped out and ran back to him. She stopped in front of him and stared at him, shaking her head. 'I go to all that trouble and you blow it straight away,' she said.

'What?'

'I do like opera as it happens. Think about it.'

He did, and got nowhere. 'I don't know what you mean.'

'You're meant to be clever,' she said. 'You're a teacher. I fix up a date and you turn her down.'

'A date? You—oh shit. Wait here.'

He ran to Rachel's car.

*   *   *

425

Later that evening, as the sun settled down on the rim of the western lowlands, the girl and the boy who were older than the oak trees and as young as saplings sat on their hilltop, as they had always done, watching the colours growing under the distant terraces of cloud.

'I have something to say to you,' said Gally.

'I might know what it is.'

'You might not. Do you know me well enough to be certain?'

'After all this time? No, probably not.'

She smiled at him, 'We still have a few mysteries. What chance do they have, all the rest of them—Mike, Fleur, Rachel? One lifetime to know someone else. It's barely enough to get started.'

'Can I try?' he said. 'Can I see if perhaps I do know what it is you want to say?'

'All right.'

'When I heard your letter,' he sounded tentative, 'and when I saw the way he was this morning, I finally realised how much we had both hurt him. I wouldn't want to hurt someone like that, someone who mattered, ever again. Is that it?'

'That's my starting point,' she said, 'but it goes much further. I think there might be another way to tackle all this.'

He waited quietly as she put the words together.

'We both know how much harder it's getting,' she said. 'You said it yourself. Everything has numbers and files and records. There are more and more rules about schools and houses and taxes and ownership. Cameras watch us and these days,

426

there always has to be an answer to the question "Who is he?" or "Who is she?"'

'It's been hard before in many different ways. We always manage.'

'It's much harder now.' She leaned her head on his shoulder. 'I think there's a better way and everybody else knows it except us. People adapt because they have such a short time. They do what they have to do to get by because they'll only have to do it once. They take the world for what it is and they don't mind because that's the only one they know. They have children and *that's* how they deal with the world—that's how they throw their spear onwards, one generation to another.' She kissed him on the cheek. 'I think that's what we should do,' she said. 'We should have children again. They'll be much better at this changing game and the world is bringing too much change.'

'But you know what happens then. They break your heart.'

'Ferney, most children stay alive these days.'

'All right, but we have them, then we get old and die and come back and we see them getting it all wrong, and—'

'That's not what I'm saying.'

'Then . . . what?'

'I'm saying enough is enough. I'm saying we should stop this time. We have children and they have children and then we stop when our time comes just like everybody else.'

'And throw away all this, you and me? All our futures? All our history and knowledge?'

She touched his face with her fingers. 'Where's it got us?' she asked him. 'Let's live in the here and now, not in the future because we don't know it

427

and not the past because we know it far too well. Let's have the most joyful life with the most joyful family and prepare them to face whatever the world throws at them. Then, when the candle flickers, let's make sure we snuff it out together and let that be our ending in the full sunlight of our love, and the best part is we won't even know we're missing anything. Let's make this the last time and the best time and find no regret in that at all.'

He took her hands. 'Do you think we can just decide to stop?'

'Who knows?' she answered, 'Let's try it and see.'

962
690
537
155
575
757
162
680
317